Marcus Mac Donald

GW00760815

The Polish WEEK

PORTIA.
PUBLISHING

Published by **Portia Publishing 2012**
ISBN 978-0-9573720-0-9

Copyright © Marcus Mac Donald

First published in Ireland in 2012 by Portia Publishing
www.portiacommunications.com

Portia Publishing is part of the **Portia Communications Group**, Dublin & Pisa.

A CIP catalogue record for this book is available from the British Library.

ISBN 978-0-9573720-0-9

Design and Typesetting by Gabriel German Carbone, Rosario, Argentina.
GPS Colour Graphics, Alexander Road, Belfast BT6 9HP.

For Mairéad – friend, lover, wife and muse – a little Brick!

When bad men combine, the good must associate;
else they will fall one by one,
an unpitied sacrifice in a contemptible struggle.

Edmund Burke

Thoughts on the Cause of the Present Discontentment

PROLOGUE

Warsaw
February 1981

The blustering wind propelled a scattering of sleet into the colonel's face, the only exposed part of his erect figure encased in full uniform and greatcoat. He slammed the passenger door of the black limousine and walked the concourse, enduring the stinging aerial rebukes. His irritability reflected the political turmoil surrounding him – ineffectual Polish leadership; the malignant Solidarity Movement; the arch traitor Lech Walesa; all of whom ignored the churning might of Soviet armour on Polish borders waiting to impose direct rule from Moscow. Weather had much in common with human nature: both were fickle and undependable.

The colonel mounted the steps to intelligence headquarters. The guard on duty pulled the door open and saluted. His briskness in returning the salute stemmed from an accident he had had a few years previously that deprived him of the two middle fingers of his right hand. Winter provided a gloved camouflage, which he extended beyond the normal period for wear. Yet his irritation was constantly fuelled by the inquisitive eyes of NCOs as they latched onto his right hand when returning their salutes – whether he was wearing gloves or not.

He made his way to the lifts. He had arrived early to initiate the process that would copper-fasten the appointment of the new prime minister. He removed his greatcoat and draped it over a hanger on the coat stand. The fingers of his left hand brushed pearls of moisture from the fabric. This would be his first meeting with the soon-to-be prime minister, General Jaruzelski. A reception in the afternoon, formal to begin with, would later relocate for a private session. He was hopeful that this was where some real business could be done. He needed Jaruzelski's backing for the substitution of the minister for culture by that sycophant Uginski. They could not afford to lose the talented minister for culture, so Uginski would depart for London to attend the concert of Polish music. It would be the only notable achievement in his miserable existence and would end in his final exit.

General Jaruzelski's promotion from minister of defence to prime minister was the initial step to curb the rot. He possessed determination and did not suffer fools. He was the only reason the Soviets were holding back. He *must* succeed! It was imperative that Jaruzelski become Head of State and he would ensure that this came to pass. It was a bitter memory for *all* Poles that the Soviets had divided Poland between themselves and Nazi Germany during World War II. But these current threats were between two communist states. Did the Soviets not see that they were endangering the People's Republic of Poland?

The colonel lifted his private phone and dialled a number. It rang on the other side of the city in the ministry for foreign affairs, passports section. An apathetic minor official answered.

"Yes?"

"You are handling the passport arrangements for this concert of Polish music in London next month?"

"Yes."

"I'm ringing from intelligence to forewarn you of a change in personnel for the concert."

There was a quick intake of breath from passports. "But the names on my list have been passed at the highest level."

The colonel ignored the alarm at the other end of the phone. "The minister for culture will not be travelling."

"Ah," the official faltered, and then resorted to curiosity. "Why isn't this information coming from culture?"

"I'll repeat what I've already said. This phone call is to *forewarn* you. In time, you will receive notification from culture. His replacement is Minister Anton Uginski – department for urban renewal."

"But – but Anton Uginski's name has been withdrawn, with others, from the official register. The man is in disgrace. I received an official circular to that effect – just yesterday. You must know that. New prime minister in – old rotten apples out."

The colonel was taken aback at the flunkey's righteous crescendo but forestalled a sharp rejoinder by reminding himself that, as deputy director of intelligence, *he* was engaged on a much more important mission of consequence and at a much more significant level. The barracking minion on the other end of the phone merely carried out orders. As a deputy director it was his privilege to initiate directives, and bearing in mind the weight of this present venture and the importance of its successful conclusion – then he must be cool, clear, incisive and *wary*.

"What is your name?" he asked with authoritative condescension, and repeated the name as he wrote it down. "Now, I have neither the time nor inclination to repeat myself – so listen. Uginski is *not* in disgrace. His name was included on the circular in error. You shall have a verbal correction this afternoon from the department for urban renewal."

"Seems an odd substitution for a cultural occasion – but who am I to say."

"Quite. Who are you to say? My function is to retrieve the situation. Your function is to rectify the error at your end. SEE TO IT!"

CHAPTER 1

Monday March 23rd 1981
Hendon, North London
9.00 am

David Brenton closed the door of No 16 Brookdale Avenue and exerted a slight momentary pressure below the key latch to ensure it had locked. He fastened the top button of his mackintosh and walked briskly towards his front gate. He repeated the sequence with the front gate, and strode down the avenue for the twelve-minute walk to Colindale Underground.

Preoccupation with systems came naturally to him, an inheritance from his years spent as a flying officer with the Royal Air Force. He considered his other inheritance from the service, the diminished response in his right eye, to be an occasional distraction.

At forty years of age, Brenton presented a slim taut figure. A decision taken nine years previously to dispense with a car, and the corresponding increase in his only form of exercise, walking, had staved off any hint of middle-aged spread. The benefits of this determination were many and varied, although aside from the obvious physical advantage, there had been the initial necessity to pound the after-effects of a divorce out of his system.

The walk to Colindale combined brevity with a sense of spaciousness, due to the expanse of Hendon Aerodrome. He was bareheaded, and his lank fair hair bounced fractionally behind his stride, the colour forming a good camouflage for the few flecks of grey that had begun to appear. He anticipated minute change in the awakening vegetation from blue-grey eyes, which a casual glance might have judged as kindly. Occasionally, they acquired a quality akin to a one-way mirror, turning him into a closed book.

He always enjoyed the feeling which the open aspect imparted, but more particularly today. The recording location   would present indifferent ventilation, confined space and artificial light. As he made his way up the steps to the railway platform, he thought the lack of daylight the greatest loss.

On the platform he joined a smaller-than-usual group, some perusing the day's headlines on tomorrow's litter. Even before he idly looked from one face to another, he knew there would not be one familiar countenance amongst them. Despite settling in Brookdale two years previously, he had socialised little; there was a certain indifference on his part to ordinary social mores that went beyond the usual English reserve.

He looked out and over towards the airfield and remembered the youthful excitement, the wonderment, the joy and simplicity of the games which had taken place with other boys and girls within its confines. There had been little contact with those outside due to the RAF security arrangements. While compounding the divisiveness, they had also imparted a feeling of privilege. A people set apart. For David Brenton, Hendon RAF Aerodrome in North London had been the centre of his formative years, a wonderful extension of his immediate family. His earliest recollection of the Aerodrome had been the feeling of reverberation in his father's living quarters, which came as a shock after the cosy sounds of his aunt and uncle's farmhouse where he had spent the war years. On the day of his return during Easter 1946, his father, Air Commodore George Brenton, had irreverently referred to the occasion as the 'second coming' – his birth on June 12th 1940 having been overshadowed by an event at Hendon of historical importance.

That night, Winston Churchill, accompanied by the Foreign Secretary, Anthony Eden, the chief of the imperial general staff, Sir John Dill and other notables, had flown into Hendon from France with the shattering news that France was on the verge of collapse and Britain now stood alone in the war.

Domestic re-arrangements followed, the most important of which was the departure of Mrs Dorothy Brenton and baby David to Mrs Brenton's family farm in Somerset.

The duration of the war hardly impinged on young David, tucked away in the comfort and security of a remote Somerset farm. Towards the end of the conflagration, this placid existence was occasionally interrupted when his father paid unexpected and, therefore, all the more exciting visits.

Hendon by contrast to Somerset meant movement and mechanical things and interesting robust noises, not that he disliked the tranquillity and rural beauty from which he had emerged. One complemented the other. It always remained a joy to swing between them as he grew older.

The rush of the train as it entered the station brought him back with a jolt. There would be a choice of seats, because Colindale was close to the terminus at Edgware. The doors opened with their familiar 'whoosh' and he stepped aboard. He eased himself into a seat on the platform side.

One late passenger ran the few yards from the entrance to the first open door, a flash of blue RAF non-commissioned energy. Brenton strained to see the face, but the airman had moved too quickly. The doors closed almost on cue and they moved off.

It was good to see at least one uniform. There had been a time when they were more plentiful, but that was before Hendon became what it is today – the first RAF Museum, which was the main reason he had been able to buy a house in the area. There was no aircraft activity at Hendon. Had there been, the realisation that it was now denied him would have been a constant irritation. As it was, the aerodrome, like its precious contents of old aircraft and artefacts, was something plucked out of time, preserved for contemplation, and therefore therapeutic. The train slowed as it crossed Finchley Road Bridge before the Golders Green stop. He caught a glimpse of the roof of the BBC Hippodrome picked out in the morning sun. He had spent time there acquiring the skills for recording music. He wondered which orchestra was assembling that morning. Possibly the BBC Radio Orchestra. In which case, the lash up of assorted microphones, cables, and ancillary equipment would be a complicated and heavy one. He did not envy the studio manager's task one bit. On the other hand, he did envy him the multiplicity of good recording acoustics available in the Hippodrome. Originally a theatre, the BBC had expertly converted it to its own needs, while retaining its basic concept.

As if to compensate for the earlier lack of passengers, Golders Green contained a superfluity of the species. Already a number were standing, although hanging might be a more accurate description of their postures. Some were dexterously manipulating newspapers with their free hands. He desultorily began to subdivide this group as the train re-started. Beside him, a trench coat swayed perilously while working away at some headline. The effort to keep his eyes glued to the print, accompanied by tiny dancing steps, never entirely in time with either the clickety-clacks, or sudden side movements of the train, seemed exaggeratedly inept. *Le Ballet Comique*? Further away swayed a Yehudi Menuhin, paper hand moving to and fro in nice style. On second thoughts – a double bass player; left hand much too high in the strap for a violinist. He tired of the game and instead tried to decipher the newspaper headlines.

The Times had a photo of two Soviet cosmonauts waving before blast off for a space link up. To the right of the photo: 'Heseltine Warns Councils as Rate Rises Average 20.5%'. Under the cosmonauts it said: 'Military Manoeuvres in Poland Extended'. Ballet Comique's *Guardian* proclaimed: 'Poland's Politburo Accuses Solidarity of Anarchy'. Across the aisle the *Financial Times* told him: 'Motorway Food as Bad as Ever'.

He turned his head to gaze out the window. Shortly after Golders Green, the train went underground. Departing from daylight into the underground never failed to impart a feeling of deprivation. The idea that the experience of descending into darkness might be of value should he ever find himself having to go down a coalmine was a fanciful notion his mother had once put to him as a small boy. As the sunshine disappeared, the train swept on and downward beneath London, and the reminiscence of his mother brought a smile to his face.

CHAPTER 2

Monday March 23rd 1981
St George's Church, London
10.00 am

Brenton walked out into the bright sunlight, glad to leave behind the electro-luminescent atmosphere of the Underground. He paused, eyes closed, and lifted his head in the direction of the sun. Then abruptly, he wheeled right in the direction of St George's Church, his recording location.

There was something about London in early spring. It had a cleansed feeling, a feeling of renewal, alive with the promise of the full flowering just around the corner. It *was* true it added something to a person's step – a welcome change after the winter's scurrying about, and a perfect prelude to the more liberating movements of summer.

It was not a recording in the accepted sense. The purpose of the tests would determine whether or not the rumble from city traffic was prohibitively intrusive. It would be a pity if it proved positive, because the organ, which had been refurbished recently, had turned out to be a very good instrument of its type. Any one of his assistants, including the present incumbent, Sarah Carlyle, could adequately have carried out the tests. He had a personal interest in this instrument however, and was acquainted with Ken Joyce, the man who had transformed the organ with meticulous care.

As soon as he entered St George's Close, where the church stood centre stage in the small eighteenth century square, it was obvious the microphones inside the church would pick up external vehicular sounds. But traffic was rare, so there was no insurmountable problem. He looked out from the church portico. The real worry would be the rumble from fast-moving traffic on the main road beyond the square. Then he noticed the large entrance door was fractionally open, despite a 'Closed' notice pinned to it. He walked in and allowed the door slam behind him. This would keep the inquisitive tourist from wandering into the building and also inform Sarah Carlyle of his arrival. He pushed through the swing door in the porch and entered the church proper.

"Hello Sarah, it's me – David." She was nowhere in sight, which meant she must be in the crypt, where he had suggested they set up their listening post; and sure enough a distant reply echoed, "Down here!"

On his way to the basement, he noticed the stereo microphone projecting from an extended microphone stand centre aisle, half way down the church. He stepped through the open doorway to the crypt and closed it. The wooden stairs stretching down before him disappeared into blackness. He waited until his eyes became accustomed to the dark, then proceeded gingerly downwards, guided by the slit of light under Sarah's door. At the bottom of the stairs, a block of dry cold air enveloped him. Damn it! He'd forgotten to make arrangements for heating. The door was wrenched open, revealing an unusually bulky Sarah Carlyle in the parsimonious lighting of the cellar.

"Taa-raaah!" she trumpeted in a mock fanfare, arms thrown wide and punctuated with a mini curtsey. Brenton inclined his head, and since it was 'darkest London' added, "Miss Carlyle, I presume?"

Under the insipid rays of the single unadorned light bulb, he realised Sarah was wearing a duffle coat at least four sizes too big.

"I apologise for the lack of heating, my oversight. But you er – couldn't have travelled here in that tent – or could you?"

"It's Jim Sherry's," she explained with a laugh. "He left it with me when he went to hire a heater."

Jim Sherry was the company's rigger, driver, technician, location man, and an indispensable cog in their recording business. 'I know every electric socket within a ten mile radius of base,' he had modestly told them '– and some I shouldn't…'

"Is the side door open?"

Sarah walked over to the mixing desk. "I locked the side door because the wind is blowing from that side of the building. It stopped the door clattering."

"How long has Jim been gone?"

"About half an hour."

"Let's move upstairs and await his arrival in more agreeable surroundings."

"Lead on Mac Duff!"

They re-emerged into the church's Georgian elegance, the relative warmth of which was attributable to the strong sun shining through its graciously paned windows. This was confirmed a moment later when he laid a hand on a cold radiator. He nodded his head in the direction of the sun's rays. "Let's sit on the sunny side."

Sarah reached the sunlit pews first, more by Brenton's courtesy than swiftness of movement. Brenton settled into the pew behind her, a little to the left, and discreetly observed her. The rise in temperature meant she could dispense with Sherry's duffle coat. She was taller than her figure would lead one to believe, but that may have been the effect of the coat. She was about 5'7. Her face – though not of classic proportions – contained a certain indefinable something; strength of character perhaps. And it seemed to centre in her green eyes, which were ... well, rather beautiful.

Sarah sat down and stretched her arms along the bench at her back, raising her head in the direction of the welcoming warmth. Her auburn hair caught the concentrated rays of light and appeared to shimmer. "This is lovely," she murmured, lost in the semi-somnolent atmosphere. The word 'nubile' crossed his mind, to be swiftly ejected, and replaced with the facts of her life: she had spent three years teaching at a kindergarten before joining the company two years ago. She'd make some man very happy – if she acquired a more flattering wardrobe – but then, would that be appropriate in the depths of St George's?

There was a loud banging on the front door of the church.

"Must be Jim," Brenton said, moving across to the aisle. Sarah followed, the effort of climbing back into the coat slowing her progress. Brenton unlocked and opened the door to reveal Jim Sherry in all his cheerfulness.

"I was wondering whether you two could be safely left together," he joked, entering with a heater under each arm.

"And why not," Sarah retorted. "Particularly with the passion damper you threw over my shoulders before you left."

Sherry grinned. "And you thought it was just to keep you warm!" He turned to Brenton and explained, "I hired these for the confinement cell. Didn't want anyone getting frost bite."

"Yes, and in order not to overload the basement socket you may have to run an extension lead from up here."

"I'm way ahead of you," Sherry cut in as he made his way towards the basement door, "Except, I've only one pair of arms. I left the haversack at home unfor –" The rest was lost in the noise of his steps descending the wooden stairs. Brenton looked at Sarah and said, "The cable must be in the van. Show him where you want them positioned. I'll slip out and fetch the cable drum." Sarah turned away and moved towards the basement. "Back to the grill," she mumbled resignedly. "Give my regards to the sun," she threw back over her shoulder.

Brenton thought her last words peculiarly applicable to his own state of mind. She possessed a disconcerting ability to make him feel… His eyes narrowed as he descended the six steps under the portico to street level, still at a loss for a definition.

The van was parked outside the church's main door. He cut diagonally across the narrow footpath to the backdoor of the van, only to find it locked. Irritation evaporated with the realisation that this was in fact an implemented company directive. He retraced his steps. Halfway through the church he met Sherry who said, "Sarah told me you went out to the van?"

"Yes, to get the extension lead. Instead I found your security arrangements are up to scratch." Sherry smiled cursorily, aware of what might have developed had he inadvertently left the van unlocked. In an effort to overcome the tense silence, Brenton suggested, "I'll walk to the van with you and bring in the cable. You can then take off for the Hall in Croydon."

"One journey to Croydon should do the trick," Sherry offered, sensing an impending task in the pipeline. His perceptiveness was confirmed as they reached the van. "I want you back here this afternoon," Brenton said. "Otherwise Sarah will be on her own, and because it's not the most cheerful basement in London, she could do with the company. After you finish here, I'll see you both in Croydon, where we'll make a start on the rig for tomorrow's orchestral rehearsal."

"No problem – I'll collect my coat this afternoon."

"Because of the tightness of the schedule, I'll have meals laid on here about six o'clock. There's a good Italian restaurant close by, and I think lasagne retains heat well." Sherry unlocked the van door. "Lasagne will suit me fine," he said. Leaning inside, he grabbed a drum of cable and scrambled back out. "But Sarah may be on one of her diets, so I'd check with her, if I were you."

"I intend to," Brenton agreed. "Does Sarah have to diet?"

"All women diet," said Sherry locking the van door. He turned to Brenton and added incredulously, "Where have you been?" An embarrassed silence followed.

"David," Sherry said, distressed, "What can I say? That's the sort of slip which, knowing some of the circumstances, could only pop out unintentionally."

"Jim –"

"No, let me finish," Sherry insisted. "I like to think of you as a friend. I hope it's mutual, and strong enough to hear what I'm about to say. I had intended bringing this up, and because of my gaffe, the present moment seems as good a time as any, and maybe better than most. What I want to say is –"He stood squarely in front of Brenton, his hands extended in a muted gesture of appeal. Throwing caution aside he said bluntly, "For God's sake David, rejoin the human race! Look, I know you've been through the mill – your marriage, and maybe plenty more I don't know about. You should've come to terms with these things by now. It's a fatal flaw, and you can't be allowed to continue in this self-imposed isolation, if not for your own sake – then for the rest of us who come in contact with you. What you need is a few good booze-ups for openers. You realise we've never had a drink together, apart from some of those snooty after-concert affairs? You seem to be glued to that crowd like nothing else in life mattered. There's got to be more to life than that." He had run out of verbal steam and to break the silence added, "I wouldn't have said any of that if I didn't feel I owed you."

There was a further sustained pause. Sherry had made up his mind not to contribute another syllable. The ball was very definitely in the other court. Brenton, whose eyes never left Sherry quietly assured, "Your friendship *is* appreciated, and I am grateful that you feel as concerned as you do. I wasn't aware I was having this effect on those around me. It's not intentional. You may be right about a few drinks, and that's what we shall do when the opportunity arises."

He bent down, caught hold of the electric cable container, and before walking into the church added, "I'm beginning to get the message. No man is an island, and all that."

Sherry climbed into the cab seat of his van, not sure whether he had initiated a process, or finished a friendship.

Brenton locked the church door behind him and moved through the porch into the building. The most immediate problem lay in finding an electric socket on the right hand wall, close to the basement door. Starting at the back wall, he worked his way along the skirting board. While attuned to the task, his mental faculty was preoccupied with what had taken place. As he passed the open door to the basement he shouted down, "I'll be with you as soon as I locate a socket." An acknowledgement issued from below. He wasn't sure what she had said, nor was he inclined to go back to find out. He spotted a socket behind a single prie-dieu inside the altar rail, inserted the plug, and fed out cable back to the basement door, down the stairs, and into the recording room.

"Are they working?" he enquired after inserting the plugs and peering across to where Sarah had dropped to her haunches, hands extended in front of the heater furthest away. There was a moment's pause before she replied, "Yes, it's started to heat."

"Good," Brenton grunted and moved to the nearest heater to check its state of health. Even before he extended his hand, he knew he was in business; an expansion click in the heater forewarned him that his journey was unnecessary. But he had a compulsion to feel the heat anyway. In order to justify his dalliance he took the opportunity to examine more minutely their basement surroundings. The room, about twenty-five feet square and eleven or twelve feet high possessed the advantageous quality of near total acoustic isolation. Three of the walls, including the wall in which the door was set, were composed of brickwork from floor to ceiling. The fourth wall, on the left as one entered, seemed to be part of a larger structure which extended beyond the confines of the basement. It was a barrel-shaped arch. The formation was not akin to either the architecture, or the Portland stone of the church above ground. It was a dark basalt-like stone used for foundations, or perhaps the remains of an even older establishment. An exception was one small centre stone, notable only because of its singular dampness.

Brenton walked to the mixing desk and suggested, "Let's get the show off the ground."

"*Ja wöhl – mein fürher*," Sarah sighed, detaching herself from the heater.

"Have you checked the microphone characteristics?"

"Yes," she replied, throwing a self-congratulatory smile in his direction. "Figure of eight – as per job spec."

"Good," Brenton nodded. "The figure of eight will pick up more of the church ambience which could be useful, since we don't wish to add artificial reverberation. Its disadvantage is that it's likely to pick up the distant rumble of traffic."

Sarah had begun to remove the coat from her shoulders. Brenton instinctively felt the urge to assist, but was surprised to find his feet did not have the same inclination. He removed his own coat to divert from his ungraciousness, which Sarah, with the advantage of a more emancipated generation, did not seem to expect. He had a heightened awareness of her eyes, and realised that his own must have been locked on hers for longer than was necessary. Turning quickly to examine the minutiae of the dark patch on the wall, he asked, "Would you mind stepping into the church and counting out a few numbers in a moderately loud voice, in order to insure the levels are correct."

"Be happy to," she cheerily responded.

"Thank you," Brenton said perfunctorily, and hearing his abruptness, added, "Shouldn't take more than a minute or two."

As Sarah reached the door he suggested, "Leave the door open – to throw light onto the stairs."

He heard the sound of her shoes as she ascended the stairs, reappearing on the speakers as she entered the church overhead. He followed their progress from left to centre. A smile hovered on his lips as she announced her position and proceeded to count up and then down from one to ten in that unmistakably well-modulated voice. Listening to her in this detached way, her voice imparted a soothing effect. Her speech on microphone confirmed levels and, as he sat down in front of the desk, Jim Sherry's admonition preoccupied his thoughts. He wondered in what way, if at all, his 'fatal flaw' impinged on Sarah. Should he broach the subject with her? No, quite definitely, no.

Assuming their modus vivendi to be a reasonable one – and Sarah had never implied otherwise – then it would be folly to undermine a relationship that was good and correct with the introduction of what was superficial and irrelevant. The job in hand became his focus again. He would ask her to take on the task of recording the organ in St George's – provided tests proved its feasibility.

The sudden clatter of female shoes descending the wooden stairs jerked him back to reality. His mind wrestled with the necessity for an explanation. He rose and turned towards the open door as Sarah came in. "Sorry for the delay," he said starkly.

Sarah approached and asked, "Did you get the levels on my voice?"

"Yes. I became preoccupied with an adjustment here." He returned to the desk and as he panned the systems left and right, turned the conversation in a new direction.

"I'd like you to take charge of the recording – if it goes ahead according to plan."

The diversion worked.

Sarah said, "I don't quite know what to say – perhaps thank you for having confidence in me."

Brenton smiled. Having overcome his inbuilt conservativeness, he was about to indulge himself and wallow in the warm feeling of gratification. Pointing to the second chair he said, "Sit down and let's talk about it."

Sarah sat on the proffered chair and asked, "When did you decide to allow me try my hand?"

"It's been on my mind for some time," he disclosed. "The appropriate job didn't arise until now."

Sarah's eyes shifted to the floor in a bid to control the uneasy movement of her feet.

"I hope I justify your confidence."

Warming to the subject, Brenton expanded, "I'd like you to understand, I wouldn't have asked you if I thought you couldn't handle it. You have a good musical ear and so far as I'm concerned, you're au fait with all the tricks of the business."

She glanced at him. "You've never said anything like that to me before."

"You weren't ready before. You've always given an impression of self-confidence. Do I now detect something less?"

After a moment's pause, she raised her head to a position rather higher than usual, and answered, "No, David, it's not something less, I'm just curious. You popped this out of the blue. I can remember early in my career how much emphasis you placed on the correct mental approach to recording sessions. I would have appreciated a little more notice of what you had in mind."

Uncrossing his legs and placing a hand on each knee, he asked, "Do you accept the job or don't you?"

"Of course I accept the job, David. But can't you see –"

"Very well," he interjected and stood up. "Because of a prior commitment, I shall not be here this afternoon. Jim will return and remain here until tests finish at six o'clock. I shall arrange for meals to be delivered here at that time. Before I depart I'll play the 'Adagio' from Bach's *Toccata, Adagio and Fugue in C major*, nothing any louder than mezzo forte. The final section is forte. Bring the tape to Croydon tonight and tomorrow I shall discuss its merits with you." He moved towards the door where he paused, and without turning round advised, "I'll give you a five second cue to start." He had pulled the door behind him and was half way up the stairs before she regained her composure.

"The unfeeling monster! I'm not surprised he's acquired the reputation he has. Must get a perverted satisfaction in walking on people. That's when he's not keeping them at arm's length!"

Brenton moved purposefully through the church towards the door in the back wall, behind which lay the narrow winding stairs to the organ loft. He gave the microphone a quick nervous look as he passed by. He felt resentment at its pervasive intrusion into what could have been, in private, a pleasant elevating experience. At the top of the stairs he stretched his arm along the wall behind the pipes and switched on. Moving round to the console, he seated himself at the keyboard and, while removing flecks of dust from his sleeve, soaked in the ambience of the instrument. The quiet reassuring hum of the wind box within which potential energy strained impatiently, awaiting the application of his hands on the keyboard for joyous musical release. The aromas of diverse old wood and historical ivory keyboards mingled to produce a faint odour of beeswax and faded lavender. Inevitably his mind returned to happier hours spent on less prestigious instruments a long time ago. There was certainly nothing more tangible around him nowadays that could serve as a means of continuity in his life. At times he felt as if his present existence was a reincarnation; with the recent addition of a disturbing ability to stand outside himself and question the psychological pressures which had dictated his change of direction.

He placed both hands lightly on the lower keyboard without depressing the notes. The diminished response in his eye made an unexpected appearance, so he switched on the keyboard light. The warm glow relaxed him sufficiently to allow his fingers find their way through the scale of G major, contrary motion, and while playing chords and short truncated extracts, select suitable organ stops.

When the tonal requirements were to his satisfaction he sat back and placed his hands on his knees. After a few moments' concentration, he turned and shouted down the church, "Starting in five seconds from – now."

Sarah heard the cue on the loudspeakers and set the tape machine to record. She noted the tape time and rapidly took her place in front of the desk, her right hand on the main fader. The music opened with the arresting notes of a mordent. Her right hand tensed as Bach's glorious answer unfolded. Then she gradually relaxed to a point where a more objective assessment of the music's beauty could be made. The interpretation, she thought, wasn't without some slight imperfection; but it was deeply musical. If one set aside their recent contretemps she would have to admit to being taken aback at his facility. As the music found its palliative way to her, she felt a disheartening exasperation. Here was someone who communicated intelligence and sensitivity in music, yet face to face was opaque and standoffish. The music changed gear dynamically and as it entered the final section, a new more forceful timbre took control. It occurred to her that the organ must be his instrument. It also brought home, in a pointedly challenging way, how little she knew about the person behind the interpretation. Something within made her wish to fill that void.

CHAPTER 3

Monday March 23rd 1981
Croydon
2.15 pm

It was said that Symphony Hall Croydon was the brainchild of Michael Pecton. It was also said that apart from managing the Hall, which he did superbly, his only contribution to a consortium which he moulded to launch the project, was the suggestion to change the name to Symphony Hall. In light of the enterprise's subsequent achievements, and according to the barometer that measures success by degrees of envy, Michael Pecton could consider himself very successful. He was intolerant of the slipshod or the second rate. Therefore, of necessity and preference, he acquired a team to perform music and manage its interpretation, whose differing personalities had one thing in common: a capacity for hard work. His negotiations with the unions when first assembling the new Symphony Orchestra, were legendary. On a quid pro quo basis, he organised long-term touring arrangements for the orchestra in East European countries, coupled with a yearly allotment to their major conservatories for British music students. In return he was given the green light to tap into the rich over-production of Eastern-bloc music academies, and consequently brought to Croydon a sizeable number of fine orchestral musicians, mainly strings, whose quality and dedication proved to be an immediate attraction, and for Pecton, an agreeable investment.

One of the negative sides of the arrangement was a union ban on the new arrivals participating in the gig scene in London, the world of the ad hoc orchestra or backing group – the gold behind the tinsel of the pop and advertisement worlds. As things turned out, it made not one whit of difference to the enthusiastic influx of Czechs, Romanians, Hungarians, and Poles. Their disciplined good humour, and in some cases, inordinate thankfulness for the attainment of a good lifestyle, endeared them to a growing circle of friends. Their combined numbers made up forty-six per cent of the orchestra.

One of the more loquacious of the group, in an expansive moment, summed up the political differences picturesquely, when he explained: "In my country ... we have a proverb which say ... 'Do not piss in shrubbery – you make microphones go rusty.'" The lack of similar ironmongery in English shrubbery was greatly appreciated.

Knitted into the package, and pivotal to its success, was a recording contract. Pecton's negotiations with one of the majors produced the small subsidiary, *Croydon Records*. It had been intended initially to float their own independent recording company, but finding themselves extended financially on central projects, their company was aligned with one of the field leaders for a fraction of the original estimate. David Brenton found himself in charge of this, and quickly came to terms with Pecton's economic requirements of down–market quickies. It was a trim, taut, somewhat meagre production arrangement, with, in Pecton's view, the admirable attributes of flexibility and cost effectiveness, which did not bite too deeply into the quality of the end product. Pecton expressed himself satisfied with an initial break-even situation. He personally directed the publicity and public relations side of the enterprise, expending a great deal of his energy in this direction. His most recent coup had taken place last year when he successfully arranged a Polish Night for the orchestra at the Royal Albert Hall. This was to be staged in five days' time.

The latest correspondence and publicity on the impending concert lay on his desk in front of him. Quickly and cursorily, he went through each item, which he then laid in one of two piles. He was halfway through a press release when there was a knock on the door. He glanced at the small clock on the desk, which read half past two. It must be Quentin Appleby for their Monday conference. Nobody else got past his secretary, Miss Maybury, without a forewarning on the intercom. He laid the newspaper cutting back on the desk and announced in his crisp evenly-pitched voice that directive which had become a byword, "Come!"

Quentin Appleby entered the room on cue, his awareness of the hilarity with which Pecton's directive was bandied about in certain quarters masked by his business-like expression.

"Good afternoon, Quentin." Pecton gestured toward the leather armchair.

"'Afternoon Michael, and for a change it *is* good. The weather, I mean."

Appleby slowly lowered himself into the arms of the chair, not through any feeling of unease or deference, but rather due to the enjoyment he derived from the opulent sound of his worsted suit in contact with real leather. Pecton leaned back into his wrap-around swivel chair, which he turned in the direction of the armchair, and laid his entwined hands across his paunch. "Are there any changes in the schedule I'm not already aware of?" He glanced across the top of his glasses in an effort to focus more accurately on Appleby, his vision blinded by the strong sunlight streaming in the window behind the armchair. Appleby brought chronological order to the sheets on his knees and replied, "There are a number of changes which do not alter the orchestra schedule. Shall I run you through the main schedule as far as D–Day?"

Pecton rose from his chair and made for the window. "Yes, yes, please do," he shot back; then, pulling the blind halfway down the window to exclude the offending rays, he resumed his position. Appleby took up, "Today, Monday 23rd –" Pecton raised a terminating hand. "Shortly before you arrived I received a number of programmes from the printers," he said. "I'd be grateful for your comments."

He reached inside the top left hand drawer of his desk, and permitting himself a gratified, "Now then," handed a copy to Appleby who also murmured approvingly. The front cover of pale matt brown contrasted effectively with a diagonal of silk in red and white, the Polish national colours. Across the top of the page it announced – *Symphony Hall.*

Appleby uncrossed his legs, the better to examine the programme. It opened on the centre page to display the order of music for the concert.

Appleby raised his eyes in Pecton's direction. "It's definitely Uginski?"

"Yes, yes – quite definitely Mr Anton Uginski. I must say I found that hiatus – after they withdrew the minister for culture's name – very tedious, not to say trying. He was patently the man for an occasion such as this, and I'm still not sure whether there is not some inbuilt slight in this substitution."

"No, no," Appleby echoed, soothingly. "I'm sure you are mistaken in that. If they wished to offend, they could have withdrawn any one of a number of contributions. Instead of which you are getting a government minister, and their ambassador, as an ostentatious seal of approval. There may be, on the other hand, shades of inter-governmental diplomacy of which we are unaware. But then, Michael, that's not our line of business. We should concentrate on what we do know and that is our undoubted coup."

"Perhaps you're right. It was so intensely irritating when they withdrew the first minister, and did not seem either inclined or interested in providing a substitute; and of course, then there was the resultant hassle trying to hold off the printers. However, we're on course now, and Mr Uginski arrives on Saturday."

"Good. It's coming together nicely."

"I did think it a trifle odd, not to say –" Pecton stopped, not for a loss of words, but reluctant to conclude.

"A little odd?" Appleby probed.

Pecton overcame his reluctance. "To pack the first box at the Albert Hall with men! Decidedly odd."

Appleby broke into a deep belly laugh. "Well yes, an all male phalanx could be open to a number of interpretations, and in that connection let's hope 'phalanx' is the nearest anybody comes to a Freudian slip."

A smile flickered on Pecton's face, "Yes, yes, quite," and went out.

His unresolved irritability resurfaced almost immediately. "You do agree there is something incongruous in placing my wife and the ambassador's wife in the next box with the other ladies?"

Appleby pulled his papers and programme to his chest, crossed his legs, and sank back into the armchair. "One must face the fact," he began slowly, "that they are sending a government minister, a move they didn't take lightly. So they call the shots. They may also have different social conventions of which we are unaware. There is the possibility that the positions in the two boxes were dictated by Mrs Uginski not being able to travel."

"All very laudable, Quentin, but I doubt very much if there is a precedent for this sort of ludicrous demarcation in the civilised world."

The latent comedian took hold of Appleby as he pondered his next piece of advice. "If you are looking for a precedent, all one need do is cross their border with Russia on May Day – you won't find many smiling female faces mingling with the heavies on the podium over Lenin's tomb!"

Pecton released an impotent sigh. "That comparison does nothing for my equilibrium, which is disturbed even further every time I think of their suggestion to place Lyle Butler, a junior minister in our government – and his wife – in the next box." The frown suddenly disappeared as, by association, he remembered a further item. "By the way, Butler has effected a meeting with the minister with responsibility for the Independent Broadcast Authority in connection with our application for a commercial radio licence. This meeting takes place on Monday April 13th, a judicious week after our hopeful triumph. I want you to keep that morning free to accompany me, and the chairman, on this most important mission. I wish to emphasise our major commitment to music, which I hope to underline with your considerable presence."

Appleby moved uneasily within the confines of the armchair, not sure whether that was a comment on his corporate abilities, or his corpulent propensities.

"Now then," Pecton picked up the schedules. Appleby raised his head from his less elevated position in an endeavour to detect the direction of the meeting, and succeeding, selected his own schedule.

He sometimes wondered whether this discrepancy in height wasn't a psychological ploy of Pecton's. He wouldn't be surprised if it were.

"Just a moment," Appleby muttered, rummaging for his diary. "I wish to make a note of our meeting on April 13th."

"I shouldn't bother," Pecton advised. "Miss Maybury will have sent you a note on the subject."

"Ah, good." Appleby realigned his sheets and started into the schedule. He rattled off all the rehearsal and recording dates and times including the move to the Royal Albert Hall on Saturday, which Pecton had decided should also be recorded.

Pecton looked across the top of his glasses and gave a brief nod of agreement. Appleby cleared his throat and continued. "The changes I mentioned earlier are minor – the first concerns this evening. There won't be a microphone balance this evening because Brenton and company are in St George's today for that possible organ recording with Shipsey during the week."

Pecton clarified, "You will see that the only days we're not using Shipsey in Croydon are tomorrow and Wednesday. That means, with satisfactory tests, Brenton will record in St George's on Tuesday and Wednesday. If we can manage it, Shipsey fulfils his contract to provide a Bach programme for disc during this week and at no extra cost."

"That's rather a heavy load," Appleby ventured.

"Rubbish. He's delighted we engaged him for the Polish Week."

"I was thinking of Brenton."

"That's a matter between Brenton and the company. Entirely outside your jurisdiction."

"Mmm. On a point of information – are those microphone rehearsals and recordings in the Albert Hall still on, if the recordings in Croydon go according to plan?"

Pecton pursed his lips, and on their release answered, "I thought of the Albert Hall as a fail-safe situation. However, the possibility of the live concert proving a more memorable occasion on disc, I just can't afford to miss." He leaned forward and placed his arms on the desk in a more intimate gesture. "May I bring you back to a suggestion you made earlier. It's a minor point, but an important one in terms of attitude. If we are using a D–Day analogy, I suggest we refer to today as D–Day and the Royal Albert Hall on Saturday as VE Day."

"A nice idea," Appleby said, brightening. "It does add a certain momentum to the week."

The contrast between the two men was both physical and one of approach. Pecton's sharp, thin, austere countenance – the innovator; a foil to Appleby's chubby affability, the smoother of problems. The orchestra had picked up the differences and produced the motto: An Appleby a day keeps the doctor away – the doctor being a reference to Pecton's recent acceptance of an Honorary Doctorate of Music; the motto itself, a commentary on their respective personalities.

Shrewdness rather than modesty indicated that Pecton not use the nomenclature in day-to-day business. But he was not above using it on the company's brochures and publicity handouts, upon which he thought it looked rather well – an auspicious start along the honours trail. The conferral was undoubtedly a 'thank you' for the annual concerts that Pecton arranged at the West Country University, and possibly a means to ensure their continuance. The concerts were organised as a two-performance event. The matinee, which was free, was for the students and staff of the university. The evening concert, a gala out-of-town event paid for the matinee. The university provided its examination hall gratis.

Quentin Appleby's demeanour could be deceptive, but those who found themselves deceived had usually been presumptuous enough to equate his courtliness with malleability, an unfortunate error, as the more opportunistic inevitably found out. His reaction under this type of duress was blunt and unequivocal, but invariably within the bounds of politeness. He had never been known to lose his temper. The nearest approach to this being a visible tightening of the lips, coupled with a fractional lowering of the eyelids, which for some, made his large brown eyes even more attractive, but for the more perceptive, signalled the need for a diversion. He made an excellent listener, and at fifty-eight, imparted a congenial paternalism to all his undertakings.

They reached the final tally on a second sheet of estimated arrival and departure times. Both nodded in the other's direction, communicating mutual satisfaction.

"Well, that's that." Appleby grunted, as Pecton clipped his sheets into an easy view rotational display to his left.

"Yes," Pecton confirmed, "Everything in order. The only imponderable seems to be St George's. By the same token, I've often thought Brenton a trifle pernickety." He turned his swivel chair towards Appleby for confirmation adding, "Don't you think?"

"Perhaps," Appleby replied easily, "But in his line of business where a miscalculation can cost thousands, I should have imagined it would pay to be fussy."

"Yes, yes, quite," Pecton replied testily. What he had hoped for was a social rather than a professional comment, and since Appleby had not risen to his cast, he moved on tetchily to the next subject. Sometimes it irked him that he had not had a say in Brenton's appointment to the organisation. It wasn't that he was dissatisfied with his work; in fact he heard nothing but good on that subject. It was the man himself. There was something vaguely unsettling about him, something he could not quite put a finger on. Was it a case of Brenton being rather too much his own man? If that were so, then it was not in an ostentatious way because that was something he could cope with, and quickly bring to heel. No, he reasoned, it came in the more subtle shape of a self-contained detachment, which, because of its studied vagueness, was difficult to apprehend.

All of which could have been avoided had Brenton undergone the obligatory interview laid on for everybody else in the company. In one salutary operation, it could have been demonstrated to whom he owed allegiance, and indeed deference. In an endeavour to reach Brenton, he had provided a desk and ancillary equipment in Miss Maybury's anteroom. The extra responsibility did not amount to anything terribly tedious for Brenton: telephone calls, messages, a modicum of secretarial, and an item they were all engaged in assembling – an archive of the company's recordings.

Pecton turned his preoccupied features in Appleby's direction, who, misreading the expression, removed from the bottom of his bundle a sheet that bore the heading, 'Additional Items.' Glancing at Pecton to judge his timing, he was encouraged by a single point on the Pecton 'yes' scale. He elaborated, "There are two or three items which I think should be brought to your attention. The most important of which is the robbery over the weekend in the recording equipment area."

"The what!" Pecton's eyebrows shot up over the rim of his glasses.

"Yes, I'm afraid so." Appleby confirmed, and while taking a breath with which to service his explanation, Pecton impatiently overflowed, "Why wasn't I informed of this before now? This could read very badly for us if the press get their hands on it, yes – yes, and it is quite conceivable that –"

"Michael – Michael!" Appleby expended his breath, unnecessarily he thought, on the interjection. It was not without effect because it produced the desired halt to Pecton's shocked response.

Appleby continued, "It is a relatively minor occurrence. Therefore, nothing we can't cope with."

"Try me – try me," Pecton prodded. "What's involved?"

Appleby moved marginally within the confines of his chair. "Brenton's equipment storeroom was opened, and three two-way radios stolen. But before I continue, I wish to dispel the impression that I may have been negligent in some way. I find it embarrassing having to point out to you that I am your orchestra manager, nothing more – nothing less, and circumventing this type of occurrence is consequently no part of my contractual responsibility. In point of fact, because we don't employ a house superintendent, it would seem to me to be part of your portfolio." Appleby's eyes closed momentarily, a disdainful punctuation of the cadence point.

Pecton moved forward within his chair and rested his arms on the desk in a placatory gesture. He opened his mouth to speak, but this time the roles were reversed and it was Appleby who broke the silence with a glumly intoned coda. "Of course I would not be averse to an extension of my contract that included the area under discussion – with the stipulation," he concluded, "that we renegotiate my salary."

To say time stood still would be a trite over-simplification, more particularly since it did nothing of the kind. However, under these particular circumstances something occurred within the flow of its latitudinal parameters that may have given Pecton this impression. One explanation could have been the mind's capacity to add a longitudinal dimension to such moments, and Pecton, never one to miss an opportunity, used the three seconds devoid of sound to process a number of propositions:

Had he overstepped the mark with Appleby? Yes. Was he overstretched on house matters? Yes. Would Appleby make a good houseman? Yes. Would it interfere with his present function? No. Was there finance available to effect a transfer to Appleby? No. Leave well enough alone? Yes.

Quentin Appleby for his part, not finding it necessary to depart from the metronomic norm, merely found time to lower his gaze from where he had abstractedly contemplated a brass-framed print of Degas' *The Musicians of the Orchestra* on the wall above Pecton's head, to meet its owner's eyes straight on.

"Yes, yes, quite," Pecton began predictably enough. "If I seem to have overstretched your contractual boundaries Quentin, let me assure you it was quite unintentional. You must be aware of the strain this Polish Week is having on me." Then, hurriedly, "Indeed on all of us."

The intercom interrupted peremptorily. Pecton pressed the illuminated button and Miss Maybury's voice announced, "Mr Brenton has arrived, Dr Pecton."

"Please tell him that I shall see him in a few moments."

"Oh, and Dr Pecton?"

"Yes?"

"You have a call from Poland coming through on line one."

"Very good Miss Maybury, thank you." He turned to Appleby and said, "I'm afraid I must ask you to excuse me, but before you depart, I wish to say briefly that the matter of house superintendent is a subject I should like to discuss with you in the future. In the meantime, could I ask you to go downstairs with Brenton, find out what precisely took place, and come back to me on it in, say –" He glanced at the clock on his desk, "one hour?"

Line one started to buzz. Appleby reluctantly, it appeared, extricated himself from his plush surroundings. As he reached the door, Pecton, having lifted the phone, placed one hand across its mouthpiece and asked, "Was there anything else of importance?"

"Nothing which won't keep," Appleby replied, and closed the door.

In the large outer office, Appleby nodded in Miss Maybury's direction and crossed the room to David Brenton's desk.

"Hello David, how are you keeping?"

"Well," Brenton indicated the chair on the other side of his desk.

Appleby seated himself in a spartan edition of the comfort he had recently vacated, and found the contrast not to his liking. "I suppose", he began sympathetically, "you've been informed of the break-in?"

"Yes. Jim Sherry left a note with a few details." Brenton nodded towards a half sheet of foolscap on his desk. "I wish Pecton would get a move on. I haven't as yet checked over the storeroom."

"I do beg your pardon," Appleby said, clutching his papers and uncrossing his legs. "I should have explained straight away. Michael asked me to go down with you and bring back the details." Brenton was already rising from behind his desk before Appleby had finished the sentence.

"In that case I'd like to get down there as quickly as possible." He moved around the desk and waited in the centre of the room while Appleby gathered together his belongings and himself.

Brenton turned towards Miss Maybury, "We'll be in the storeroom area, Miss Maybury."

"Very good, Mr Brenton."

The decorous formality was an overt manifestation of the particular style with which Miss Maybury ran her office. Not just everything well done and in its proper place, but correctly labelled. She felt, however, within the confines of her small coterie of friends, that the approach of a sixtieth birthday empowered her to refer to Messrs Pecton and Brenton as 'My two boys'. The reference was a diffused mixture of the maternal and the indulgent, the cornerstone of many a successful secretary. Her two boys responded in kind for differing reasons. Apart from her good secretarial qualities, Pecton recognised that she managed to impart a particular tone to general and personal proceedings, which he found agreeable. He attributed this to her correct manner of address, which imbued him with a comfortable feeling of acknowledged status. Brenton on the other hand was closer in spirit to Miss Maybury's mode of social interaction, which precluded intrusive banter. Despite this, their mutual respect meant genuine warmth of feeling flowed between them.

As the two men walked towards the outer door, Appleby signalled the necessity to dump the schedules in his office. Brenton held the door for him.

"Be with you in a moment," Appleby murmured as he eased by.

"I'll go ahead and open up," Brenton replied, closing the door behind him. He turned right in the corridor without waiting for a reply and headed for the stairs. At the bottom he strode diagonally across the main foyer to the right hand entrance to the auditorium.

Without slackening pace he brushed through the swing doors and entered the auditorium. In the half-light its unusually sombre atmosphere made no impression; his mind was fixed on the storeroom beyond the exit doors at the other end. When he arrived at his destination, he checked first to see if either of the double-doors were susceptible to outside pressure, and drew a blank. Using his key he entered the room, looked briefly around its contents and, detecting nothing out of place, moved to the microphone press in which the three short-wave radios should have lain. He produced a second key and opened up. They were not in their usual positions. A quick glance over the remaining shelves confirmed the information in Jim Sherry's note. He placed an elbow on a convenient shelf, and with his thumb and forefinger was tweaking his chin, deep in thought, when Quentin Appleby padded through the open door.

"Any luck?"

"'Fraid not." Brenton turned back toward the press and proceeded to eliminate the remaining items against an inventory list on the back of the door. Starting from the top, it took a few minutes to get through the lot. Removing his hand from the final item he resumed his former position and mused, "Nothing else missing."

Appleby moved between him and the iron-barred window. "That's good news at any rate."

"Well – yes and no."

"Ah. There's a further problem?"

"Indeed. A number of them in fact, but the most intriguing one – supposing it was a robbery – is why they would remove three relatively inexpensive pieces of hardware and leave the more expensive ones."

"That *is* strange," Appleby said, moving closer to the press to determine what constituted expensive in the engineering world. "Mmm," he mumbled softly in a downward glissando, "Microphones and things."

A fleeting smile came to Brenton's lips. He turned aside lest he offend Appleby, and moved into the centre of the room. Serious again, he approached the window and examined its bolted rigidity, and more closely its perimeter. "No sign of interference or movement here," he concluded, turning back to face Appleby. "Does security know about this?"

Appleby's face lit up and his mouth widened into an outright grin. "Excuse the laugh, it just occurred to me that it's my turn to answer yes and no. Jim Sherry told them there might have been a break-in and I took the liberty of asking them to look out for anything in the building that might support such an assumption. But they don't as yet know what exactly is involved."

"You did well."

"Once you've confirmed the disappearance, fill them in on the situation. Pecton said he's not calling the police because of possible newspaper publicity."

"That request has a hollow ring to it, since he damn well doesn't have to replace the equipment."

"I'm sure if you try to understand his point of view, something could be worked out."

"Something could be worked out," Brenton said reflectively, "but not out of my budget."

"I'll see what can be done." Appleby moved towards the door. Over his shoulder he added, "I'll be seeing him in half an hour, so I'll relate what you've just said. How long do you intend staying in the Hall?"

"For the rest of the evening. I thought I'd connect the stereo mic in the ceiling for a mini-listen to tonight's rehearsal."

Appleby ambled out into the corridor and threw a "See you anon," over his shoulder. Brenton did not reply. His mind engaged in a quick scan for information he knew he should have imparted to Appleby, or was it Pecton – or maybe both. He suddenly clicked his fingers, ran to the door after Appleby, who at that point having despaired of a parting salutation, had quickened pace. Brenton shouted, "Tell Pecton St George's is almost certainly on. I'll have confirmation tonight."

CHAPTER 4

Monday March 23rd 1981
St George's
6.30 pm

Sarah heard the side door slam at the top of the stairs. A dull thud, and then the sound of descending footsteps. She threw her own door wide open, but the meagre light that trickled out made hardly any impact on the darkness of the stairwell.

"That you Jim?"

A dark suited form began to materialise and said, "No, my dear." As the figure took a more definite shape, Sarah realised the man was negotiating the stairs holding a large tray in front of him.

"I'm the rector," the man announced.

"Do let me help. I didn't realise you were carrying a tray." Sarah moved to the bottom of the stairs.

"No, my dear. I've managed as far as this, I can manage the remaining few steps."

She stepped aside as he reached the ground floor and the grey-haired, neat, slight person of the Reverend Rupert Pryce propelled his overburdened, concave gait into the recording room. He paused briefly and, coming to terms with the absence of an available table, placed the tray on one of the chairs.

"I must leave this down for the moment," he expelled, with obvious relief.

"We're using your tables for the desk and tape machine," Sarah explained.

Relieved of his task, he turned to face her and his features took on a more benign expression.

"My name is Rupert Pryce," he began, "and I most sincerely regret the lack of light on the stairs. It must be a dreadful nuisance for you. Particularly for a young lady."

"How do you do, I'm Sarah Carlyle."

Mr Pryce nodded his head in greeting. "I feel obliged to explain," he continued, "that it's not just a matter of replacing an electric light bulb. The wiring is faulty and needs renewing. Under the circumstances – accidents and such," he underlined sotto voce, "I thought I had better deliver your meal in person. I must confess I felt a certain distress when Mr Brenton informed me on the telephone that we had a young lady working under these conditions. Might I suggest that you keep this door open at all times to allow some light onto the stairs."

"Yes of course, Mr Pryce, that's a sensible suggestion."

He extended one hand in the direction of the tray, and arranging his features interrogatively added, "I was under the impression there would be two of you here. At least that is what the restaurant people intimated when they delivered this to the rectory."

Sarah's hand rose involuntarily to cover her mouth.

"Oh – I see what's happened, they were asked to make the delivery to the church. As it happens, that's why I'm on my own. My colleague Jim Sherry left here at about 6.15 to try and locate them. They were to have been here at six o'clock."

Mr Pryce smiled benevolently and extended both hands in an unconsciously clerical gesture. "I had another reason to cross the road to see you. I received a message on my telephone from your Mr Brenton, which he asked me to deliver to you." With eyes blinking rapidly and a deep frown etched across his normally bright face, he groped around in the voluminous right hand pocket of his jacket until he found a folded sheet of notepaper, which he pulled out in triumph and handed to Sarah.

"What time did the message arrive?"

"I would say," the rector pondered, raising an eye heavenwards, "I would say about twenty minutes ago."

Sarah continued to run the paper fold between finger and thumb. Her reluctance to read the contents stemmed mainly from a feigned indifference. The trouble was, the longer she prolonged the inevitable, the more convinced she became that the note contained nothing more than the usual terse command. Besides, what was unlikely face to face could be ruled out absolutely through a third party, and as if to point up the futility of the exercise, the final piece of tape ran through the tape capstan, and with a combined mechanical-electronic click, the machine automatically switched its recording mechanism off.

"Excuse me," Sarah said, turning towards the tape deck. "I must spool off my last tape."

"Why yes of course!" Mr Pryce found relief in having the sudden noise explained.

While resetting the tape through the machine, the sound of someone moving through the church upstairs came across through the speakers. The movement was accompanied momentarily by a snatch of some recent pop tune, which, as soon as she heard the voice, Sarah knew heralded Jim Sherry's return.

Now in a more relaxed frame of mind, she began to read Brenton's note. She moved directly under the light to decipher some aspect of the writing as Sherry came clattering down the stairs. When he reached the bottom step, he caught sight of the food tray.

"I see the bloo-" and on seeing Mr Pryce, "-ooming nosh got here before me," he corrected himself hastily. "Hello Mr Pryce."

"Good evening – Jim isn't it? Before it runs out of my mind … since you collected the church keys this morning, may I presume you'll be responsible for their return?"

"Yes, that's correct Mr Pryce," Sherry answered, glad of the change of subject.

"Well then, neither my sister nor I shall be in the rectory this evening after seven o'clock, so if you would, please drop the keys through the letter box." He moved closer to the door and added, "I have one or two things I must attend to in the church, and I presume you two wish to start on your meal before it becomes cold. I'll drop down to see you before I depart, if I may?"

"Of course," Sherry responded.

"Mr Pryce", Sarah enquired, "Is it alright if we leave the equipment here? The possibility of our recording during the week seems to be quite good, indeed I can say from a technical point of view it's on. The only uncertain element appears to be the availability of Ronald Shipsey, the organist."

Mr Pryce gleefully returned from the doorway. "That's a nice surprise. Mr Brenton told me Mr Shipsey was standing by, and that it all depended on what you, Miss Carlyle, had to say."

'When Brenton hands something over,' Sarah reflected, 'he hands it over.' She held out the note and informed them, "It's on then, starting tomorrow afternoon."

Mr Pryce stood between the two, his head nodding in benevolent delight from one to the other. Then his face assumed an expression of anxiety and he refocused on Sarah.

"My dear, you are forgetting your meals. They may have started to turn cold by now."

Sarah stepped towards the tray. "Let's start straightaway. Did I see a bottle of wine peeping out from a basket there?"

Sarah cast an eye around the room they were standing in. "I'm sure," she remarked, "This room would pass muster as a good wine cellar."

"It's interesting that you should say that," Mr Pryce said. "We have reason to believe there may have been a wine cellar on the other side of this wall. I shall show you something which will undoubtedly interest you." Marshalling his thoughts, he peered at them across imaginary spectacles.

"As you are possibly aware, this church was built in 1732." He turned his head back towards the area of the dark wall, and raising his left hand to emphasise the point said, "This wall, and its similarly endowed adjuncts, form part of the remains of a previous religious establishment – belonging to Benedictine nuns I am told. At the dissolution, or shortly after, the building fell into disrepair, because the building was of no great architectural merit. Then in the late 17th century, it was converted to the needs of the wine trade. The crypt here, as you were quick to notice Miss Carlyle, presented certain characteristics necessary for the safe storage of wine."

He moved closer to the wall and motioned to them to follow. He placed his hand on what was pointedly a particular stone, about chest level, and smaller than the surrounding blocks.

"Now watch closely," he said. When he pressed on the stone, it moved with ease into the wall, about an inch. He looked back to savour the surprised expressions behind him, as a large part of the wall moved inward. The aperture, now wide open, was about five feet high, and the same in width. Mr Pryce stood aside, a smile of triumphant amusement on his face, encouraged by the incredulity of the others standing behind him.

"Needless to say," he chuckled, "this contraption was not any part of either religious establishment. Its significance lies in the wine trade's need of a secure inner sanctuary, so to speak, to store the more expensive and rare items. Unfortunately, the lighting inside is afflicted in the same way as the light on the stairs outside – on the same circuit; but if you step through after me, your eyes will become accustomed. Mind your heads coming through," and he disappeared inside.

"After you," Sherry declared gallantly. Sarah shot a look at him before taking the plunge. From inside, she looked over her shoulder to watch Sherry taking his initial steps. He was repeating the motions she had gone through a moment before – hands outstretched, apprehensive foot movements, head held back.

Mr Pryce's voice sprang out of the darkness. The extra reverberation indicated a larger area than they had just left, built with similar material as the wall through which they had just gained access.

"If you face the light, and then slowly turn away, you may get some idea of the area involved. The ceiling is five or six feet higher than the room outside. It is, in fact, the floor of the church upstairs. I should also mention the interesting point, that this floor on which we now stand, was not a crypt in the original church. It was the ground floor, but due to the way residue of one sort or another can build up over a period of time, it gives an impression of having sunk. If you know anything of archaeology you will understand."

"My eyes are beginning to come to terms with the dark," Sarah whispered, and then wondered, "Why am I whispering?"

Still not fully acclimatised, Sherry asked, "Are there any steps in here, or are we completely on the flat?"

"Completely on the flat," Mr Pryce answered. "Have you noticed how very cold it is in here?"

"Yes!" came the combined reply.

"Well now, I must bring the tour to a close. I have one or two small jobs that I must attend to rather urgently, and presumably you have likewise."

Outside once more, Sarah gave an involuntary shiver. "That was petrifying!"

"Pity the light wasn't working," Sherry added, rubbing his hands briskly.

"Yes," the rector agreed, "but since you will be here over the next few days, I shall bring a lamp, so that you can see it again in more detail – and hopefully less rushed circumstances."

He pulled the door closed. It moved inexorably into position, with the gritty self-assurance of an alligator's jaws.

CHAPTER 5

Monday March 23rd 1981
Croydon
7.50 pm

Brenton sat in the most unobtrusive position in the auditorium. Nearer the stage in a better listening position would have drawn attention to himself; further back in the darkness of the stalls, he would have had to endure less perfect acoustics.

The stage was bathed in the warm embracing glow of hidden overhead spotlights. Musicians had started to emerge, one by one, but as rehearsal time drew nearer there was more movement and they were entering the stage area in twos and threes. Their animated conversation grew louder in a useless attempt to top the growing volume of instruments being warmed up. They ranged in intricacy from the barking de-de-dee of the oboe, to the more convoluted indulgences of members of the strings. He heard Freddie Parker's French horn before he espied its owner. When finished with brisk scales, he invariably announced his satisfaction with the same familiar quote from Strauss' *Till Eulenspiegel*.

Brenton's mood lightened. Sitting alone in the half-light, he found the unfolding spectacle absorbing. How was it possible that so many disparate strands of humanity could be moulded into a unified musical force? Tradition – or perhaps discipline? More like a balance of both. The undisciplined cacophony should have had a sharpening effect on his senses, like a good aperitif. Unexpectedly, lack of a recent meal, coupled with physical and mental tiredness, combined to produce the opposite.

The oboe began to emerge and dominate with a continuously sounding A for a general tuning. The other members began to play copycat with the A and related harmony notes. They reached a frenzied climax and faded to a hushed expectant silence. A solitary, familiar voice rose to fill the void. The comfortable solidity of Quentin Appleby stood beside the podium and introduced the visiting Polish conductor, Jan Komorski. To polite applause, the maestro stepped from behind Appleby and mounted the podium. His tall, blond, bespectacled frame acknowledged the greeting. His appearance seemed to impart extra length to his arms. Brenton would have guessed his age to be mid forties. He knew it to be thirty-six last birthday. Bearing in mind the patriarchal society in which Komorski lived and worked, his rise to academic eminence in the University of Krakow at such an early age spoke well of his abilities. Whether these extended to conducting remained to be seen, and heard, because strangely, he was not listed among the top ten Polish conductors. Komorski raised his arms to begin and a moment later launched into Elgar's Symphonic Prelude, *Polonia*.

The arresting martial opening startled Brenton momentarily. His drowsiness returned however with the introduction of a soothing Polish melody. His eyes glazed and changed the scene to a yellow impressionistic glow.

"David!" Brenton's head jerked up from where it had lain on his chest. A perturbed Jim Sherry stood in front of him in the next row of seats. The music on stage had come to a tumultuous halt, the pedal notes of the organ reverberating around the walls of the Hall, a continuation of what had been running through Brenton's head moments before.

"My head," Brenton placed his forehead between finger and thumb of his left hand.

"You ok?" Sherry bent forward, grasping the back of the seat in front of him; then remembering the purpose of his mission, he exclaimed, "Pecton asked me to give you this note as soon as I saw you."

Without lifting his head, Brenton held out his hand.

"There *is* something the matter," pressed Sherry. "Are you feeling all right?"

Brenton looked up at Sherry with one eye open. "Nothing more than a bloody awful headache." He tore open the envelope and read the brief note. He looked up again, both eyes open.

"Pecton foots the bill for the missing two-ways. Where's Sarah?"

"Upstairs in the control room listening to the tapes she recorded earlier in St George's. Can I get her for you?"

"No." Brenton rose from the seat and indicated that they move to the aisle. He turned to Sherry and almost apologetically added, "I thought perhaps she might carry some aspirin."

Sherry grinned and asked, "Have you been drinking without telling Uncle Jim?"

There was no response. Eventually, Brenton said, "Let's bail out of here as smartly as possible. I want you to lash up my usual quota of mics, two extra condenser types, plus one for the piano front of stage. Leave them labelled and standing in the wings."

"Got it."

"Here are my keys to the store room. Be sure and lock it each time you leave. I'll go upstairs and have a listen with Sarah."

He handed Sherry the keys. When he reached the short access corridor to the control room, he saw the door was open, although no sound emanated.

"You there, Sarah?"

"Yes, David," came the absorbed reply, and as he came through the open door, "I'm listening to some of the George tapes."

"Ah, good."

"To tell the truth, I won't be satisfied until you've had a listen."

He came around the control desk and stood behind her. The tape continued to roll. She became aware of his proximity, which did not help her powers of concentration. His voice, when he spoke, confirmed his closeness in a curiously tingly way. She thought, 'Why aren't all conversations like this.'

"Seems ok," Brenton said. "Are they all as clean as this one?"

"Yes. This is one we recorded from 4.35 pm. It contains a Heathrow jet which I checked before you came up, and it does come across on tape – but not intrusively."

"I shouldn't worry. That particular take off direction is not frequently used, and tomorrow the wind is forecast from the opposite direction –

so nothing to worry about." He moved to one side and, with an apologetic demeanour asked, "Do you by any chance have some aspirin?"

Sarah grabbed her shoulder bag and started to rummage. "Not actually aspirin, but if it's for neuralgia or a headache I do have these." She handed over a small packet.

Brenton extracted two. "I'm sure they'll do fine. I should have explained I've a large headache." He returned the packet. "Thanks. Would you excuse me a moment while I go downstairs for a glass of water?"

"They should act fairly quickly."

He strode briskly through the open door calling back, "Thanks again." She relaxed, and sank back into her swivel chair. Placing an elbow on each armrest she propped up her chin with clasped hands. She picked up another tape. Thank goodness the encounter had gone well. After this morning's wrangle, she'd been more than a little apprehensive. Not that she felt differently now; she didn't. But it was difficult to feel angry with somebody who had clearly put the incident behind him. Actually, that was something in his favour. He wasn't the type who held a grudge. She turned to place the final tape on the machine. Her fingers wound the tape through the capstan and tape heads. Really, she mused, there was little point in listening to the final tape. The others had proved satisfactory and she still remembered the aural conditions under which this last one had been recorded. But then 'Decisive David' hadn't heard a lengthy piece yet. Or was he leaving that decision to her? She would have preferred if he'd stayed a bit longer to listen. His face had seemed unusually drawn and grey. Hopefully, he wasn't on the verge of catching some bug or other – this week of all weeks.

She pressed the replay button and sat back. There had hardly been time to resettle when she heard Brenton and Sherry at the bottom of the stairs. From the snippets of conversation that wafted ahead of them, she gathered Michael Pecton to be the subject of their debate. Brenton appeared first in the doorway.

"Sarah, Jim and I are going for a coffee before Mrs Wheeler puts the wraps on the canteen. Are you interested in grabbing a cup?"

"Love to." Sarah rose from her chair behind the desk.

"Switch the tape off until you return," Brenton advised.

The trio moved quickly across the entrance foyer and up the stairs on the opposite side. Because the orchestra had returned to the fray, they had the canteen to themselves.

Brenton was first to the counter. "Three coffees if you please, Mrs Wheeler." Mrs Wheeler's matronly face flashed a smile in their direction. "Evenin' Mr Brenton. You lot are a bit late." She reached for three cups from a recess behind her, and threw in her well-intentioned but inevitable question, "Workin' 'ard?" And looking more perceptively at Brenton, "'Hope not too 'ard!" She placed them all on the counter.

"Thank you," Brenton said. "Surely you must know by now Mrs Wheeler, we don't work – we just sit and listen."

Mrs Wheeler laughed wheezily. "Whatever it is, my son, you look like you could do with a good rest or an 'oliday." Mrs Wheeler rang up three coffees on the till and Brenton turned to the others behind him. "This one's on me," he stated, and returning to Mrs Wheeler, "Actually, what I could do with at this moment is a sandwich."

"Sorry love, I've only cakes left." She pointed towards a tray of confectionery at the end of the counter. "Any of those take your fancy?"

Sarah removed her coffee from the counter. "Thanks David, Jim and I will grab a seat." They found a centre table. "He does look rather peaky," Sarah said, looking in the direction of the counter.

"Not surprised," Sherry replied, removing the cup from his lips. "He hasn't eaten since breakfast, he told me. Only remembered a while ago."

Sarah adjusted a third chair at the table as Brenton approached. He sat down and they mutely surveyed his balanced diet – a Banbury bun and two aspirin. The aspirin disappeared in quick succession accompanied by sips of coffee, which left the main course for his delectation.

The lack of conversation began to have an unsettling effect on Sarah and Jim Sherry. Sarah finished her coffee and rose from the table.

"I'd like to finish that tape as soon as possible," she said addressing

Brenton, "and if it's not too much trouble, I'd appreciate it if you could listen to some more of it." Heading for the door she threw back a "Good night" to Mrs Wheeler who responded in kind.

Brenton, seemingly impervious to admonishment or blandishment, said to Sherry, "I want you to drop me at Hyde Park tonight."

"I could go out to Hendon if you wish."

"I'm staying in town tonight, Lancaster Gate will do fine."

"You staying with friends?"

"You could say that."

"When would you like to leave?"

Brenton drained his coffee with subdued relish. "Just as soon as I've reassured Sarah on her St George recording."

"I'd intended calling in for a pork pie and a pint of bitter on the way. Care to join me?"

There was a moment's pause. "That's a good idea – mention of food has set my salivary glands in motion."

The sound of impatient shunting crockery insinuated itself from the background. Brenton cast a quick glance in Mrs Wheeler's direction, and then at his watch. "We'd better not overstay our welcome," he said, rising to his feet. Sherry quickly followed.

"Good night Mrs Wheeler," they chorused, making for the door.

"G'night gentlemen," she echoed, managing to feign reasonable surprise at their departure. As they crossed the foyer, Brenton asked, "I presume you have a particular hostelry in mind?"

"The Ranelagh, across Chelsea Bridge. They have a nice buffet, and it's on the way to Hyde Park."

"Good. This shouldn't take more than a few minutes."

They had hardly set foot on the stairway to the control room, when an agitated Sarah materialised at the top of the stairs. "Come quickly!" she called excitedly. "There's a row taking place on stage!"

Brenton bounded up the steps with an alacrity that left Sarah and Jim Sherry somewhat taken aback. When they came in after him, they saw he had already opened the first two channels on the desk, to which he had earlier plugged up the auditorium ceiling mic. He looked intently towards the stage, as the sounds of a shouting match came across on the speakers. Sherry came up behind and, while endeavouring to peer through the haze on the window, said, "That's some barney."

Brenton brusquely increased the loudspeaker volume. Sarah, visually picking up where she had left off, saw the same white-haired trumpet player, Jack Lesko, now standing and shouting even more loudly at the conductor. Komorski stepped down from the podium and, escorted by the orchestra leader, Arthur Liddel, swept off stage. They were replaced immediately by Quentin Appleby, who mounted the podium, and in the course of taking control, used the first intelligible words to come across on the loudspeakers – "Quiet please!" He raised both hands in the air. "May we have some quiet, please."

The loud hum of conversation began to fade, only to recommence as Arthur Liddel came back on stage. He approached Appleby, whispered something in his ear, and resumed his seat. Appleby made a half-hearted attempt to raise his arms in the air again, giving the impression that the first attempt had drained his energy. He began speaking at a low volume.

"…and I find it distressing … to have to reiterate that which was made known to every member of this orchestra individually; and that is … the door to my office is always open, and I'm always available to discuss group or individual grievances. Which brings me to the …"

"I will not sit here and suffer the insults of that communist dog!" Jack Lesko was on his feet again. Appleby raised a placatory hand to Lesko.

"Jack, this is not the place to discuss your grievance. I want you to pack your instrument and come with me to my office, where we can talk in private." Appleby turned to Arthur Liddel on his left and, stepping down from the podium, directed, "Take over the rehearsal until the maestro returns."

Liddel stepped onto the podium and commanded, "From the top, ladies and gentlemen."

Further discussion had been snuffed. Appleby moved side stage and waited for Lesko.

Brenton turned away from the window. "That was rather nasty, the more so when one considers the significance of the week ahead."

"Was that Polish they were hurling at one another?" Sherry asked.

"I'd say so," Brenton answered, "not because I recognised it as such, but in the knowledge that the protagonists are both Polish."

"Is Jack Polish?" Sarah inquired, surprised. "I was under the impression he was British, but that may have been because of his age."

"Yes, he's Polish," Brenton confirmed. "But he is rather different from the recent influx, both in age and outlook. He's one of the expatriate Poles who settled in Britain after the last war."

"I see."

"And where did he acquire the handle 'Jack'?" Sherry wondered.

"His name is actually Jan," Brenton disclosed. "I suppose the native population's inability to cope with the unusual changed it to Jack."

"I hope he's not in trouble," Sarah said apprehensively.

"I hope not," Brenton agreed. "He's a decent chap. His outburst, I'm sure, can be explained. Speaking of trouble, if we don't get cracking on your tape – I'm in trouble." She smiled, and motioned to the chairs behind the desk.

She clicked off the input from the concert hall below and turned on the tape output. They listened intently to the final fifteen minutes of the tape, noting here and there occasional distant sounds, none of which, they agreed, would have a direct influence on the recording.

"Excellent," Brenton pronounced as the last of the tape ran through the machine and tripped the off switch. "I wish you the best of luck tomorrow."

———

Sherry, who had whiled away the time with the day's paper, lifted his head. "Did you see this article about the bloke who records strange sounds and voices in certain old buildings around the country?"

"Yes," Sarah responded immediately. "I read that while we were in St George's, and I must say I was tempted to leave a tape rolling there during the night – the fire hazard pulled me up."

Brenton turned to Sarah. "I expect you have your own transport?"

"Yes, I'll wrap up here – you two go ahead."

"Could I make a brief run through your schedule for St George's tomorrow, Tuesday? Ronald Shipsey will be ready to start at 3.00 pm and will be available until 10.00 pm tomorrow night. He's acting as his own music director. You'll need to keep a tight rein on the time allowance on each item. The time allowances will be attached to the initial tapes, which I'll issue you with here tomorrow at 1.00 pm. So there's no necessity to surface here before that time. I can't give you the printout now because the draft only reached Miss Maybury this evening, shortly before she departed. Is that ok?"

"Yes, that's fine."

"Right then." Exiting past Sherry he added, "See you outside in a few minutes."

———

Sherry waited until the sound of Brenton's footsteps had faded before disclosing with unabashed pleasure his success in persuading Brenton to accompany him for a drink and a bite to eat.

"You didn't?" she asked with some astonishment.

"I did," he proclaimed with relish.

"I congratulate you. Who would have thought it possible! How did you manage it?"

"Not quite sure – I just said I was going for a drink and a pork-pie on the way home, and would he like to drop in with me – and his Highness said yes."

"I take it you're driving him home. It's a long way to Hendon."

"He's not going to Hendon tonight. Staying with a friend at Lancaster Gate."

"Lancaster Gate? A friend?"

"Yes. That makes it very handy for me."

Sarah returned abruptly to the tape machine and started to fidget with the controls.

"I can see that will be handy all round – did you see the vari-speed control for this thing?" she asked in a sudden spurt of annoyance. Sherry advanced to her side and, surprised at her inability to see beyond the top of the tape deck, pointed out, "Look, there it is hanging down behind the deck. Are you using it now?"

"Yes. I thought I'd roll a tape during the night, at the slowest speed available – like our friend in that article. Which means – the tape will run until two or three o'clock in the morning." She bent down and inserted the vari-speed.

"You don't believe that rubbish?" Sherry rebuked. "How could it possibly happen?"

"I'm not sure, but the theory behind it is interesting."

"Yes? I didn't get that."

"Briefly, depending on the coefficient of absorption of the building materials in a building, sounds emitted years before are somehow reactivated under certain unknown criteria, and released once more into the surroundings. I don't expect anything to happen while the shower on stage are blasting away," she nodded towards the orchestra. "But when they pack up and close down the Hall and silence takes over ... well you never can tell what might happen. I just have to make a start and find out. I know the building isn't as old as St George's but I must start somewhere." She hunched up her shoulders in exasperation. "Look Jim," she said directly, "You'd better move smartly if you're not to miss that handy gig with David."

"You're right," he admitted, and made for the door. "Wouldn't do to keep his Lordship waiting. See you tomorrow in St George's."

Sarah opened the channel to the concert hall microphone, and saw that Komorski had taken over rehearsals again, minus Jack Lesko. She took a rough level of the proceedings and switched the tape to record. She quickly wrote a note to David, explaining the insertion of the vari-speed in number one tape machine.

She slowly and tidily placed the note under the main fader and, feeling rather at sea, considered, 'Man proposes but God disposes.'

CHAPTER 6

Monday March 23rd 1981
Croydon
10.10 pm

Outside, Jim Sherry found the night enshrouded in an almost tangible blackness; its only concession to human susceptibilities was a slight rise in temperature.

He stepped back into the shelter and light of the stage door to adjust his duffle coat and throw its hood over his head. He smiled, as a residue of Sarah's perfume found his nose – an ethereal reminder of her occupancy of the garment during the morning. Trying to pinpoint the source led to frustration, and without success, he stepped out into the downpour, which damped down any residual male ardour.

He reached the van on the trot and rooted in his outside pockets for the keys, only to remember he had transferred them to an inner pocket. "Sod it!" he growled, unbuttoning the coat and sacrificing any remaining fragrance to expediency and an inclement rain god. He jumped aboard and slammed the door behind him; as the sleeve ends dripped onto his hands, he started the engine and roused the heater into action. The wipers and lights visually confirmed the wretchedness. He engaged gear and moved up to the stage door, keeping the engine running.

Brenton emerged as the heater began to emit strong wafts of warm air. "Low ceiling," he observed as he settled himself into the cosy surroundings.

"In that case, mind your head," Sherry cautioned, swinging the van through the exit and out onto the roadway. They moved through Croydon towards the A23. The tyres hissed through the running water, which alerted Brenton to possible trouble ahead in St George's. He studied the splattering rain on the driving window a while longer before giving voice to his fears.

"You know, this damnable rain was the one thing I didn't allow for."

"Who can?" Sherry replied. "I often think the forecasting lot decide on the toss of a coin."

"The effects of a downpour will be picked up on mics in St George's ... on the large area of window glass."

"Yeah, I suppose it will."

A brief silence followed. Brenton took up, "You don't seem particularly put out."

"Worrying about it now will put me out that much more if it happens."

"I'm trying to think of an option in the event of a cancellation."

"Why don't you try and leave the whole caboodle behind you for one or two hours while we refresh our bellies and minds in The Ranelagh?"

"Because, essentially, that's one of the differences between my job and yours. I'm expected to anticipate and circumvent job problems."

"Does that mean it's going to be pork-pie à la St George? Because if it is …"

"I'm thinking aloud Jim. I shouldn't have brought it up on the way for a drink."

On a winning wicket, Sherry badgered on. "If it happens ... it's an act of God, in a house of God, and Shipsey will have to heave to ... or whatever organists do when they throw out an anchor."

A brief laugh, and then the left turn on Streatham High Road took Sherry's concentration. Clapham Common came and went, not worth a second glance under the wet circumstances. Clapham Junction – the train-spotter's paradise – came into view. Did it hold the record for trains passing per minute, Brenton mused. Was it odd that he didn't have a yearning to go there as a boy? But then the adulation of one's own region was always paramount. The Midland had been his be-all and end-all. Although, he did have a grudging regard for the Great Western ... the sunshine holiday line to his Aunt and Uncle's place in the South-West. Copper and brass of the Great Western; Crimson of the LMS; echoes from the past; gone like a good deal else of value.

Perhaps it was wrong to think of things past as having gone. Change was the diligent acolyte of time, this life's unyielding master of ceremonies.

They entered Queenstown Road, Battersea Park to the left and Battersea Power Station somewhere out in the mists to their right. He'd read recently that it was to be preserved as a piece of industrial archaeology. Seemed like preserving last week.

"Did you see that blind bastard?" Sherry muttered a tad excitedly. "Must have singed the rollicking paint!"

They moved across Chelsea Bridge. Sherry took his eyes off the road long enough to look Brenton up and down. "I'll say one thing for you. You're a cool one. How can you sit there with the old stiff upper, after that scalded cat tried to replace the side of the van?"

"Because, old man," Brenton smilingly enjoined, placing an elbow across the back of his seat, "if it happens, I could only conceive of it being an act of God, and therefore in no way a reflection on your abilities. If it happens."

Sherry grinned into his rear view mirror, and pulling into a vacant space in Ranelagh Grove, conceded, "Tou-bloody-ché!"

———

The welcoming warmth of The Ranelagh meant they could dispense with overcoats as soon as they found themselves a place to sit. When their food arrived not a word passed between them for several minutes. Feeling refreshed, Brenton began to take note of his surroundings. There was a pleasant lightness to the atmosphere. "This is your watering hole, then?" Brenton asked.

"It's one of those places I like to take someone special."

Brenton pushed his empty plate away and replaced it with his glass of ale.

"I'm suddenly feeling … special," he said sarcastically, sitting back into his seat and resting his hands across his middle. Sherry laughingly scoffed at the suggestion. "Don't get carried away – special means you pay the bill."

"Mercenary as ever. On the other hand, I feel honoured to sit in the same surroundings in which you've been wining and dining Miss Maybury." Brenton replied.

"What's her first name? I've never once heard it crop up."

"Patricia."

"Patricia? Sounds almost human. I'm surprised it's not Prudence!"

"She's not a bad sort. I'm quite fond of the old girl. She comes from, or as I like to think, has broken out of, an overly-protective, sheltered home environment where the very idea of the ladies of the family lifting a finger was anathema. Whether due to changed circumstances or again, as I would like to think, through her determination to do something useful, Miss Maybury in middle age pulled the chocks on her undercarriage and took off. With a minimum of fuss she settled down and equipped herself with the commercial basics. With her deep love of music, she gravitated in Pecton's direction and he, never one to miss an opportunity where class is concerned, flagged her in."

Pausing long enough for his mind to flit from administration to the operational area of the Hall, Brenton said thoughtfully, "I'm sorry Sarah isn't here with us, but frankly, I had just one urgent wish in Croydon this evening – to hit the sack after a bite to eat. I'm really bushed."

"You looked that way earlier on – I suppose the food juiced you up."

"I feel a deal better, but I expect that's only a temporary respite."

As Sherry was raising his glass, he caught sight of a familiar face on the way in.

"Hello, isn't that one of the orchestra coming towards us?"

Brenton followed his line of vision and recognised the new arrival, "Ah yes, Joe Abraham – plays the fiddle."

Abraham approached, and had almost passed before his eye latched onto the two ensconced. His tall prematurely balding frame came to a halt. "Our recording experts!" he exclaimed in pleased recognition. A quick glance around, and he added, "Minus the distaff side of your business – more's the pity."

"Care to join us, Joe?" Brenton invited, and as the Irishman accepted and sat down opposite, Brenton explained, "We dropped in for a quick one."

"Same here," Abraham replied.

The waitress materialised to sweep away the crockery and take Abraham's order for a pint of Guinness. "It removes the dust of Symphony Hall," he grinned.

"The rehearsal's over then?" asked Sherry.

"Yes – and an exciting rehearsal it turned out to be."

"Jack Lesko you mean?" Brenton queried.

"Yes. Poor old Jack; most of us still haven't a clue what it was all about. The consensus is, he picked up a remark of Komorski's in Polish to Reptarski – you know, the bassoonist – which Jack took to be politically objectionable."

Still struggling to place the antagonists in identifiable camps, Sherry asked, "Does this mean one is communist and the other anti?"

"We don't know what happened," Brenton lightly objected. "And until we do, we reserve judgment. What we do know is, Jack is one of a group of Poles who remained in this country after the last war because of their feelings of alienation from the political system instituted in Poland. He possibly feels antagonistic towards a man such as Komorski, a pillar of the establishment, albeit academic, and foolishly gave vent to his feelings."

"By God, he certainly gave vent," Abraham agreed. "The pity is, it was all in Polish."

"I'm sure it will all be settled amicably," Brenton said shrugging.

"Amicably?" Abraham replied sceptically. "Jack has been suspended for the week."

"No – not suspended. He's been asked to take the week off on full pay," Brenton corrected. "And what could be more amicable than that?"

"To an indifferent so-and-so like myself, it would be a Godsend, but for Jack – it is after all a Polish Week, and to be told to make yourself scarce didn't help."

"What about Komorski?" Brenton enquired. "Any repercussions when he returned?"

"I'd say he was shaken, he looked very pale. On the other hand it's difficult to tell with an austere lizard like that."

The evening wore on and the conversation diminished to the extent that during an exchange of thoughts on Komorski between Sherry and Abraham, the Irishman nodded towards Brenton over his glass of Guinness. Draining his glass, Sherry poked Brenton's ankle with his foot, and perceiving a reaction from the corner of his eye, resumed his conversation with Abraham.

"Did I nod off?" Brenton mumbled, shifting his weight to a new less constricted position.

"I think we all could do with some rest," Abraham said, throwing back the remains of his drink.

The rain had eased but had become even more wetting. It dictated brief goodbyes with Abraham and a race to the van for Brenton and Sherry. They bundled inside.

"This rain could be a problem," Brenton complained. If it had to rain tomorrow, he hoped for Sarah's sake that it would be this more timorous variety, its audibility being negligible.

The engine fired and roared a defiant shout at the night. Even the van, it seemed, was delighted to shake some of the wet from its exterior. As they negotiated Pimlico Road, Sherry enquired, "Lancaster Gate wasn't it?"

"Yep."

"Am I right in thinking it's a lady soloist tomorrow?"

"Maria Wohlicka."

"Does she arrive tomorrow?"

"She arrived late last night."

They turned right into Sloane Street for the run up to Knightsbridge.

Brenton started to ruminate on the schedule. A nervous turn of anticipation ran through him. Over the years he had come to accept the arrival of the uncertainties, the interdependency of orchestra, conductor, soloist and recording agent. They were all savants in the service of an unpredictable mistress – music. The consolation was the assurance that the day he lost this apprehensiveness would be the day he lost a good deal else besides his ability to record music. He mustn't forget to explain that feeling to Sarah. She would be extremely apprehensive because it was her first solo. He decided he would drop in to see how it was going for her after the session in Croydon.

Guessing Brenton's wavelength Sherry asked, "When do you start recording?"

"Tomorrow afternoon. The rehearsals continue tomorrow morning until lunch. Maria Wohlicka joins the band after lunch; hopefully we'll stick something on tape after 3 o'clock."

Sherry looked ahead into the night and eventually asked, "There's one part of your work I don't understand. How come when you get a good microphone balance with the orchestra, you don't photograph, or at least note, the desk readings and mic positions – and then you're in business for as long as it holds up?"

Brenton smiled tiredly and peered out in the same direction for an answer. "Change," he said quietly.

The van slowed as they reached the Alexandra Gate to Hyde Park.

"Is that an explanation or a demand?" Sherry prodded.

"Everything changes from moment to moment. The acoustic, the reverberation, the concentration, the interpretation, the intonation – they all move and change."

Sweeping through Alexandra Gate, they entered Hyde Park and headed towards Victoria Gate on the other side of the Serpentine.

"So you're not quite so placid sitting at the desk as your outward appearance might suggest," Sherry ventured.

"If you have a knot in your stomach, it should not, under the circumstances, appear on your face. A good *Ton Meister* must react and respond instinctively to minute imposed changes in the short term, and in the long term to technological change. If he – or she, come to think of it – can't, it's curtains. The same can be said of life generally. The juices or sap of life induce change."

They swayed with the van as the vehicle wove through the S-bend across the Serpentine.

"Bus crews are more philosophic than we give them credit," Sherry remarked.

"In what sense?"

"You know when a bus breaks down and comes to a stop. They always say – all change!"

Brenton grinned. "Tou-bloody-ché!"

They exited through Victoria Gate and, leaving the relative darkness of Hyde Park behind them, turned left under the brighter street lighting of Bayswater Road.

"Where exactly?" Sherry asked crisply.

"Over there," Brenton pointed. "Lancaster Gate Underground will do nicely."

Sherry pulled the van over to the right hand side of the road and rolled to a halt outside the underground entrance. "Mission accomplished," he announced, drawing on the brake.

"And quite an agreeable mission it turned out to be," Brenton replied, closing the top button of his mackintosh. He opened the passenger door and stepped out into the weather. Brusque good nights were exchanged and the door slammed shut. Brenton stood waiting on the pavement as Sherry engaged gear, turned the van, and headed back the way he had come. He glanced in the rear-view mirror to catch a momentary picture of his mentor still standing in the rain in the same position.

"Dear God," he muttered. He shook his head. 'Course, Brenton could've nodded off again. Anyway – obvious he wasn't wanted there. Couldn't understand people who didn't come clean. What did he take him for – the office gossip? Couldn't be taking the tube, or could he? No. Probably getting ready to do a Gene Kelly up Lancaster Terrace – singing and dancing in the rain. Did he have a bird stashed up there?

Wouldn't be surprised. A good-looking bloke like him had his needs. If it was true, someone was going to get her fingers singed. Bloody underhand way to go through life. But then, he always had been shadowy. Pathetic! Who in his right mind would spend a night out, yet hardly manage to keep his eyes open.

The van cut a line through the wet murk towards Southwark. It was swallowed up and quickly lost to sight in the enveloping drizzle.

CHAPTER 7

Tuesday March 24th 1981
Croydon
8.30 am

Brenton felt satisfied he had made the correct decision to start the day with a walk through Croydon rather than Hyde Park. Around the next turn he would already be in sight of Symphony Hall. The temptation of the park had been its immediacy and the battalions of daffodils to be reviewed; but he had seen enough of the trumpeting heralds in suburban gardens to feel adequately compensated. Last night's rain had ceased for the moment. Low sullen clouds scudded by overhead, hustling to another location with the bluster of the new day. The bracing conditions brought to mind Shakespeare's thoughts on the subject:

'Daffodils that come before the swallow dares

And take the winds of March with beauty!'

He felt good. Better than he had felt in quite some time. Refreshed might be a more apt expression of his feelings, both in body and mind. Tuesday March 24th 1981, the day the cobwebs were blown away.

From his waking moment that morning, he had been trying out a new idea in his head. In the shower and over breakfast, it had become clear to him: it was time for a new direction. The music he would undoubtedly miss – the bright side of the moon as it were, but it was inextricably a part of the other half of the entity, the cancerous subverted side of his world. The decision to move in a new direction wasn't prompted by any self-gratification, it was more a form of social surgery – the elimination of an alienating sense of duty. He had reached a point within its numbing labyrinth where the dividing line between duty and accountability had blurred. Beyond that point, duty took on the efficiency of a machine, rather than the functional responsibilities of a rational being.

He swung past the traffic barrier to the Hall, still in a state of preoccupation. "'Mornin' Mr Brenton!" the security man barked from the hut. Brenton snapped to and, recognising the voice behind the treated glass, replied "'Morning, Charlie."

He resisted the impulse to stop and enquire about the missing equipment, which, he persuaded himself, had nothing whatever to do with Charlie Primrose's disarming capacity to stun even the least fastidious with an alarming variety of aromas accumulated during the previous evening's social jousting. He continued around the side of the building, safe in the knowledge that the latest score on the break-in would arrive on his desk early that morning, if it were not already there.

Inside he made for the stage area. He thought he detected Sherry's inquisitive head protrude from the far stage-exit door.

"That you, Jim?" he shouted.

Coming into view, Sherry replied, "Getting the mic stands ready."

Throwing a cable to the floor, he approached the conductor's podium, below which Brenton was standing. "No hiccups so far," Sherry announced smiling broadly, and then added, "You don't seem to be any the worse for last night's downpour."

Brenton smiled and said, "I'm on my way upstairs for the fan mail. Continue here with the rig. Plug up what you have there, starting clockwise with the strings behind you, and finishing on the floor here with the solo mic." As he was turning away he added, "I see Pecton's in – so I'll have a credit note for a trio of two-way radios for you in the control room when you arrive."

"Fine."

———

"Good morning, Miss Maybury."

"Good morning, Mr Brenton. Dreadful weather last night."

"Yes, it *was* rather damp." Brenton nodded towards the inner sanctum. "Is he inside?"

"Dr Pecton left for the boardroom with Professor Komorski about ten minutes ago."

"Mmm," Brenton raised an eyebrow while flicking through his in-tray.

"If it's the equipment business you're worried about," Miss Maybury correctly interpreted, "Dr Pecton suggests you replace them, and bill Symphony Hall."

"In that case we'll shop locally, and leave some business, not to say good will, in the area."

There was nothing of world-shattering importance on his desk, so he rose and moved towards the door. "I'm going over to the control room," he informed Miss Maybury, "in case anybody's looking for me."

In the control room his eye lit on the note penned by Sarah the previous evening. He sat down at the desk to read its contents and looked over at the tape machine to which it referred. A full tape had run through the machine he observed, and now lay inertly on the right-hand spool. He removed the vari-speed control from the machine and left the tape for Sarah to attend to. Moving to plug up the microphones to the desk, he heard Jim Sherry ascend the stairs.

"All finished on stage," he announced entering the room.

"Any problems?"

"No problems."

"Then I can go downstairs and make a few final adjustments. I'll give you identification on each mic, which you will mark up on the desk. Then I'll check out the store room."

"I'll do that if you wish."

"No. I have a job for you after you mark up. Go to Miss Maybury and pick up an advice note for three two-way radios. Try the local electronic outfits. If they don't match what we've got, go further afield. If I say don't disappear down a black hole, I know you'll appreciate I may need you here later on this morning."

"That's fine."

"Make sure they're as near the original spec as possible."

"Right."

"See you at the break," Brenton said, departing.

On stage, he was just in time to interrupt the audible efforts of two attendants, guided by the librarian, Tim Cranshaw, as they pushed the piano into position. "Hold it chaps – you'll damage the cables," Brenton yelled, rushing forward. He kicked one cable forward out of reach of the heavy instrument as it rolled to a halt.

"Sorry, David," Cranshaw apologised. "The piano tuner has been standing by to have a crack at it, and he doesn't have much time to spare before the shower start to come on stage." Cranshaw then addressed the attendants. "As you were, and in the same direction." He beckoned on the moving piano towards the front centre stage and then dismissed the attendants with a request to send in the tuner. "Piano position all right for you?" he asked Brenton.

Brenton turned from where he was adjusting the first string mic. "Yes, spot on."

Cranshaw moved over to stand beside him and, after looking back to see if the tuner had appeared, asked, "Can we meet sometime this morning, David? Coffee maybe? I feel certain –"

"Am I coming across, Jim?" Brenton directed into the mic.

Even before Sherry replied affirmatively on the talk back, Cranshaw had backed off.

"Sorry – didn't think you were in communication."

He turned towards the sound of approaching footsteps and greeted the tuner. "She's all yours, George," and moved towards the stage door.

Brenton called, "Tim, coffee break will do fine."

Cranshaw gave a thumbs-up without looking back.

Even as the tuner commenced his checks, the growing human activity offstage began to overflow on stage. Brenton wound up his own checks finishing with the piano solo mic, over which he bade Jim Sherry bon voyage, and with a wave of his hand in the direction of the control room window, set off for the equipment storeroom.

Rounding the corner to the base, he was not surprised to find a member of the security staff outside the door. "Morning Thompson, you have a report for me?"

"Yes, sir."

"Let's move inside."

Thompson produced his master key, unlocked the door, and they entered the storeroom.

———

Jim Sherry bounced out the side door and almost collided with Sarah. "That's the first nice thing to happen today!" he beamed, catching Sarah before she pitched sideways. Recovering, Sarah gasped, "I wish I could say the same."

"I knew you were coming through the door. I took a chance and grabbed the opportunity, so to speak, to –"

"Jim Sherry, remove that soppy expression from your face. Save it for the unsuspecting."

"Why are you in so early?"

Sarah considered for a second. "I suppose I'm a bit fidgety about the recording in St George's."

"Interesting," Sherry murmured, a faint smile appearing. "That confirms something I learned last night."

"Oh. Did David mention my recording?"

"Not directly, though I know he is concerned for you. Actually I found out recording butterflies are not confined to one's first recording."

"That's consoling, if maybe just a little worrying."

"I must go," he said suddenly. "I'll see you at coffee then?"

"Next time ring the bell on your bicycle," Sarah advised moving towards the door.

———

The control room was a priority. She must remove the vari-speed from the tape machine, and any evidence of her unusual recording aspiration of last night. Twelve hours ago it had all seemed so interesting and intriguing. Today she had her first professional recording, so something more rational was called for.

She found the control room empty. But her note had been removed from where she had left it, and presumably read. A quick look at the tape machine confirmed this – the vari-speed hung inertly out of circuit. The prospect of a further entanglement with David was depressing. She removed the tape and threw it into the re-use box; slowly, the frown that creased her forehead melted to accommodate a smile. She looked down at the tape where it lay abandoned in the re-use box. Retrieving it from the box, she attached it to the tape machine. Her fingers lightly and deftly entwined the tape and pressed the rewind button. She *was* curious.

Brenton appeared in the doorway. "Ah – the 'distaff' side of the business."

"That's a rather sexist term, don't you think?"

"Perhaps," he agreed, sitting down and stretching his legs under the desk. "But any observations you may have on the subject should be directed to Joe Abraham. He used the expression last night when enquiring about you. Oh – and good morning." Sarah considered him for a moment. A good scream might have lent a modicum of release to her feelings. She swallowed, and, she hoped, with a steady voice answered, "And good morning to you."

"You're in a little earlier than expected."

"Yes. I thought I'd collect the tapes, have a coffee here, and do some leisurely shopping on the way to St George's."

"Sensible enough. While we're alone, I'd like to say – if you have any problem – give me a call."

His eye caught the spinning tape. "Is that a St George tape?" he asked.

"No, it's a tape I stuck on here last night."

"You recorded some of the orchestral rehearsal?"

"Well yes – and no," Sarah replied with increasing irritation.

"Good God, either it is, or it isn't."

"It isn't!" Sarah almost shouted. "If you had given me a moment, I was about to explain how I had pandered to my curiosity, having read that article on phantom sounds in yesterday's newspaper."

"I see. Why didn't you say so in the first place?"

"I was afraid you might have thought the idea childish."

"On the contrary. It's already been the subject of two articles in a trade magazine. I would certainly be interested in your findings – provided you approached the subject with a degree of rational inquiry."

Sarah relaxed visibly. "I must get a hold of those two articles. If I ring the magazine, might they supply back numbers?"

"Presumably. If not try the public library."

Looking down into the hall, Brenton was just in time to see Komorski raise his hands to commence the day's rehearsal. He switched to the output from the single stereo mic as the first notes came across. "If you wish," he called over the music, "use headphones to listen to your tape."

"I'll do that," Sarah agreed, removing a pair from the wall rack, and slipping the vari-speed back into circuit.

Brenton set about recreating the sounds in the hall. He opened the music score, his eye not really searching for detail. Immersing himself in the general sound, he inhaled the music with the dependent gratification of the addicted. A re-awakened ability to 'feel' music, as distinct from an appreciation of it, had once more become an element of his perception. The discrepancies of the elemental sound were now not just obvious, but irritating. He began to seek clarification in the music score, and open spotter channels on the desk – add a little more woodwind here – diffuse the cello sound there. Pulling a sound together was not unlike some of those extraordinarily complicated knitting patterns his mother had embarked on at times, in which it seemed, half a dozen needles projected from a mangled mass of wool, out of which she had created, with a nonchalance which belied the accompanying clicking frenzy, splendid masterpieces –

"David!"

"Yes?"

Sarah removed the headphones to stand beside him. "I – I'm not sure what to make of this." She held the headphones in front of Brenton. "I think you'd better have a listen."

"In the middle of a balance?" he enquired irritably.

"It's serious interference of a curious variety, and possibly repetitious."

Brenton noted her earnestness. "Very well – let it roll." He switched the desk to tape output. Last night's Chopin rehearsal came across in the same basic sound with which he had started today's balance. After listening for a moment or two he judged, "Apart from the crummy sound, nothing of note here."

"No, wait a moment," Sarah insisted raising a hand. The tape continued to roll. It played for a further minute.

"What exactly are we listening for?" Brenton asked wearily.

"I'm sorry, I'll spool back to where I last–" A sudden interruption of telephonic speech over music cut in. "There it is!" she exclaimed.

Brenton remained rooted to his seat.

The blast of male speech lasted five seconds. The tape continued to run. After a further trouble-free period of two minutes, Sarah asked, "Shall I spool back?"

"Yes, do." he answered, without looking around, "Back to that speech, and put the machine on repeat."

Sarah complied, and with Brenton's unacknowledged acceptance of the importance of her discovery, tapped in her instructions to Memory 1. The machine dutifully obliged and proceeded to repeat the sequence.

"I was wondering why I couldn't understand a word," she murmured. "He's not speaking English."

'Or French, or German' she thought on the repeat.

Brenton turned suddenly. "Spool back to where you think this stuff starts."

Sarah spooled to fifteen minutes from the start of tape. Almost immediately there occurred a twelve second interjection.

"Give me that again," he demanded.

"Sounds a bit like Russian," Sarah mused, re-spooling, "Or that fracas – Polish perhaps."

The tape continued to play, interrupted occasionally by short bursts of rasping speech.

"Stop the tape for a moment. Does anybody else know about this?"

"No – with the exception of Jim, of course."

"He's listened to this?"

"He hasn't listened, just knows about my recording it."

"Good," he said, seemingly relieved. "I want you to transfer that section from your slow-speed tape to–" he rummaged in a cardboard box at his feet, "–to this cassette."

Sarah took the proffered cassette and moved aside as he made to leave the room. Passing between her and the desk, he grasped her arms and with a degree of enthusiasm which surprised, said, "I'll explain sometime why I'm so very grateful you recorded that sequence."

Sarah regarded him round-eyed; he let go of her arms.

"I'll be back in fifteen minutes," he said moving away, and to cover the lack of explanation continued, "Oh, and before it slips my mind, your St George tapes are in that box under the desk." And he was gone.

———

Sarah busied herself with the transcription. 'I'll explain sometime'. Was this the prospect of a change of relationship? That gleam in his eye. She had never seen that intensity there before – and his sudden departure, at what both knew to be a critical period in the putting together of a sound. That was disturbing really, because she knew he would ordinarily consider this sort of absence irresponsible. He was therefore behaving out of character. Was he in trouble because of her discovery? And as a result, not going to return! Was this where she was suddenly and precipitously thrust to recording stardom? Should she be listening to the orchestra rehearsing below?

'If he wasn't coming back' she reasoned, 'he wouldn't have asked me to do this job. Of course he's coming back.'

———

For the second time that morning, Brenton passed Charlie Primrose at the front gate security checkpoint. Pleasantries dispensed with earlier in the morning, they now exchanged judicious nods. Turning in the opposite direction to which he had arrived, he kept to the same side of the road until he approached and entered a public telephone kiosk.

Prefixing three digits before a London number provided unencumbered access to a subscriber who answered immediately. A cool detached female voice directed him to state his category after the signal. He placed his digital watch close to the telephone transmitter and pressed a button on one side. It emitted the first phrase of Oranges and Lemons. There quickly followed a short succession of electronic clicks, which terminated when a male voice commanded – "Start now!" Brenton cleared his throat. "David Brenton – Special Operations, for the urgent attention of the director of D Division. Indications of a possible wet job beginning to emerge in Croydon. Visiting Polish government minister Anton Uginski a likely target this coming Saturday at a concert in the Royal Albert Hall. I have on tape intermittent, one way, duplex-type conversation for collection and translation. Request the services of a watcher for Jan Lesko – that's L-E-S-K-O of 18 Bognor Road, Bromley. Photo to be collected with tape. I request a meeting with you this evening, after 1800 hours. Please confirm with courier. Thank you."

He replaced the receiver and, without removing his hand, stared intently at the telephone. His mind avoided the consequences of his phone call and perversely dwelt on the feeling of unreality that speaking to a computer, or any kind of answering and recording service imparted. Catching a movement out of the corner of his eye, he looked out to find another customer staring curiously in at him. He stepped outside and held the door for the elderly man in dungarees.

"I'm afraid I was daydreaming," he apologised.

"Well for some," the man muttered, brushing past.

Brenton retraced his steps. The wind blew directly in his face, dissipating the residue of the flippant comment. He walked on, head bent into the wind. The threat for which he had prepared and waited ten years had begun to emerge. Hardly an auspicious start to the proceedings, particularly when one considered the fortuitous manner in which the last piece of information had arrived to confront him – thanks to Sarah.

The lucky break meant that with the translation of the tape, he would have insight into his adversary's intentions, and they were as yet unaware of this advantage. Uginski, the communist Polish minister for urban renewal was the undoubted target; he had twice heard his name mentioned on the tape. That gave him about four days to sort things out. Not a great deal of time, but if it hadn't been for Sarah, it could have been much tighter. And Sarah? She must not become entangled in this thing – at any cost.

Fortunately, she would be preoccupied with St George's until Wednesday night. After that she must be found something to do outside of the concert; and after that again? Invite her to some light-hearted show in town, and afterwards, dinner in exotic surroundings. 'I have an excuse now – but first things first.'

His pace began to quicken. Facts began to marshal. His raison d'être had advanced and been recognised. Battle order had begun to take shape.

CHAPTER 8

Tuesday March 24th 1981
Croydon
11.00 am

Brenton reached the arterial corridor, then hesitated. He turned right in the direction of the orchestra changing-rooms and equipment storeroom. He produced a key, let himself in, and relocked the door from inside, leaving the key in the lock. Lifting the wall telephone, he dialled the control room. Sarah answered.

"David here. Everything all right?"

"I've finished the transcription, if that's what you mean."

He heard the edginess in her voice. "I'm speaking from the equipment room – I'll be along shortly."

"Looks like the orchestra is about to break for coffee."

"In that case, I'll see you in the restaurant. Bring along the cassette. After you've removed your George tapes, put that original recording of yours in the same box under the desk."

"Ok."

"Thanks old girl, see you in a few moments."

In terms of endearment, Sarah thought that could be considered gushing. "Very good, David," she replied, on an impulse adding, "Bye."

Brenton replaced the receiver and turned to the microphone press to unlock it. He inched his hand up inside the upper right hand corner of the seven-foot high cupboard until it came in contact with a small metal button. He pressed it until there was a minute movement on the top outside. He placed a chair at the right–hand side of the press, mounted it, and noiselessly pulled out a three-inch high drawer from the top. His fingers ran through a card index until they came to LESKO. With one fluid motion he checked Lesko's photograph and stored it in an inside pocket. This stuff would have to be moved to higher ground. It was becoming too much like open house around here. He double-checked the closed drawer.

As he turned to step down, the door handle was pressed down. He froze, and saw the handle return to normal. The action had been slow and deliberate. In the absence of any further movement, he swiftly and quietly reached the door, and with one quick motion, unlocked and threw it open.

The person who had turned his back on the door seemed to rise fractionally in the air, clutching a microphone stand in one hand and three boxes in the other.

"Bloody hell!" Sherry's eyes shot around. The final syllable was lost in the non-plussed reaction.

After a moment's silent exasperation, Brenton waved Sherry inside. "Sorry about that, thought I'd caught our burglar."

Jim Sherry slowly shook his head. "Where do I dump these new two-ways?"

"The mic press," Brenton replied. After they were tucked away, Brenton locked the press door and they made for the restaurant.

The hum of conversation was audible from outside. It was always cheering to approach the restaurant when the orchestra was in recess. Perhaps the strictures on verbal communication during their working hours necessitated a redressing of the imbalance through plenty of animated conversations during coffee and meal breaks. Brenton and Sherry walked through the open door and were enveloped in the lively din. On their way to the counter they were on the lookout for different people.

"Wot'll it be gentlemen?" Mrs Wheeler greeted. "Tea or coffee?"

It turned out to be coffee for Sherry and tea for Brenton. Sherry motioned towards the table at which Sarah, Anna Bretcu and Joe Abraham were already seated. On the way Brenton placed his tea on Jim Cranshaw's table. Sherry made to get an extra chair when Brenton intervened.

"Don't bother, Jim. I'll sit with Cranshaw, if you don't mind. Had a run-in with him this morning and I wish to patch things up." He exchanged morning pleasantries with Anna and Joe. Turning to Sarah, he added, "I'll relieve you of that item now, if you like."

"I have it here." She reached for her shoulder bag beside the St George tapes at her feet. Brenton was relieved to receive it enclosed in an envelope. "If I can manage it, I'll drop by St George's later in the evening."

Cranshaw obligingly stubbed out his cigarette and drained his coffee, as Brenton sat opposite and drank deeply from his tea.

Captain Mortimer Timpson Cranshaw, ex director of Music Royal Artillary, was first to speak. "Sorry, old chap. That was inept on stage this morning."

Brenton took another less gulping mouthful. "Aaah," he sighed, slowly surveying the surrounding tables, "I really needed that." His gaze turned to rest on Cranshaw's scrubbed and deceptively youthful countenance. "Luckily no harm done, Tim. Have you anything positive to report?"

"Nothing very definite, I'm afraid. But I can't shake off the queasy feeling something's coming down. In trying to reduce the feeling to component parts, I come up with four unconnected incidents, which in isolation might cast a shadow, but whose cumulative effect add up to, shall we say, an alert."

"Let's have 'em."

"The first two are hardly worth bothering about, but, because the second two are more promising, I'll leave nothing out. The first snippet concerns Appleby, and to a lesser degree, Pecton. They're glued to Komorski like limpets. Appleby has moved into Komorski's Kensington hotel. The second concerns Anna Bretcu who has been snooping around in some unlikely places." Cranshaw cast around him before getting to the point.

"By a stroke of luck, while driving up to the entrance this morning, I noticed a member of Polish intelligence drive by. He's on our circulated list. His name is Lutowicz, a member of their embassy trade section. I checked on my car list, and he was driving a known non-diplomatic registration. And finally, last night after you departed, Komorski had a visit from two members of the Polish Government in Exile. Gate security rang the library. Wished to know where Komorski and Pecton were. There was no reply from his office. Quite open about it – gave their names, Prolow and Cerniaski. Said they had an appointment with Komorski, who turned out to be in the board room with you-know-who plus Appleby."

"Nice work, Tim. Combining your information with what I acquired this morning, I can confirm we're no longer on standby." Brenton picked up his cup and bent forward fractionally, "Consider yourself on full alert."

Cranshaw remained motionless apart from an involuntary grin.

"Steady on," Brenton muttered. "This isn't a damn paper chase."

Cranshaw's face regained its customary gravity.

Brenton continued, "There's a pub about a mile down the Addington Road called The Pigeon Loft – on the A212. Make sure you're there for lunch and I'll fill you in on my end."

"Excuse me, Mr Brenton," one of the waitresses intervened. "Mrs Wheeler asked me to tell you, reception rang to say there's a Mr Smith at the side door to see you."

"Thanks. I'll be along in a few moments."

The girl removed the cup and saucer in front of Cranshaw and moved to the next table.

"I've already missed more of the rehearsal than I can afford," Brenton said, moving his legs out from under the table. "I'll push along. I want you to insert your quartet into the computer. Give me a second to make an exit, and then go outside and do it."

Cranshaw lit a further cigarette to help pass the moment and ponder the implications. A sudden burst of hilarity from three or four tables away distracted him. Looking over he saw the Bretcu-Abraham group was the source of the mirth, though Bretcu was obviously laughing because she felt she was expected to.

As the restaurant was beginning to empty, he heard Jim Sherry remonstrate, "On the other hand, suppose you found you had to administer mouth to mouth resuscitation to Charlie Primrose!" More laughter.

"That's nauseating," Sarah cried, yet she was unable to match her disapproval with an appropriately serious expression. "And besides,

I'm sure poor Anna here hasn't an idea what we're talking about."

Sarah then asked, "Are you interested in languages, Joe?"

"I have a smattering of a few languages – and I find it absorbing to detect influences and movement, one on the other, down through the ages."

"It's a pity I didn't have you with me this morning when I tried to determine the foreign language I inadvertently recorded last night."

"Maybe I could still assist?" Abraham suggested.

"Is this your ghost recording?" Jim Sherry asked.

"Yes. Unfortunately instead of a ghost, I somehow picked up a telephonic conversation on tape." Sarah went on to describe the motive behind her experiment.

"Seems to be an engrossing subject," Joe Abraham agreed. "What language do you suspect?"

"I'm not quite sure – Slavic of one sort or another. In any event, further investigation will have to wait until my recordings in St George's are completed."

"I take it you're not working with us here?"

"Not for two days. We're using Ronald Shipsey during the afternoon and evening to record an album on the organ in St George's, so as soon as you lot take yourselves back to your Chopin, I gather up my bits and pieces here," she said, patting the tapes and shoulder bag, "and take myself off to St George's."

"Which should be soon, if the few still remaining are anything to go by," Sherry observed.

"Good grief Anna – let's go!" Abraham suddenly rose from the table with alarm. As the restaurant had started to empty in dribs and drabs a short time earlier, they were so absorbed in their own company, they'd failed to notice the ebb in customers. The two caught up with the tail of the exodus and removed the last twittering of chitchat from Mrs Wheeler's domain, leaving it to the more purposeful sounds of lunch preparations.

Tim Cranshaw was furious as he emerged from the stage door. The clock at the entrance read 1.20 pm – he was going to be late. He took the most diagonal route possible to his car.

He ducked into an ageing red MGB that coughed politely after an initial demand. On a second application, and with the assistance of a stream of blistering invective, it more readily obliged – with a self-righteous roar. Slamming into first gear, he negotiated the entrance and pointed its nose in the direction of the A212.

Cranshaw's position as librarian was an exacting one. Apart from the obvious tasks such as filing, retrieving and indexing, which were fundamentals in a library, he provided a liaison between the orchestra's requirements and outside agencies such as publishers, arrangers, composers, copyists, and the like. Allied to this, and no less taxing in terms of time, was his position as assistant manager to Quentin Appleby.

This entailed a certain secondary contact with Pecton who normally used Appleby as an intermediary. Today had been an exception. Pecton had made direct and urgent contact with Cranshaw before he left the Hall for lunch. The meeting had been short, sharp and abrasive.

Cranshaw turned left onto the A212 proper, which because of the less confined driving conditions enabled him to make a corresponding increase in speed. The row with Pecton was directly attributable to a divided allegiance. His loyalty, in so far as he could spread it, should not have been called into question. What it came down to basically was – two into one won't go, or put another way, two masters into one subordinate. Uncle David plus Papa Doc equalled trouble. Behind him fumed the Doc, ahead awaited Uncle, simmering away quietly, a trifle below boiling point. It took a further fifteen minutes of sharp driving before he reached what resembled Brenton's description of the rendezvous. He pulled off the road and swung into the first available space. Anxiety to meet Brenton precluded an appraisal of the establishment's architectural merit, or even a stab at the reason for the unusual name. In pristine innocence he raced to the entrance where his ears picked up the strains of *Royal Garden Blues* from a jazz trio inside. He entered, intrigued, a pigeon among the cats.

Circling the interior for the second time, Cranshaw's eyes met

Brenton's as he emerged from the men's room. He winced at their grim expression and quickly closed the distance between them.

"Sorry about the delay, old boy – absolutely nothing I could do about it," he apologised, sitting down.

"Really?"

"Had a to–do with Pecton before I left. Wanted me to collect the soloist, Maria Wohlicka, at her hotel and bring her to Croyden, and he was not in any mood to take no for an answer."

Brenton's expression relaxed.

The jazz trio finished their number and a waiter materialised, notebook at the ready. They both ordered onion soup, and a liver pâté with toast.

"Obviously," Brenton said, returning the menu, and reverting to the original subject, "Pecton was obliged to take no for an answer, since you're here?"

"Yes." Cranshaw confirmed with some pride. "The whole interview was doubly irritating because he was asking something of me I should normally be delighted to do. Maria Wohlicka has an enviable facility on the piano – if one can judge by the recordings she has made. I was looking forward to meeting her."

He observed his intertwined fingers, and suddenly cracked his knuckles. "Pecton on the other hand I can do without – today included. The end result was damned unpleasant. The silly bugger suggested I was being disloyal, which did not exactly send me away singing."

"We can't afford to antagonise Pecton. Let's hope a conflict of interest doesn't arise again." Brenton asked quizzically, "For the record, what excuse did you offer?"

Cranshaw looked somewhat taken aback that the question should have been asked, but replied expansively, "I explained I had an appointment with a dear uncle, which was not negotiable."

"Nice one," said Brenton. "Which reminds me, it wasn't because of its inconvenience I brought you out here. The high level of sound insures privacy of conversation." Cranshaw drew expectantly closer. Brenton continued. "Due to Sarah Carlyle's single-minded pursuit of an unlikely theory on sound regeneration, we have in our possession a recording which may well turn out to be a rehearsal for a wet job this coming Saturday. The language spoken, I suspect, is Polish; and while my knowledge of the language is superficial I did catch the expected Polish minister's name twice."

Cranshaw emitted a sharp excited little laugh. "What extraordinary good luck."

"Yes – and we must use it to full advantage."

Cranshaw signalled the waiter and ordered a whiskey in coffee. "Care to join me?" he asked. "It will help me stay the course in the Pecton *Puissance* when I return."

"Perhaps I should," Brenton said.

Between sips Cranshaw remarked, "Strikes me as odd – I mean, considering the credentials of the recipient. Who or what are we looking for?"

An involuntary frown creased Brenton's face. "I'm afraid that's the bad news. Despite it seeming to point in the direction of Polish nationalists in exile, I consider it wide open until we receive or uncover some further information, such as the tape transcript for instance."

"How in God's name did Sarah Carlyle come by the tape?"

"After I left last night, she ran a tape which picked up a duplex type transmission in the hall on the single stereo mic in the ceiling."

"What type of transmission is that?"

"From a two-way radio. The duplex system uses different wavelengths to transmit and receive, which enables a pair to hold a simultaneous conversation without all those over-and-outs one normally associates with a simplex transmission. For us, with the duplex, it's only possible to overhear one side of the conversation – whichever side one happens to be tuned into. Let's hope what we have on tape is the more revealing side of the conversation."

"This means you've a single voice on tape?"

"Yes. Although difficult to detect, because of the bad quality – without doubt – it's the same voice."

Brenton replaced the empty coffee cup in its saucer. "I've the same arrangement running now in the hall, at a faster speed in case of a repeat performance. I'm not using the ceiling stereo mic in the music recording, so I have it plugged directly into a tape machine."

Cranshaw withdrew a gold cigarette case from an inside pocket. "Mind if I smoke?"

Brenton shook his head.

He selected and lit a cigarette, and then asked through a haze of smoke, "Does this point to your missing two-ways?"

"Unfortunately, no. Ours were the simplex type and would have presented both sides of the conversation."

"Pity – might have tied in nicely."

Brenton agreed, crumpling his paper napkin.

The jazz trio concluded their final number. Brenton looked at his watch. "Time to get back to Croydon. I'll take a lift to some point near the Hall – I've a number of things I wish to pass on to you."

They inserted themselves into Cranshaw's two-seater and briskly moved towards Croydon, leaving rather less rubber on the road than on the outward journey.

"Y'know", Brenton considered, "I'm beginning to question whether or not Symphony Hall was the best progression from the Royal Artillery for you."

Cranshaw's normally firm jaw dropped open. "Good God! Why ever so?"

Brenton stared steadily ahead. "Can't help thinking a stint with the Red Arrows Aerobatic Team might have been a more practical arrangement – if only to eliminate my embarrassment when endeavouring to explain further up the line the absolute necessity for your outrageous speeds around South London. To say nothing of your inevitable collection of tickets for speeding." Cranshaw tried to look penitent, but couldn't contain a grin. He eased his foot on the accelerator. "Sorry, old man. Came out here in something of a rush – suppose the adrenalin's still flowing." The car slowed to the lawful limit. Paradoxically, Brenton now felt the contrast a trifle sedate, but said nothing further. Better to arrive eventually rather than courtesy of the local constabulary.

"Tim," Brenton recommenced more seriously. "I want you to go through every locker in the hall, male and female."

"This evening presumably – after the orchestra finishes?"

"Yes."

"Will I have back up?"

"Thompson will accompany you. I filled him in this morning. He'll have a miniature camera for anything you may find of interest. Don't remove anything. If you find time, extend the search to cover Pecton and Appleby. If that's not possible –" Brenton shrugged. "Well, with luck I'll take care of those tomorrow. Keep an eye open for technical equipment, literature, correspondence, photographs, the usual."

The car turned off the A212 and slowed further. Cranshaw looked questioningly at Brenton. "I don't wish to bring you too close."

"Pull up after the next junction – it's a fast fifteen minutes from the Hall. My schedule this afternoon slots in with the orchestra's until they finish at four o'clock. I'm then part of a confab with Komorski – Wohlicka – Pecton – Appleby – until about five. I have an appointment with our section director for six o'clock – so if you have anything of importance to impart – you'll find me in his office. After which ..."

The car eased into the kerb, Brenton pulled the door's release cord, extracted himself, bent back in and concluded, "After which I'll leave a number at the usual phone. Oh – and good luck this evening."

His walking pace was dictated by the necessity to meet Maria Wohlicka before she went on stage. It was tempered with the obligation to present an unflustered and confident appearance to the musician. Performing artists became wound up before a performance, some more than others. They required around them calm, self-assured professionals in order that their pent up energies be channelled directly into the music and not dissipated on unnecessary distractions. His energies would be channelled into going on the offensive – but without breaking cover.

CHAPTER 9

Tuesday March 24th 1981
2.15 pm

Preconceptions can be misleading, as Brenton was reminded on being introduced to Maria Wohlicka. Appleby performed the introduction with panache. "Our Mr Brenton," he affably exuded, raising his arm theatrically as Brenton joined the small assembly in the soloist's suite. Advancing to shake the musician's proffered hand, Brenton was struck by the seeming frailty of her frame. He had initially made the mistake of thinking the bulk of her assistant presented the more likely if less appetising candidate. But the firmness of Madame Wohlicka's handshake questioned his concept of fragility. From a face framed by a head of close-cut brown hair, flecked with grey, a pair of dark blue eyes stared back into his own, dispelling any residual doubt he had had on the lady's fortitude.

"I am glad to meet you." Her tone was resolute, the accent markedly Polish. "Mr Appleby says good things about your work. We will work well together." She smiled, released his hand, and returned a cigarette to the corner of her mouth.

The gathering included Pecton, Kormorski, Cranshaw, the leader of the orchestra Arthur Liddel, and Madame Wohlicka's robust companion who hovered, disapprovingly it seemed, in the background. Appleby once more obliged and made the introduction. "David Brenton – Lina Zukowska."

Comrade Zukowska nodded sullenly from afar. Brenton reciprocated brusquely. Arthur Liddel excused himself saying, "Must get the tuning going," and Pecton enquired of Brenton, "Everything in order?" He was rewarded with an affirmative nod before Cranshaw intervened to ask Brenton, "You received the music scores?"

"With the exception of the Kilar," Brenton replied.

"The Kilar's a bit of a dismal story, I'm afraid. Nothing has arrived in the way of music scores. I'm trying to solicit the aid of Professor

Komorski with a few telephone calls to Warsaw."

Maria Wohlicka brushed stray ash from her clothes and murmured, "It will be all right – it will be all right."

Cranshaw eyed her speculatively and mumbled, "Hope that's not their version of all right on the night."

Brenton said, "These things usually turn up – in the end."

"Mr Cranshaw," Madame Wohlicka said peremptorily, "In Poland, Komorski is what you say here – well placed. The music of Kilar *will* arrive."

Brenton noted the strength of character; the information on Komorski; and Cranshaw's underestimation. Appleby approached and suggested it was time to get the afternoon's session underway. Madame Wohlicka agreed, and Brenton wished her success before excusing himself.

En route to the control room he had a brief word with Jim Sherry, and a quick visual of the stage. He flopped into the chair at the desk. On stage, introductions had already taken place and the 1st Movement rehearsal was about to commence. The morning's orchestral rehearsal had sounded uninspired and bland. Whether this was due to his balance, Komorski's interpretation, or Chopin's orchestration, remained open to conjecture. He had resisted the consequent urge to seek the missing element by electronic means. Experience had whispered a less precipitous approach, and now, as the piano made its first entry, it became increasingly apparent that his hunch had been correct. The piano was so completely filling the void as to push his other problems momentarily from his mind. The missing ingredient had been the diminutive Madame Wohlicka. It was fresh and youthfully vibrant. The mood was infectious because the orchestra's response was to cosset rather than perfunctorily support. Drawing the piano a little more into the picture, he looked down into the hall in admiration and felt a tingle of anticipation. He was experiencing an emotion, which, had he dared to think about it, had not been with him since he participated in intercept scrambles over the North Sea. The exercise then had been to turn away the occasional Soviet Badger or Bear sent to probe Britain's air defence system. Now the exercise was to capture the artistic endeavours of those below him on stage.

They were rising so superbly to the piano, it wouldn't surprise him if they put the 1st Movement on tape immediately after this run through. In this state of heightened awareness he hoped he would prove as successful on the ground as he had been in the air – and fulfil this apotheosis of the nineteen-year-old Chopin, who first performed the work in public during this same month of March, one hundred and fifty–one years ago.

After listening to the recording in the control room, Madame Wohlicka, Professor Komorski and Brenton joined Appleby and Pecton in the latter's office. "Yes," Pecton said expectantly from behind the expanse of his mahogany desk. "Was everything to your satisfaction?" He addressed first Kormorski and then Wohlicka.

"Some little things," Komorski sighed, wagging his hand and pulling a face.

"And some big things," Wohlicka interjected as they took their seats.

"Yes – yes?" Pecton threw out in alarm.

Wohlicka leaned forward in her armchair, one eye tightly closed against spiralling smoke from the dangling cigarette in the corner of her mouth. "And the big thing," she remonstrated with the aid of her gyrating cigarette, "– is how very musical the whole performance was."

Audible sighs of relief all around.

"Yes-yes-yes!" Pecton enthused. The buzzer sounded on his intercom, to which he predictably responded, "Yes?"

Miss Maybury's voice answered from the other end. "Comrade Lina Zukowska is here to join Madame Wohlicka?"

Pecton looked at Madame Wohlicka and asked, "Yes?"

Her response was to turn on Komorski and open fire in Polish.

This brought two red blotches to the maestro's cheeks, and a smile to Appleby's face. Pecton seemed transfixed by the rapid movements of the soloist's cigarette, and Brenton thought he had never heard so many 'yeses' in such a short space of time.

Komorski hurriedly replied in Polish and then rose to his feet. "Sorry," he said turning to the others, "a little problem." On his way to the door Madame Wohlicka further instructed him, "And she will stay out there until I am finished." Through a blast of smoke and ash, she spat out "Pfeff!" and gestured dismissively. There was a collective pause, until Appleby enquired, "How did you find the piano, Madame Wohlicka?"

"Very good. Very fine," she said, obviously glad to return to the subject of music. "A little stiff here and there, but that is because it is a new piano."

"Is there anything can be done about that?" Pecton asked Appleby, to which the soloist replied, "Nothing. It is part of a new instrument, and with the help of Mr George, is a very very small part."

Pecton sought Appleby's clarification over the top of his glasses.

"The tuner," Appleby supplied.

"Ah George, yes, yes, of course." Pecton nodded his head vigorously.

Maria Wohlicka continued, "The instrument makes very good sound, and it makes good sound from bass to treble – what is the expression?" she asked, crinkling her eyes.

Brenton suggested, "Evenly?"

"Exactly!" she confirmed with satisfaction, reopening one eye. "Piano soloists live more dangerously than other soloists," she expanded. "We cannot bring our own instruments with us. So during our travels we meet the good, we meet the bad, and one time I meet the dangerous!" The gathering responded with amused laughter. "But in this case, I am sorry I don't own your instrument."

Gratified, Pecton rejoined, "How kind of you to say so."

"No – no." The soloist shook her head, only pausing to light a new cigarette with the remains of the old. Appleby civilly stepped forward with an ashtray and placed it on her armchair.

"No," she recommenced from within a new smoke cloud. "– I speak frankly. If piano is bad, I say piano is bad." She waved vaguely in the direction of the outer office, "I am told I speak my mind too much – but I only say truth. Like life, it sometimes hurts – but only to those who are afraid of truth."

The door opened. Komorski entered alone and resumed his seat.

"Everything is correct," he assured Madame Wohlicka, and without waiting for a reaction, suggested that they address themselves to the 1st Movement recording.

"You were saying," prompted Pecton. "There were one or two small things which, I take it, you were not pleased with?"

"Yes," Komorski considered. "During some of Comrade Wohlicka's *rubato* sections, I did not feel I was in control."

"Did this come across on tape?" Pecton asked Brenton.

"Not at all," Brenton answered. "I thought it unusually accomplished."

"Comrade Professor," Madame Wohlicka asked, "Over what were you not in control? The orchestra, the piano, or both?"

"Where you used *rubato* – both," he answered testily.

"In that case, the two of us had better go over the 2nd and 3rd Movements before we meet the orchestra again and smooth out our problems, because the problem is between us."

"I feel you are pulling it around too much."

Madame Wohlicka's eyes opened wide. "Comrade Professor," she began in an ominously low voice, "I am not one of your pupils. You are looking at a professional who has performed this work, to the satisfaction of my public, more times than I wish to remember. The first time was my debut at the International Chopin Contest in Warsaw."

"Which you did not win!" Komorski peevishly snapped.

Her eyes narrowed and she removed the cigarette from her mouth. "If second place was good enough for Vladimir Ashkenazi, it was good enough for Maria Wohlicka," she remonstrated. "And I wish you to remember, I am the one with a reputation to lose. You are the one trying to make a reputation, and on – my – back!" With vigorous taps on her shoulder, she emphasised each of the last three words, scattering ash all over her clothes and the chair.

The weak afternoon sunlight exaggerated the amount of dust sent ceilingwards. Pecton's eyes darted quickly between protagonists and perceiving a lull, said placatingly, "Please – please – let us break for refreshment." He sprang from behind his desk with surprising alacrity. Making towards the soloist, he said, "David, let us accompany Madame Wohlicka to the boardroom."

He took both the musician's hands in his, and with more compassion than Brenton thought him capable of, said, "My dear, let us repair to the boardroom for some well-earned refreshment."

Madame Wohlicka rose, transformed it seemed, by the sudden attentiveness. "That would be nice," she sighed, and as if to hasten normality stuck the cigarette back in the corner of her mouth. As they moved to the outer office, Pecton asked Appleby to serve Kormorski refreshments from the cabinet.

"Miss Maybury," he appealed on his way through, "Coffee, etcetera, in the boardroom – *now*."

Brenton held the door to the sombre refinement of the boardroom as Pecton ushered Madame Wohlicka through towards a seat at the polished solidity of the board table. Closing the door behind him, he realised that the shape that rapidly materialised out of the gloom of the corridor was none other than the ubiquitous Zukowska.

Giving the lie to her bulk, she executed a nimble *pas de cheval* through the narrowing gap, and followed Pecton and Wohlicka into the room, leaving a disagreeable fug of jaded mothballs in her wake. Against his better judgment, Brenton coughed a warning.

Neither of them picked up on it. Pecton settled Madame Wohlicka into a seat and, turning to address Brenton, almost collided with Zukowska. He recovered enough to ask Madame Wohlicka, "Do you need your assistant with you?" Wohlicka's eye fell on the unwelcome presence; holding her forehead in her hand, she emitted a groan.

"Yes, yes, I see." Pecton nodded, and turned to Zukowska. "Please be good enough to assist Miss Maybury with the coffee," he said sharply.

Zukowska remained unmoved until Madame Wohlicka translated into Polish. There was a moment's hesitation before Zukowska turned, and with obvious bad grace, retraced her steps.

Brenton closed the door and joined the two at the table.

Madame Wohlicka removed the cigarette from her mouth. "Already I am missing her," she sighed with weary sarcasm.

"I can understand why you would," Brenton smiled. "She's undoubtedly the life and soul of the party."

The soloist threw him a questioning look.

"A gorgon might be nearer the mark," said Pecton. "Why do you put up with her?"

"Do I have a choice?" she asked sardonically, as they sat down one on either side.

"I am having her for breakfast, I am having her for dinner, I am even having her while I am asleep because we share the same bedroom."

"Does she speak English?" Brenton asked.

"I have never heard her," Madame Wohlicka replied, "and I do not ask."

"Yes, quite," Pecton said, rising. "I'll go out and see how the coffee is coming along. David, stay here with Madame until I return." Then he took Brenton aside and murmured, "Try and make her amenable to a retake. We're working on an apology from Komorski to her. We'll be along shortly."

Brenton collected an ashtray from the sideboard and placed it on the table in front of Madame Wohlicka. "Ah, thank you. Mr Pecton was worried about my cigarette?" she asked with a laugh. "His beautiful table might get burnt, eh?"

"He was worried to find we were neglecting you," he countered, and sat beside her. "May I ask you, Madame Wohlicka, are you under some kind of pressure from Comrade Zukowska?"

The soloist's attention was drawn to the window opposite into the afternoon's gentle surrender to evening. The blustering weather of the morning had given way to more placid conditions. Just when Brenton thought she might not have understood correctly, her mind returned to the room and she murmured, "I want no trouble – maybe I say too much already."

"I only ask in order to try and smooth the obvious difficulties."

She drew deeply on the cigarette and deposited a precarious length of ash in the tray. "There are always difficulties. There will always be difficulties," she said with a certain resignation.

Brenton hoped he wasn't up against Slavic fatalism. "Nobody as distinguished as you are," he said with slow deliberation, "should have to suffer the petty indignities you're enduring at the moment."

She patted his hand. "I have the feeling – you are a good man," she said wryly.

"May I say it distresses me to see you so upset. I wish you to know that I am your friend, and you may call on my assistance at any time – for whatever reason. However, I won't mention the subject again."

The door opened after a brisk knock. Miss Maybury entered and, holding the door wide open, announced with apparent disdain, "Coffee." Mrs Wheeler breezed through with a laden tray and Zukowska followed bearing another tray with mixed sandwiches and Black Forest gâteau.

After attending to Madame Wohlicka's needs, Brenton asked, "Why do you think Professor Komorski is dissatisfied with the 1st Movement?"

"I don't know. His reason seems not to be a musical reason – but a personal reason, which we can work on. What I do not like is to work on something which is already good."

Pecton, Appleby and Komorski entered and joined them around the top of the table. They seemed relaxed and in good humour. Pecton unobtrusively summoned Brenton from his seat, which Komorski immediately occupied and engaged Madame Wohlicka in serious conversation.

Pecton asked, "Did you succeed?"

Brenton shook his head. "She feels – and I can't help agreeing – the take is musically sound and we should press ahead."

"Damn!" Pecton muttered irritably. "I'm sorry I didn't find time to listen to the replay. I don't suppose there's anything about the balance?"

"No. They both expressed satisfaction."

Pecton's face suddenly brightened. "Yes, yes, of course." His eyes refocused on Brenton. "We'll listen to the tape once more!"

Somewhat taken aback Brenton said, "I'll make arrangements for a replay."

"Aren't you interested in re-listening?"

"Ordinarily, yes. Remember, I do have another recording to contend with in St George's."

"Yes, yes, quite. Well then, make arrangements and I'll put it to our visitors."

Brenton moved to a telephone on a secretarial desk to contact Jim Sherry, and Pecton moved over to Wohlicka and Komorski.

"Excuse me," he politely interrupted. "I have a suggestion to make. I haven't heard the 1st Movement yet. Would it help if we all re-listened to the tape, I wonder?"

They agreed – Madame Wohlicka reluctantly. "You see," she said, "I have been thinking on the 2nd Movement since we finished the 1st."

Komorski shifted noisily in his chair. "I will feel good when we re-do the 1st Movement," he insisted.

The pleased expression vanished from the soloist's face. "I understood we would make a decision after listening to the recording," she protested.

"I have already made that decision," Komorski rancorously confirmed.

"This is ... this is offensive!" Madame Wohlicka cried.

Komorski reverted to Polish and addressed Comrade Zukowska on the other side of the table. The result was startling. Zukowska barked a staccato burst of Polish invective in Madame Wohlicka's direction. The soloist threw her hands in the air and gave a sigh of resignation as they fell back onto the table.

Embarrassment enveloped the non-Polish members around the table. To varying degrees, they had all treated the voluminous piece of baggage with disdain; but it was she who had turned out to be the hierarch of the Polish group. It was like a fairy story turned on its head. The wicked stepmother gets the better of Snow White, or Little Red Riding Hood cops it with the Big Bad Wolf.

Brenton found it difficult to avert his eyes from where the soloist sat ill-at-ease, peering at reflections on the window glass. He felt sorry for her, but there was nothing he could do about it. He would hold onto that morning's tape. The chances of a better recording under the present depressed conditions were remote.

CHAPTER 10

Tuesday March 24ᵗʰ 1981
Room 16 MI5 Headquarters
Gower Street
5.30 pm

Brenton gave the door of Major Frank Hempson's office a perfunctory knock and entered. Inside the ante-room, Sheena Barrett, Hempson's Australian secretary, greeted him with a beaming "Hello, David." He acknowledged the greeting and sat down opposite her desk. From this vantage point, he was the beneficiary of a mildly erotic display, from it could be said, down under.

"I'll tell Major Hempson you're here," she said engagingly, reaching for the telephone and once more rearranging her long shapely legs. "How are things in the music world?"

"You could say they're perking up," Brenton responded with amiable irony.

Sheena Barrett held the phone in abeyance and jested, "Yes, you could say that – if the extra traffic through the office this afternoon is anything to go by." She pressed the button, "Yes, you – Ah, Major Hempson, Wing Commander Brenton to see you… yes, straight away." She replaced the receiver and waved towards the inner door. "You're on, Commander." He stood up, regretting the disappearance of the vision from down under. As he exchanged the sweetness of the anteroom for the acidity of a pipe smoker's abode, he wondered about Sheena Barrett's display. Was it intentional?

Major Hempson rose from behind his desk and extended his hand in greeting. Brenton grasped it with enthusiasm. He didn't meet his boss very frequently, but when they did meet, their salutations were cordial.

"Good to see you David," Hempson began. "A spot of bother in Symphony Hall?"

Brenton crossed his legs and proceeded to unburden himself of the day's events. As he was talking, Hempson initiated the ritual of victualling his pipe, which was accompanied by an occasional "Umm" of encouragement, as he fed tobacco from a porcelain jar on his desk into the pipe bowl. Having struck a match, the flame began to release the leaf's aromaticity. But the rate of conflagration was slow and tantalising – would it or would it not light? Then, just as the fingers holding the match seemed on the point of being enveloped by the flame, Hempson – with a deftness that turned Brenton's anxiety to irritation – extinguished the match with a sharp puff of blue smoke. He added a further "Mmm," as he sank back into his armchair.

Frank Hempson fitted the popular conception of what a Guards Officer should look like. His ruddy complexion proffered what had once been a long straight aristocratic nose; now, at fifty-eight years, it had moved up a notch to imperial. Even more convincingly, his chin, of fine proportions, culminated in an accommodating ledge, the sole function of which could only have been the support of a bearskin chinstrap.

Brenton uncrossed his legs as he drew to the end of his monologue and concluded, "– and apart from the tape translation, that's the lot from my end."

Hempson put his pipe to one side and extracted a typewritten sheet from the papers in front of him. "Here we are," he said softly, and handed the transcript of Sarah's recording across the table to Brenton. "Have a look."

Brenton gave the sheet a sharp flick and refocused. It read:

Duration – 14' 10"

1.   If you hear me – do not look in my direction.

[0' 5" interval

2.   If you hear me correctly – raise your hand and stroke your nose.

[0' 47"

3.   I will not speak when there is silence on stage.

[1' 18"

4.   Uginski sits on your right.

[4′ 18″

5.   Has there been any reaction from either side of you?

[0 14″

6.   Shake your head if negative.

[0 10″

7.   Good.

[3′ 03″

8.   Raise your instrument in the direction of Uginski.

[1′ 05″

9.   Make the minister welcome.

[0′ 52″

10.   Uginski is yours *ad libitum.*

[1′ 36″

11.   You have a lot to do just now.

[0′ 10″

12.   I will sign off.

"That's an interesting collection of instructions," Hempson said.

Brenton watched him for a moment as he relit his pipe with a quick flourish. "For me, two items arise. The first is – *ad libitum* which is normally delivered as *ad lib,* and has also become a frequently used musical term. In this instance I take it as a direction to the recipient to carry out their instructions – *in whatever way necessary.* The second item points up an omission in my report."

Hempson emitted an interrogative "Oh?"

"I neglected to tell you of a break-in to our storeroom last weekend, which I thought unconnected with our problem, but in the light of this transcript I've had to revise my opinion."

"Go on."

"Three two-way Simplex radios were stolen. I incorrectly assumed the type used in the transmission to be Duplex, because I didn't hear a reply on tape." Brenton pulled his chair forward and laid the transcript on the desk. "As you see – all the replies on this were by sign language."

Hempson removed the pipe from his mouth and tapped his lips. "A curious lack of judgment in our adversary's opening move. Pinching equipment suggests they are arrogantly corrupt – or worse, amateurs."

Hempson rose and, fondling his pipe, moved to the window. "Which confirms that your position is still secure." he added with satisfaction, jamming the pipe back in his mouth The view from Hempson's window stretched out to embrace London University and the British Museum. On a fine day the Houses of Parliament stood out against the skyline, but the diminishing light reduced their sharp profile to a Turneresque suggestion.

Hempson turned and said, "I accept there is something afoot, and I also accept we pull out the stops. There is, however, another dimension to this, which may give rise to two further developments. Anton Uginski, as a guest in this country, shall be afforded appropriate security cover – but because of the possible risk to his life, I shall take the matter, through our director general, to our political master. I would hope the outcome of that meeting might be a recommendation to the Polish authorities to cancel. This is the course of action I shall push because it will remove the reason for possible political embarrassment. If the recommendation is accepted – then I shall further recommend that the cancellation be kept under wraps until the last moment."

Brenton had a sudden vision of Pecton's face, had he been privy to this last piece of information.

"This will give us, in the short time available, a chance to unravel what we can of the problem." Hempson re-seated himself and asked, "Do you have any suggestions?"

"I have requested a watcher on Jan Lesko."

"Yes. I received that this afternoon, and he shall have one, after roll call tomorrow morning. Again, because of the time scale, I also sent in a request for a phone tap. We may not use it, but it will be there tomorrow in any event."

"I intend interviewing Lesko some time this evening. I'd like to have his version of the on-stage row with Komorski."

"Could be useful."

"I also recommend you have the two Government in Exile chaps questioned – Cerniaski and Prolow. They had a confab with Komorski, Pecton and Appleby in Croydon. I'd like to know what went on there."

"I'll arrange that tomorrow morning." Hempson made a further note on a pad in front of him. "Cranshaw and Thompson are fully conversant with the situation?"

"Yes. I've launched them on a search of orchestra members' lockers this evening."

Hempson nodded at the transcript. "What's your initial impression?"

Brenton picked up the paper from the desk. "Setting aside for a moment the implications of the words spoken, the voice on the tape spoke from inside the auditorium – in order to see the responses of his accomplice. The silent partner would appear to be a member of the orchestra – or if not, was at least facing the same direction as certain members of the orchestra, because only from these positions within the orchestra would Uginski be on one's right. The reference to an instrument and the inquiry about a reaction from either side would seem to place him or her in the body of the orchestra. If this is correct, then I should imagine the two-way radio on the orchestral end was hidden, and they used one of those small insert ear pieces for listening."

Hempson said, "Makes sense."

Brenton continued, "I think we should lay aside the possibility of a Kamikaze effort; that kind of thing is more achievable at close range. We should see this as an assassination attempt – a subtler effort with music as a supportive background. May I keep a copy?"

"Yes," Hempson lisped, before removing his pipe from between clenched teeth. "Hold on to the one you have. This goes back to translations for clarification." He scribbled a note on the head of the transcript and returned it to an envelope. "Now, moving to personnel – how many Poles in the orchestra?"

"Six," Brenton replied.

Hempson opened a new page on his jotter.

"Jan Lesko – third trumpet," Brenton spelled out the surname. "Edward Mopak – rank and file cellist; Jerzy Kazimierz – percussionist; Henryk Hisiel – principle viola section; Stanislaw Reptarski – bassoon; Wanda Polascka – rank and file violin. Lesko is a Free Pole. The rest are recent arrivals."

"And so?"

"Apart from an age difference, there are the inherent political differences."

"I wouldn't put conversion to Lesko's political leanings beyond the bounds of possibility. My hope is that the conversion would be a natural progression – given time."

"Only one of the newcomers – Reptarski – has joined a London Polish society, and I've had doubts about that gentleman's bona fides."

Hempson sent a stream of smoke in the direction of the window, and when satisfied that his effort would not reach the target, returned to Brenton. "We have two suspects – identities unknown. One speaks Polish – the other comprehends Polish. If we assume for a moment one of them is Lesko –"

"That's what doesn't equate!" Brenton interrupted. "Lesko had already left the Hall, under a cloud, when the radio interruptions took place."

Hempson placed his elbows on the desk and cradled the pipe in his hands at the top of the equilateral. "Are you sure?"

"Absolutely. I checked out his movements. He left the building in a blinding rage, a good deal before the transmissions started."

"Interesting. He may have arranged that little operation before he left, or perhaps it could have been pre-arranged."

"Why then, assuming for a moment Lesko is part of the arrangement, why blow his part in the operation with the outburst?"

"Brenton old man, we seem to be dealing with amateurs, which the Polish community here undoubtedly are, at least in the business of political assassination. This imposes an element of unpredictability. Your interview with Lesko will be on a personal rather than official basis?"

"Yes."

"I have a meeting tomorrow morning with those of our people covering ethnic groups. This is fortuitous, because the meeting was arranged three weeks ago. Even then, Poland was placed top of the agenda on account of the strong Government in Exile reaction in Britain to the Polish government's overtures for the return of General Sikorski's body to Poland. I'll have the Polish deliberations of the meeting delivered to Cranshaw tomorrow afternoon for your consideration." Hempson took a look at his wristwatch. "I'm dining at my club this evening. I expect you could do with a bite, so if you'd like to join me, we could rake over the general background to our problem."

"Can't think of a more agreeable way to discuss the background," Brenton replied, as Hempson shook out the remains of his pipe in a metal container.

"I'll ring down for the car." Hempson reached for the phone. "And by the way, don't send any further open phone messages into the computer. We've had indications the Russians may have a radiotelephone intercept mechanism in operation. I thought of mentioning it because you may have reason to use it in the next twelve hours. Use normal encoding procedure. You should have a memo presently from the traffic sector."

CHAPTER 11

Tuesday March 24th 1981
The Athenaeum
6.30 pm

The Athenaeum admirably fulfilled the requirements of a gentleman's club. It provided a tranquil, civilised oasis, within which its members could view the outside world with varying degrees of mutually sympathetic indignation.

"This way," Hempson hastily directed, pointing towards a reading room. "In here," he commanded, opening the door. The room, of gracious proportions, was empty. Hempson permitted himself a sigh of satisfaction, and ushered his guest towards an alcove beside a window. He pressed a wall button before sitting down opposite Brenton.

"Brenton old man, you are not a member of a London club."

It was a statement, rather than a question.

"I'm not," Brenton admitted, "Where do you think I'd find the time, Major?"

"It's not a matter of time, old man. It's a matter of coming events."

Brenton's eyes creased inquisitively.

"Apart from the Albert Hall –" he began.

"That's it you see," Hempson cut in. "You're unable to see beyond your tight little circle in Croydon." Hempson laughed lightly as Brenton's face turned apprehensive. "I jest Brenton, I jest. But –" he raised an admonitory finger, "the jest may contain a shadow of reality, and the reality is – you've run an efficiently tight operation out there, which hasn't gone unnoticed."

"That's kind of you to say, but what has that to do with coming events?"

The door opened and a member of the staff moved deferentially across the room towards them. "You rang, Major?"

"Good man, Jackson. Under the circumstances," Hempson nodded conspiratorially towards the door, "I take it we may have a pre–dinner drink in here?"

Jackson smiled in collusion. "Yes, of course Major. The usual?" he enquired archly.

Hempson turned to Brenton. "Whisky?"

"Whisky will be fine," Brenton agreed.

"In which case, might I make a recommendation?" Without waiting for an answer, Hempson expanded, "Bushmills – a beautiful job. First became attached to it while on a tour of duty in Northern Ireland. They keep a few bottles in store for me here. Don't you, Jackson." He cocked an eye in Jackson's direction.

"Oh, yes sir – indeed we do, Major."

"So, bloody well jump to it, Jackson. Don't keep us on tenterhooks – and bring the menu when you return."

Jackson moved towards the door with obsequious alacrity.

"Make them doubles, Jackson!" he fired after him. Returning to Brenton, he added, "Not a bad chap, really."

"Coming events?" Brenton prompted.

"Yes," Hempson cleared his throat. "I've put your name forward for a position on the Board of Trustees of the Royal Air Force Museum in Hendon."

Brenton released the shadow of a smile. "It's not my birthday, Major. What's the occasion?"

"Brenton, in some respects you are –", his fingers fluttered across his chin, "– perhaps engagingly naive," he concluded. "Single-minded, was our initial impression, if my memory serves me correctly, and I won't pretend it didn't play a part in your being marked out for selection to our merry band."

Brenton said nothing, while continuing to observe him attentively.

"What I'm trying to say is, you have a capacity to bury yourself in specifics to the exclusion of the broad-spectrum, and I have to confess, I took advantage of your disposition – until now. With Cranshaw in position, the pressure to have you continue in your present capacity is off." Hempson allowed a few seconds for ingestion.

"I'm informing you of these matters now rather than later, because there's a possibility your cover may be blown during the next few days. If that happens, I don't want you to feel any remorse. In any event, you're moving out and up; and now seems as good a time as any to place my cards on the table."

Brenton's mouth opened to speak.

"Don't say anything just yet, Brenton. I need to explain. Naturally, Cranshaw must be kept under wraps. This shall increase pressure on your position, with possible consequent exposure."

Jackson materialised with drinks on a tray and menus tucked under an arm. Before he had an opportunity to deliver them, Hempson asked, "What's the beef like, Jackson?"

"Excellent, Major."

"Fancy a spot of beef, Wing Commander?"

Anxious to return to the subject of conversation, Brenton readily agreed. Jackson dispensed the whisky and departed with the unopened menus.

"I've been aware of your interest in that business out in Hendon," the Major recommenced, "and I thought it might be some compensation for having organised the set-up in Croydon in such exemplary fashion, not the least of which was your ability to keep your head down over an extended period."

"This is quite extraordinary," Brenton said with quiet sincerity. "My immediate reaction is to accept your offer, and let the consequences take care of themselves. But –"

"But nothing!" Hempson retorted paternally. "We'll drink to that."

They both raised their glasses.

"The Home Office has already made the recommendation to the Secretary of State for Defence, and he has accepted the recommendation. The position won't come through until mid-summer, but I dare say you have the strength of character to contain both yourself and the information until then."

"Absolutely."

"Well now. If I may take this business a step further. What would you say if I suggested proposing your name for membership of the club here?"

Brenton paused reflectively. "I'd have to say that the lack of acknowledgment of my birthday over the past number of years has been more than compensated. They all seem to be coming together."

"Splendid," said Hempson. "Of course, I don't mind telling you that an agreeable aspect of your acceptance is the fact that you'll no longer have to doss around in some of our safe houses after a late evening in town."

Brenton threw his head back in a surprised laugh. "You've had me tailed?"

"Word gets around old man, word gets around."

"I don't suppose the expense is insurmountable?"

"Why should that be a burden to someone who's been drawing two salaries for a decade?"

Brenton would normally have rewarded such a personally intrusive observation with silent disdain, but Hempson's generosity outweighed any offence he might have given.

"Come along Brenton!" Hempson chivvied, "Let's not get bogged down in a golden silence." Suddenly bending forward, he asked more confidentially, "You're not in some sort of financial bind?"

The open concern restored Brenton to a more amenable frame of mind. He smiled and said, "No, Major, no financial trouble. The answer however does involve finance. It's also rather personal."

Hempson sank back and said. "You'd rather not say?"

"On the contrary," said Brenton, "I feel now might be a good time to open up on the subject." He took a mouthful of whisky and settled back into the recess of his armchair. "I hesitated, Major, because of my own reluctance to communicate matters of a family nature ..."

"Damn it Brenton – nobody appreciates a tight lip more than I do, more particularly since I've worked through a period of extraordinary self-doubt and recrimination in the service myself. Remember, you're looking at the man who recruited you."

"I'm deeply grateful for the museum appointment. You know my father was stationed at Hendon and I have great affection for the place." Brenton took another mouthful of his drink and placed it to one side. "When I undertook Croydon, I had no idea it would be as protracted as it turned out. In order not to become acclimatised to the extra income, I hived off the Croydon salary for investment in a family farm in the West Country. In doing so, I was able to turn a financial bonus towards a family commitment."

"Very laudable, Brenton. You guarded against a reliance on an inflated remuneration. It's something I would have expected of you. Your realignment during the year won't quite match your present salaries, but it won't be too far short. If I may be equally frank. Farming is a business which, if well managed, should produce a good return. As things take shape during the year, you shall have more time on your hands. Some of it will be taken up in Hendon; the remainder could, with profit, be applied to your family farm. With regard to club expenses – they should not present an impediment to someone of your financial standing. Splash out Brenton! People in our profession have a need to emerge from the shadows on occasions. We all have a need of a few freckles. If I may be permitted a turn to the macabre – you know, when you become a member of the Athenaeum, your chances of being buried in Westminster Abbey increase appreciably. Sixty-nine of our members have been so honoured. That in itself should be something of an inducement." Hempson took a mouthful of whisky.

"However, to get back to the matter in hand, I wish to go over the background to our present business before going in to dinner. How much do you know about General Wladislaw Sikorski?"

"Not a lot – apart from his being leader of the Free Poles during the last war, and his death in a plane crash off Gibraltar in, I think, 1943. Oh yes, and he's buried in Newark cemetery."

"Yes, that's the bones of the matter – if you will forgive the unintended pun. And now to put flesh on it. You're already aware of unofficial approaches from the Polish authorities to have Sikorski's body returned to Poland?"

"I received that information in a memo."

"To bring you up to date. Those soundings have now become official, with a formal request."

"Increasing the pressure," Brenton guessed.

"Yes," Hempson agreed. "A curious aspect of these negotiations – and that seems to be the road we're going – is that until recent times, the Polish government preferred to regard Sikorski as a non-person. This was understandable because to do otherwise would have given grievous offence to their Russian masters, who are unforgiving of Sikorski's wartime row with Stalin over the Katyn massacre." Hempson drained his whisky.

"Therefore a fundamental change in relationship between Poland and the Soviets has taken place, which has enabled this request to be made. Another intriguing element in the shift is that the underwriters, so to speak, would appear to be the Roman Catholic hierarchy in Poland. They, we are told, are preparing a place in the Wawel Cathedral in Krakow for Sikorski's remains."

"Is there a connection here, I wonder?" Brenton asked. "The conductor engaged for the Polish concert, Komorski, hails from Krakow."

"In a secondary sense, perhaps. It has no bearing on the presented battle order, but keep it in mind."

"The connection may have been made manifest with the two Government in Exile chaps – Cerniaski and Prolow."

"Good man, Brenton. I'd forgotten that meeting in your welter of data; that was one of their unofficial meetings. They're very anxious to seek the support of the Polish population here, and to a limited extent they've succeeded. But before elaborating on that part of the jigsaw, let me present the government's thinking on the transfer."

Hempson cast a glance at his empty glass. Catching the look, Brenton asked, "Shall I ring for a refill?"

"Not now, Brenton, I'd prefer to get through this without Jackson's assistance. Now, as I've said, there seems to be a shift in relations between Poland and Russia. Her Majesty's government would like to see this rift widen. Indeed, they see General Sikorski's body as an instrument to drive the wedge deeper. At the same time, they must take cognisance of the Government in Exile, which has pointedly taken the view that, until Poland re-emerges as the free democracy for which Sikorski fought, his body should lie undisturbed in Newark. To discourage a move, from whatever quarter, to disinter without lawful authority, his grave now has round-the-clock police protection."

"Justifiable under the circumstances," Brenton nodded.

"The Polish prime minister, General Jaruzelski, is desperately in need of a catalyst to counter the wide wave of disenchantment throughout Poland, the focus of which is centred in the Solidarity Movement. This remarkable marriage of workers and intellectuals spells doom for Jaruzelski unless he achieves the unthinkable: the reform of the incompetent and corrupt Polish Communist Party." The door opened and Jackson announced dinner.

"Good man, Jackson," Hempson acknowledged, inclining his head in the direction of the announcement. "We'll give the claret a few more moments to breathe." Hempson turned fully to check that the door had closed, and returned to his subject. "So far, I don't have any evidence of nefarious intent from any of the Polish associations," he said, as his chin suffered the indignity of over-emphatic squeezes between his thumb and index finger. "That's not to say there isn't a great deal of apprehensive anger, particularly from the military associations." He gave a sigh of dissatisfaction. "It all seems to point to freelance hot-heads."

Brenton's hand reached for his own chin sympathetically. "May I take it you'll be looking after the Polish societies?" he asked.

Hempson nodded. "I'll put together the information from that end. Patently, the main arena is Croydon and finally the Royal Albert Hall, and the further we move through the week, the more this will be so. Everything else is ancillary."

Brenton reached for his glass and asked, "In the event of a need for extra hands – where do I stand?"

"You don't, old man," Hempson dismissed. "After all, if I have my way, Mr Uginski won't be attending, and if at the end of the day you don't achieve one hundred percent success, at least we'll have tried to take the only prudent course – prevention." Hempson uncrossed his legs and placed his arms along the length of the armrests. At their curved ends, his fingers tapped an impatient little tattoo. "Let's not delay any further, Brenton, I think our wine should be just right."

CHAPTER 12

Tuesday March 24th 1981
Bromley
8.30 pm

"Hello, Jack." Brenton did not have to fake a salutation where Jack Lesko was concerned as they had a strong mutual regard. On this occasion however, when Lesko opened his front door, he put it on ice. "Did they send you?" he asked with obvious distaste.

"Easy on, Jack," Brenton said lightly. "Do you honestly believe I'd undertake such an errand?"

Lesko eyed him frankly. Then, with a glance next door and across the road at his neighbours' semi-detached homes, he said, "You'd better come in."

In the taxi on the way out to Bromley, Brenton had wondered what sort of reception he would receive. He had not been looking forward to the meeting because he knew the Pole would feel embarrassment, perhaps even feel he was being snooped on. Jack Lesko was a proud man, methodical in his ways, but with a capacity for emotion. As an orchestral musician, this fitted the bill. After World War II, Lesko had demobbed in Britain and married an English schoolteacher, Ada Rawlings. They were blessed, if not with children, then with an undiminished affection, which in late middle age continued to shine out like a beacon in a sea of human disaffection. They were at once an inspiration – and an irritant.

"Please, go straight through to the kitchen," Lesko directed in accented but impeccable English. "I was drinking a cup of coffee – will you have one too?"

"I'd be delighted," Brenton quickly accepted, entering the kitchen.

The room combined a cooking and dining area. Its practical elegance spoke munificently of two unencumbered incomes. Lesko gestured in the direction of a large impressive oak table, which mutely proclaimed his original family ambitions. Brenton sat at the table and watched him prepare the coffee.

"Ada is attending a parent-teacher meeting and won't be back for an hour or so," he said without looking around. "Do you take sugar?"

"One spoon, thanks." Brenton took note of the almost palpable animosity exuding from Lesko's back. He had to find out quickly whether it was directed at him, or Symphony Hall. Lesko turned, reluctantly it seemed, and joined Brenton at the table passing him a steaming cup of instant coffee.

"Like to tell me what happened, Jack?"

Lesko looked long and hard at Brenton. The silence stretched for so long that he was about to take another tack, when Lesko finally answered. "I'm not sure I wish to answer that question. Surely if you did not see and hear the commotion, you would have heard talk about it?" he charged with bitterness.

Brenton sipped his coffee to give Lesko's anger time to subside.

"I've heard so many differing versions of the event – I'm totally confused. I did see and hear the final moments of the row ... but I couldn't possibly make up my mind until I hear your side of the story."

Lesko seemed to simmer down at this nod in his direction.

Brenton continued, "The confusion, I imagine, is due to everybody's ignorance of your native tongue, the language in which the dispute took place."

"Not everybody," Lesko corrected emphatically. "Remember there are five other Polish members in the orchestra."

"They didn't want to know, and even less to become involved", remarked Brenton, "You must know the new breed by now."

Lesko received this with sullen chagrin, eventually acknowledging its correctness with a curt dismissive nod of his head. "Look," he said suddenly. "I am sick to death of this whole affair. You know I wanted to resign?"

Now it was Brenton's turn to be taken by surprise, and it showed. Lesko responded with a further disclosure. "And did you know that

Appleby and Pecton were so shook up that they refused to accept my resignation? At least until things cooled down. They didn't suspend me; I was informed that my services would not be required during the week."

Lesko stood up and paced around the room. "Me – a Pole! And my services are not required during the Polish Week!" He brought his fist down on the table with a bang. "They can paddle their Polish Week up the Vistula for all I care."

Brenton tried to diffuse the situation. "Don't do anything rash. Just ignore the political element that's making itself felt. You're probably better off away from the event, since it's so obviously touched a raw nerve."

Lesko now looked at Brenton with open anger; clearly he was about to erupt.

"Take a moment," said Brenton placatingly. "Talk me through what happened."

The Pole exhaled. His eyes coldly fastened on Brenton's. "You lot never really understand, do you?"

Brenton held the look but declined to reply, knowing he would eventually get an answer to the loaded question.

"You lot never really *try* to understand – if it doesn't suit you to," Lesko asserted. The two sets of eyes still held each other. The Pole continued, "Except when you receive a kick in the crotch. But in that case the offence is immediately bracketed under 'Not Cricket'." Lesko leaned close across the table. He narrowed his eyes. "Or," he said softly, "If some of your revered institutions are mocked." He relinquished eye contact with a mock inspirational look at the ceiling, and returned with, "Like the monarchy for instance." He sought the ceiling again, and added, "Or a Guards regiment." Lesko drew back from the table. "Now there's a funny thing," he said, reverting to normal voice and posture. "Mention a British regiment in a bad light and – boom! – you'll find the bowler gets nasty."

Brenton couldn't contain himself any further. "What in hell's name has any of this to do with Croydon?"

Lesko drew himself erect in his chair. "It has this to do with Croydon," he said folding his arms. "Invite an enemy to your table and expect to be insulted."

"Does that specifically refer to me?" Brenton asked sharply.

Lesko realised his statement had a second connotation, and quickly reassured his visitor. This took some of the wind out of his sails, and finally he decided to unfold his version of events.

The enemy, Lesko informed Brenton, was the Polish communist entourage presently encamped in Croydon. Even at this point in the proceedings, he argued how provocative and inappropriate it was to invite communist usurpers from his homeland to Britain – lending them legitimacy. Brenton tried to steer him in the direction of the on-stage outburst.

"Even if I agreed with the sentiments, there's nothing I could have done about it. This decision was taken at a much more elevated level, and whether I like it or not, I have to get on with the job."

"But," countered Lesko, "If you invite an enemy, don't be surprised if the hospitality is abused. This is what has actually happened. After the coffee break on Monday evening," Lesko continued, "Komorski returned to the podium and started bantering in Polish with Reptarski, the bassoonist."

Brenton relaxed a little. Lesko had started his version of events; he sat back and nodded encouragingly. Once Lesko started, the flow seemed unstoppable.

Lesko had not been inclined to earwig, because he detested Komorski and preferred to ignore the conductor's inanities. However, it impinged on him that Komorski was talking about the rehearsal of the Elgar which they had finished before the coffee break. Then the conductor began to make comments about Elgar. As sometimes happens where a large collection of people are engaged in animated conversation, there was a sudden lull in proceedings and clear as a bell he heard Komorski – still speaking in Polish say – 'As with the music, they should put away the toy soldiers outside Buckingham Palace, and while they're at it, they should put away the toy Queen.'

In Lesko's opinion this was a most serious and cynical breach of etiquette, and since nobody else had noticed, he felt obliged to remonstrate. "I jumped to my feet. I knew the insult had not been understood. I couldn't believe my ears. I stood staring at the dog for a few moments. My reaction to his insult attracted his attention and we stared at each other. Komorski broke the spell by asking Reptarski was I Polish. I answered his question by shouting, '*Psiakrew! Psiakrew!*'"

Lesko rose from the kitchen table and paced the room. "Basically it means dog's blood!" he snapped. He paused and then sighed, aware that his interjection had been heavy-handed. "Look," he said simply, "I just boiled over." He rubbed his nose and added mulishly, "I'm not apologising to anybody."

"Are Pecton and Appleby aware of what you overheard?" Brenton asked.

"Of course. They immediately demanded an explanation."

"And what was their reaction?"

"Pecton, the pompous idiot, tried to make light of it. It was patently clear, he said, the conductor was referring to the red coats of the guardsmen, which have been reproduced all over the world on toy soldiers."

"And?"

"I asked him what he thought his 'toy Queen' might make of those comments if they were brought to Her Majesty's attention."

Brenton's mouth twitched, but Lesko felt that the seriousness of the subject prohibited a reciprocal softening of attitude.

"Damn it, David," the Pole continued, "I do believe you also would have accepted the dog's insult. I can't believe it! What is the matter with you English?"

Brenton beckoned him to sit at the table. Lesko sat down expectantly on the vacant chair.

"Jack, my reaction wasn't in any way due to Komorski's snide remarks," he began. "Your 'toy queen' comment conjured up an abject picture of Dr Pecton's punctured ambitions for possible future royal honours."

Even this prospect did not seem to lighten the event for Lesko. The reference either went over his head or he deliberately chose to ignore it. "I can tell you," he dourly divined, shaking his head, "– it does not auger well. No, it does not auger well."

"In what respect?"

Lesko's head ceased its movement and he looked disbelievingly at Brenton, "For Poland." he contemptuously replied, "For Poland, of course!"

The depth of his feeling was transparent. Brenton felt trapped. This would normally be the point where he would rise and extricate himself, and leave the man to his private thoughts. Increasing his unease, Lesko now threw him a jaundiced look. "I expect you also think the thousands of Poles who came to this country, came to fight for England?"

Brenton tried to accommodate the question with a shrug of his shoulders.

"They came, my friend, to fight for Poland!" Lesko pronounced with a sense of pride – then added more quietly, "That's not to say we were all chauvinistic in our motives. To a man," he emphasised, "we thought of England as the moral guardian of Europe, and at that time, the last shining light in an enveloping sea of misery. Perhaps I should say Britain – but so many refer to this Kingdom as England."

Lesko looked at Brenton in mute appeal but came up against a brick wall. He ploughed on regardless. "We came to Great Britain and fought the good fight, on land and in the air. Naturally, we felt privileged to be allowed to do so. After all, you allowed us to bring our government here with General Sikorski at its head and commander in chief of our forces." Lesko became thoughtful. "We were content in the knowledge that we were in the country and part of Winston Churchill's fighting machine – the same man who had championed our cause. If history has taught us anything, it is the meaning of the words 'partition' and 'obliteration'."

"Yes," Brenton agreed. "Polish history does present a dismal litany in recent times; but that's no reason to be totally pessimistic. Look at all the emerging colonial nations –"

Lesko interposed, "You, in your condescending wisdom, give me an example of nations which have thrown off foreign domination. You are facing a man whose country is still under foreign domination, and not likely to get out from under it in the foreseeable future."

"Russia had to overrun Eastern Europe to defeat Hitler," Brenton countered.

"That is only half the story," Lesko shot back.

Brenton observed the clenched hands and the heightened colour. Reluctantly, he decided that he'd have to hear him out.

"Any nation which invades another, with territorial gain in mind, must be considered an aggressor. In 1939 my country was invaded by Germany *and* Russia," Lesko said, shaking his head. "As a result of the Ribbentrop-Molotov Pact, they split Poland between them, but before Russia had time to enjoy the spoils, Hitler decided he needed further space and invaded Russia. What I say now should have had a bearing on our destiny at the end of the war. Poland was the only continental country that did not have personnel attached to the German Wehrmacht. Another reason was the discovery of the mass murder of Polish officers near Katyn. They had been captured by the Russians in 1939. About 4,400 unfortunates, each one shot in the back of the head. What sort of barbarians could contemplate such an undertaking – but then they did it to their own – so why shouldn't they do it to someone else?" Lesko paused to take a deep breath; Brenton resigned himself for an ineluctable history lesson. Somehow he'd have to find a way of eliciting the information he was after.

"As you may know, I was with the Polish contingent in Italy during the last war under General Władysław Anders." Lesko reopened his World War II encounter. "The majority of the troops in his second corps were Poles from what was then Eastern Poland and today is Russia. They had been captured by Russia in 1939 and were transported there. When Hitler attacked Stalin, the Government in Exile in London negotiated their release and decided they would make up the bulk of what became known as the Second Corps under General Anders."

"I had forgotten that episode," Brenton remarked. He lowered his eyes and cast around in his mind for a way of terminating the potted history of Poland in the Second World War, but Lesko beat him to it.

"Before that influx," Lesko pursued his theme determinedly, "there had been a previous flow of Poles into Britain to join the Royal Air Force. They were members of the abandoned Polish Air Force, and when they arrived, they formed 303 Squadron – which became known as the Polish Squadron. It was to play a significant part in the Battle of Britain. When they joined the RAF and began training on British aircraft, they couldn't believe their luck. The Polish aircraft with which they had tried to defend their homeland were obsolete in comparison with the German machines; but the Hurricanes and Spitfires in which they trained surpassed everything they had come across previously. Their new–found enthusiasm became so boundless that they disobeyed RAF orders by following invading Nazi bombers back across the Channel."

"Yes, I've heard reference to those episodes in the RAF," Brenton smiled.

"As it turned out, this would acquire for 303 Squadron the highest number of hits in Britain. It would subsequently be seen that they had contributed to eliminating half of the Nazi bomber fleet in the process." Jack Lesko emitted a sigh of satisfaction. He looked Brenton straight in the eye and pronounced. "You are undoubtedly aware that the culmination of the Battle of Britain brought with it the cancellation of the German invasion of Britain."

Brenton considered this. "It was appreciated, of course."

"I've become completely disillusioned with international politics," Lesko retorted. "From Neville Chamberlain's 'Peace in our Time' – which in effect dismembered Czechoslovakia – down to Britain's present invitation to Polish communists."

Brenton found himself wondering about the extent of Lesko's anti-communism. Was he a hardliner? One way or another he'd have to find out if Lesko's stance had more concrete ambitions.

"There had been talk during the Italian Campaign," Lesko picked up on his personal contribution in the Second World War. "Radio news revealed the successes of the Red Army on the Eastern Front and most of this talk centred on speculation over Russia's motives towards

Poland. Some of this apprehension was fuelled by Polish couriers who used Italy as a staging point for entry to Poland. Their anxieties were taken on board; but even when they were subsequently disregarded, a certain naivety – an unwillingness to believe anything other than good of Great Britain and the United States – meant that ultimately nothing was done."

Lesko's mood was sombre now as he ruminated – almost to himself – on the first time, the very first time, doubt had insinuated itself into his mind.

"It was a doubt that led to questions soldiers knew they shouldn't be asking. It was insidious: a growing awareness that the moral superiority of the West was a chimera. Reaction set in, and then came the self-recriminations after the battle for Monte Cassino."

Brenton held up a questioning hand. "What do you mean?"

"It may have started ten months before that," Lesko responded. "We'd been stunned by the news of General Sikorski's death in a plane crash off Gibraltar on July 4th, 1943. There wasn't a free Pole alive who didn't feel the loss, or in another way, feel politically naked. A few even found it impossible to speak of the General in the past tense. Sikorski had been Poland's Charles de Gaulle and like de Gaulle he was imbued with a high sense of destiny. Lesko suddenly broke off, overcome with emotion.

Brenton tried to move beyond his own embarrassment. "And?" he prompted.

"In 1944," Lesko took up quietly, "the Russian juggernaut ground to a cynical halt outside Warsaw, to witness the annihilation of the Polish Home Army by the Germans. They watched, and waited, for three agonising months, from the other side of the River Vistula, whilst the Flower of Poland was wiped out. I have become so bitter about all this," Lesko said with tired resignation. "At times I've felt I would have been better off if I'd never left Poland. The pull to return is still there ... even today. I wouldn't have met my good lady, of course. But then, as the saying goes, 'What you've never had ...'" He fell into a thoughtful silence. Brenton didn't interrupt it.

"Ada keeps me on course," he took up. Brenton nodded. "She's a steadying influence," Lesko added. "Another influence has been the 'Russian Quartet' factor," he suggested cryptically, looking at Brenton for a sign of recognition. He received a negative shake of the head. The prospect of the hackneyed story induced the first friendly expression on Lesko's face. "A quartet is what is left," he confided, "after a Russian symphony orchestra goes on tour to the West. The same is true of Poland," he continued more soberly. "The spectacle of ordinary folk escaping from communism is that system's greatest indictment and my anchor here." He looked around his well-appointed domain, of which Ada was such an important part, and smiled at his good fortune. As exiles went, this one was golden. "I have often thought," he said frowning, "that General de Gaulle staved off any ambitions America and Britain may have had on France at the end of World War II. Before the Germans had completely left Paris, de Gaulle slipped in and set up shop. Britain and the US had to acknowledge the huge popular acclaim he commanded, and with good grace accepted the fait accompli. He gave France back its pride. When he was recalled to office, he guided – and on occasion even goaded – his country back to pre-eminence in Europe." Lesko rubbed his forehead; Brenton could see he was getting worked up again. "You see," he said, speaking quietly and deliberately, as if trying to keep his emotion under control, "Sikorski came from the same mould: independent and alert. He could have achieved the same for Poland, and Poland would have given him its all."

They both drained their coffees in silence. Then Brenton steered him back to the first time he had been assailed by doubts.

"It was on the Italian campaign," Lesko recalled, "Between Naples and Rome, when things ground to a halt against the massive defences of the Gustav Line. The first four months of 1944 amounted to a bitter and bloody stalemate. Initial Allied probes found the German defence system well defended. The most conspicuous and commanding position in the Line was Monte Cassino. It stood sentinel at the entrance to the Liri Valley and overlooked the Via Casilina to Rome, which gave it great strategic importance. I remember it well, Saint Benedict's monastery looking down from the top of the mountain on the scrabble for life taking place below. It was almost one and a half thousand years old. It was a home both to monks and priceless works of art. But, as the days stretched to weeks, the Cassino sector began to acquire a certain notoriety."

"General Mark Clark's 36th Division suffered terrible losses trying to cross the River Rapido; it was the first major setback. Actually, it was a debacle. The Rapido event was later to become the subject of an American Congressional inquiry and there are those who say it was the reason Mark Clark did not reach the top post in the United States military establishment."

Lesko rose and refilled their two cups with coffee. After his first sip he continued, "The second phase began with the introduction of Lieutenent General Sir Bernard Freyberg's New Zealand Corps. The Corps included the British 78th Division, the 4th Indian Division and the 2nd New Zealand Division – all well seasoned and very durable outfits. Freyberg was from New Zealand and didn't willingly take orders from anyone. This upset Clark and Alexander. He initiated all-out frontal assaults. When they took a number of bad reverses, he cast around for an explanation other than the obvious: he surmised the Germans must be in possession of the monastery – therefore, bomb it. Mark Clark and Alexander found Freyberg's charge unsubstantiated, but Freyberg insisted, and to Clark's eternal shame he let his subordinate have his way. Here was the ultimate in witless vandalism. Freyberg set about flattening Monte Cassino – a beacon of civilisation which had actually felt the presence of the man Benedict, whose role sparked the first light of post-Roman social organisation, which in turn inspired men such as Gregory the Great and Augustine of Canterbury – and it disappeared in an ignominious cloud of dust. When that dust settled, the Germans felt they could now occupy the rubble with impunity, and what had previously been awkward to defend because of its restrictions now became the defensive position par excellence. Thanks to Freyberg."

Lesko placed his elbows on the table and cradled his chin in his hands. "You possibly already know ... eventually the Poles took Monte Cassino."

The conclusion was delivered in a deadpan unemotional tone. "That is not to convey that we were better than anybody else. The climax came about as a result of a major thrust on another sector. The Germans on

Monte Cassino became out-flanked and on the night of May 17th they withdrew. Strategy had succeeded where might had failed."

Brenton grimaced and opened his mouth to respond, but Lesko got in before him.

"What I'm getting to is –" he removed his hands from his chin, "Our country was about to be swallowed by your ally. At the same time we became guilty by association with an act of wilful destruction. A monastery that we in Poland looked to for inspiration was pulverised before our eyes. Anticipating the event, the Nazi army, which had raped and looted Europe, was provided with the opportunity to save the transportable treasures of Monte Cassino and move them to safety. This was a major role reversal and we didn't care for it." Lesko resumed resting his chin in his hands. "Four thousand Poles were lost in our brush with Monte Cassino," he sighed reflectively. "And those of us who survived, lost our homeland."

Brenton let a decent passage of time elapse before asking, "Do all your compatriots in this country feel as you do?"

"Yes," Lesko replied, and then qualified, "To varying degrees of course, but yes, we all feel we were let down. If we were worth going to war over – surely we were worth brokering peace for too?"

"You were correct – as things turned out. But that's little consolation to you now," Brenton said.

Lesko raised a speculative eyebrow.

"The proposal to transfer General Sikorski's remains back to Poland," pushed Brenton, "Has it been discussed by your association?"

Lesko's smile dissolved into inquisitiveness. "How do you know about that? I was under the impression it was a secret suggestion."

"It was – until different Polish organisations also put them on the agenda for discussion. May I ask the result of your deliberations?"

"I don't think it would be letting any cats out of the bag if I told you the vast majority – with whom I agree – opposes the idea."

"Look, we know what's going on inside Poland. We know the people are sick and tired of the dull grey purgatory of a communist state. Marvellous on paper, hideous in reality. The perverse aspect of the philosophy is – the idea is not new."

Lesko permitted himself a knowing smile. "We're back to Benedict," he said quietly. "His system of community has worked successfully for a millennium and a half. Although, in fairness it must be said, Benedict's rule has the distinct advantage of having been instituted for the greater glory of God – and its membership confirmed without coercion."

"You really do detest communism."

"Yes," Lesko acknowledged with a tinge of pride. "And my detestation is only equalled by my fear of Russia. Thank God they did not take to capitalism, they'd probably rule the world today."

"Jack, have you any close friends in the orchestra?"

"That's an odd question."

"It's not, if you consider my position in Croydon: I'll find myself defending your stance without knowing who your allies are."

"Those who speak for me are my friends – the rest do not matter."

"That makes me feel secure," Brenton reacted sarcastically.

Lesko considered this for a moment before saying, "I've no close friends in Croydon – just good working relationships."

"What about the young Polish members?"

"I maintain a paternal interest in their general welfare. But David, you see before you a man drawing to the end of his useful life as a musician. There's a very wide generation gap – socially speaking. Nevertheless, we all manage to make good music together."

"If the opportunity presented itself Jack, would you do damage to the cause of communism, and in particular, Polish communism in whatever way possible?"

"Yes. I would."

Brenton registered the stark admission. To maintain the momentum, he crashed into the next question. "How – what would you do?"

"You ask that question as if you expect me to do something."

"I'm curious as to the extent of your feelings."

"They take me a long way – at least on this subject, I assure you."

Lesko shrugged. "But they've never had an opportunity to become reality."

The front door opened and Ada Lesko shouted from the hall: "It's me, I'm back."

"We're in the kitchen," Lesko called.

Mrs Lesko's head materialised around the opening kitchen door. "I wondered who the 'we' could be. Hello David, you're about the last person I expected to find here – especially after what you did to poor Jack."

"Ada," Lesko hastily interposed, "David and I have gone over the situation and I can tell you he had no part in what happened."

"I'm very glad to hear that. Just one moment while I put away my hat and coat."

She disappeared into the hall cloakroom.

"I really think I should go," Brenton said, rising from the table. "I've already encroached enough on your hospitality… And Jack, have a think about what we discussed earlier."

CHAPTER 13

Tuesday March 24th 1981
St George's
9.45 pm

Ronald Shipsey listened to the recording of the first take of the organ in St George's until the reverberation of the last note died away. He said, "That's the take I like."

"I agree," Sarah confirmed. "Although there's very little between it and the second take. Pass me the tape box, Jim."

Jim Sherry threw his magazine to one side and brought over the tape cover. Sarah made an additional note on its label.

"Could I interest anyone in a drink?" the organist enquired, rising from his seat. "Your gloomy surroundings here make it an absolute necessity, and we should quite easily find a pub before closing time."

"That's kind of you," Sarah said, "but quite honestly, I'm far too exhausted. I'll pass for tonight, we'll have a celebratory drink after the final recording."

"Yes, that would be nice," he agreed. "How about you, Jim? Would you care for a drink?"

"I'd care very much," Sherry said. "Unfortunately, duty calls in another direction."

"Duty?" Shipsey echoed.

"I've a date," Sherry replied cockily, "with one of the girls in the orchestra!"

Sarah cast an indulgent look in Sherry's direction.

"Ok – ok," he laughed. "So she also wants her lighting fixed."

"That's more like what I got from Miss Bretcu," Sarah said. "It was me she came to about her problem, remember?"

"Catch on," Sherry said, somewhat taken aback that the male banter might have been misconstrued. "I'm just delighted to be of some help to the girl."

"That's better, and more like the Jim Sherry I know," Sarah said more agreeably.

"I'll press on then and see you tomorrow," Shipsey said, moving towards the door. "Thanks for your nice sound production."

He disappeared into the gloom of the stairwell and clattered up the wooden stairs into the church.

"Did Mr Pryce say we could leave everything as is?" Jim Sherry asked.

"Yes, everything as it is," Sarah confirmed. "It's at least as safe here under lock and key as in our so-called impregnable fortress in Croydon."

"Right then," he said. "Anything I can do before I go?"

"Not a thing. You could perhaps take the tape with the acceptable take on it and drop it into Croydon tomorrow."

"No problem."

"I know you're anxious to answer the call to *duty*, so toddle along, and remember – behave yourself!"

"Aren't you leaving?" he asked uneasily. "I mean, the place has to be locked up and that."

"I'll lock up tonight," Sarah assured. "I'd like to re-listen to take two before crawling home to bed."

"Reliving the glory," Sherry smirked.

"Yes ... partly," Sarah said with a touch of pride. "I'd also like to make sure that there's nothing I've overlooked, and the way to do that is – alone."

Sherry made for the stairs, but before closing the door advised, "I wouldn't leave it too late – might upset the rector's schedule."

She switched the desk to the microphone input and listened to Sherry's indeterminate whistling retreat through the church. The front door slammed, and then slammed a second and evidently successful time, leaving only an electronically exaggerated quiet. The urge to fill the emptiness took hold of her. She switched back to tape input, reeled on the tape, and dropped into a chair to listen. The ability to listen objectively was enhanced when one was alone. She liked what she was hearing; it confirmed her opinion of the initial balance.

She needed David's admiration like a flower needs the sun, and this was a beginning. The tape finished and she switched the speakers back to the upstairs microphones. While replacing the tape in its cover, her attention was drawn to a vague squeaking noise on the loud speakers. She drew closer to one of them, not sure whether she had heard correctly. A trick of the imagination, she concluded, after a moment or two of negative response. Then, it was there again, this time distinct and clear – crepe soles on the polished floor of the church.

Eliminating David, Jim Sherry and Ronald Shipsey as exponents of this insalubrious mode of footwear, Sarah scrupled about the possibility of the Reverend Rupert Pryce. But there was only one way to find out. She bounded out and up the stairs.

———

After the bustle and noise during recording, the church seemed intimidatingly quiet and sombre.

"Is that you Mr Pryce?" she enquired boldly, anxious to break the silence.

Her voice pointed up the admirable acoustics in the building, something for which she had earlier rejoiced, but now could only feel unease and silence.

Beyond the front door the faint rumble of London night traffic impinged. She made an impulsive move in that direction, but stopped abruptly when she heard and then saw a fleeting figure dart from behind a pillar at the back of the church and reach for the light switches inside the front door. The church plunged into darkness.

It happened so quickly. She stood where she had halted in disbelief, expecting the lights to return, but the only thing to return was the sound of crepe soles on marble.

With as much firmness as she could muster, she demanded, "Who's there!" Her voice bounced off every nook and recess. It returned unacknowledged to ridicule in an exaggerated echo; then once again silence.

A sudden screech from a jolted table at the bottom of the church rent the stillness. Sarah went rigid, and at once felt vulnerable. The cloying sound of crepe soles recommenced, then entered the aisle, hypnotically holding her attention. She knew she should be moving in the opposite direction; knew it was lunacy to remain standing where she was standing; even knew she was wasting precious seconds arguing with herself. She turned and groped her way back towards the glimmer of light from the basement door. Closing it to deny the intruder a point of direction, she rushed to the side door at the top of the stairs. It was locked – the keys were in the basement. Panic began to control her actions as she scampered down the stairs. Misjudging the final step for the ground floor, she pitched forward and struck the floor with a thud. Painfully, she gathered herself together and staggered into the recording room, but the keys were nowhere in sight.

The steps approached the stereo microphone in the church. Sarah listened to them on the speakers, almost expecting the shoes to emerge disembodied. The microphone transformed the more eccentric frequencies into a series of obsessive squeals until one shoe collided with the mic stand. The explosion on the speakers jolted her. She began a frantic search, scattering newspapers and tapes in mounting dread – spied the keys on the handle of the recording desk – snatched them up and raced for the stairs.

Half way up, the door from the church began to open, cutting her off. With an involuntary cry she groped her way back down into the recording room. There she tugged at the tape machine to jam the door. She froze in her efforts – remembering the wine cellar.

The footsteps began slowly to descend the stairs, the spongy soles massaging each step. Her hands scrabbled in a two-handed search somewhere under the damp patch on the wall for the keystone. She found it, pressed it, waited an agonising three seconds before squeezing through, then put her back to it and pushed. It closed with a palpitating reluctance and locked home with a low igneous grunt. She closed her eyes. Convulsed in uncontrollable shivering, she sank to the ground. Every fibre of her body affected by terror. She found it difficult to focus on any aspect of what had just happened.

Opening her eyes, she was overwhelmed by the darkness of her surroundings. Unable to make out any distinguishing features in front of her, she turned, and was relieved to see the perimeter of the stone door outlined with a thin sliver of indirect light. Placing her ear to the outline, she picked up sounds of movement from the other side of the wall. Hearing the sounds so close induced a feeling of nausea. To control her quaking body she sat down and embraced her knees.

Sarah was not sure what period of time had elapsed when she became aware that her shivering owed more to the bitter cold of her surroundings than the feeling of terror. Her extremities felt chilled and stiff. She rose and listened at the door – not a sound. Which doesn't mean he's left, she reasoned. But she did feel secure. He would have come through by now had he known how to gain access. She started to jump up and down and clap her hands to her body. 'What wouldn't I give to have Jim Sherry's duffle coat,' she thought as she danced. After five hops, she reached for the wall to steady herself, perplexed to find her legs inclined to buckle. Delayed shock, she suspected. The perimeter crack surrounding the door drew her attention once more. She listened for half a minute without detecting a noise. Her ear tingled with cold from the stone door. Turning her other ear to the crack, and folding her arms for insulation, she listened again. Not a whisper of movement, until she fancied she heard a distant ambulance siren, which suddenly pleased. The microphones in the church were still transmitting into the room next-door. The urge to listen and catch occasional sounds from the outside became irresistible. An impatient toot toot on a car horn nearby relieved the feeling of isolation and sometime later in the immediate area of the church, the cheerful yap! yap! yap! of a small dog lifted her spirits in the dark.

As she withdrew her ear, she felt acutely the loss of those mundane and previously considered irritating sounds. Never again would she complain about barking dogs or late night car horns – ever!

Surely there must be some way of opening the door from inside? And the means to do so should lie in the same location as the keystone on the other side. But there was no suggestion of movement in the masonry. She extended the search on both sides and finally gave up due to the pain and numbness in her hands.

The cold was now so intense it was physical. Her hands and ears hurt and her body seemed locked in a rheumatic crouch. No longer affected by outside distractions, she was compelled to face the implications of an extended stay in the cellar. Her response was immediate and spirited.

She started to rub and clap her hands furiously in an effort to turn the encroaching tide. When they responded encouragingly, she transferred her energy to rubbing her ears and stamping her feet on the floor. The trouble was, when she moved her attention from one part of her body to another, the unattended part began to freeze again.

There was only one solution. She'd try a pre–hockey match warm up, and take it easy in case she felt weak. Here goes, she encouraged herself. Out … in … out … in … left arm and leg moving in opposite direction to right arm and leg. It didn't seem too strenuous and she had gone beyond five hops. Out ... in ... out ... in ... The rhythm brought back a remembrance of the ancient theme embodied in the last piece they had recorded on the organ. Bach's Chorale – *Nun Komm der Heiden Heiland*.

"Nun ... Komm ... Nun ... Komm…" – she exhaled on each hop. Which expanded inevitably to encompass the opening first line: "Nun ... Komm ... der ... Hei ... den ... Hei … land."

She managed six further renditions before halting for rest. Not any warmer – but not any colder.

When David first told her she was to record the organ recital, she had gone over the background of the works to be recorded. And while she already knew the English translation to be '*O Come Thou Saviour of the Gentiles*', the information that the Latin original went back to Saint Ambrose, a fourth century bishop of Milan, she had found enormously interesting.

"*Veni … Redemptor … Gentium!*" She shouted into the dark, with a defiant satisfaction in the knowledge that she was now part of a continuous stream of vocal exultancy across sixteen hundred years.

The cold began to bite once more and she resumed the exercise. Trying to capitalise on the continuity of feeling, she made a number of attempts to marry the Latin to the melody, all unsuccessful. She stopped after the fourth try, as the timing was completely askew and left her genuinely bewildered, until she remembered that Ambrosians couldn't possibly have rendered the hymn in anything other than modal plain song. The original had to be somewhat different to what was sung today. She resumed in German because it had already worked well. This time she felt the exercise might succeed in keeping the cold from penetrating further. To conserve her energies, she stopped singing and instead just breathed the three first lines in chronological order:

Ve-ni-Re-dem-tor-Gen-tium.

Nun-Komm-der-Hei-den-Hei-land.

O-Come-Thou-Sav-iour-of-the-Gen-tiles.

On the sixth rendering of the trio she stopped. A trifle warmer, but how long could she keep jumping up and down. For as long as was necessary she supposed, and resumed before any debilitating thoughts on her prospects took hold. Her ear picked up distant sounds. She jammed her ear to the crack. Footsteps! Leather-clad footsteps clearly audible in the church.

"Sarah!" Her heart missed a beat when she heard Brenton shout her name.

The door at the top of the stairs opened faintly. "Are you down there, Sarah?" he called.

"Yes – Yes!" she shouted as loudly as she could, through the door crack.

An ominous silence.

"I'm here! Down here!" she pleaded, her mouth pressed against the aperture.

The door upstairs closed faintly. "He's coming down." Then she heard his footsteps re-enter the church. "O God no," she mumbled followed by a whispered "David?" Then she screamed, "David! I'm in the cellar!" But even as she yelled his name again, she knew it was useless. Yet she shouted again, and again and again, until with his steps

129

fading towards the porch, the possibility of a further twist in events momentarily silenced her. She stared fixedly at the glimmer of light along the door crack. Through clenched teeth she pleaded, "Please don't switch the lights off." Hands clasped, she implored, "Please, oh please, leave the lights on."

The dull clunk of the front door signalled Brenton's departure.

Sarah stood mesmerised before the thin line of light. Her face twitched in a brief smile of gratitude. She was so absurdly thankful for this remaining contact, her finger found and followed a small part of its outline in admiration. Imperceptibly, the cold of the wall reached into the marrow of her finger, and brought back the totality of what had happened. Instead of the vigorous physical response with which she had counteracted the cold and gloom until then, there was nothing. Her arm swung listlessly back to her side. The temperature took physical possession of her body and from within, began to shake her violently. She sank to her knees. Silently the tears coursed down her cheeks.

In the darkness, a last vestige of endurance scratched at the silence. "O Come" she whispered brokenly, "Thou Saviour of the Gentiles."

CHAPTER 14

Tuesday March 24th 1981
St George's Rectory
10.30 pm

Just as he felt he should give the bell on the rectory door a second ring, Brenton heard approaching footsteps in the entrance hall. The door opened tentatively, throwing a widening sliver of light across the doorstep.

"Ah, Mr Brenton," the Reverend Rupert Pryce gushed, pleasantly surprised. "How nice. You've had a change of heart and decided to drop by after all." He opened the door fully and said, "Please come in."

Faced with the rector's warm persuasiveness, Brenton's reluctance melted, and he stepped into the elegance of the pale blue Wedgwood hall.

"You're returning the keys, I take it," the rector enquired. "Would you care to join me in a sherry?"

Brenton gave the invitation cursory consideration and declined with the geniality an invitation to sip sherry demands. "Regarding the keys," he continued, "my answer unfortunately is again no." He discarded the mask of civility. "I've come from the church," he added, "where I found the lights switched off, except in the basement; the front door unlocked; nobody on the premises, and the equipment van departed."

Mr Pryce placed a single finger across his lips as if in a futile attempt to conserve his affability. "My word," he murmured.

"And now that I know the keys have not been returned," Brenton added briskly, "I'm returning to the church to try and make some sense of it."

"Right enough," Mr Pryce said recovering, "Your tidings seem to present a jumble of contradictions." He frisked his pockets and continued, "I should like to accompany you, if you don't mind. There may be something I could point out, or put my finger on. If you would be kind enough to wait a moment I'll collect a second set of keys." Brenton nodded and the rector, with obvious preoccupation, retreated back down the hall. When Brenton stepped outside from the rectory, he almost expected to see the van in place outside the church, and shadowy signs of movement from within its lighted windows. But there was nothing: no van, no sign of movement – only the lighted windows. And it was he who had switched the lights on."

This was either negligence of outlandish proportions or ... what?

He clenched his fists within the pockets of his overcoat in frustration. His anxiety alternated with anger as his mind jumped from one explanation to another. Unable to remain still, he re-entered the rectory hall, paced the length of the carpeted section, turned and retraced his steps to the doorway. He performed this exercise with increasing irritability until he heard the rector's footsteps emerge from the recesses of the house.

"Please excuse the delay," Mr Pryce sighed. "I thought I had better bring an electric torch in case of further exigencies."

The clergyman's finicky adjustments to overcoat and scarf precipitated Brenton's move outside. They walked in silence to the church.

The interior was exactly as he had left it. They closed the front door behind them and continued into the centre of the main aisle, where the microphone boom projected into the air. Brenton felt part of the atmosphere of the basement had seeped into the main building. "Seems unusually gloomy, Mr Pryce?"

"Perhaps it's because one does not normally see it at this time of night. Also, not all the lights are switched on," he said, eyeing the brass chandeliers.

"That might explain it." Brenton turned towards the main door. "When I first entered, I had great difficulty finding the light switches. Obviously I didn't find them all. Which reminds me," he said, turning to face the rector, "The only light that was switched on, was the light in the basement."

"Very careless," the rector admonished. "Particularly when they were aware of the condition of the wiring in the crypt."

"There are too many careless things to add up to anything other than something out of the norm." Brenton threw a questioning look at the stereo mic. "Let's take a look in the crypt," he suggested. "It may throw up a clue of sorts."

They moved across the church to the crypt door in the sidewall.

"I understood you to say you'd been down to the cellar," Mr Pryce queried.

"No," Brenton said, opening the door and ushering the rector through. "I came as far as the landing here and shouted down."

Mr Pryce averted his eyes from the dull light at the bottom of the stairs and enquired, "There may have been someone lying injured down there?"

Brenton pushed past the rector and down the stairs. The disarray of the recording room jumped into focus as soon as he walked through the open door. Mr Pryce joined him a few moments later. "Seems a trifle untidy," he observed.

Ignoring the comment, Brenton walked to the centre of the room and said, "Something very unusual's happened here. Not under any ordinary circumstances would either of the people involved have departed and left this mess." He lifted an item of debris from the floor. Mr Pryce, who had joined him in the centre of the room said, "I don't understand. What has happened?"

"I'd like to use your phone, if I may. I think we should contact the police. Whatever happened, I hope it was without injury." Brenton moved to the door and turned to survey the scene. "Look," he said sharply. "The equipment hasn't been switched off." He briskly disconnected the plug. With their life support gone, the speakers emitted an electronic gasp and expired. Then he froze as something else caught his attention. But it wasn't the stereophonic punctuation. "What a curious sound," he said softly. "Can't be the equipment. I've just switched it off."

The rector cocked an ear. "I must confess, I can't hear anything," he said, after a moment's listening.

"It's possibly of no importance. I'd better make those calls as quickly as – no wait, there it goes again ... listen."

They both held their breath and listened.

"Yes," the rector nodded, "I believe I do hear something."

"Do you recognise the sound Mr Pryce?"

"Can't say I've ever heard it before."

"We should determine its source."

They moved around the room in an endeavour to locate the intermittent sound. Brenton stopped at the basalt wall and said quickly, "It's coming from the other side of this wall. Someone's in there!"

The rector hurried to his side, and with frightened incredulity asked, "Behind the wall?"

"Yes. Behind the bloody wall!" Brenton fumed. "There's somebody in there. How do we gain entry?"

The rector mutely approached the keystone and pushed. He was only partly mollified by the surprise on Brenton's face as the large stone wall began to move. It made a grating sound as it slowly opened to reveal an inky black entrance. Their eyes adjusted to the gloom, and then they made out the shivering, semi-conscious form of Sarah Carlyle. Together they knelt down to her. Slowly and with great gentleness, Brenton raised her to a standing position. Feeling the sudden cold of his surroundings, he suggested, "Let's move outside."

They moved into the warmth of the recording room. Brenton removed his overcoat and jacket and drew them around Sarah's shoulders, while Mr Pryce closed off the aperture behind them. Seeing Brenton's efforts to warm Sarah, the rector removed his scarf and tied it around her head explaining, "A high proportion of body heat exits through the top of one's head."

Sarah clung to Brenton, eyes closed. Brenton gently patted her head, which was resting on his shoulder, and eventually she murmured something. It was immediately recognisable as the sound that had attracted their attention. "Good Lord," Mr Pryce exclaimed, "That's a Bach chorale she's endeavouring to sing!"

The mumbled attempt had been reduced to two words – *"Nun Komm – Nun Komm,"* and with an exhausted sigh, disappeared altogether.

"It's one of the items she recorded this evening," Brenton whispered.

"Dear me," Mr Pryce said, looking with wonder at the closed eyes. "I wonder what happened?"

"We won't know that until she's recovered a little."

As he caressed the back of her head, Brenton became conscious of the body outline pressed against him. It felt unnervingly supple, smooth, and somehow, deep, the antithesis of the sinewy veneer he knew his body must present to her.

He tried shifting his position to alleviate the embarrassing advantage, and provoked a muttered response from Sarah. Her eyes fluttered open and closed again accompanied by an exhausted, "Thank God it's over."

"I think we may take you up on your invitation to a sherry," Brenton gently primed the rector.

"Why, of course," he enthusiastically responded. "Would it help if I brought it over here while Miss Carlyle recovers?"

"It's better if we move her from these surroundings as quickly as possible."

Drawing away, Brenton took in Sarah's face and observed, "I don't think she should be allowed fall deeply asleep. I'm going to waken her and walk her to the rectory."

"Very well," Mr Pryce agreed. "I'll lock up as we proceed."

With the rector's assistance, Brenton positioned Sarah on one of the chairs. As he knelt beside her, he nodded in the direction of the basalt wall. "That's quite an Aladdin's cave you have there. Would Sarah have known about it?"

"Unfortunately, yes. I showed both Miss Carlyle and Mr Sherry its location yesterday, purely as a curiosity of course. How she managed to incarcerate herself I find difficult to understand. It's a rather tricky procedure to operate."

"Before we leave Mr Pryce, I suggest you make a thorough search inside: we're still down one body – Jim Sherry."

"Good Lord. Yes, of course," and the rector, torch in hand, reopened the wall door. Moments later he re-emerged brandishing the lost keys, but without further distressing news. Brenton gently brought Sarah to her senses and they slowly made their way through the church, across the square, and into the rectory.

———

Mr Pryce ushered them into his sitting room, where he straightaway concerned himself with rejuvenating and replenishing the embers of his coal fire. That settled, he turned to Sarah to renew his attentions. Brenton had eased her onto a sofa facing the fire.

"I do believe," the rector observed across Brenton's shoulder, "the palms of her hands have some very nasty abrasions."

Brenton took her hands in his. "Must have taken a tumble," he concluded. "Do you have any ointment?"

"Of course," the rector confirmed, already on his way.

He returned with an antiseptic cream and plasters, which, with Brenton's assistance, he administered with extreme care. Sarah winced once or twice during this operation, but otherwise remained silent.

———

In the muted lighting of the classically proportioned cream and amber room, Sarah's face lost its extreme pallor. But it had taken on a translucent sheen that startled the rector sufficiently for him to suggest brandy rather than sherry. "Its medicinal properties," he arcanely whispered.

After an initial spluttering cough, she slowly sipped the drink with such obviously beneficial results, that Brenton felt free to ask some innocuous questions, which, as the minutes went by, were answered by Sarah with growing confidence. Her bouts of shivering ceased.

During a pause in the one-sided questioning, Sarah unexpectedly asked, "Don't you wish to know what happened?"

Brenton considered this, and said, "Only if you think you're up to telling us."

"My dear," Mr Pryce drew Sarah's attention, "Would a woollen rug to wrap around your legs be of assistance?"

"The fire is beautifully warm," she said simply.

"How are you feeling?" Brenton asked.

"I'm feeling wonderful – now that I'm amongst friends." Hearing his inclusion in the collective, the rector's smile reached its apex.

"Things got a little unfriendly, did they?" Brenton gentled probed.

Sarah again reflected. It was difficult to draw the thread of events together. Her inclination had been to repress all thoughts and feelings on the subject. It was even more difficult to find a point of commencement, each incident demanding its own priority. But, as with all endeavours, it was important that she start at the very beginning. Suddenly the sluice-gate opened. From hesitant beginnings, the frequency of syllables increased to flood the room with graphic details, imponderables and questions, all demanding answers.

"And yes," she said, "I threw a lot of stuff around the room when I was searching for the keys. I upset almost everything except the box of tapes, come to think of it."

Brenton looked perplexed. "But there's no box of tapes in the recording room. Did Jim take them away?"

"No, definitely no," she said emphatically. "I asked him to take the successful recording and deliver it to Croydon tomorrow. I held the other takes and the new tapes in the box."

Brenton looked over to where Mr Pryce had seated himself on the chintz sofa.

"I'd like to take another look around the church. I may have overlooked something."

"Please don't leave me alone," Sarah implored.

"Don't worry Sarah," Brenton hastily reassured. "Mr Pryce will stay here with you. I'll only be a few minutes."

"Of course," Mr Pryce agreed. "You'll be nice and comfortable here beside the fire."

Brenton collected keys and torch and left for the church.

The rector busied himself refurbishing the condition of the fire in front of which he had encouraged Sarah to settle. Mr Pryce was not au fait with the underlying importance of the conversation Brenton had initiated with Sarah, but, in order to continue along similar lines, he brought up the subject of his uncovering of the hidden wine cellar, and apologised for having done so. For a protracted period, Sarah remained silent. The rector didn't know whether this was a continuation of her initial silence, or a reaction to what he had just said. He replaced the fire tongs and sat in the seat beside Sarah without adding anything further. Had he gone too far? Sarah's eyes took in the rector's countenance, which at that moment was contemplating the resuscitation he had effected on the fire.

"Where would I be now, if you hadn't shown me where to hide?"

The rector beamed at Sarah's answer to his apology. "We must pass that on to Mr Brenton when he returns."

———

When Brenton got back from the church, he sat down beside Sarah and Mr Pryce went off for some tea and biscuits. A short while later he reappeared with a laden tray and handed out the refreshment.

Brenton asked Sarah, "You did say there'd been a box of virgin tapes in the basement before you locked yourself into the cellar?"

Noticing the fatigued reaction, he apologised and suggested postponing the questioning until tomorrow.

"Sorry," Sarah, said. "I know how important it is to rehash everything."

"If you could – it would make a difference," Brenton said. "You see, there's no tape of any description left in the recording room."

This information imposed a thoughtful silence on proceedings, which Mr Pryce was moved to break. "Perhaps Mr Sherry...?" Brenton's dismissive expression drew him up short.

"Sarah," Brenton asked, redirecting his attention. "Can you throw any light on the disappearance of the tapes?"

Sarah thought on this for a moment and then replied, "You ask that as if it's my fault."

"If I did, I apologise." He pinched the bridge of his nose between thumb and index finger, and then recommenced. "If I said the tapes may have been the motive behind the intrusion, what would you say?"

"Relief. I believed ... I was the..." She gave a shiver of loathing, and looked away.

"Do you understand why I'm concentrating on the tapes?"

Sarah shook her head slowly. "No," she said, searching in her bandaged hands for an answer. "Well – yes, maybe I do," she corrected and, looking directly at Brenton, continued, "You're concerned about the tapes because it's the lesser of two evils."

Mr Pryce offered more tea, which was accepted, and he departed for the kitchen with the empty teapot. Brenton leaned towards Sarah and more confidentially explained, "You're right to some extent. I can't at this moment prove the intruder was interested in the tapes. But I am, as the police might put it, following a definite line of enquiry. I can't elaborate on that. Please believe me. I am not trying to save your feelings."

Sarah turned over the proposition and said, "I believe you. Convince me."

Brenton nodded his head in acceptance. "I want you to cast around in your mind," he said, "For anything out of the ordinary, or something that may have struck you as odd. I also want you to allow me to be the judge of their relevance to events."

"I'm afraid nothing extra-ordinary," she said.

The rector returned from the kitchen and, hands clasped, begged leave to withdraw from their company for twenty minutes or so. "I've an elderly couple in the vicinity whom I drop in on every evening." They both thanked him for the opportunity of a further twenty minutes of recuperative time, and assured him they would remain at the rectory until he returned. When the front door closed, Brenton rejoined Sarah. "May I take you through today's schedule?" he asked, trying to keep the sense of urgency from his voice.

"If it's not long," she answered with a suppressed yawn. "I'm falling asleep."

"Of course you are," he agreed. His tone was sympathetically hearty. "Best to get this out of the way."

"Besides," she limply pointed out, "isn't this a matter for the police?"

"If you spill it out now, I can fill in the details for them, and they won't have to bother you."

"In that case ..." she said resignedly.

Brenton paused to select the least taxing yet unobtrusively pertinent question. "Did you discuss your recording here with anyone today?"

Sarah's eyes crinkled in recollection and tiredness. "I spoke to everyone I met about St George's. I was very excited about it. Still am."

"From this morning on, name names."

She endeavoured to reassess her earlier social to-ing and fro-ing and after a few moments recollection proceeded. "In Croydon – Jim Sherry. Then you – in the control room, then –"She ran her fingers through her hair in frustration. "– then ... I find it so hard to concentrate. Yes, then Mrs Wheeler,"

"Mrs Wheeler?"

"When I arrived in the canteen for coffee, she asked me if I was running away with the box of tapes. I felt obliged to explain." Sarah smiled shyly. "Well ... maybe I was delighted to be able to explain," she said with a shrug of her shoulders.

Brenton joined in the low-key amusement. "Do you know," said Brenton, "I believe I felt exactly the same way on my first solo." And then cryptically added, "Both times."

"Both times?" Sarah echoed.

"Well," Brenton said slowly, obviously returning from reminiscence, "The more recent first solo was with the BBC Concert Orchestra in

Golders Green. The previous first solo was in an RAF Chipmunk – so long ago it seems like ..." He gazed beyond Sarah. "It seems like –" he shook his head and murmured, "– yesterday."

"You were in the RAF?" Sarah asked, brightening.

"As they say – that's a story for another day."

"And you flew?" Sarah continued, eyes a little wider.

"Yes," Brenton said, back in control. "And like your syntax – it's past tense. Let's return to the present and Mrs Wheeler. Were you alone or in a queue?"

"In fact," she said remembering, "I was alone. The orchestra had already arrived and were seated."

"And the conversation with Mrs Wheeler?"

"Entirely flippant."

"What happened next?"

"Accompanied by a box of tapes and a cup of coffee, I joined Joe Abraham and Anna Bretcu at their table."

"And that's where Jim Sherry and I came in?"

"Precisely," Sarah sighed with satisfaction, mistakenly thinking the end had been reached.

"You mentioned St George's?"

"Of course I mentioned St George's!" Nettled, she resumed the account. "They wanted to know why I was lugging a box of tapes around. And as I've already explained, maybe I wanted them to ask."

Brenton knew it was time to ease off, but 'need to know' won out on 'no to needs', so he braced himself for any adverse reaction she might unleash as he pressed further. Unexpectedly, she recounted the items of conversation without rancour.

The first subject – a description of the recording location in St George's, was followed by Jim Sherry's introduction to Anna Bretcu, followed by disparaging remarks about Charlie Primrose, followed by Joe Abraham's offer to translate the foreign language on the tape she had recorded. This was greeted by a sharp intake of breath from Brenton.

"Can I stop you there?" he almost whispered. "Are you saying that everyone at that table is now aware that you recorded radio interference in Polish?"

"David, what's going on?" Sarah's drowsiness faded and she regarded Brenton with growing curiosity. Brenton shook his head. "Don't press me on this. I'll explain everything when the time is right. You have my word. In the meantime I want to impress on you what I should have said this morning. This voice recording is of the utmost importance. Please do not open your mouth on the subject again without first checking with me."

He took her hand in his, and held on to it while the apprehensiveness remained on her face. "I didn't even know it was Polish," she complained, "Not definitely at any rate. How did *you* find out?"

"It's Polish all right."

"Is what I went through tonight somehow mixed up in it?"

"I'm not sure yet. Who brought up the subject of the tape, you or Abraham?"

Sarah hesitated, and then replied with conviction, "I did."

"Could you have been overheard from surrounding tables?"

"I've no idea, I suppose so if someone were listening intently."

Sarah looked exhausted. Brenton knew any further questioning would not just be counter-productive, but harmful. "Sarah," Brenton said tentatively. "I think we should postpone the St George recordings until after the Polish Week. There's just too much at stake."

"Absolutely not! There's no guarantee I'll manage to get an acoustic match – and anyway, I'm not chickening out of anything. Brenton compressed his lips and said nothing. He then agreed to her request. Her depleted physical and mental condition was not something he felt inclined to argue with. After a good night's sleep she would be in better shape and more inclined to see reason. But somehow, deep down, he knew his assessment to be off-course. Sarah had been through a harrowing experience, and her frank admission of both misgivings and aspirations deserved respect. So, whatever she wanted, or requested – that was ok with him. If she insisted on resuming tomorrow he would agree and accordingly make provision for discreet protection, which meant contacting Special Branch tonight for an armed officer. On second thoughts, a uniformed officer would fill the bill. Prevention was better than cure, and the ostentatious presence of a Metropolitan bobby should do the trick.

Mr Pryce let himself in the front door, and cautiously inserted his tremulously smiling features around the door of the sitting room. All had gone satisfactorily, he beamingly informed them, and he trusted everything was as satisfactory here.

Brenton explained what he proposed to do about taxis, and the rector punctiliously repeated the edict, lending it an air of verisimilitude.

"You," he indicated in Brenton's direction, "take a taxi to Miss Carlyle's flat. You then ring the rectory here," he pointed to the phone in the hall, "and Miss Carlyle, leaving her car safely parked outside, takes a taxi to the flat?" he enquired.

"That's it," Brenton confirmed. "I'd like to call a taxi now, if I may." Mr Pryce escorted him to the phone, where he initiated his guest into the eccentricities of the rectory phone: the dial occasionally stuck on seven going up and two going back.

Once Mr Pryce had returned to the sitting room, Brenton – despite the vagaries of the phone – made two calls. The first ensured a police presence the following afternoon; the second assured him a taxi in fifteen minutes.

Before departing Brenton remembered to tell Mr Pryce that there were tickets for the Saturday concert in the post for him.

CHAPTER 15

Tuesday March 24th 1981

Chiswick

11.30 pm

As soon as Brenton went to insert the key into the door of Sarah's flat, it eased open of its own accord. The light on the landing illuminated a jagged fracture on the inside of the wooden doorjamb. He pushed the door fully open. Even without the light on, the disarray was obvious. Brenton quickly groped around for the light switch and was lucky enough to connect immediately.

A quick glance through the crack into the lighted hallway revealed further disorder, but no lurking intruder. He cautiously entered the small square entrance hall off which three doors lay open; from these, strewn household items spilt over into the hallway. The door on the right led into a bathroom. He clicked on the light, but it was relatively undisturbed. The shower curtain fluttered lightly. He swished the curtain aside to reveal a partially opened window.

The door on the left led into a sitting-cum-dining room. He picked his way through the debris to another door on the far side. It led to an unoccupied, narrow and debris-strewn kitchen. Not unexpectedly, the bedroom presented an equally sad sight. The job on the hall door had all the hallmarks of an amateur – a junkie looking for a quick hit? The wanton destruction and truculence with which the objects had been thrown about confirmed this. He returned to the living room. Selecting the kitchen doorway as the widest observation point he tried to detect some underlying pattern to the chaos. Some idiosyncrasy – some small giveaway, something, anything – that might tell him what had happened. Back and forth, his eyes took in the room's scattered disorder, the bulk of which was attributable to Sarah's considerable collection of books. An ormolu clock gracing the mantelpiece caught his eye. He glanced around to see what else had survived the onslaught. A Chinese-type vase stood inviolate on its pedestal in a corner. The television, an obvious target, looked pristinely into the room. The list grew. A hi-fi set intact; yet the records strewn about. Three wall paintings askew, but no more than that.

It was the same in the hall. The contents of a coat rack thrown about, while a miniature Venus de Milo on the hall table stood untouched – in so far as any statue without arms can be considered unmolested.

So much for the junkie theory. In the kitchen he found further evidence to support this: a five-pound note and some loose change in a perspex jar on an accessible shelf. He dwelt on the aimlessness of the deed, and then wondered whether it had been haste that had dictated the destructive momentum.

And what were they looking for? But he already knew the answer. The Croydon recording, he murmured as he held the phone with his handkerchief and dialled Special Branch. He requested a dusting crew. It might just be possible to catch and match a stray fingerprint.

And Sarah?

She had been persistently present in his mind, waiting patiently for his full attention. He couldn't delay any further. They must be anxiously awaiting his phone call in the rectory. His reluctance to make the call stemmed from a fear that Sarah might not be able to cope with this further intrusion; underlying this, however, were feelings of guilt that barracked his self-assurance by insinuating the doubt that he should have been able to prevent what had taken place.

She must be told. There was no way around it. She had to be told, and quickly. He would try to divert her attention, but first he must extricate her from the rectory without letting them know there was anything amiss.

When a taxi pulled up smartly alongside the kerb, Brenton felt prepared. Sarah alighted and as the taxi moved away, he asked, "Everything ok?"

"Yes," she reassured him, "Now that I'm safely back."

"I've bad news on that front," said Brenton. The smile vanished from Sarah's face. "What do you mean," she blurted out.

Brenton felt if he could manage to get beyond this point quickly, the remainder would be easier. "When I arrived, I found your place had been broken into, and things thrown about." The haunted, hurt expression of St George's reoccupied Sarah's face. She whispered, "This is too much."

Her demeanour turned to anger. She made to move past him towards the entrance. Brenton's hand quickly caught her elbow.

"Yes," she asked irritably, "Is there something else?"

"There is, actually."

"What more could there possibly be?" she implored, breaking free of his hold.

"Could we take a stroll down the street?" Brenton gestured with his dismissed hand.

Sarah looked aghast. "My apartment has been broken into – and you ask me to go on a nocturnal jaunt? No thank you!" and she brushed by. "There are now a number of rather pressing matters to attend to – not the least of which is the police."

"Sarah!"

The change in his tone induced a momentary halt. She half turned and tilted her head interrogatively. Brenton moved towards her. "The police are already up there dusting for finger prints."

The unexpectedness of the disclosure produced an immediate and prolonged silence. Brenton, now beside her, continued "And they work more efficiently when they're not disturbed."

He took hold of her more amenable hands. "Sarah, you've been through a couple of really dreadful experiences today. I dearly want to fill you in on another dimension to what you've had to put up with. It may assist in explaining aspects of what happened, and perhaps help you to come to terms with events." He squeezed her hands. "Can we take that stroll?"

"I've been rude David," she said, relenting. "Let's take that stroll."

———

The night was fresh and dry. Invigorating if one happened to be moving; enervating for the solitary and sedentary. They were not much bothered by either motor or pedestrian traffic at that hour, so they felt free to talk. Their footsteps sounded like a multiple game in a hardball alley. Brenton took the unusual liberty of placing his arm across Sarah's shoulder. She found it comforting and warm and hoped it would stay there. For Brenton it rekindled the excitement that shot through him as he held her in his arms after her emergence from the hellhole in St George's. It nagged at him that this high was the result of a traumatic experience for Sarah. It was unsatisfactory that feelings of such intensity should be wholly reliant on Sarah's traumatic experiences.

He withdrew his arm.

"Put your arm back," Sarah said matter-of-factly.

"What's that?"

"I said, put your arm back."

Brenton replaced his arm, and was surprised how much he had missed the warmth of the bodily contact.

"I need the extra heat across my shoulder." She looked up and added, "Hope you don't mind?"

"I thought perhaps my arm had become too heavy."

"Absolutely not, she murmured. "Besides, that's what arms are for."

—————

He knew he was treading the tightrope of transition. Behind him lay the comfortable if sterile attitudes he had come to rely upon. He had no wish ever to experience emotional trauma again. Yet, to savour what was beckoning presupposed a willingness to acknowledge the theory of probabilities. So, he must also find within himself the means of opening up to the one emotion from which he had retreated with such wretchedness.

"Uncharted love," he supposed.

Sarah looked up. "That's an odd thing to say. But then anything with love in it can only be good."

Despite her good humour, Brenton felt a slight limpness in her body.

"I think we've gone far enough," he suggested.

"You said you had something to explain."

"I have," he agreed, "but it can wait until we get to that nearby café."

They stopped walking and faced one another. Sarah asked with concern, "Is it in a dreadful condition?"

"Nothing which can't be replaced, I'm sure," and then more truthfully, "There are a few things broken." He took a look at his watch. "Come on, let's grab a quick cup of coffee." He indicated the late night coffee shop. "We can get a taxi back to your place afterwards."

———

Brenton brought the two coffees to a formica-topped table beside a window. He grimaced at the first sip.

"Too hot?" Sarah asked.

He shook his head. "Dog rough!" he gasped. "I now know how taxi drivers manage to stay awake."

Taking his eyes off two melancholy inebriates inside the door, Brenton leaned across the table. "I'm not sure how to begin," he confided. "In any event, what you're about to hear is in strictest confidence. You've earned the right to know, and I have absolute trust in your discretion. It's possible I could have saved ourselves a lot of hassle had I taken you into confidence earlier. But of course that's easy to say in retrospect."

Sarah raised both hands from the table, stopping him. "I'm not sure I want to hear this. I'm tired ... I need sleep."

Her grumpy rejection quickly brought him to the point.

"Sarah," he said stiffly. "This concerns your personal safety."

Something in his tone made her sit up and listen.

"I'm not who you think I am," he recommended. "I am, in fact, an officer in the security service. MI5."

He allowed time for digestion and then continued. "When you recorded those one-way directions in Polish on Monday night, you inadvertently became involved in an attempt to subvert the security of Great Britain. The intrusions in St George's and the break-in at your flat were efforts to retrieve those tapes."

The glazed expression on her face stayed put.

"Are you all right?" he asked, noting the lack of response.

"I can't take anymore," she answered unemotionally. "I just can't absorb what you're telling me. You seem to be saying you're some sort of James Bond, and earlier you told me you had been in the RAF. It's all too much. The only thing I'm positively sure of is," she indicated unhappily at the table, "If you don't take me home I shall fall asleep right here on the table. Right here –" she emphasised, "– before your very eyes."

Brenton rose to his feet. "Drink some of that muck," he appealed, "It would have kept Rip Van Winkle awake. I'll be back in a minute with a taxi."

Sarah was not much concerned how long the search took. She spread her arms on the table, lay her head down, and closed her eyes. It only seemed like five seconds when Brenton returned to shake her gently awake.

"That was fast," she mumbled, staggering to her feet with assistance.

As they fumbled their way towards the door, the two tipplers thought they recognised kindred spirits, and joyously wished them happy dreams – the older one breaking into a tearful rendition of 'Good Night Irene'.

In the taxi, Brenton resumed a protective role and placed his arm around Sarah, this time without prompting. She snuggled closer, and inched about until she found the most comfortable position. She muttered, "I don't care what condition the room is in. I'm going straight to bed." The taxi driver cast an amused look in his mirror.

A growing feeling of warmth spread throughout his being. He sank back into the seat and hoped the driver had lost his way. All too soon they drew up outside Sarah's place.

Walking Sarah to the flat was going to be difficult. Brenton asked the taxi-driver to give him a hand as far as the lobby. Once there, he called down Sgt Broadbent. The taxi driver departed and the three of them made their way up to Sarah's flat. If she wasn't fully awake before walking through her front door, the chaos behind it did the trick. She dropped down on the sofa and, looking dumbstruck about her, said, "All my poor little things."

"You've finished your job, Broadbent?" Brenton asked the detective sergeant.

"Yes sir, we finished about ten minutes ago. Newman took away the possibles and I'd like to take a set from you and Miss Carlyle for reference."

"Let's get that out of the way and then we can assist in a quick clean up of the flat."

During the clean up they insisted Sarah remain on the sofa while they took instructions on replacing and generally re-imposing a basic order to the room. It became apparent that all of her collection of tapes had disappeared. Broadbent continued in the hall and Brenton started on the kitchen. Sarah asked permission to begin in the bedroom, and they finished in about the same order. It wasn't perfect, but then it never was for some time after a break in.

"There's the matter of the front door," Brenton drew Sarah's attention. "Until the lock is repaired, what would you say to a live-in guard on the premises? I'd like to start, with your permission, and perhaps Newman or Broadbent might take my place in the morning."

"Certainly sir," Sgt Broadbent responded. "What time in the morning?"

"Eight o'clock?"

"Eight o'clock it is then." Broadbent moved to the door. "Good night, Miss Carlyle. See you tomorrow morning," Brenton accompanied him to the front door.

"I suppose a chair against the door will do for tonight?" Broadbent suggested.

"Yes," Brenton agreed, "Something like that. Don't ring the bell when you arrive. Miss Carlyle hasn't a duty until the afternoon. I've tried to dissuade her. We'll have to wait and see how she feels when she wakes up. Good night, Broadbent. Oh, by the way, could I ask you to bring along a razor?"

———

"It's nice to feel protected." Sarah greeted Brenton when he returned to the living room. Patting the sofa she said, "I've nothing better to offer you than my trusty sofa. I'll get you some blankets."

"That's fine. I don't want you to go to any trouble."

"No trouble," she said as she re-emerged from the bedroom with an armful of blankets. "The only trouble," she said, dumping them on the sofa, "is my lack of energy to make the bed up."

She looked for understanding, and was rewarded when he said, "I shouldn't have allowed you do as much as you've done. Off to bed," he instructed. "And leave me to my own devices."

"Would you mind? I can't wait to lay my head down." She looked back from the doorway. "Interesting. You and me under the same roof." And she vanished into the bedroom.

———

He set about laying out and tucking in the bedclothes. The sofa would not accommodate his length, but that shouldn't present a problem. He hung his jacket and tie across a chair, placed his shoes underneath. Checked the table lamp and set his watch alarm. He pulled the bedclothes under his chin.

So much had happened during the day that it took some time before his mind steadied sufficiently to enable him to concentrate on any one aspect of the day's proceedings. He accepted this as part and parcel of the responsibility he was now shouldering. It should be tempered, he kept telling himself, with Hempson's assurance that Minister Uginski would not be attending. Nevertheless, what had been contemplated for Uginski had a chilling brashness about it. He did not like admitting to queasiness, but lying there in the dark, he knew what the heavy feeling was, like an indigestible ball in his stomach. It was accompanied by a film of perspiration that propelled him restlessly from one side to the other, which eventually infuriated when the bedclothes became detached and wound up in a knot on one side. He stepped out in exasperation and remade the bed. Before getting back in, he overcame his reluctance and stripped down to his underclothes. When he climbed in, he felt cooler and more relaxed. The mind should be a blank if one wished to drop off smoothly, he remembered being told as a child. That night he found the formula impossibly difficult. He was facing a looming grey void, armed with nothing. No idea where the threat was coming from – just a blank, grey nothing.

He turned once again, opened his eyes, and saw the open door into the hallway. He could see its outline clearly, and the blackness of the hall beyond. There had been a suggestion of light earlier, which must have come from under Sarah's door, and she had now switched off; funny to think of her asleep in there. Had she thought about him before she closed her eyes, as he was thinking about her? A warm companionable glow replaced the queasiness of the void. How long had he known her? It seemed like a lifetime. What he now found intriguing was the indifference they had shown one another when they first met. All good professional spit and polish, but yes, he thought indifference covered it accurately. He supposed it would not be worth commenting on, had there not been this change. Had the indifference been a subconscious reaction to the possibilities? Sarah had all the attributes he would have considered prerequisites in the matrimonial stakes: attractive, mentally and physically; interested in music; liked the countryside. A sharp mind – and an interest in literature, as he had found out tonight. The fact that he could think of her without turmoil, and reflect on love, meant that he had probably come through his metamorphosis after the divorce. Whether he was ready for more of the same remained an open question. The fact was, Sarah had grown on him gradually. From indifference, through awareness of her natural optimism, to admiration of her self-assuredness and attractiveness. She was a cheerful person to work with, radiating her own brand of sunshine. She had proved herself a friend in a number of ways, the most memorable being the instance when she had approached him with, as she termed it, a problem.

Pecton had asked her into his office on an occasion when she had needed access to Miss Maybury's files. He had put a thinly veiled proposition to her for a flow of information on recording procedures in general, and on David Brenton in particular. She became disturbed about the ethics of this procedure, and after some soul–searching, came to him with the problem. He had persuaded her it was a childish attempt at gossip on Pecton's part, and to play him along. The arrangement insured a feed of what he thought Pecton should know, and a return of inside stuff he might not otherwise have obtained.

It continued for a while in this fashion until she found it had become irksome. He couldn't fault her on the decision, and he acquiesced. She just wasn't the type. Would never have made an agent, never mind a double. Pecton on the other hand had found the innocuous tittle-tattle of riveting interest, because he threatened dire retribution when told of its cut off. He was not able to touch her of course, because of the contractual tie-up between Croydon and the recording company. It had given Brenton pleasure to make her aware of this, and the incident succeeded in cementing a firm bond of regard. He remembered thinking at the time – the girl is rock steady, and he had never had any reason to change his opinion.

And that was what he murmured as he closed his eyes. 'A good friend. A rock-steady good friend.' He switched on the grey screen. Sarah's image came into focus. Contentedly, he eased off into a deep and satisfying sleep.

CHAPTER 16

Wednesday March 25th 1981
Chiswick
7.00 am

The day began for Brenton when the alarm on his watch came on at 7.00 am. His eyes opened slowly to confirm the unusual location and rediscover his state of undress, which he hastily put to rights before he tiptoed to the bathroom.

In the kitchenette, he quietly rustled up toast, marmalade, and a mug of coffee, decaffeinated he noted. Munching contentedly, he was drawn to a small-framed photograph of Sarah in characteristically jolly mood. It had been taken in a rural setting. Her companion was a young man of, he had to admit, handsome appearance.

Despite all attempts to ignore them, his eye kept turning back to the happy couple. Eventually he had to acknowledge they disturbed him. There was a palpable intimacy between the pair. Pausing in front of the photograph, he looked closely at it again. They were happy. They were content. And their exclusiveness rankled.

The wall clock said five minutes to eight. He busied himself removing the chair holding the front door closed, and then returned to the living room to await his relief. His overnight had been an intrusion, looking and peering at intimacies that should not have concerned him. He was fidgety and anxious now to purge the experience. Broadbent's knock on the door provided the opportunity.

"Did you bring a razor?" Brenton whispered. The detective produced a packet of plastic razors and Brenton disappeared into the bathroom.

"That's better," he said, reappearing a few minutes later. "I'd forgotten how difficult it was with ordinary soap."

"I could have –" Broadbent started.

"Not necessary," Brenton assured. "I don't expect Miss Carlyle to surface before lunch. So the first thing you'll have to contend with will be the chap to fix the door."

"If I need to get in touch, should I ring Croydon?"

"Yes. If I'm not available, ask for Cranshaw."

"Very good, sir."

At the front door, Brenton requested, "Escort Miss Carlyle to St George's this afternoon – if she expresses the wish to attend. Introduce her to the constable on duty."

———

In the taxi on the way to Croydon, Brenton felt his emotional problem ebb as the location of the security issue loomed. Inside Symphony Hall, he headed to the stage area in pursuit of Jim Sherry and Thompson. He doubted Cranshaw would be in yet. He found Thompson first.

"Find anything of interest last night?" Brenton enquired.

"A blank on the walkie-talkies. The usual insight into social arrangements, and a fair amount of correspondence. The photographs have been despatched for developing and translation."

"Damn!" Brenton muttered. He had expected some indication of the previous day's illicit transmission. It didn't make sense that the perpetrators would carry the equipment around on their persons after the transmission. But today's rehearsals would present an opportunity, and this time they'd be prepared.

"I want you to collect Cranshaw's binoculars, and between the two of you, set up a viewing post in the tape-edit room alongside the orchestra. You won't be observed if the room remains in darkness. Ask Cranshaw to meet me at coffee break."

He tracked Jim Sherry down in the control room. Ignoring Sherry's greeting, he came straight to the point. "You have responsibility for unlocking and relocking all outside locations. What happened last night in St George's that you were unable to fulfil that requirement?"

"What do you mean? What are you talking about?"

"Precisely what I said. There was a foul up, and I need to know who was responsible for it."

Sherry shook his head, mystified. "I'll talk you through my part of the operation, then."

Through the consequent cross flow of information, Brenton satisfied himself that the breach in procedure had been in good faith; Jim Sherry's umbrage turned to shocked astonishment when he was told of the incident.

"That must not happen again," Brenton insisted.

"It won't," Sherry abjectly agreed. "She seemed, somehow … like the cat with the cream, and I didn't wish to bruise her new-found fervour an' all."

"When you left the church, did you notice anything out of the way?"

"Can't say as I did. No lurking shadows or anything of that sort." He scratched his head in thought. "The door … the front door, that is, was more difficult to close than usual."

"Difficult?"

"The door needs to be slammed to close properly. I had to slam it a couple of times."

"Did you ensure it had closed properly?"

"I'm fairly sure I did."

"Did you check that the door had closed or not?" Brenton persisted.

Sherry took on a chastened look. "I can't be certain about that."

"Then we have an explanation for this," Brenton withdrew a soiled piece of cardboard from his pocket. Sherry looked at the object. "I don't see the connection."

"This was placed between the door latch and the striker plate."

"Preventing the latch going home?"

"I found it on the ground in the entrance porch."

"And it was put in place sometime before I came out?"

"That's my guess," Brenton said.

The stage area began to fill, necessitating a brisk check of microphone lines. Brenton's phone rang. Miss Maybury informed him that Michael

Pecton intended visiting them to follow the second take of the Chopin. He arrived shortly before the conductor and soloist walked on stage.

"Yes, David," he began fussily and, disregarding Jim Sherry, surmised, "You have yesterday's Chopin take?"

Putting aside the underlying threat in the question, Brenton replied, "I do. As an insurance against –"

"Just as I'd hoped," Pecton cut in, "Yes, yes, just as I'd hoped."

His voice falling to a murmur, he then confided, "Relations have deteriorated even further this morning." He nodded his head in the direction of the stage. "They're not even on speaking terms now. The prospect is terrifying and very unfair. It's difficult enough to keep the train on the tracks without the addition of this unedifying display of vilification – yes – and I hope it doesn't communicate itself to the orchestra."

Brenton turned to Jim Sherry and asked him to take up his position off-stage in preparation. Pecton resumed the Komorski versus Wohlicka saga. The latest and not entirely unexpected development was the obligatory inclusion of Lina Zukowska wherever the soloist made an appearance. Pecton felt Zukowska's demeanour to be overpowering and unnecessarily intimidating. She would, if she persisted, cast a shadow over what was supposed to be a festive occasion. This was another aspect which would quickly communicate itself to the orchestra, and that was why he must hear this take and come to a decision on how best to proceed.

The phone rang again. Appleby informed Brenton that the protagonists were standing by. Was he ready to record? With the affirmative, conductor and soloist walked on stage, Komorski crudely ahead of Wohlicka's small figure. Lina Zukowska's off-stage presence was felt as far as the control room, and the conductor's lack of etiquette noted on stage, because as he raised his arms to begin Maria Wohlicka was greeted with a flutter of tapping applause – much to Komorski's chagrin. He impatiently rapped the music stand with his baton to bring it to a halt, but the orchestra pointedly chose to believe he had joined in the tribute. It was best to put a good face on things, so he masked his rancour and, without making visual contact with the subject of their flattery, united with them to give it the appearance of a unanimous accolade.

Not alone was the episode embarrassing for Komorski, but it also set off deep personal alarm bells. He was not devoid of awareness; the blandishments thrown in his compatriot's direction were an unsolicited testimony to her ability, and quite detached from the personality. He knew that at the end of the day, soloists performed to and for an audience, but between a morning rehearsal and an evening performance, they must run the cauterising gamut of appraisal by fellow musicians. The soloist who emerged from that experience unscathed had good reason to feel thankful. Only those who were gifted enough to receive the *summa cum laude* of their peers were due the admiration of all. Komorski reluctantly took note and raised his baton.

———

Every journey had a beginning, every beginning an end. And even if it took just one step to initiate – as the old Chinese proverb had it – there was another dimension to embarkation that separated the epic from the uninspired. It was knowing when to take that first step. The conductor was not without this quality, but his over-riding concern was merely to start proceedings, and this priority was inadvertently communicated to and absorbed by the orchestra. Subsequently, he made frantic efforts to convey his feeling for the music, but to little avail. He never surmounted that initial impression of careless impetuosity. This was one performance Komorski wished would never end, for the upsetting reason that he had not the stomach to face the aftermath. Sweat coursed down his face, entered his eyes, engulfed his hands and finally detached the baton from his grasp. Like a ticket collector without his punch, he fumbled his way to the last bar, excused himself to the leader, and walked off stage on the pretext of not feeling well.

Coupled with the indifferent interpretation, Komorski's exit registered an apoplectic five on the Pecton scale. He rose from his seat on a fountain of harried 'yeses' and hurtled from the control room, instructing Brenton to go to the soloist's suite.

Brenton reached for the phone and dialled Tape Edit. Without identifying himself, Thompson informed him, "Am in position and active; I haven't spotted anything of interest; but I know what I'm looking for." Brenton replaced the phone and made his way downstairs.

———

Maria Wohlicka ignored the three sofas and sat upright on a straight-backed chair, a hand on each knee. An unlit cigarette drooped forlornly from the corner of her mouth as she brooded on recent events. With sullen satisfaction, Lina Zukowska observed the distressed artist from the depths of a sofa. Brenton's entrance hardly impinged. The soloist eventually responded to his enquiries with, "A disaster ... a disaster."

Brenton consoled, "We still have yesterday's recording."

"Every time we play, it gets worse," she complained. "If Komorski played the piano, and I conducted, it could be no worse!"

"May I get you a coffee?"

She looked at him beseechingly. "In the name of God, get me a box of matches. My jailer here will not allow me to leave the room."

Brenton was indignant on her behalf. "Of course, of course. How are you for cigarettes?" he asked, opening the door.

"Just get me matches," she shrugged.

Brenton stuck his head around the door of the conductor's room. Pecton greeted him with a frenzied, "Dismiss the orchestra for a coffee break – yes, yes – and find Appleby!"

His original quest made him pause.

"At once!" Pecton urged.

Deciding the restless mass of the orchestra was more in need of immediate attention, he complied without protest. On the way, he nearly collided with a bustling Appleby travelling in the opposite direction. "What happened?" he panted.

Brenton put him in the picture. Appleby said that he would tell Pecton the orchestra had been dismissed and Brenton proceeded to the canteen on his errand for Maria Wohlicka. His early arrival startled Mrs Wheeler. "Something the matter?" she asked. He warned her of the imminent influx and she hastily organised her two assistants.

"Seeing as how you've time on your 'ands – wot can I get you?"

"Two coffees and a box of matches," Brenton answered simply.

"That's the sort of daft combination'll keep me wondering for the rest of the day." She rang up the price and thanked him again for his early warning. As he left the canteen the first musicians began to arrive.

———

In the soloist's suite, he placed the tray on a table and handed Maria Wohlicka one of the coffees. She took a brisk sip, placed the cup to one side, snatched up the matches, and determinedly engaged in ignition. Brenton picked up the remaining coffee before Zukowska could claim it and retired to another sofa. He hadn't long to wait before his ears were tingling with Zukowska's raucous reaction.

Madame Wohlicka offered her own coffee to the overbearing thug; it was crudely rejected. Jumping to her feet with a briskness that demonstrated her bulk to be efficiently muscular, Zukowska stormed from the room.

"So she needs a drink," the soloist shrugged her shoulders philosophically; "Perhaps she should use the fire hose in the hall."

Brenton smiled. "I hope it won't rebound on you."

"You mean be hard for me?" she queried.

"Yes."

"It couldn't be harder for me than now," she said. "Can we be overheard in here?" She glanced around the room.

"No, not at all."

Her eyes glittered. "I have to tell you quickly. I am not returning to Poland. I could be hurt because of what happens here. You may not understand that reason. I think perhaps you do, and I want you to arrange for me – do you mind?" She sketched a smile and then added, "I can't take any more. Zukowska is ..." She paused for the right word,

"Frightening! And whatever she says about me if I go home could mean the end of my performing career."

Brenton said, "I knew you were unhappy, and I'm sorry it has come to this. Of course I'll assist. May I suggest that nothing happens until after your performance on Saturday night? To anticipate would make a difficult situation impossible. Is Zukowska returning to the room here?"

"Yes, she has gone to get coffee."

"I shall arrange a safe exit for you sometime after your performance on Saturday. If possible I shall tell you what form it will take. If I find it difficult to speak to you alone, be prepared after you finish. You will be taken to a safe house until the others depart on Sunday."

"I feel ... afraid. It is a big step. In this country I shall be alone."

"Not entirely. Most of the Polish societies are based in London, and someone as gifted as you are will never be alone for very long."

The door opened and Zukowska re-entered brandishing a coffee. She renewed her tirade as she made her way to the sofa and was only cut short when the phone rang. Looking for a position to place cup and saucer, she spilt coffee on her hand before reaching for the phone, only to find Brenton already grasping the receiver. Her nails slowly broke the skin of his hand and remained embedded there until Brenton's heel cracked down on her instep. She released her grip with an audible gasp and hobbled to her sofa. Brenton placed his bruised hand in his jacket pocket and raised the phone to his ear with the other. It was Pecton commanding their presence in the conductor's room. He heard very little of what Pecton said, just the general drift, because his throbbing hand fleetingly brought to mind the predicament of the Bulgarian émigré who broadcast to Bulgaria from London, and who had had a lethal dose of poison administered by the Bulgarian secret service with the prod of an umbrella. He dismissed the idea in this instance as being too dangerous personally to the donor – although bearing in mind what an unmitigated bitch Zukowska was, an anti-rabies injection might not have gone astray.

"Pecton wishes to see us in the conductor's room," he told them.

When they arrived, Appleby had joined the group.

"Professor Komorski has not been feeling well," Pecton, told them, "so we must do what we can."

"What is this?" the soloist asked, "Are you abandoning?"

"No – no," Komorski blustered. "I felt unwell for some reason. I will be all right."

"He refuses to see a doctor," Pecton said in exasperation.

"Have you a deputy conductor until he recovers?" Maria Wohlicka asked pointedly.

Komorski turned on her in a fury. "How dare you suggest such a thing! How dare you!"

"You see?" the soloist flared up, "Already he is better. Now you see him with his strength back."

"Please – please," Pecton appealed. "Let us try and be calm about this." He clasped his hands and pointed out, "I cannot allow this concert to deteriorate to the complete shambles you seem intent on its becoming."

There was a knock on the door. "Come," Pecton invited, and Cranshaw stuck his head in. "The Kilar music did not arrive in the morning's post," he announced.

"Later," Pecton irritably dismissed.

"But you said –"

"I said later!" he shouted. Instantly repenting of this uncharacteristic lack of aplomb, he added more amenably, "There may not be any need for Kilar's music. I'll see you as soon as I can spare the time." He closed the door on Cranshaw and started to pace up and down the room, his chin resting on his clasped hands. Appleby too was cut short when he made an attempt to contribute.

Four pairs of eyes followed him back and forth for half a minute. He stopped in the middle of the room, seemingly satisfied with the destination his thoughts had taken. Appleby was told to fetch the orchestra leader. Turning to Komorski and Wohlicka, he demanded that the animosity between them cease. "If it does not and there's a continuation of this nerve-wracking unseemliness, then I shall cancel the event."

He let the consequences of this sink in, and then took up. "I have too great a regard for Polish music and the good reputation of my organisation to allow either to head into a public fiasco on Saturday."

Komorski was told he would have to undergo a medical examination; the conductor protested but eventually backed down.

The door opened and Appleby ushered in Arthur Liddel, the orchestra leader. Pecton cleared his throat. "As we all know, Professor Komorski had a weakness this morning. He now insists he is fully recovered and ready to resume, but I would like to have a medical opinion to ensure that all is well. I hope this will take as little time as possible." He turned to the orchestra leader. "I have just informed the others, yes, and this information is in strictest confidence. I am considering abandoning the Polish Week if the animosity between conductor and soloist continues. If there is no progress this morning, I shall ring the Polish embassy to inform them of my decision."

The silence in the room was absolute. Brenton understood the heaviness weighing on the occupants. To contemplate obliterating two years' of intricate negotiations and diplomacy took resolve of breathtaking proportions; it left a vacuum of confusion in its wake. Brenton thought he detected a minute tremor on Pecton's lower lip.

"Starting with Professor Komorski," Pecton motioned in the conductor's direction. "How do you suggest we retrieve the situation?"

Komorski threw a disconcerted glance at Zukowska and considered. Eventually he said, "I have not been feeling very well. This makes me very irritable. For that I apologise. My condition has affected some people more than others." He nodded in Wohlicka's direction. "I keep telling myself I will get better, but that does not seem to have happened. I am sorry for that."

Pecton turned to the soloist. "And you, Madame Wohlicka, how do you think you could retrieve the situation?"

She jumped to her feet with a pained expression, dropping her handbag on the floor. "I am without cigarettes," she groaned.

"Good God," Pecton muttered. He had already dispatched Appleby to get a doctor, so he turned to Brenton. "Would you oblige?"

Brenton rose and was immediately joined by Madame Wohlicka, who in turn was joined by Comrade Zukowska. Brenton escorted them out the door. Pecton passed a quivering hand across his face. "Hadn't expected she needed cigarettes that badly," he snapped. He honed in on the leader. "Arthur, I'd like to hear your comments in light of what you've experienced and heard."

"Well," Liddel started, and then paused to clear his throat. "In light of what I've heard, the problem – while not resolved – has at least been identified. I refer to the maestro's evident indisposition, which has had the effect of making his interpretation somewhat rigid." He bowed in Komorski's direction. "It must be very difficult to manage such a strenuous programme under the circumstances."

"Yes, yes, quite," Pecton approved. "I think, Professor, we should leave so that you can get some rest – and yes – reflect."

———

In the corridor Pecton came to a halt, which demanded a similar if expectant reciprocity from Liddel. He removed his steel-rimmed glasses to polish them. He looked younger, more vulnerable, or as Liddel thought, like a surgeon without his scalpel.

"Arthur, I found your assessment revealing." He replaced the cleansed spectacles and assumed again a clinical air of authority. "I wondered whether you wished to add anything further in private?"

"I can tell you, the orchestra is not particularly taken with the maestro's cavalier treatment of the soloist. If she were incompetent it might be understandable – if jolly well ungentlemanly. But Madame Wohlicka has a truly great talent."

"Yes, quite. And we now have to contend with the knock-on effect of a wasted morning's work." Pecton looked directly at Liddel. "I think you may as well tell the orchestra we shall not resume until after lunch. Hanging around on the off chance could prove counter-productive, and we're going to need all the good will we can muster to get us through to Saturday. Remember, not a word – except about Komorski's indisposition. And tell Madame Wohlicka and Brenton I'm waiting for them in my office."

———

Passing through the outer office, Pecton brusquely directed, "Miss Maybury, get me Cranshaw."

He threw himself into his armchair and grabbed the orchestra schedules from the rotational. He ran his finger down the week until it found Kilar, opposite Thursday morning. He emitted an audible moan. "Tomorrow morning! Cancellation seems attractive."

Cranshaw barely allowed the syllable "Come" to issue, before he was inside and facing Pecton.

"The Kilar is scheduled for tomorrow morning," groaned Pecton. "It will have to be shifted, and the obvious swap is with Friday afternoon's Elgar. The Elgar is shorter than the Kilar, which leaves a more flexible morning available for possible Chopin retakes tomorrow." Cranshaw looked up from his schedule and acknowledged the soundness of the suggestion.

"Good. That is what we'll do, then." said Pecton with finality.

Cranshaw rose to depart.

"Inform Appleby of the change," he was instructed. The buzzer sounded. "Madame Wohlicka, Mr Brenton and that woman," Miss Maybury announced, with something close to open rebellion. Cranshaw held the door for the trio.

"I trust you have adequately replenished your tobacco stocks," Pecton enquired.

"No," the soloist misunderstood. She shook her head, liberally distributing cigarette ash across her bosom. "I bought cigarettes," she explained, transferring by hand the ash on her blouse to the anonymity of the plush carpet.

From behind his desk, Pecton became more than normally aware of Zukowska's presence. It would be difficult to be circumspect under the circumstances, but then why should he be circumspect? All cock-ups had originated with the visiting party. He slammed the top drawer of his desk and spat out in Zukowska's direction, "Because of the bungling of the Polish contingent, I've had to change tomorrow's Kilar with Friday's Elgar." He turned to Brenton. "Please take note," he underlined in a robotic monotone.

"I think you're wasting your energy," Brenton replied.

"That's uncalled for."

"I refer to our friend's command of English." Brenton glanced in Zukowska's direction.

"Yes. Quite," Pecton conceded. "In that event let us concentrate on Madame Wohlicka. Now then, I have asked the others what they might do to make the Chopin better. I now ask you."

The soloist erupted in a volcanic cloud of coughing ash and smoke.

"What is this? What is this, eh? You want I should conduct with my feet? And maybe polish the piano when I finish!"

"Madame Wohlicka," Brenton appealed. "You misinterpret Dr Pecton's question. He wishes to know where you think the fault is."

Maria Wohlicka considered this for a moment. "To me ... the answer is so obvious. I feel ... well, I feel you are idiots or ... you have ..." She let the words hang.

"Ulterior motives?" Brenton suggested.

"No – no," she shot back dismissively. "I mean – wrong."

"Yes, quite," Pecton said. "Perhaps you could elaborate?"

"Perhaps you could ask your orchestra!" she countered.

"I already have. I want to hear it from you," he persisted.

"Listen to me," she started aggressively, while attempting to light a new cigarette with the old. Pecton rushed with an ashtray to prevent the fall-out reaching his carpet. "I come to you with a reputation. A reputation that has been achieved perhaps longer than you can remember. I have recorded this work for record. You must know that. You have to get permission from my record company to record this concert, no? All my recordings have been satisfactory. So I come to you as old hand ... Experienced old hand," she stressed, her tone deceptively calm. "And if I come to you as a professional," her voice suddenly rose, "I expect you to be professional in return!" She blew out a long column of smoke and shook her head aggrievedly. "And that includes protection of my reputation from bad recordings."

Unexpectedly, she moved over to Pecton's desk, leaning on it with her hands. Zukowska jumped to her feet as well, but Brenton placed himself between the two women.

"Who is the director of music here?" entreated Maria Wohlicka. "Who is it that cannot see and hear what is happening?"

Zukowska emitted a low growl, which Wohlicka ignored. "Answer me – answer me!"

"I think we should all sit down," Brenton suggested, "and discuss it coolly and calmly." He gave a warning squeeze on the arm of the distraught Pole.

When they had sat back down, Pecton said, "I take your point Madame Wohlicka, I take your point. But please try and see our side of the story. You see, when I accepted this undertaking, I assumed I was accepting a harmonious and congenial package." He searched his mouth for saliva. "Am I now correct in thinking you and Professor Komorski have never performed together in public before?"

"Never!"

The phone rang. Pecton took a message from Appleby. The doctor had arrived and was now in attendance on Komorski. Returning to those in the room, he declared, "I must at least try and find a solution. Madame Wohlicka, I am about to return to the conductor's room. What should I impress on Professor Komorski?"

"More than in any other composer, the piano dominates Chopin's concertos. Komorski does not support that role."

"Very well," Pecton acquiesced from the open door. "I ask you to remain here until I negotiate that point with the professor."

"It does not negotiate! It is a fact from its birth," she pointed out, "Either he bows to art, or you have shambles."

———

Whether through the wonders of modern medicine, salutary experience, or Pecton's earlier threat, Professor Komorski proved amenable to suggestion. The soloist was summoned to the conductor's room, where instant cordial work commenced around the upright piano, and a more Chopinesque approach to the work was hammered out.

Brenton excused himself and sought out Cranshaw. When they met, he disclosed the additional hazard facing them as a result of the soloist's proposed defection. If this became known, then the stability of one faction and the reputation of the other would be threatened.

CHAPTER 17

Wednesday March 25th 1981
Croydon
2.00 pm

To hear a well-honed machine motoring impeccably was an exhilarating experience. They had not travelled very far into the 1st Movement when Brenton turned to a transformed Pecton and exclaimed, "By God, we're motoring!"

This time the timing was perfection and the motor was firing sweetly on all cylinders. As soon as the final chord died to the obligatory five seconds of silence, there was an eruption of congratulations. Even Pecton's frugal smile as he rose from the desk enhanced the atmosphere, particularly when he issued his imprimatur in the shape of a protracted solitary "Yes."

"I suggest we continue immediately," he said, on his way to the door, "while common sense prevails."

———

They sailed through the remaining movements of the concerto with an invigorating opulence of sound. A beautiful rendering of the work produced a splendid recording, and in the end they found themselves with ten minutes in hand and once again on schedule.

"A perilous step towards the abyss, and an exhilarating dance along its brink," Pecton subsequently remarked.

———

After a diplomatic visit to the conductor's room, Brenton left for a pre-arranged meeting with Cranshaw and Thompson in the tape-edit room.

He was very anxious to find out whether Thompson had seen anything of importance from his vantage point overlooking the orchestra. Cranshaw's glum shake of the head told him everything.

It could only mean the opposing team had decided not to play that day.

Cranshaw had been in touch with Hempson during the morning. Hempson's latest communiqué was that the Polish societies in Britain had renewed their disaffection at the Home Office with a further representation to the Home Secretary on the subject of Sikorski's remains. Another item concerned the visit of the Free Poles, Cerniaski and Prolow, to Croydon last Monday evening. "Our info", said Cranshaw, "is that the visit was at the invitation of Professor Komorski, which suggests that the conductor is an unofficial Polish government intermediary. Neither side", Cranshaw continued, "wishes to be seen to engage in official talks so it's all very unofficial and cards-close-to-the-chest stuff. The Government in Exile chaps almost certainly turned down whatever Komorski had to offer."

Brenton said his visit to Jack Lesko the previous night corroborated this. Then, when one saw who effectively controlled the visiting entourage, the Free Poles' aversion became more understandable. "Which brings me to a further matter," Brenton added. "Maria Wohlicka's proposed defection."

"What have you got on that?" Cranshaw enquired.

"The best opportunity will be presented after the concert on Saturday night, before or during the reception," Brenton suggested. "Any move prior to that would interfere with our primary concern." He paused and then added, "Tim, you'll need to find out the Polish party's itinerary and intentions after the concert. Ideally, Maria Wohlicka should just disappear ... with our unobtrusive assistance. However, if a dust-up is on the cards, so be it. I think the lady is deserving of our overt assistance, if the covert variety proves difficult to implement."

"I suppose I shouldn't be surprised," said Thompson. "She's been made a rag-ball of, by all accounts. Makes you wonder why they brought her over."

"In order to make the greatest musical impression. She is known internationally and would therefore attract the respect of the British public. Her handicap would be ... that she knows her worth, and would not lightly accept second-rate from any quarter. On top of which," Brenton gave a wry smile, "my guess is that she's lapsed on her Communist Party dues."

"A lapsed atheist?" Thompson mused.

"Hempson also asked me to tell you the tape translation is correct," said Cranshaw.

"*Ad libitum*," Brenton murmured with slow deliberation, "Is there any music in the programme marked like this?"

"Not that I've noticed," Cranshaw replied. "'Course, there could be a bar marked *ad libitum* which didn't impinge ... Is it important? Do you wish me to rummage around for you?"

"I do," Brenton said. "It's a doubt I'd like eliminated."

"Certainly," Cranshaw agreed. "The Kilar has yet to arrive, come to think of it, and it's a complete unknown. I have to trot over to Heathrow this evening. There's a strong possibility it's on an Aeroflot flight."

"That's unfortunate," said Brenton. "I'd intended the two of you to continue the search of the Hall this evening. Any chance you'll finish early at Heathrow?"

"I'll be okay on my own," Thompson said.

"I don't doubt that," Brenton assured. "Nevertheless I think back-up is always prudent. How about it, Tim?"

"'Fraid the time is a little indefinite," Cranshaw said with regret. "What happened was, they failed to offload the music on a through flight. It wound up in Cuba and it's now on its way back courtesy of Aeroflot. So it's important I should be there, particularly after I turned down Pecton's last request."

"I agree. If you weren't there it would draw attention. So –" Brenton turned to Thompson, "– you're on your own."

"That's no problem." Thompson shrugged. "I have every right to be in any location in this Hall."

"Right then." Brenton addressed him directly. "Top of the remaining locations to be searched are Pecton's and Appleby's offices. Don't take chances. We have further opportunities on Thursday and Friday. Who has the camera?"

"I have," Cranshaw replied and then turned to Thompson. "Come down to the library and collect it." He reached for the binoculars. "I'll take these along for safe keeping."

At the door, Brenton asked, "Anyone try to gain entry while you were here?"

Cranshaw shook his head. Thompson said someone had tried the door while he'd been on his own.

"Any idea who?" Brenton pressed.

"None. But come to think of it, there was no noise whatsoever. Normally you'd hear some sort of clatter outside the door on the parquet floor, but this time, absolutely nothing."

Brenton paused to consider. "Remember," he said, "It should be as late as possible this evening. Make sure the principals have departed. I'll be in St George's until recording finishes tonight."

———

Under the portico of St George's, Brenton was pleased to see the solid presence of a police constable. He showed his Symphony Hall ID and was admitted to the church. Ronald Shipsey and Sarah were absorbed in a replay, while Jim Sherry sat in a corner completing a crossword. Brenton made signs that they should not interrupt their appraisal and listened in as Sarah and Shipsey exchanged notes, glances and comments in response to the unfolding music. This was the first time he had had a chance to observe an audio protégé in action and it filled him with a sense of achievement. The transfer was so obviously successful, it augured well for more ambitious projects in the future. When the change came, as Hempson had intimated to him over their drinks at the club, it was good to know he wouldn't leave a vacuum behind. He felt a sudden and inexplicable twinge of regret. This he attributed to the perversity of human nature, which given time, unsettled even the most accommodating achievement or satisfying accomplishment. Two days ago he had been prepared to leap into the whirlwind of total change; today, the determination was tempered by cautiousness. He needed to find a new equilibrium.

He felt rather than saw the intimacies that passed between Sarah and the organist, and knew that only for the emergence of the security threat, he would now be sitting where Sarah was sitting. But that was not what disturbed him, nor what he desired. More than anything else, he desired to sit where Shipsey was sitting and feel himself to be at the centre of her attention. Was that too much to expect?

He followed Shipsey's disagreeable over-familiarity with increasing irritation, until common sense provided a more pertinent answer: Shipsey was enchanted with his own music-making. But he continued to find the performance faintly unsettling – until a further reason presented itself. It was Sarah's first recording, and quite naturally, she felt excited. What was this bile, which was unaccountably rising within him and blinding him? It would be annoying at the best of times. Now, when clarity of thought was essential, it was a bloody disaster.

The replay finished and the congratulations flowed in both directions. Brenton suggested that it was a suitable moment to break for tea. He dismissed a delighted Jim Sherry and told him to leave the equipment until the following morning.

"Half past nine, or nine thirty ... whichever is more suitable," Sherry whimsically offered, and was gone.

Shipsey stipulated that he did not want anything terribly heavy in the way of a meal, so the remaining three elected to go to the appropriately named 'Tea Cosy', a small place around the corner on the main road. Suitably enough, they ordered tea and three omelettes. The organist, who was first to finish, then excused himself saying he was going for a re-invigorating walk and would see them back in St George's in fifteen minutes.

Sarah waited until Shipsey was out of earshot and then asked, "What was all that about last night?"

Brenton smiled at the abrupt gear change. Here was no fawning professional enquiry; no social fluttering of eyelashes. Here was a sincere personal question, which in its tenor, might to the casual listener suggest a certain intimacy. He should have felt charmed, but somehow it didn't register as such.

"Before I answer your question," he said, "How are you feeling?"

"I'm feeling fine," she reassured. "When I'm not thinking about the two episodes yesterday, that is. The recordings keep me fully occupied and I'm thankful for that."

"Good," he said, relieved. "Last night you took a hammering, physically and mentally, to such an extent that I was surprised to see you here today."

"The alternative was to spend the day moping around the flat. I couldn't have tolerated that. Besides, I slept 'till noon and feel the better for it."

"Mr Pryce and I were very concerned about you last night."

"I know – I know," she said brightening. "That was the nice part of it. I shall never forget Mr Pryce's sitting room, the warmth, the beauty of the room, and the kindness of you both."

"You were, I imagine, in a state of shock," he said gently. "Which meant you couldn't or didn't wish to take in everything I said." Sarah straightened up in her chair and, with a tincture of apprehensive curiosity, remembered a warning delivered the previous night.

"Ordinarily," continued Brenton, "you should not have been involved in what's going on. But the fact is, you are." He proceeded to outline as much as he felt she needed to know of events.

"Now I remember," Sarah said slowly. "Seems like a bad dream."

"Indeed."

"Are you suggesting my life may be in danger?"

"I'll come to that in a moment," Brenton said softly.

"Please come to it now!" Sarah urged.

Brenton shifted anxiously. To deflect her growing unease, he suggested they move outside. On the way back to St George's, he again took the liberty of placing his arm across her shoulder. "They're frantic to get their hands on the tape," he whispered.

"They?" she asked, "Who are *they*?"

"Indications suggest a hardline element in the Polish community in Britain."

"Presumably, that's why I have police protection?"

"Round the clock – until this is resolved."

"That's reassuring. Are you part of this protection?"

"When I'm with you, I'm part of your protection rota."

She shot an enquiring look in his direction. "You're protecting me now?"

He thought he caught a faint aroma of lipstick, which, if she were wearing any, seemed transparent or non-existent. "Yes, I'm your protection for this evening."

"Mmm," she murmured contentedly. "Espionage, or whatever we're engaged in, does have its compensations."

———

The remaining three items of Bach took until nine o'clock to finish: three sets of Toccata and Fugue, including the well-known D minor BWV565. This Shipsey left until last, imparting an air of triumphal finality to the event.

Brenton closed the installation down and informed the satisfied participants that concluding refreshments awaited them in the rectory. Mr Pryce greeted them at the door with congratulatory effusiveness and Sarah once more found herself in the warmth of the rector's sitting room. This time its elegant 18th century aesthetics struck fully home.

No sooner had conversation got under way than the phone rang. Mr Pryce left the room to answer. But the call was for Brenton – and no, they had not given their name.

After a couple of minutes, Brenton re-entered. "There's been a serious accident at Symphony Hall," he said quietly, looking at Sarah. "Would you mind driving me out to Croyden?"

They left the rectory amid much tut-tutting from Mr Pryce and commiserations from Shipsey.

———

Sarah drove a car well, Brenton discovered on the way. Why he should have expected otherwise, he could not have answered. "Thompson's been shot," he told her.

"What!" Sarah cried, nearly losing her concentration.

"In actual fact – he's dead."

"I knew something very serious had happened as soon as you returned to the room." Sarah's eyes flicked in disbelief between Brenton and the road.

"Look, I'm sorry to drag you even further into this mess, but as I've already explained, I'm your protector tonight, so you don't leave my side without a very good reason."

They approached the Hall where blue flashing police lights beat a cheerless welcome.

"Pull over behind that police car," Brenton directed.

Sarah pulled in and asked, "Aren't we going into the Hall?"

"Thompson was shot in that telephone kiosk." He indicated the brightly lit facility further down the road.

Brenton got out of his car and spoke to the driver of the police car in front. Then he returned to Sarah. "Don't move until I get back," he warned. As Brenton made his way to the inspector in charge, he noted that the area in the vicinity of the kiosk had already been cordoned off. The cordon was now in the process of being extended to include the whole road. Near the other end, Symphony Hall stood back from the roadway and in the darkness presented a brooding unlit mass.

Detective Inspector Blackmore was in charge, and expecting Brenton. They moved to the kiosk in which Thompson's slumped form lay. He opened the door to allow Brenton a closer inspection and without warning removed the woollen blanket covering Thompson's face. Brenton felt his stomach lurch and backed off from the kiosk. The inspector dropped back the blanket covers and said, "Not a pretty sight, eh?"

Brenton made no reply.

"We'd like to remove the body now, if that's all right with you, Wing

Commander?" Brenton nodded. He moved further away in a futile attempt to erase Thompson's face from his mind. A single bullet had obliterated his nose, and Brenton's sudden impression had been Thompson's eyes, frozen in a startled reaction above two gaping, sticky red mouths, from which the life force had ceased to flow.

As the ambulance containing the remains moved slowly down the road, Det Insp Blackmore explained, "Young motor cyclist made the discovery. Parked his bike there", he pointed, "and thought he'd come upon a drunk. Until he opened the kiosk door, that is," he added complacently.

Brenton turned towards the empty phone booth. "Was Thompson shot before he had a chance to make his phone call?"

Blackmore tucked his chin in like a prize-winning pouter pigeon and clasped his hands behind his raincoat. "Phone was off the hook when we arrived, Wing Commander."

"Did you manage to trace his number?" Brenton asked with urgency.

"Of course we traced the number, Wing Commander –"

"Look," Brenton cut in, "for Christ's sake cut the wing commander bit. Can't you understand? Thompson was a colleague and friend. I left him in good spirits just six hours ago, and to have him presented in that condition …"

"Sorry about that, sir," said Blackmore, rising gently on his toes. "Thought you lot were used to this sort of thing. All I know is that we'd hardly arrived here to start investigations, when all hell breaks loose. First Special Branch arrive in their swift anonymous chariots. Then, what I would call the trenchcoat brigade arrive. So you see, *sir* –" the emphasis was underlined by a twitch of his chin, "I've hardly had time to do anything constructive – what with this guided tour and that guided tour, and this heavy and that heavy, and now you, sir. I'll tell you one thing," he drew himself up to his full height, "This is murder, and it will be treated as such."

"Well," Brenton replied blandly, "We're on common ground, then. That's exactly what you will do – treat the matter as murder. I think you'll find your commissioner will take the same line."

"Doesn't make sense," Blackmore remonstrated. "A security guard in a concert hall is murdered, and every spook, save in your presence sir, every spook within a six-mile radius turns up in my lap."

Blackmore had succeeded in purging Brenton's queasiness. He indicated the road leading to Symphony Hall. "Let's take a turn down here, and I'll explain what is and is not expected of you."

"That would be very helpful. Always as well to know when one is standing on toes."

They began to stroll side by side. "I am also assuming, Inspector", Brenton took up, "that you're not so naive as to believe Thompson was just a security guard."

"Perhaps," Blackmore acknowledged, a tight smile hovering over his face.

"I also work in Symphony Hall," Brenton continued, "yet you address me as 'Wing Commander' and are fully aware that I represent security out here. Inside that establishment," he nodded towards the dark edifice, "I am nothing more and nothing less than their director of recordings – David Brenton. Let's keep it that way. If you can carry out your investigations under those playing rules, then we're going to get along fine. The same strictures apply to Thompson. I shall give you every assistance in your investigation and indeed wish you luck. It's a particularly nasty piece of work."

"Indeed," Blackmore admitted darkly. "Whoever the perpetrator is, he blasted off into Thompson's face at close range."

This confirmed Brenton's own summation. In the ensuing silence, Thompson's darkened features bore down on him. "Thompson was carrying a camera," he told Blackmore. "Apart from the contents of the film being a security risk, it might provide a clue to his murderer."

"It wasn't on him," Blackmore said.

"In that case, ring this number – Charlie Primrose. He can let you into the Hall and Thompson's locker."

"Good," Blackmore muttered, placing the card in his notebook.

"Did you say you managed to trace Thompson's phone call?"

"We did," Blackmore said, searching again inside his notebook. He extracted a loose leaf of paper and handed it to Brenton. On it was written the Security Computer Access Number – SCAN. Thompson must have managed to get through to the computer, Brenton guessed. Hence the sudden unbidden appearance of Special Branch and the security service.

"Number doesn't make sense," Blackmore observed.

"I wonder what Thompson was ringing about,"

"Mind if I hold onto that, sir?" Blackmore demanded, holding out his hand.

"Not at all," Brenton extended the piece of paper, but released his grip on it before Blackmore's fingers had closed over it and it flew into the air on a gust of wind. "Damn it!" Brenton cried, as it fluttered from sight.

Blackmore pursed his mouth in barely-concealed resignation. "Perhaps you might consider telling me what was behind the call when next we meet. Tomorrow perhaps?" he pressed, with professional tediousness.

Brenton nodded.

————

There was a tap on his shoulder. "Oh, it's you Chisholme," Brenton said to a slightly built man of indeterminate middle age, sporting a dark brown velour hat and a fawn knee-length crombie overcoat.

"I was duty officer this evening when the alert came from communications," Chisholme said. "The poor bugger'd only managed to transmit an ID, when he was shot. It's all on tape."

"I was wondering who was representing our trenchcoat interests. Are you assigned to me?"

"'Fraid not. Having made contact with you, I've to make a dash now for Hempson's hacienda to fill him in."

Brenton rubbed his chin in thought. "When you meet Hempson, say I'll catch up with him later. Part of my function this evening is protection for the other member of staff whose life has been endangered. From a security point of view I feel exposed in the party's flat. I'm unarmed. The surest means of an undisturbed night's rest would be under compound security, and the nearest I can think of is RAF Biggin Hill. Ask Hempson to flex a little muscle and get us two beds inside – bearing in mind the protected is female."

"With your background that shouldn't present a problem. I'll say nothing about the wasted opportunity."

"I do have a lot on my plate right now, Chisholme."

"Of course, of course. Poor old Thompson; didn't know him too well, and of course you did. Is there anything else you want to say to Hempson?"

"Tell him the police under Det Insp Blackmore will investigate the death on a non-political level. Blackmore will need a note of exemption and an explanation from his commissioner, who should be informed that Blackmore is to be allowed to sit in on certain of our relevant deliberations. I'm available from four o'clock tomorrow afternoon."

"That the lot?"

Brenton nodded and turned to go. "Don't take all night about it, Chisholme," he added, "I need some shut-eye rather urgently."

———

Sarah needed a lot of persuading not to return to her apartment for the fundamental requirements of an overnight. Eventually she gave in, with the promise from Brenton that she could return the following morning accompanied by Special Branch. She would require the necessities for at least three days. Brenton's persuasiveness centred on the security aspect, which Sarah realised needed very little elaboration after what had happened to Thompson. There was a sinister capriciousness to what was taking place, but it was made bearable by her faith in

Brenton's ability to deal with it. This in itself presented one further metamorphosis. She now found difficulty in focusing on him as the particular person she had known and grown to admire. It was as if she were meeting him for the first time, having already met him in some other shape or form; and this sojourn at Biggin Hill? David was indeed becoming larger than life, and she felt correspondingly in awe of their developing relationship.

"Next turn on the right," Brenton advised, "We're about half way."

"Biggin Hill is the Battle of Britain Airfield?"

"One of the World War II RAF airfields. The airfield is no longer run by the RAF. They use a block of buildings as a selection centre for aircrew."

"Interviews and the like?"

"Yes."

"And how can they put us up if it's an administrative centre?"

"It's called Officers and Aircrew Selection Centre, and the hopefuls stay there for a few days during preliminary interviews, assessments and medical examinations."

The car headlights caught the two guarding angels in its beam as they arrived at the entrance gates to Biggin Hill, a Spitfire on the left and a Hurricane on the right. They never failed to impress. Brenton directed Sarah through the gates towards reception. At reception Brenton asked for the station duty officer. A few moments later Squadron Leader Peter Evans entered. He grasped Brenton's hand and said, "Great to see you again, David."

Sarah was introduced and, at the squadron leader's invitation, they made their way behind the candidate's club, where about twenty-five new arrivals were relaxing, to the smaller and more intimate surroundings of the officers' mess. Evans introduced his guests to two fellow officers sitting at one end of the room. Brenton said he presumed Hempson had been in touch to warn of their impending visit. Evans confirmed receipt of a call just before they arrived. He had been told they were travelling 'light' and organised some basic toiletries to tide them over, which were gratefully accepted and then deposited in their rooms. The squadron leader excused himself as he had to finish off assessment papers. Breakfast formed a parting subject. Reveille was at 6.30 am and breakfast at 6.45 am sharp, he warned.

They returned to the mess.

"Why did you leave the RAF, David?" This was not the question to send Brenton to bed a happy man. But he realised belatedly how his decision must have aroused curiosity in the casual outsider.

"It's a long story," he began.

Sarah snuggled up and said, "I think I'm going to like this."

"Unfortunately, it's not a very edifying tale, but if nothing else, it will explain certain aspects of my life which, on the face of it, must present something of an enigma."

He took hold of his drink and steadied himself, like someone unexpectedly asked to sing a song.

"My father was in the RAF and was station commander at Hendon. During the war my mother and I stayed with an aunt and uncle in Somerset. After the war, we returned to London. I went to boarding school and was then lucky enough to gain a place at Cranwell – the RAF Training College. I was commissioned and appointed to pilot training, and assigned to a lightning squadron. Then at twenty-four I got married and everything seemed set for a normal career in the service. In actual fact things started to come apart."

Sarah shifted away from him to observe his face. He didn't meet her eye and kept looking rigidly ahead. Clearly, he was holding something back. But she'd just have to let it go – it wasn't the right moment.

"I had reached the rank of wing commander," Brenton took up, "so some well-disposed superior supplied information on a vacancy in our embassy in Moscow as assistant to the air attaché."

It was almost, Sarah thought, as if he were reading from a rehearsed speech.

"Then in 1969, I was sent to Moscow. The embassy circuit I found disconcerting at the best of times. If I had been eased into the lifestyle earlier in my career, I might have come to terms more easily with its seeming artificiality, but at thirty years of age I found it difficult to adjust. I also found the restrictions on travel in Moscow very frustrating. I'm not sure whether I was open to alternatives; in any event on my return to London I was recruited to the security service to undertake what I'm engaged in at Croydon. My interest in music was a key factor. My wife, on the other hand, had taken to diplomatic life like a duck to water. She revelled in it. When I resigned my commission and returned to London to train with the BBC, she was devastated.

Looking back on it now, I may not have been very understanding, but then I'm not sure I understood myself. Certainly I was less than frank about what I was engaged in. I felt I couldn't open up, and what started as a misunderstanding, very quickly moved to mistrust. Finally, at thirty-one, I found myself separated and later ... divorced."

Brenton dashed back the remainder of his drink to dilute the memory.

"I hope the security service will be as kind to you as you've been to it." said Sarah. "You do realise your dedication cost you your marriage."

"It might appear so superficially. There were other reasons, which drove her in one direction, and me in another. And when I think about it, I probably knew the choice I made would break the marriage."

"I take it you weren't as open on the subject with her as you are with me?"

"Never mentioned security."

"But why?"

"My wife was, and presumably still is, an inveterate chatter-box. You on the other hand are not. My wife was never involved, nor wished to be involved, in anything I did. You on the other hand are deeply involved in what I do. You've even had the misfortune to become involved in my security lash-up."

Had he gone too far? To pour out his private life and personal feelings with such abandon? The wonder was, he felt the better for having done so. It was tantamount to verbalising his inhibitions and hang-ups. In that respect, he had gone too far because he was losing a part of himself. Yet he was happy. He knew he was happy – and light-hearted about the future. He realised that he had never in recent times thought about the future. Always the past.

"And another thing," he said, "I feel I'm missing out on fulfilment, and it's time I filled the emptiness."

Sarah placed her arm inside his. "Can anyone apply?" she whispered.

Brenton embraced her. "New plans," he replied softly, "new beginnings."

They left the mess hand in hand. He escorted her to the door of her room and, holding both her hands, said, "I must add one thing before we say goodnight. You give me hope for the future."

With an imperceptible movement their arms enfolded, clasping one body to the other. Brenton found the answer to every questioning nerve end in his body on Sarah's lips.

CHAPTER 18

Thursday March 26th 1981
RAF Biggin Hill
6.30 am

Morning came sooner than expected, with a briskness only matched at boarding school. Sarah fell on the RAF toiletries in a preoccupied numbness, and with Brenton, joined the gung-ho training candidates at 6.45 am for breakfast. Brenton was introduced as wing commander, which considerably dampened the ebullience of the assembly.

After breakfast they drove to Croydon where Brenton arranged to have Special Branch escort Sarah to collect essentials for a three-day sojourn.

———

In Symphony Hall the main topic of conversation was Thompson's death. The crime had made the front page of most of the dailies and the telephone box figured prominently in photographs. One zealous paper, unable to get a photograph of the original, had even stuck in a photograph of an indeterminate relation. Appleby spoke to the orchestra before work commenced, informing them of what had happened. Det Insp Blackmore, they were told, was in charge of the case and would interview every member. They were asked to give their full cooperation.

Pecton had earlier primed Appleby, Brenton, Liddel and Cranshaw as to how far they could go in associating Thompson with Symphony Hall. Which was not very far, as he saw it, and he thanked providence the crime had not happened on the premises. He wondered what Thompson had been up to out there when he should have been inside minding his own business.

Until he arrived in Croyden, Cranshaw hadn't been aware of what had happened. Brenton explained there had been little point in disturbing his night's sleep since the matter was firmly in the hands of the police.

"Pecton has requested a meeting during coffee break," Brenton said. "Something about new developments – can you cast any light?"

Cranshaw's eyes narrowed reflectively. "'Fraid I can't. Pecton said nothing to me on new developments."

"Right, Tim. Keep your eyes and ears open. Remember, we won't have a replacement for Thompson."

Having rearranged the recording of the Elgar for Thursday morning, Pecton stuck with this change in order to allow Professor Komorski and Cranshaw time to go through the Kilar, which had arrived the previous night in Heathrow. Elgar's *Polonia* had already had an airing on Monday to sort out misplaced parts and notes. It had not been heard very frequently, but Pecton thought it particularly appropriate to have an English orchestral comment on the country in whose honour the concert was being given. After Monday's rehearsal he was not displeased and wondered why he had not heard the piece before. He turned to Appleby and chivvied him to get things moving. When Komorski strode on stage, he had already darted back to his office.

They had not gone very far when Sarah entered the control room. Brenton set about explaining the techniques and technology he was using. If Sarah worked alongside him on the sessions, he might feel confident about letting her take rehearsals, in the event of having to be in two places at once. The pleasurable side effect was that he would have her by his side for the duration. Half an hour later Komorski signalled his readiness to record; shortly after that, they had their first take under wraps. Komorski suggested a further take for good measure, and then a break for refreshments.

———

Pecton had coffee and biscuits laid on in his office. "I had almost agreed to this request," he said, as he tossed a typewritten letter across to Brenton. "But then I wondered if it might interfere with my Saturday concert."

The letter was from Polish radio and sought permission to transmit the concert live in Poland. As Brenton finished reading, Pecton continued, "Yes, yes. If we could oblige – without incurring any extra expenditure, mind – it would be jolly nice, and another feather in our cap."

"It's certainly possible," Brenton considered. "But whether at this juncture –"

"In that case it's on," Pecton cut in. "I like the idea. It's further publicity, and good publicity which may counteract this disgusting business down the road."

"Look, I find this particular turn in the discussion distasteful. Your lack of sympathy for Thompson leaves me cold."

Pecton smarted. "This is outrageous," he blustered. "Yes, yes, particularly when I'm the one who organised sympathy for the man's widow. I had Appleby out with the unfortunate lady last night! I haven't heard you were out there, although I know you found time to snoop around Symphony Hall after the tragedy."

"I was told what had happened while in St George's. Naturally I came over."

"Who told you?" Pecton asked quickly.

"The police," Brenton said carefully.

Pecton's eyebrows arched sceptically. "The police?"

"Yes, the police." Brenton replied, his voice dangerously low. "Somebody must have told them Symphony Hall was recording in St George's. It wasn't you, I take it?"

"I didn't inform anyone of your whereabouts."

Brenton paused and rubbed his nose. "All I know is – I was in the company of the Reverend Rupert Pryce, Ronald Shipsey and Sarah Carlyle in St George's rectory, when the police rang and said there had been a serious accident outside Symphony Hall to a member of the staff. What was I supposed to do – ask for tickets to the policeman's ball?"

"You – you could have asked who was damn well speaking."

"If someone's been damn well injured, I'm not interested in which policeman's damn well speaking!"

"When the police rang me, I didn't mention your name – and neither did they. There's something awry in your explanation, and I intend getting to the bottom of it." Pecton reached for the intercom and asked Miss Maybury to contact Insp Blackmore, who was operating from the boardroom. He paused to allow this development to sink in on Brenton and when he thought there was nothing further to be gained, abruptly changed direction. With controlled vindictiveness he breathed, "Make arrangements for transmission to Poland."

"No," Brenton laconically replied.

Pecton jerked back into his armchair. "Are you refusing to transmit?"

"No."

Perplexed and bewildered, Pecton cried, "You're trying to sabotage the transmission!"

Brenton sighed. "Allow me to explain," he replied. "The technical situation in the Albert Hall is first class. There are permanent transmission lines out from the Hall. There is no reason why Polish radio should not have our output –"

"So?" cut in Pecton, poking with petulant fussiness at the glasses on the bridge of his nose.

"So, from our end no problem; but what you don't realise is, the BBC are the agents in this country for transmissions to sister organisations. Lines go from the Albert Hall to –"

The intercom interrupted, and Miss Maybury announced Insp Blackmore.

"Damn," Pecton hissed before pressing the talkback. "Please send in Insp Blackmore."

Blackmore opened the door and was invited to sit down in the armchair opposite Pecton. "Do you know David Brenton?" Pecton enquired.

"We've met," Blackmore grunted, settling in between the leather arms.

"Before we move to the subject that involves you, Inspector, might I finalise a problem which we were discussing before you came in?"

"Certainly," said Blackmore, and proceeded unselfconsciously to take in the decor of Pecton's office.

Pecton's unsympathetic eye honed in on Brenton. "Yes – now then."

"We were leaving the Albert Hall with transmission lines which wind up in the BBC", Brenton took up, "and are then distributed either into their own system or sent abroad. This dimension involves a BBC presence at the venue. If they accept responsibility for transmissions, they require a personal input."

"This is ridiculously complicated."

"Only to those who are ignorant of the normal procedure. There is still time to organise lines into Poland, if you act straight away, and particularly if there is immediate pressure from Polish radio and government. But *you* must initiate the procedure," Brenton emphasised. "The other element, the presence of a BBC studio manager, will assist in the overall problems I face in the Hall. These people are experts in the music field and are aware of all the quirks and foibles of the place. The problem at this late stage is whether there's a manager available. I'll pull a few strings."

"How much will all this cost?"

"Nothing. The BBC attends on a quid pro quo, and Polish radio pays for the lines."

The nervousness faded from Pecton's eyes.

"Are you going to move on it?" Brenton asked.

"It's on," Pecton replied and pressed his intercom. Blackmore moved impatiently in his chair as Miss Maybury entered. "Do you know, Inspector," said Pecton, "I've quite forgotten what it was I called you for."

Miss Maybury advised Brenton that the orchestra had restarted rehearsals. He rose and turned to address Blackmore, who had also stood up. "Dr Pecton was wondering how, and why, the police rang me in St George's about Thompson's murder."

Surprise registered on Pecton's face, but failed to obliterate his curiosity. Blackmore, his face inscrutable, turned to Pecton. "May I ask sir, why you are interested in Brenton's being contacted by phone?"

Pecton blustered. "Yes, yes, you see nobody knew he was there, and I was wondering –"

"Seems a very trivial reason to ask for my intervention. Are you sure, sir, there isn't some other reason?"

"Oh no," Pecton hastened to assure, "no reason at all. Just curiosity."

"If it reassures you, Dr Pecton, we found a note in Thompson's coat pocket which told us David Brenton was in ...?"

"St George's," Brenton supplied.

"The same," Blackmore agreed, and brushed past and out.

Brenton followed. Catching up, he thanked Blackmore and headed for the control room. Blackmore watched his disappearing form. "No problem," he muttered, once again tucking in his chin. "You now owe me one, my son, and if that means the co-operation of the trenchcoat brigade – no problem."

Sarah lifted her eyes from the Szymanowski score when Brenton entered. "I took the liberty," she said, indicating the rehearsal of Szymanowski's 2nd Symphony coming from the loud speakers. "Stay where you are," Brenton smiled, and sat down beside her to pick up the point in the score. It was not a work either of them was familiar with. Brenton remembered he had had a Szymanowski piano piece when he was at school. Perversely, while Szymanowski's music had evaporated, he still remembered the accompanying notes describing the composer's birth into a wealthy family and his contrasting death in poverty. He was born in the Ukraine, and when the Bolsheviks broke into his family home in 1917, they threw his grand piano into a lake. As it became clear that the rule of the proletariat was to be even less edifying than what had gone before, the Szymanowski family moved to a newly independent Poland and the more hospitable environs of their fellow countrymen. Brenton wondered if there wasn't a jab contained in the choice of composer. The programme, he had been told, was a chronological presentation of Polish music, with an opening comment from the host country courtesy of Elgar.

The Elgar had been Pecton's choice, as they were incessantly informed. This suggested the remainder must have been the visitors' choice. The fact remained that Szymanowski had preferred Poland to the Soviet Union, and in some quarters this in itself constituted a snub.

"Arthur Liddel has quite a lot of solo work," Sarah said, as the leader's violin soared above the general tumultuousness of the 1st Movement. "The movement opened with a violin solo," she continued, "which came across rather well on the repositioned piano mic."

"Sounds good," he agreed, as the violin solo faded and submerged.

The Szymanowski 2nd Symphony had two movements. The 1st was about fourteen minutes in length, so the morning provided ample time to rehearse and record it. Even allowing for a retake of the opening solo, which Arthur Liddel requested, by lunch they had it all under wraps.

Brenton and Sarah went to the canteen where Jim Sherry and Cranshaw joined them. Cranshaw seemed a little agitated when he sat down. Mistaking his unease, Brenton explained the extent of Sarah's involvement and the consequent need for close protection. Cranshaw acknowledged this with a curt nod but remained tight-lipped. Eventually he reached inside his pocket, extracted a folded note and passed it across the table to Brenton.

He toyed with his shepherd's pie as Brenton's eyes took in the contents with growing alarm. "Good God," he groaned. The note read: 'Unable to dissuade Poles. Minister Uginski's visit going ahead.'

The 2nd Movement of Szymanowski's Symphony No 2 was about twenty-four minutes in duration. It was marked *Lento* and its wistful chromatics reinforced Brenton's feeling of helplessness. It would take the remainder of the afternoon to record, with the possibility of an over-run into Friday morning. For the first time he wished he did not have to record, but he had no choice; he'd have to see the remainder of the afternoon through, and only then begin to get to grips with this disastrous change of circumstance. There were so many questions bubbling away unanswered inside his head, and his sense of unease, he knew, was to the detriment of the music. Sarah noted his absorbed preoccupation. He asked her to keep an ear open in case he missed some point in the score. The balance seemed to work, but because it was an unfamiliar work there could be fine distinctions that were eluding him. This was no time to be short on concentration.

At four o'clock, Komorski decided to call a halt. He wanted to listen to all the takes again before convening on Friday morning. That meant Brenton was free to take the second eavesdrop tape to the edit room with Sarah for a fast-spool check.

Brenton registered a rush of adrenaline as soon as the quick splashes of sound indicating speech on tape emerged. He shot Sarah an apprehensive glance. "Here we go," he muttered. A moment later telephonic commands in Polish came across at normal tape speed. He grabbed a phone, booked a Polish translator and arranged a parking permit for Sarah's car at MI5 Headquarters in Gower Street.

At Gower Street, he accompanied Sarah to a table in the canteen and then disappeared to leave the tape off for translation. Observing her surroundings, Sarah thought the faces and chatter wouldn't have been out of place in any normal refreshment area in a London office. She wasn't sure what she had been expecting at MI5 HQ, but definitely not this anticlimactic sense of the mundane. What did secret service officials look like? Maybe all the trilby and suspender-belt types were off lurking around Paris or Berlin …

Brenton arrived back at the table unnoticed. "Come and meet Major Hempson. We'll take the lift to his office."

His invitation startled Sarah. But Hempson was all charm and sympathised with her about the distressing ordeal she'd been through. "There is also the problem of your safety," Hempson added, with a certain placating smoothness, "and our consequent obligation. This business can be devilishly harsh and frequently untidy."

Sarah suggested that as she was already a part of the arrangement, she knew how she could assist unobtrusively.

Hempson sought consolation in his tobacco jar and Brenton's views on the subject. As he methodically transferred leaf from jar to pipe he listened carefully. Brenton confirmed that they were under lock and key each night in Biggin Hill. The advantage in having Sarah stay on duty was its deception. If she left now, questions would be asked.

At this juncture, Hempson objected, deception was an unnecessary ploy. With the Uginski visit definitely on, an ostentatious display of awareness might be what was wanted. "However, we shall discuss that option later in the evening," he said pointedly in Brenton's direction.

Another advantage, Brenton considered, was the ability to move while recording, should the necessity arise. This could only be achieved if Sarah were in situ.

Sparks alighted about Hempson's person, as he gave vent to a ferocious lighting of his pipe. "Well now," he murmured, subsiding into a more relaxed position. "If you find you have reason to move, be damned to the recording – move!"

The Major and Brenton studied one another across the desk. Hempson suddenly perked up and, pointing the stem of his pipe at Brenton, said, "I think, old man, it will be all right." Turning to Sarah he said, "I must warn you, we cannot accept responsibility for any injury you may receive. I have suggested a course of action, which you have chosen to put aside. I can offer you Brenton here, as a bulwark against the rising tide."

He raised one eyebrow questioningly.

"I accept – unreservedly," Sarah said.

"Good." Hempson rang his secretary Sheena Barrett and arranged to have her take Sarah for a meal. After which they would return to Gower Street: Sheena Barrett to record the minutes of that night's meeting – Sarah to await Brenton's exit from the same meeting.

———

"Cranshaw should have arrived before now," Hempson muttered, and moved over to a sideboard against the opposite wall. He withdrew a bottle of whisky and two glasses. "Cheers," he said, raising his glass at Brenton. Evidently satisfied with the condition of the bowl of his pipe, he struck a match and, as the head sparked into flame, declared, "Miss Carlyle –" There was an irritating interval of rekindling, and then he took up. "I dare say Brenton," he managed to get across between puffs, "you shall have your hands full there."

"I don't understand," Brenton hedged, uncertain of the implication.

A purposeful, assessing pause ensued, within which Hempson indulged his senses with the lolling tobacco smoke. "That is not the answer I'm looking for," he eventually said. "In fact, that is not an answer at all, Brenton old man."

During a further pause, Brenton sought to retrieve the situation with a quick explanatory stab. "What I mean is –"

"I know now what you mean," Hempson cut in. "What I expected was an assurance that Miss Carlyle would not interfere in the smooth running of this operation." Hempson paused to observe an embarrassed Brenton, and then continued more amenably, "I am obliged to ask you – are you involved with Miss Carlyle?"

Brenton's mind raced through the practical application of Hempson's legal mind, and its incisiveness; then to the self-immolation in which he had deposited himself; and the retreating possibility of a recovery. Come clean, seemed as good a rallying cry as any.

"Sarah Carlyle has come to mean a lot to me," he stated.

"Good man, Brenton," Hempson mumbled as he stoked the contents of his pipe bowl. "Seems a nice gel."

The tension in the room cleared, and then the outside door was heard to open, followed by two sharp knocks on Hempson's door. "Ah, Cranshaw. Could you go and see if our refreshments are ready?" He laid his pipe aside and leaned across the desk towards Brenton.

"I want this little fairytale to last happily ever after – understand? I want that nice young prospective immobilised for your sake, her own sake, and mine. You can catch up on lost time after business. I don't want any of my people without their disciplined objectivity in place, and you, old sport, are in the process of losing yours."

What he had in mind was close protective surveillance. And before Brenton could protest at the intrusion, Hempson copper-fastened the proposal by pointing out that under no ordinary circumstances would similar facilities have been extended to someone outside the fraternity.

"I'm protecting my position," Hempson confessed. "I'm ordering you to do likewise. You're under the impression that I wish to have Sarah Carlyle withdrawn totally. In actual fact, I want Sarah Carlyle out of the action, but under your thumb. It makes sense. Nothing should be overlooked, particularly in view of what you shall hear tonight. I should also point out that I detect a divergence of approach between us. This I'll wear, up to a point. After all you're the man on the spot. However, it will be noted. I've given permission to have Miss Carlyle with you, under the aforesaid conditions. Of more importance, ultimately, is your approach to the business in hand. Correct me if I'm wrong: you'd prefer to approach by stealth, whilst I'd prefer an ostentatious display of protectiveness."

The gap was there, Brenton had to admit. But the other side was unaware of the headway MI5 had made thanks to the two-way recordings; they were also unaware of any shortcomings or discrepancies in MI5 strategy. That was why he was reluctant to reveal his hand. Instinctively, he preferred to keep them in the dark; it was always the best policy.

"If you knew who the other side are, I might have a modicum of sympathy," Hempson taunted. "We'll see. Maybe you'll change your mind presently."

Cranshaw staggered in with a large tray of sandwiches and tea. Before starting, Hempson thought it appropriate to say a few words about Thompson. "He is very much in our minds just now, and perhaps even on our minds," he acknowledged in Brenton's direction. "Because you recruited him from the RAF, undoubtedly it's affecting you more than the rest of us. I'd like to say this – the man's unswerving loyalty and his innate conscientiousness should be sufficient motivation to see us through this business successfully."

Hempson went on to explain why the obsequies would be delayed. "How much does his widow know about Thompson's involvement in the fraternity?"

"Nothing at all," Brenton admitted. "He played it close to his chest."

"In that case, you two look after the home front. I'll have the welfare section take up where you leave off – a few weeks after things settle down."

Hempson indicated the sandwiches and asked Cranshaw to pour tea. "You're already aware that I haven't been able to dissuade Minister Uginski from attending. Nobody on our side has actually communicated with Uginski or his ministry. That chap Lutowicz – a member of their trade section here – is handling everything in London. An odd choice for a cultural event, but as we know, he's also a member of their intelligence group, and there's no knowing where intelligence chaps pop up. Not wishing to give too much away, I'm afraid I underestimated his capacity to read between the lines, with the result that his response was a sceptical negative. My intermediary was Chief Superintendent Morgan Laymott from Special Branch. I supervised the interview through a one way mirror where I found it difficult not to enter and shake Lutowicz by his Saville Row lapels."

"What information did you give the Polish embassy through Lutowicz?" Brenton asked.

"They were informed that we are very alarmed by some of the feedback we're getting from Polish reaction in Britain. They were told some of this might be rash enough to amount to assassination. For their part, they're desperate to make this programme a bridge-building exercise, in pursuit of which they have already made contact with the Government in Exile. This presumably refers to Prolow and Cerniaski, who were interviewed today and told us they had flatly turned down the Komorski proposals."

Cranshaw, who had uncovered the Prolow-Cerniaski visit to Croydon, asked what part Pecton and Appleby had played in the negotiations. The answer was – no direct input. They were facilitating a Kormorski request and providing the facility and venue for what they saw as a worthwhile diplomatic move.

Hempson then expanded on information he had received from sources within the Polish societies and community. Nowhere was there any hint of what Hempson referred to as "hanky panky". The whole impetus of Polish reaction in Britain was towards a boycott, which indicated what had already been assumed: a small, determined group of hardliners.

"Or –" Brenton pondered, "Somebody or some organisation of whom we are as yet unaware."

Hempson sighed, reached for his pipe, and accompanied it to the window. "That's a second group of possibles of whom we're unaware."

Brenton felt the gap between them widen further. Hempson continued, "I'm beginning to understand how our Polish opposites would have misinterpreted." He turned back to face Brenton. "All of which reinforces my approach rather than yours – don't you think?"

"Shouldn't we tell them what we have on tape?" Cranshaw asked.

"No," Hempson said bluntly. Puffing strenuously, he returned to the desk. "That would break a very elementary principle, Cranshaw," he reprimanded. "Never give anything away. Not even with our friends across the pond do we automatically share information – unless it is to our benefit."

He pondered this a moment. "However," he continued, "I can see why you suggested that, Cranshaw – it does seem to be to our mutual advantage. But I think we shall hold on to it a while longer."

"I'm glad to hear you say that," Brenton said, "It keeps our options open." He cleared his throat with tea and asked, "Would you elaborate, Major, on the Polish reason for scepticism."

Hempson knocked the remnants of his smoke into a receptacle under his desk and poured a further cup of tea. "Their main thrust seemed to be the need to resolve differences between the Polish government and the Government in Exile. The communists have always found the Government in Exile an embarrassment, and in certain instances an impediment to better relations with the West. Their irritation has been demonstrated in the past with a fairly constant stream of vituperation against the exiles in the Polish press, which in itself is a form of flattery. The new man – Jaruzelski – wishes to demonstrate even-handedness. He is obliged to, if he has ambitions to continue to do business with Western banks, to whom he is deeply indebted. The Poles are desperate for hard currency and Western technological know-how. They feel, therefore, that they must come to terms with the exiles before progress can be made. While their ideological Mecca is to the east, they know their commercial salvation and economic renaissance lies to the west. A first step along the road of regeneration would be recognition of Sikorski as a national figure. If they can demonstrate acceptance of a non-communist fellow countryman, and institute a shrine in his honour with the active collaboration of the Church, there is no knowing where it might lead. The intriguing part is – do they have Moscow's permission? Trouble is," Hempson, concluded, "the Poles in exile have rebuffed every overture. All of which seems to have made the communists more determined to make the concert a musical, social and political success."

Cranshaw said, "I can accept that they may be anxious to make the thing a success, sir, but I doubt if that extends to foolhardiness. If it ends in the manner we anticipate, then it's a disaster for them, and it's curtains for us. We must tell them."

"Let's try and put a perspective on the carnival," Brenton proposed.

"I'm aware there is very little time. I'm also very conscious of the easy option, and its temptations."

"Not an easy option," Cranshaw objected. "It's the correct and expedient thing to do."

"Yes – quite so, Tim," Hempson judged. "Let's see how David expands on that."

Brenton put forward an image that had taken shape in his mind. "It's like … attending a circus. Watching a trapeze act. The artist turns out to be Uginski. He's been ordered to perform and hasn't been told the safety net has been removed."

Hempson's eyes glazed over. "How about we leave the delights of the Big Top," he suggested unhelpfully, "and get back to the reality facing us on the ground?"

'Damn it,' Brenton thought, 'this isn't about Hempson's susceptibilities – it's about political assassination.' He sat forward. "Look," he said brusquely, "I've already written down an assessment. It needs to be looked at and addressed."

Ignoring the gratified surprise on Hempson's face, he pulled out a crumpled piece of paper from his pocket and, holding it under the rays of the desk lamp, began to read:

1. Inconceivable that a national security agency when informed of impending trouble on an away match, would not respond protectively. Something amiss in Polish security?

2. Presuming the Poles in exile are involved, from what section would the threat materialise?

(a) Hardly from the elderly and diminishing group of original Poles who in the process of drawing nearer their eternal reward are more intent on expiating their sins.

(b) Hardly the new younger generation of British-born Poles whose ambitions lie in consolidating the considerable contribution their fathers made to the British way of life. This is not to diminish their feelings for their homeland.

3. What would perpetrators from (a) or (b) gain from assassination?

(a) The elimination of senior members of the abhorred Polish communist government.

(b) Publicity for exile cause.

(c) Adherents to the movement.

What would perpetrators from (a) or (b) lose as a result of assassination?

(a) Movement curtailed.

(b) Goodwill of British public.

(c) Loss of the recognition Her Majesty's government accords the Government in Exile.

4. The new Polish arrivals are an unknown quantity. They have not, with one exception, integrated with the resident Poles. This may be due to pre-entry pep talks, if their group had included a member of Polish intelligence. Assuming that that is the case – why would they score an own-goal against Uginski? Another possibility is a coterie of disgruntled and embittered anti-communists who would need outside assistance to become effective.

Hempson asked to see the paper. After a moment's perusal, he nodded his head.

"Lutowicz is a member of the Polish intelligence service. They, of course, play ball in a different code, and therefore more closely match the ground rules of MI6."

"And point one does not therefore arise?" Cranshaw suggested.

"You misread me," Hempson answered with a smile.

"Lutowicz's change of address takes him out of the business of protection, and very definitely places him in the business of 'hanky-panky'." Hempson arched conciliatory eyebrows in Brenton's direction. "Which places a different emphasis on David's first point," he directed in Cranshaw's direction. "Well now," he continued, "bearing in mind Lutowicz's real designation, if we join point one and point three, we may be on to something of interest."

Hempson requested Brenton to subject this connection to more searching criteria. He passed on to the next item with the warning that time was not on their side.

"Battle order," he commanded. Brenton and Cranshaw expectantly inched forward in their seats.

The major and Brenton were again the main speakers. Hempson advocated a saturation of the Royal Albert with a conspicuous uniformed presence. Brenton questioned whether this might antagonise both the Poles and the Home Office. Agreement was finally reached to saturate it with plain clothes from Special Branch. Hempson put in train the purchase of strategically placed blocks of two and three seats. He felt compromised to a degree and, before leaving the subject, expressed the fervent hope that the arrangement would work. "For both our sakes," he added ominously. Which brings us to the final item – the piano soloist, Madame Wohlicka."

Hempson picked up Brenton's note outlining details, and prefaced discussion with a word of caution. He would not countenance any official involvement, and instanced a number of recent assisted defections to the West that had come unstuck. This was a social rather than a political move, which should need very little assistance to put into effect. "All she has to do is walk away," Hempson said.

Brenton immediately disclosed the demeanour and dimensions of the soloist's escort.

"I understand your feelings for the lady's predicament," Hempson judiciously replied, "but it is my conviction that the more disaffected there are over there, the sooner the system will change."

"Can we do anything to assist?" Brenton asked pointedly. Cranshaw rowed in with, "She is quite intent sir, and if we don't control the situation, it's possible she may get in our way."

"You are very persuasive, gentlemen. I shall see what can be done to assist." He bent forward to ascertain the quantity of tea remaining in the teapot.

"Don't bring the subject up at the eight o'clock meeting," he warned, and dispatched Cranshaw for a further pot.

CHAPTER 19

Thursday March 26th 1981
MI5 Headquarters, Gower Street
7.00 pm

The committee-room door opened and Sheena Barrett entered. Hempson raised his head questioningly and, receiving the expected response, proceeded to open the meeting.

"Gentlemen, this is Mrs Barrett, the secretary to this meeting. Please be seated and let us commence."

Hempson sat at the head of the oblong walnut table, Sheena Barrett at a small escritoire to his right. Blackmore and Chief Supt Morgan Laymot from Special Branch settled in opposite Brenton and Cranshaw. They listened attentively as Hempson outlined events. Blackmore assessed the information in silence and intuitively knew he was the only person at the table receiving the information for the first time. The story as outlined seemed far-fetched and to a large degree unsubstantiated; they were relying on signs that appeared to him somehow contrived. He had to admit to relying on signs in his own area, but they had an aroma, he could smell them. He debated whether he should stop Hempson and ask him to clarify a point; in the event he let him continue. What he found difficult to determine was how much of this unfolding drama was the truth, as they saw it, or a diversion as he was meant to see it.

"... and that's as much as I can properly reveal at this time," Hempson concluded. "I would like to assure you however that if, in the course of solving Thompson's murder, a conflicting point of security arose, I would put aside the impediment to further your case."

"You being the arbiter?" Blackmore asked pointedly.

"Look here Blackmore –" Hempson reined in, "we have our hands full with this business. It's already become a trifle untidy and we're glad to have your assistance. We've lost a good chap in Thompson. I note your anxiety and admit there have been times when instruments such as *habeas corpus* have been, how shall I say? ... fudged. But that instrument is not in place in this instance, I assure you. Which means you have complete freedom to pursue your lawful duty. The involvement of the Metropolitan police lends an air of probity and strength to proceedings, and I don't mind admitting, lays something of a smoke screen across our bows. This should help both agencies because there will be two sets of information accruing."

"And you again will be the arbiter," Blackmore pursued.

"Of course I'll be the arbiter," Hempson testily confirmed. "Not much point in having a security service if we haven't security of tenure, old man. And don't go mixing us up with the prima donnas in intelligence. We are Britain's defence against foreign strikers. If under certain circumstances the rights of the individual are submerged in the collective – well, it keeps the fabric of our society intact and indirectly preserves the rights of the individual," he concluded. "So without further ado, let us proceed. What have you got for us, Inspector?"

Hempson sat back in his chair and carefully extracted his smoking utensils. Blackmore checked his arrangement of papers. "Right," he began, with the quick adjustment of chin that always preceded his pronouncements.

"I've completed interviewing all members of Symphony Hall who had reason to enter the Hall yesterday, Wednesday March 25th. A small number of outsiders entered the Hall and left again after varying periods of time, mostly of brief duration. All had quite legitimate reasons to visit and all checked with security control at the front gate, with – er – Mr Primrose, I believe." He checked his notes and then continued. "Most of the orchestra members left the confines of the Hall when the orchestra was dismissed. A small number remained for various reasons, the last of whom took their departure around six o'clock."

"May we have their names?" Brenton requested, pen at the ready.

"You may," Blackmore acknowledged pedantically. He sighed silently like someone asked to contribute to an unworthy charity. "Four in number," he elucidated and, after what seemed an inordinate period of time, revealed, "The leader of the band – Arthur Liddell. He stayed back to go through the music for the following day. That the norm?" he asked Brenton.

"Yes."

"Then there was Virgil Mascombe – plays the double bass?" Blackmore again checked with Brenton. "He had a meeting with Appleby and Pecton on some question of discipline."

"I can confirm that," Cranshaw said.

"Left the precinct about 4.30 pm. Liddel left about fifteen minutes later," Blackmore added. "Er – Reptarski," His finger found the next name on the list. "Plays the er –"

"Bassoon," Brenton supplied.

"Is that what it's called," Blackmore accepted nonchalantly. "Anyway he was mucking about with the instrument. Says he'll have to bring in an extra one for the remainder of the week because of an intermittent fault on the one he was using. He left at about six. Finally – Anna Bretcu. She was hanging about waiting to meet your man, Jim Sherry." Blackmore nodded in Brenton's direction.

Brenton's eyes narrowed. "Sherry was in St George's until 6 pm yesterday."

"That's right," Blackmore observed. "She said she had made a mistake – thought he was upstairs in the control room. Wanted to tell him the electric light he fixed the other day is now working perfectly." Blackmore looked at them interrogatively.

"Have you anything on the upper echelons?" asked Brenton.

"I was coming to that," replied Blackmore with asperity, "– if you'll allow me the opportunity."

Glances shot around the table; an unobtrusive shake of the head from Hempson forestalled any hasty replies. But Blackmore's attitude was becoming increasingly irritating. He recommended, "That left three upper echelons, as you put it. Pecton, Appleby and Komorski." A piece of fluff on the sleeve of his jacket attracted his attention. He studied it a moment before removing it with pained indignation. "And two lower echelons, as you might say: Thompson and Primrose."

The plodding delivery could not have been the inspector's normal method of expounding. Brenton had already seen the brisk side of Blackmore, and it did not equate with the calculated performance to which they were now being subjected. He controlled his indignation.

Eventually they were told Pecton and Komorski had left the Hall at 6.30 pm for Komorski's hotel. Appleby left at 8 pm – the same time Primrose was locking the front gates and leaving for home.

Laymott asked, "Does that mean Thompson was locked inside?"

"No," Cranshaw corrected. "There's a side gate for which he would have had a key."

"The Hall is closed to motor traffic", added Brenton, "after the front gates are closed."

"Who else has a key to the pedestrian entrance?" Hempson asked.

"All security have access to a key," Cranshaw said. "One resides in the check point. There's another in the orchestra manager's office."

"There are also a number of personal keys issued", Brenton elaborated, "for members of the organisation who have reason to stay longer than most or arrive earlier. I'm a key-holder, Tim is another, as are Liddel, Appleby and Pecton."

"Does any of that assist you, Blackmore?" Hempson asked.

The inspector raised his eyes from the notepaper on the table in front of him with the wariness of an endangered species.

"No," he said perfunctorily.

"Let's press on," Hempson murmured. "These are points which are relevant to the police investigation and will be capably handled by Inspector Blackmore. Are there any questions you'd like to ask before we move on?" he enquired of Blackmore.

"I think I have everything I want," he replied, and then added, "for the moment."

"I should also ask if there's anything in your investigations so far you might like to make us aware of."

Blackmore paused, and then said in an off-hand tone, "I do have something which may be of interest." He reached for his briefcase and carefully extracted a medium-sized brown manila envelope. "Last night I did as you suggested", he nodded at Brenton, "and requisitioned Mr Primrose. He escorted me inside the Hall, where I took the opportunity to examine Thompson's locker."

"Yes?" Brenton observed him with growing interest.

"Among its contents – which I now hold – was a camera." Blackmore pursed his lips significantly. "The camera contained a film which I had developed. The resulting three photos – the rest were unexposed – contained shots of items which –"

"Damn it – show them here," Brenton demanded, and snatched them from Blackmore's hand. He hurriedly tossed the three enlarged photos onto the table. "The two-way radios," he whispered, and then shouted, "The two-way bloody radios! How long have you been carrying these around?"

"I received them this afternoon," Blackmore solemnly divulged.

"And you sat on your obdurate backside knowing this could be the break we're looking for?" Brenton asked incredulously.

"Gentlemen – gentlemen," Hempson intervened. "We do have a lady present."

Brenton swallowed his anger, then turned and apologised to Sheena Barrett.

"Inspector," Hempson peremptorily claimed Blackmore's attention. "You are obviously labouring under the misapprehension that it may just be possible to trifle with a director in Her Majesty's security service. If that's the case, then I must point out to you that it would be a gross misreading of my powers – not to say influence. It would also be the start of a reckless journey for an ambitious officer such as your good self. A transcript of this meeting will arrive on the Home Secretary's desk tomorrow morning, and thence to the attention of the PM – indicating, thereby, the importance Her Majesty's government are attaching to these proceedings." Hempson smiled acidly across the table at Blackmore. "Got the drift?" he politely enquired.

Blackmore shifted self-consciously in his chair.

"Back to business," Hempson indicated in Brenton's direction.

"Thompson must have discovered the hiding place of the stolen two-ways. He took photos and, it's my guess, after stashing the camera in his locker went outside to phone in an alert."

"Why couldn't he have done that from inside?" Blackmore asked.

"For a number of security reasons," Hempson said. "Take it from me Inspector, in going outside Thompson was complying with standing orders. Now then Brenton, what have you gathered from those photographs?"

Brenton scrutinised them once more. "Not a lot," he considered, and slid one of the trios across the table in Hempson's direction. "As you can see, Major, there is very little of their surroundings in the photos. A possible location might be a drawer." He handed the picture he was looking at to Blackmore and Laymott. "That blurred straight line across the bottom of the photo may be the front of an opened drawer."

"What do you propose?" enquired Hempson.

"I propose we get back inside the Hall as quickly as possible and try to match the photo to a location."

"Very well," Hempson replied. "Cranshaw, you will undertake this task, and Chief Supt Laymott will supply an armed backup. Anything else?" he asked Brenton.

Brenton directed his answer to Cranshaw and Laymott. "Thompson stayed in the Hall on Wednesday evening with the express intention of sweeping Pecton's and Appleby's offices. I suggest you start with them and see whether you can match anything with what you've got there."

He turned to Blackmore. "Is there anything you'd like to add to their shopping list?"

"A small calibre hand gun," Blackmore promptly replied. "It should be removed with the usual precautions. Let me know straight away if you're successful, and I'll have a warrant issued tomorrow morning."

"Tomorrow morning," Hempson groaned.

Blackmore heaved a sigh of tried patience. "Ok, Major – you've scored your point." He turned to Laymott. "I'm particularly interested in a round of ammo that might be lying around. And take note of anything else you think might tickle my fancy."

The discussion switched to Morgan Laymott's report on the sweep of Sarah Carlyle's flat. He stated that they had drawn a blank on finger prints, but Det Sgt Broadbent had established the presence of a number of fresh, well-defined rubber-soled imprints on the parquet floor in the entrance hall. He also mentioned that the mortice lock on the door was open, and the intruder only had to lean heavily on the retaining lock to gain entry. The conclusions drawn were: the perpetrator knew Miss Carlyle was not present in the flat; he suspected he did not have a lot of time and dispensed with the niceties; the extent of the mayhem indicated growing desperation and perhaps disappointment.

Brenton thanked Laymott for the contribution and agreed with the conclusions. The footprints he found interesting, and noted they could not have been his because he wore leather-soled shoes. He asked permission to check with Miss Carlyle who was present in the building.

On his way to locate Sarah he reluctantly admitted he had a dual interest in determining the ownership of the male imprints. The cosy photograph in Sarah's kitchen jumped to mind rather more readily than he liked to admit. He was thankful his query would have the appearance of official interest.

———

"Sarah, I have a number of questions I wish to put to you on the break-in to your flat."

Noticing his tension, Sarah invited him to sit down beside her, as there was a professional detachment in his approach she needed to bridge. She began to fill him in. No, she only used the mortice lock when inside the flat, and even then there were times when it was not in place until bedtime. And yes, she agreed, that would have to change.

About the rubber-soled shoes, she didn't know what to say. Pressed with the necessity of determining whether the imprints belonged to their quarry, she revealed that her brother was the only male to use the flat – and that was infrequently.

With a lighter heart, Brenton asked when he had last been in the flat.

"About four weeks ago. He managed to get two tickets for the Royal Opera House, came up to town, and we both went. Afterwards he slept on the same sofa you slept on."

"If it's four weeks since he was with you, then the prints in your hall can only have been our adversary's."

In any event, Sarah doubted her brother wore crepe-soled shoes. The only occasion in recent times she had come across that particular type of footwear was ...?

"St George's!" she realised with a start.

Brenton closely questioned her on the sequence of events in St George's, which had started with the faint, rasping sound of crepe soles.

———

This fresh information was shared immediately with the others. All agreed they now possessed some more pieces in the mosaic of identity of their shadowy opponent. He had been careless enough, or so pushed for time, as to walk across one or other of the muddy rectangles of grass in front of Sarah's block of flats. He had accumulated enough clay in the process to indicate a size 8 or 9 shoe in which the sponge rubber sole was appreciably extended.

That would suggest either a tall man with neat extremities, or a squat man of substantial girth. Nobody in the block had noticed anything out of the normal. Endeavouring to put a body in the shoes, Brenton returned to Blackmore's mention of outsiders entering Symphony Hall, and requested names.

Blackmore was methodical enough to have had the list typed up. In the middle of an otherwise predictable collection of names, one stood out from the others. The Polish intelligence officer, Lutowicz, from the trade and culture section, who came to see Professor Komorski. "He does have a quite legitimate if improbable reason for attending," Hempson remarked. "Anyone catch sight of the fellow's footwear?"

There was no response. Blackmore asked for Lutowicz's dimensions. Coarse, stocky appearance, suggested Cranshaw, standing about 5 ft 8 or 9 inches in his shoes; couldn't be considered overweight, in that his bulk appeared to be serviceable muscle.

Brenton handed across the table a small photograph of the Pole.

"Could be our man," Laymott considered.

"And presumably holds diplomatic immunity?" Blackmore grumbled.

"Presumably," Hempson confirmed, without raising his head or interrupting his flow of writing. Blackmore emitted a "tsk" of annoyance, which brought Hempson's scribbling to a halt. Turning to Brenton, he said, "Lutowicz will have a watcher on his tail from tomorrow morning."

Brenton shifted restlessly in his chair, remembering an unresolved point that had been niggling since his brush with Pecton that morning.

"Inspector," he addressed Blackmore, whose eyes were still taking in Lutowicz's photograph. "Thank you for your perceptive grasp of my predicament in Pecton's office this morning. The fuss arose," he continued, "because Pecton somehow found out about my presence outside Symphony Hall after Thompson's murder. Which begs the question: how did he find out?"

An amused smile spread over Blackmore's face. "Let me assure you, Wing Commander, that your cover isn't blown – at least not to my knowledge."

Charlie Primrose, it transpired, had phoned Pecton to ask permission for overtime to be paid if he were to accompany the inspector to Symphony Hall. During the telephone conversation with Pecton, Blackmore heard Primrose mention Brenton's attendance in passing.

Brenton nodded slowly. One question remained. "You told Primrose you received his whereabouts from me?" Blackmore's features hardened. Brenton hastened to defuse the difficulty with an assurance that his intention was merely to tie up a loose end. The detective inspector appeared to accept this, although the uncertainty produced a momentary pause in the flow, which was interrupted by the delivery of the second Polish transcript. The translator laid the typewritten sheet in front of Brenton and excused himself. Brenton scanned the results of this second eavesdrop as Hempson directed Blackmore to answer Brenton's question. "Better not to leave it untidily up in the air," he murmured. Brenton reluctantly withdrew his eyes from the transcript and brought them to bear on the inspector. He was recompensed with a curt "Yes."

Three heads turned in Hempson's direction. The director impatiently demanded, "Yes what?"

Blackmore's gaze desultorily followed the others to come to rest on Hempson. "Yes – sir?" he provocatively enquired.

Hempson's perceptible intake of breath prepared the room for some form of retribution.

"Inspector, leave this building immediately and return to your desk."

Blackmore's stolid expression dissolved into aggrieved surprise. "I don't take orders from you!"

"That is not in dispute. What is required of you is that you vacate my cabbage patch and return to your own. There you will receive further orders from some senior Metropolitan bigwig. Whether you accept these new orders will again be entirely up to you."

Chief Supt Morgan Laymott was clearly discomfited. His position in Special Branch strategically placed him between the Metropolitan police and the security service. He was well qualified to referee, and as he moved to intervene, he only hoped he had not left it too late. "Perhaps it would be a good idea to have a break," he suggested.

"I think not," replied Hempson coldly.

Laymott then asked that he and Blackmore be excused for a few minutes. This Hempson agreed to.

When the door closed behind them, Hempson indicated that Sheena Barrett record their absence in the minutes.

"Won't this present a possible breach in security, sir?" Cranshaw enquired bleakly. "I mean ... if he's taken off the case, he'll be a floating mine of information."

Hempson aerated his pipe bowl with a match end. Eventually, he responded, "Who said he was off the case?"

Cranshaw's perplexity produced an uncharacteristic stutter. "B-but, I understood ..." he managed, while pointing to the door through which Laymott and Blackmore had recently passed.

Hempson's assessing countenance soaked up Cranshaw's naivety.

"What I require", he stated with slow deliberation, "is an awareness of each other's problems and areas of operation. Blackmore has reached the end of the road on that one. I blame myself really. I should never have allowed anyone of inspector rank in on these meetings. But then he came with quite a good reputation. Pity." He laid aside his pipe, which had acquired an irritating gurgle.

"Well now, what I propose here is that invaluable civil service device known as 'bounce'. We bounce the problem further up the line – up as far as the chief constable, if that's what it takes."

Hempson was about to make Blackmore a foot soldier by installing a chief superintendent at committee level. Apart from the advantage of removing Blackmore and concentrating his energies where they were most needed, there was also the business of paying Laymott the compliment of having an equivalent rank from the police. "Anything of interest from translations?" he enquired of Brenton.

Brenton shrugged. The transcript contained one banal question and an imperative. He passed the paper to his director, who was equally underwhelmed by 'Can you hear me' and 'Don't stare in my direction'.

"Perhaps you might rustle up Laymott," he asked Sheena Barrett.

———

Laymott brusquely sat Blackmore down at the table in the interview facility. "What in God's name are you at?" he demanded, and threw himself into a chair opposite. Blackmore set his jaw with dogged predictability. Incensed, Laymott insisted, "You're bloody destroying yourself!"

The detective inspector honed in on the emotion he picked up behind Laymott's anger. "I don't understand," he ploddingly feigned. "Is there something in these proceedings that frightens you?"

This affront took Laymott aback. He sat looking into Blackmore's face for some sign of indebtedness and found only arrogant contempt. Curtailing a gut reaction, he unemotionally asked, "So, what are your feelings about this case?"

Blackmore raised sceptical eyebrows. "Is this off the record?"

"Yes."

Clearing his throat Blackmore said, "I think they're pulling the wool."

"You must have a good reason for that."

"I have," Blackmore confirmed, and quoted, "'A just man who gives way before the wicked is like a polluted fountain or contaminated spring'. They don't frighten me," he added defiantly.

"So?" Laymott gave a dismissive wave of his hand. "You're a brave detective inspector given to rash conclusions."

Blackmore's chin twitched. "If you'll excuse me," he said, and stood up.

"Sit down!" Laymott roared across the table, which vibrated with the thump of the chief superintendent's fist. When the dust had settled, Laymott remarked, "You still haven't afforded me the courtesy of an explanation."

Blackmore understood 'explanation' to be admonitory. He would endure its inquisitional undertones in order to placate Laymott's rank. They were, after all, part of the same police force, holding similar warrant cards, and accountable to the public through their commissioner. The same could not be said of the MI5 wallahs. God knows to whom they accounted. Was this the kernel of his feelings? Accountability? Only partly. He knew as an individual he could expect every other decent individual to join with him in a surge of abhorrence at the secret and underhand methods used by these agencies. While an integral part of the police, the Branch was regarded with disdain by the orthodox side of the force. They were derisively referred to as the 'politicals'. So, he was now expected to offer an explanation to this political officer – who would tattle back to his masters-in-subterfuge. What was required was support from his Chief Super. He would demand it on the morrow.

"I'm still waiting," pressed Laymott.

Blackmore re-arranged his countenance into unassailable righteousness. "There is nothing to explain, sir, beyond a burning desire to get to the bottom of this abomination."

"Admirable," Laymott raised the joined palms of his hands towards his face and for a few seconds rested his lips on the tips of his fingers. "Nothing wrong with a bit of zeal," he evenly considered. "No, nothing wrong there."

He looked steadily into Blackmore's face. "What I *am* afraid of –" he took up tentatively, and then abruptly decided on a different approach. "See here, Blackmore," he recommenced more briskly. "Zealots are a turn off. To borrow one of Hempson's expressions – they wind up untidily. Which brings us to your present predicament."

Blackmore's feelings overflowed. "The only aspect of this panto that interests me, sir, is the apprehension of Thompson's murderer. This, I shall continue to be very single-minded about. I won't brook any interference from any source whatsoever. If that makes me a zealot – so be it. Come what may, I shall do my duty."

"Blackmore – I don't have much time, so listen carefully."

The chief superintendent sat back into his chair. He no longer cared whether Blackmore sank or swam, but he would give it one final shot. "What this comes down to is power," he cautioned. "We possess the power to arrest – the power to search under warrant – the power to charge with crime and felony. We are the guardians of public order. MI5 are a different kettle of fish. They exist by necessity, in a world of shadows and reflections. They are the guardians of the realm's security. Their powers are not as overt as ours. They have no powers of arrest for instance – they leave that to us. They shun publicity. They wilt in the limelight. They must never take a bow in public."

Laymott held a pause and then continued, "It takes unusual character and dedication to operate in that vacuum. Although a comforting compensation is its proximity to real power. They possess direct and frequent access to the prime minister. She listens to what they say, and with good reason. If they wish to put a stop to your 'due process', one arrangement would be to have the Attorney General state in parliament that your investigation poses a security risk. End of story. Yet you, with breathtaking rashness, proceed to annoy the citadel's inhabitants."

The audacity suddenly presented itself in a quirky light. Laymott laughed. "The irony is, the man you seem to be endeavouring to demolish – Hempson – is the one who insisted on you lot being allowed in. It's really Branch territory, but Hempson objected because our involvement might have blown their cover. It's our show – and we stepped aside. By rights, I should say nothing and allow you to make a horse's arse of it – which you seem intent on doing. But I'm too much the policeman to allow a fellow officer bring the force into disrepute."

There was a knock on the door, Sheena Barrett stuck her head around. "I was wondering where you'd got to. There's a cup of tea in there."

Laymott said they would be along shortly. "Remember Blackmore," he concluded, "Where the security of the realm is concerned, absolutely nothing stands in the way. And that includes conscientious detective inspectors who happen to be here by invitation. If there's one further irritating squeak from you – there'll be a smell of burning flesh as your arse cannons up Gower Street. Let's go and see if you still have a case."

———

"I'm putting you down, Brenton, for this meeting with the Home Secretary tomorrow afternoon –" Hempson was saying and entering on a note pad, when Laymott re-entered the conference room. Blackmore shadowed him closely.

"I think I can report progress," Laymott began, without taking his seat.

"In a moment," Hempson frowned and continued writing.

"I require your full support," he stipulated, looking directly at Brenton. "It's possible our combined weight of argument may make an impact. In any event, it will be our last chance to extract some arrangement for Saturday – other than what we've been landed with."

Hempson turned to Cranshaw. "You shall be fully engaged elsewhere." He then continued more generally, "What's next on the agenda? Ah yes, Laymott – you were saying?" he asked, without inviting the chief superintendent to sit down.

"I was saying", Laymott recommenced, unable to hide the weariness in his voice, "that Det Insp Blackmore may be more amenable to change."

"More amenable to change?" Hempson enquired sharply. "What precisely does that mean?"

"It means", Blackmore interjected, "I am now aware of the broader element surrounding this case."

"Glad to hear that," Hempson said. "And to facilitate your perceptiveness, I'm inviting your Chief Super to attend these meetings. This will enable you to give your end of things your undivided attention. All right?"

Blackmore produced a silent nod.

"You'd better sit down and join us," said Hempson.

The meeting resumed with a discussion on the security arrangements for Saturday night. Laymott's latticework of armed Branch men would not be altogether in radio contact on account of audience limitations. So a back-up method of visual contact was worked out. Brenton requested that the radio frequency used for communication be as far as possible from that of the antagonists' radio frequency. Before he closed the meeting, Hempson mentioned there was one unresolved question. Fixing a detached yet expectant gaze on a photograph of his Sovereign adorning the opposite wall, he directed Brenton to put his question once again.

Blackmore shifted uneasily on his chair and confirmed that he had in fact given Brenton's whereabouts to Charlie Primrose.

Hempson's eyes returned to focus on the gathering. Without even a glance in Blackmore's direction, he closed his book with a snap. "Meeting closed, gentlemen."

CHAPTER 20

Thursday March 26th 1981
Cromwell Road
9.00 pm

When the evening television news began, Maria Wohlicka reached for her packet of cigarettes. She had been unusually abstemious and had not smoked for the previous thirty-five minutes. This was more a tribute to the beguiling influence of the science-fiction film than any determination on her part. So, as soon as the outer-world intrigues had resolved themselves in a satisfying denouement, she quickly lit a cigarette and realised that she had only three smokes left in the packet. A quick look over her shoulder told her that Lina Zukowska was still asleep, sprawled like an indisposed walrus on the sofa. Zukowska's staying power was very low when confronted with television she could neither understand nor relate to.

Maria Wohlicka stood up and, taking a deep drag on her cigarette, began to pace up and down the room. There was still no sign of a return to consciousness from the sofa, so she sat down again to consider the impasse. Her eyes flew to the television; she turned up the volume to maximum and then immediately switched off. The desired response was instantaneous.

"It was getting a bit violent," Madame Wohlicka explained to a startled Comrade Zukowska, whose return to reality was effected with slow blinking movements. Once again in control, she rasped, "What else can you expect from capitalist rubbish!"

"That's true," the soloist diplomatically conceded.

"So why do you watch this dung?" Zukowska demanded, striding to the centre of the room. The sudden movement, coupled with the verbal pincer, called for a more rational response. "Entertainment?" suggested Maria Wohlicka.

Zukowska's eyes switched from meanness to anger. "It takes little to entertain the simple!" she bellowed. Maria Wohlicka cringed. The thought of people in adjoining rooms overhearing this further rumpus depressed her. In truth, she could not say what she felt; along with her contempt for Zukowska, she blamed herself, and this was difficult to cope with.

"That is very true," she said weakly.

Bored with the topic, Zukowska returned to the sofa from where she glared in the soloist's direction, awaiting some further irritation. The pianist prayed for tranquillity of sorts, and to take her through the intervening period, she lit up another cigarette.

She now had two left and tried to control the growing desperation. "I need cigarettes," she demanded in a rush. A sour gleam shot through Zukowska's eyes. "You stinking bitch," she slowly observed, allowing herself a deep grunt of satisfaction. Maria Wohlicka forbore to point out that Zukowska's personal hygiene was straight from the Dark Ages.

"What is it to be?" she insisted, trying to maintain her self-control. "Do we go down to the kiosk in the foyer, or do I ring for room service?"

Zukowska leaned back on the creaking sofa and considered this. She had developed a liking for the fawning subservience of the hotel staff, mistaking courtesy and efficiency for obsequiousness. It was certainly a contrast to the mutinous irritability with which customers were greeted back home.

More parsimonious council prevailed however, since she also had to answer for any unnecessary profligacy, which included the leakage of hard-earned, hard currency during her stay.

"We go to the kiosk," she announced, and then sneeringly taunted, "I have to exercise my charge."

"Oh, is that what you call it," the soloist incautiously enquired.

"Out!" Zukowska shouted, and to emphasise the urgency, whipped up her woollen jumper to rummage in a vast expanse of bosom for the room key.

They arrived in the foyer to find the kiosk closed. Maria Wohlicka's disappointment was keenly balanced by Zukowska's glee, but not to be outdone, the soloist asked at the reception desk about its re-opening later in the evening. She drew an apologetic negative, the receptionist explaining that the facility was an independent concession.

"There is a 24-hour newsagent up the street on the corner of the first turn right," the pretty girl directed. Zukowska baulked at the prospect of a walk in the open attired in jumper and skirt, but relented when assured that the shop was only a six or seven-minute walk.

Outside, Zukowska strode out like a Russian guardsman and must have known that she was setting an impossible pace for Maria Wohlicka. After a futile attempt to match the speed, the soloist gave up with a wave of her hands. 'Is there no end to the woman's accomplishments?' she thought, as she fought to catch her breath. 'Now she believes she is a racing elephant. If she keeps going like this, soon I'll be alone.' She strained to keep her compatriot in sight. 'But what do I care,' the soloist reasoned. 'She is supposed to look after me. Do I now have to run races as well as play the piano? Maybe she wishes to defect, in which case I will go home to Poland and tell them how fortunate we are.'

The soloist resumed walking in the same direction. She hadn't taken six steps when she, and everybody else within earshot, were assailed from the other side of the street with a bellowing barrage of Polish. The artist stopped and searched the street opposite for a sighting of Zukowska on the other footpath. 'My God – now she can fly,' she moaned.

Zukowska had crossed the street further up, and come back down on the other side to observe Maria Wohlicka. It was a manoeuvre entirely in keeping with the woman's disposition, and should have come to nought as soon as the pianist started to walk in the correct direction. Not to be denied, Zukowska initiated a salvo, which attracted attention on both sides of the street. The pianist's uncomfortable demeanour was attracting the curiosity of those in her vicinity, so she continued in the direction of the newsagent; Zukowska immediately lumbered across the street in pursuit. Her reckless disregard for the four-lane traffic brought her to the attention of a bobby who materialised just as Zukowska grabbed Maria Wohlicka's arm in a numbing grasp.

"What have we here, then?" the constable demanded.

The two Poles looked at him askance, one uncomprehending, the other with agony on her face. Zukowska made a move to pull the soloist towards the hotel. The constable barred their way and radioed for backup.

"One moment, madam," he addressed Zukowska. "Please release this lady and explain what's happening here."

"What is he saying?" Zukowska seethed, without releasing her grip.

"My arm – my arm! He says release my arm!"

The constable directed Maria Wohlicka to inform Zukowska that if she did not comply with his request, he would charge her with obstruction and assault.

A police car glided silently to the kerbside and disgorged two further constables. Zukowska now realised the episode had taken on an extra dimension and released the soloist's arm. The bobby greeted his colleagues and explained what appeared to be happening.

Zukowska ordered Wohlicka to walk back to the hotel. She refused, but realised that sooner or later she would have to face Zukowska in their room. Well, she would face whatever had to be faced with the aid of some new cigarettes.

"I must insist, madam," the constable addressed Maria Wohlicka as the only one to have spoken English. "What's going on here? Otherwise I shall have you both taken down to the station, and that would be an unpleasant experience for a lady."

Maria Wohlicka squared up to the young constable and explained that they were both Poles. She was the soloist on the Saturday-evening concert at the Royal Albert Hall and badly in need of fresh cigarettes. "And this is my keeper," she finished up, turning in Zukowska's direction. "Not that anyone in this part of the world understands what that means."

"Madam, I would consider it a privilege to escort you for your cigarettes," the bobby gallantly proposed.

"What are they saying?" a sullen Zukowska enquired.

"They are saying they wish to arrest you," Madame Wohlicka supplied. "Laying your hand on another person without their consent is a major crime in this country."

"Tell them I have your consent."

"Make your mother proud. If I tell them that, they have both of us on another major crime, creating a nuisance. I will explain it as best I can." She turned towards the constable. "This hag is a political policewoman," Wohlicka matter-of-factly began. "Her job is to make sure I do not do anything political while performing in your country. Even though I would love to stick a pin in her –" She pointed to her own posterior, at which the policemen broke into amused grins, which broadened when Zukowska thought she had better join the jocularity, "– if anything bad happens to her, it is bad also for me. Do you understand?"

They thought they did, but to underline their concern the bobby stood in front of Zukowska and, wagging a finger, asked Maria Wohlicka to translate: "One further incident –" he said sternly. Which Miss Wohlicka blithely translated as, "You are a disgrace to your country!"

"– and I shall be forced to take the matter further!" Which became, "– and this lady prevented your deportation!"

Zukowska blustered in protest.

"That's right," Wohlicka shook her head, "Keep going the way you are and maybe we both get tickets home." Silence prevailed.

"Shake the militiamen's hands and say you are sorry," she directed Zukowska, "and let us purchase the cigarettes as directed."

Two of the policemen got back into their patrol car and the helmeted constable delivered a parting salute in Maria Wohlicka's direction.

———

The Poles moved up the street at a more sedate pace. They arrived at the turn right as a further splatter of rain descended. The blazing neon lights of the newsagent stood out. Zukowska told her to go to the shop for her cigarettes; she would be sheltering with other pedestrians under the first floor of an office block standing on concrete stilts.

The transaction did not take long and within moments Maria Wohlicka was back on the street, the cigarettes safely in her handbag, staring at the English currency given in change. She ran the last few feet of the narrow side street to gain the shelter of the office block and, still preoccupied, stood behind one of the concrete pillars endeavouring to make sense of the coins in her hand.

She had been out of sight for some moments before Zukowska realised that something was amiss. Elbowing aside a young couple standing directly in front of her, she barrelled off to the newsagent's. With a growl of disappointment, she backed out of the shop, bringing a rack of postcards to the ground. Outside she looked up and down the side street in disbelief, seeking confirmation that this was just a momentary aberration.

In the meantime, Maria Wohlicka had moved through the disbanding crowd to where she had last seen Zukowska, in the process moving out of sight. The next junction down the side street seemed like a possible route to Zukowska, and she took off to check it out.

The crowd under the shelter was thinning and still Maria Wohlicka could not manage to locate her tormentor. She shrugged her shoulders and walked out into the night.

Zukowska had traversed both ends of the street in a desperate effort to catch a glimpse of the soloist. A feeling of desolation swept through the Pole as she made her way to the kerbside. She knew she was in deep trouble. What she needed to do was collect her thoughts and shed the feeling of fear that gripped her.

Back in the hotel foyer, Zukowska wrote out a telephone number on a sheet of the hotel's notepaper and handed it to the receptionist. The number was answered and Zukowska asked for Lutowicz. When he came to the phone she told him what had happened. His numbed silence elicited a rapid "Are you there?"

"I'll be with you as quickly as possible," the Polish intelligence man muttered, still trying to put together a strategy. "Be at the entrance when I pull up in the car." Zukowska would have liked to go to her room for a jacket, but felt constrained and so held her position at the entrance until Lutowicz pulled up outside.

When she sat into the front of the car, Lutowicz demanded a repeat of what she had already told him. "Leave nothing out," he emphasised.

As he put the car in gear and moved out onto the street, Zukowska related the episode with the police; this was met with a groan. "You keep your eyes on the left side of the street, I'll look after the right." They vigilantly traversed the route to the newsagent. They had to succeed. The alternative was so bleak he found it terrifying to think about. Yet all the while the consequences were there in the back of his mind. Major defection causes Polish government to pull out; months of planning which Polish intelligence had put in – wasted.

Lutowicz clicked his fingers with sudden inspiration. "Let's get back to the hotel and see if she's taken any of her belongings. There may be something which might tell us where she's gone."

If he could only make contact with the pianist – even by phone – he might be able to arrange something. At this moment he would agree to almost any demand – give any concession – provided Wohlicka played the concert and did not rock the boat. She had to be there. The ambassador would blow a fuse, but his problem was minor compared to what faced him. Of course he understood one was in the public domain; while the other ... actually that was a positive aspect. Nobody knew about it – not even the Polish government. They were to have been surprised with a successful fait accompli, when everything had been signed, sealed, and the bodies delivered. Would Wohlicka have gone to the Polish embassy? That was a possibility. She knew no one in England, one of the reasons she had been selected. She might indeed have attempted to record a protest with the ambassador about their heavy friend sitting beside him.

Lina Zukowska had her strong points; unfortunately her shortcomings were very near the surface and liable to break through when delicacy was called for. He mulled over which location to head for, and decided on the hotel. A discreet call to the embassy was a priority. He must also ring Quentin Appleby. His listening post might pick up a whisper in Croydon. Yes, he would operate from Zukowska's room for the moment.

———

When Zukowska went to collect her key in the hotel foyer, Lutowicz was already making his first call on one of the pay phones. As an intelligence officer he held influence in his embassy, so when he made contact it was under the prearranged guise of a newspaper enquiry.

No, he was told, Wohlicka was not staying at the embassy; this dashed his hopes that she had gone there to complain. The second call found Quentin Appleby. Lutowicz explained that Comrade Wohlicka had disappeared, so the underlying event was on hold. Zukowska was standing behind him when he replaced the phone. She turned and led the way to her room.

"Have any of her things – clothing I mean – been removed?"

Zukowska opened one of the wardrobes. She brushed her hand along the meagre collection of garments and said, "No – nothing removed."

"What about her performance outfit? Is it still there?"

"Yes."

"Did you see it?"

"I saw it!" Zukowska said belligerently. She turned to the clothes rack and pulled out the sleeve of the evening gown.

Whether through uncontrolled impatience, or wretched workmanship, the sleeve came away from the gown and hung limply from Zukowska's extended hand. Lutowicz's jaundiced expression changed to incredulity. Zukowska threw the sleeve back into the wardrobe.

"You know," Lutowicz continued, "I don't think she would have walked out without making some provision for an extended stay."

"What do you mean?" Zukowska asked, beginning to feel a wind of change.

"Look around you," Lutowicz invited with exaggerated charm. "What do you see? You see –" Moving to Wohlicka's bedside table, he made a sweeping gesture, "valuable personal effects: her bedside clock," he touched the clock with deferential affection, "her earrings, and –" he gloated, "a ring."

He turned and faced Zukowska.

"What would all of that suggest to you?" he demanded, his tone hardening.

"You are going to tell me anyway," Zukowska scoffed.

"I am telling you – and it is also going into my report," Lutowicz sneered. "I am telling you, these are signs of someone who left suddenly."

He returned to the bedside table and spread his arms broadly. "This can only mean you did something to make her run. What did you do? You are not telling me everything."

The drawer in the table drew his attention. He opened it and cried, "Look, she even left her cigarettes!"

"What are you doing with my cigarettes, Mr Lutowicz?" a familiar voice enquired. Maria Wohlicka stood in the doorway of the bathroom dressed in a bathrobe and with a towel wrapped around her head in a turban.

Lutowicz's jaw dropped, but he spluttered his way back to normality as quickly as he could. "Comrade Wohlicka –" he breathed, hands half extended in the pianist's direction. "I dropped by to make sure you have everything," he beamed, now clasping his joined hands to his bosom like a gratified hairdresser. "Cigarettes? Matches?" he offered, still unable to come to terms with his luck. "How are you fixed for drinks?" he asked, assuming the cosseting aloofness of a Maître d'.

Maria Wohlicka walked questioningly to the bedside table searching for her most prized possession. Her mother's wedding ring was still where she had left it and she rapidly restored it to its usual place on her finger.

"You have been here all evening?" asked Lutowicz.

"I have had a bath and washed my hair," she said between puffs. "Before that I went outside with Comrade Zukowska for cigarettes."

A puzzled expression enveloped Lutowicz's face. "And the two of you returned to the hotel?"

"I returned on my own." Comrade Wohlicka said matter-of-factly. "I assumed Comrade Zukowska was watching me from afar – as she occasionally does." With unexpected suddenness, Zukowska moved on the pianist and crashed her closed fist across the side of Wohlicka's face.

The sharp crack momentarily froze the three of them.

Maria Wohlicka collapsed across the bed – out cold.

"You've just proved you're the lunatic I always thought you were!" Lutowicz shouted. "This woman", he added, bending over the prone figure, "has to represent her country on Saturday night." He drew back in horror and roared, "I think you've broken her jaw! Ring for the embassy doctor – you imbecile." The security man was in uncontrollable shock. "Move! Move you bison's turd!" he screamed.

He sat down on the bed. "Before the concert," he moaned a number of times. The fat sow could do anything she liked after the concert, but before! He placed his head in his hands.

———

The embassy doctor ordered the pianist to hospital for x-rays. By this time her face had swollen appreciably and her right eye had acquired a dull black frame. She could speak, which assisted in the matter of a good prognosis. Shock, the doctor thought, was what the patient would have to cope with; this in turn would keep Lutowicz and company on tenterhooks for a while.

"May I smoke?" Maria Wohlicka asked the houseman as he walked alongside the wheelchair on their way from x-ray. "I don't encourage it," the young doctor replied, but seeing the entreaty in the patient's one good eye, he relented. "Of course, if it helps you cope with your ordeal – why not. You have a room to yourself, so you shan't disturb anyone else."

In her private room everybody was asked to leave, which they did in a state of relief, having ascertained there were no broken bones. The nurse plumped up the pillows and made sure her patient was comfy and snug. The doctor showed her how to operate the remote control for the television.

On her own, and puffing delicately on a cigarette, she uninhibitedly clicked from one channel to another – purely for the fun of it.

"It should not be the norm that one has to go to hospital in order to feel good," she reflected. "But if the people outside the hospital are as nice and kind as those inside – I am going to be very happy."

CHAPTER 21

Friday March 27th 1981
Croydon
9.30 am

"David," Cranshaw called with unconcealed excitement from the control room door. He greeted Sarah in passing, and threw a music score on the recording desk. It read, Kilar/Krzesany. "Have a look at this."

Brenton picked up the score of Kilar's Symphonic Poem and said he was thankful the music had at last arrived, particularly since Komorski had declared his satisfaction with the Szymanowski Symphony. This left the Kilar to be recorded. The work was about 17 minutes in duration, so it shouldn't present a very arduous task.

"The last two pages," Cranshaw urged, as Brenton began to leaf through the opening. The final pages parted with the assistance of a book mark which Cranshaw had inserted, and the first thing to catch Brenton's eye was the organ entry marked – *ad lib*.

Brenton's eyes widened. "Here we go," he said softly. Material evidence had seemed so excruciatingly reluctant to emerge that the sudden appearance of this sought-after directive was akin to the unexpected arrival of a long-lost friend.

"Yes, indeed," Cranshaw concurred.

"Anybody like a coffee?" Sarah asked, with the cheerful diplomacy of the outsider. The offer was taken up distractedly, so Sarah left them at it, poring over the score.

They found the last two pages were a repeat of the previous sixteen bars for the strings, with the directive: 'Continue playing without conducting, *molto appassionato* until complete breaking off.' The percussion section was asked to: 'Introduce gradually as many songali, sheep bells, triangoli, crotali, cencerros, *campanelli da messa*, etc, as possible.' The effect would build up to a cacophonous finale of bucolic fervour.

"What do you make of that request?" Brenton asked, pointing to an inscription for the brass on the final bar: 'Players may gradually raise the bells of their instruments and stand up slowly.'

"À la Glenn Miller," Cranshaw laughed, peering across Brenton's shoulder.

The humorous banter continued a while longer, much of it due to the release of tension. Earlier, Cranshaw had revealed that he had nothing to report on his search of Symphony Hall. A look through the control room window told Cranshaw things were building up on stage. He beat a retreat and relieved Sarah of one of the coffees on the stairs.

Kilar's Symphonic Poem, Brenton explained to Sarah between sips of coffee, recaptured the rustic joy of a Polish festive occasion in an original *Krzesany*, a rural and boisterous spree with dancers making sparks fly with metal-tipped clogs. "It should amount to a convulsive, not to say, percussive seventeen minutes," Brenton speculated. "I've been told the final 16 bars are a repeat of the previous 16 bars and are not conducted, because it's where all the bangles and percussion join in with varying rhythms and noise to create a festive country jamboree.

The phone rang and Jim Sherry told Brenton the spot mic on the percussion was in position and plugged up. Appleby followed to say the maestro was about to go on stage. Komorski greeted the orchestra from the podium with a disenchanted brusqueness. The orchestra wasn't aware that Komorski's preoccupation centred on the question mark hanging over Comrade Wohlicka's ability to perform on Saturday, and whether or not a replacement for the Chopin should be found. He had not as yet told Symphony Hall of the dilemma, preferring to wait as long as possible to see what progress Comrade Wohlicka made. It would be a trying imposition to begin with another soloist, and that was what Symphony Hall would insist on: another know-all, keyboard prima donna.

He would make his mind up at lunchtime when he was due to meet Lutowicz, who would hopefully bring a good report.

"And finally," he droned, "if you turn to the last bar … Number 749 … you will see a written direction: trumpets, trombones and horns."

This bar was located, and he then turned to the woodwind. "This directive will also include the woodwind from bar 747. "The direction reads," he instructed the section, "'The players may raise the bells of their instruments and stand up slowly'."

"Like us to wear clogs and dance?" Bertie Cramly, the second clarinet, quipped.

The irony eluded Komorski. He turned to the bassoon section and asked Reptarski to explain.

A pale imitation of amusement briefly flickered over the conductor's face; it abruptly disappeared as soon as he raised his arms in the air. The first run-through of the Kilar commenced.

Brenton noted the extra directive for the woodwind and, with Sarah turning the pages, set about knitting a sound together. A superficial look at the score had given the impression of an overweening preoccupation with the chord of D major, coupled with a reluctance to move from any chord, once established. However, as the piece progressed, a certain subtlety of melody manifested, and it romped along with a hypnotic rhythm to reach a hilarious free-for-all at the end. Bertie Cramly injected an element of pantomime to the climax, the bell of his clarinet performing elaborate arcs in the air like a demented jazzman. The clarinettist remained standing, and with a number of others, continued gyrating.

Komorski ignored the larking and started tidying up imperfections he had found in the run-through; this allowed Brenton time for a few adjustments, including two on-stage mics, which Jim Sherry attended to when an opportunity arose. Irrespective of the involved proceedings, the tenth directive of the first transcript tape floated on the surface of Brenton's mind. 'Uginski is yours *ad libitum*'. It was difficult to equate what had been conceived as a festive occasion with the planned brutality, but from what he had heard of the finale it would present an ideal opportunity. He still was not in a position to answer the question – for whom? All he could do was concentrate on how.

The strings had neither the cover nor opportunity for such an undertaking. That eliminated Edward Mopak in the cello section, Henryk Hisiel – viola, and Wanda Polascka – violin. The percussion section would have obvious opportunities. They had freedom of movement within the section, and would be constantly changing instruments. That presented Jerzy Kazimierz as a possibility. The prescribed number of percussionists for *Kreszany* was six. Pecton had objected to the three extras on monetary grounds, suggesting it was unsatisfactory to pay for three extras that would stand around doing nothing until the last bars of the final item.

For once, Brenton found it expedient to side with Pecton – three fewer bodies to process. Another to be discounted was Ronald Shipsey on the organ. He was one of those people whose preoccupation with music precluded any interest in anything else; besides, he would be sitting with his back to the orchestra – as did most organists. Which left the brass and woodwind. What did Komorski's inclusion of the woodwind in the fun and games of the last few bars amount to? An attempt to make as many as possible feel good? Hardly. If he found it difficult to feel and express fun himself, why allow someone else a chance to express it, especially when uncalled for in the score. The extension allowed the bassoonist Stanislaw Reptarski a certain freedom of movement during the *ad libitum*.

Which brought back the consideration – Pole to hit Pole. He reluctantly admitted the proposition Pole to hit Pole only made sense in terms of exiles versus communists. Yet, apart from the Sikorski thing there was not a whisper to support that connection. Was it a preparation in the event of an adverse decision on Sikorski? Had Jack Lesko a holding group in position in the orchestra? So many questions – so little time. What was pertinent was that the attempt would come from within the orchestra. He still found it difficult to believe the Poles in Exile would pull the plug on everything. Yet the alternative, that Polish communists would bump one of their own, seemed equally absurd. What a bloody mess. The important element to hold onto was that the attempt would come from Poles. Whoever and whatever they were would hopefully float to the surface.

Brenton was asked to prepare for a take. Komorski received a 'red', and they set off along the boisterous road to *Krzesany*. All went well until they reached the climactic *ad lib*. The lack of bodies in the percussion section became apparent. It then took some time to arrange the most equitable distribution of the numerous instruments amongst the inadequate number of percussionists. The hassle generated drew down on Pecton's head the disgruntled acerbity of all on stage – 'cheap skate' being one of the less intemperate comments. They had a second bash, followed by a third, before Komorski broke for coffee and a listen to a replay.

The conductor found the lack of continuity of any one percussion instrument unacceptable and demanded a meeting. Before the meeting took place, Miss Maybury buzzed to say Insp Blackmore wished to see Mr Brenton.

In the boardroom, Blackmore sat impassively at the head of the table. "I've acquired information which may prove to be important." He waved Brenton to a chair beside him. The position alongside of, rather than across from, was significant because apparently the barriers between their interests had been lifted. Blackmore had asked for and received a copy of Lutowicz's photograph after the previous day's meeting. Armed with this, the detective inspector had begun an intensive, late evening questionnaire in the vicinity of Symphony Hall. Amongst the copious amount of trivial and negative replies, a single positive identification stood out like the Post Office Tower. The lady in question had been returning from visiting a neighbour. Close by her own home, a complete stranger, prior to opening his car door, had rudely brushed her aside. What had particularly annoyed the witness was the lack of an apology, coupled with the man's brutish irritation. The collision had riveted her attention on the man's face, and she was vehemently sure that the photograph and her antagonist were one and the same. No, she could not identify the second man because her indignation had centred totally on the person in the photograph – Witold Lutowicz.

"Lutowicz has to be interviewed," Brenton urged.

Blackmore readjusted his chin. "How do I achieve that distinction, bearing in mind the gentleman's political status?"

Brenton's expression was inscrutable. "Politely?" he ventured.

There was a pause. Then Blackmore's face crumpled in a grunting laugh. Brenton continued, "He can't afford to get shirty about a request for information. His government badly wants to hold this concert, so to a large degree he should feel obliged to cooperate. If you could find out whether Lutowicz has a visit to Croydon on his schedule this afternoon, that could turn out to be a revealing encounter. He can't appear to flout a legitimate enquiry; plus, he won't want to precipitate circumstances that might lead to the identification of his companion. I'll lay a pound to a penny his chum doesn't hold diplomatic immunity."

"I can hardly make direct enquiries", Blackmore pointed out, "without alerting our opposites, enabling them to take avoiding action."

Brenton nodded. "I'll nose around and see what comes up. I'll be in touch before I depart."

———

Back at the meeting with Pecton, Komorski and the three percussionists, Appleby had joined the assembly during Brenton's absence. He sat in beside Sarah, who whispered the bones of what had taken place. Pecton had capitulated on the matter of the three extra percussion players – which had ruffled Appleby's feathers because, as he said, this was the latter end of the week and he would be forced to engage the leavings of every other London-based orchestra. Which in effect translated into – with forethought, this could have been avoided. The meeting presently drew to a close. Out of the corner of his eye Brenton noted Pecton engaging Komorski in conversation. He heard the conductor say he was having lunch in the canteen. He had arranged to meet a member of the Polish embassy there – Mr Lutowicz.

———

Brenton made a similar lunch arrangement with Sarah, having first shared his news with Blackmore. The drill was – when Lutowicz entered the canteen with Komorski, Blackmore would then enter, greet Komorski, and request a meeting with Lutowicz.

It seemed a relatively straightforward manoeuvre, but as Brenton removed his lunch from tray to table and sat down opposite Sarah, he conceded nothing in life was ever straightforward.

Unexpectedly, Jim Sherry joined them – which perhaps proved the point. Putting a positive gloss on the unwitting intrusion, Brenton persuaded himself that a trio might be less noticeable than a duo. Another more evident plus was Sarah's immediate brightening of spirit when Sherry transferred his salad and soup and sat down.

"How's it going?" Sherry earnestly enquired, and then piously added, "The recording I mean."

Sarah laughed and poked a finger in Sherry's ribs. "Nice to see you, cheeky!"

"Can you spare the time for an answer?" asked Brenton, eyebrow arched. "Now that you've branched out into musicians' domestic lighting repairs."

Sherry re-arranged his features into contrition. "You know," he considered, while dunking bread in his soup, "there is a cruel streak in both of you, an' truth to tell –" he started to chew noisily, "I am loving it!" Sherry's eyes were suddenly drawn to the canteen entrance. Brenton followed their movement and saw three members of the orchestra enter: the tall erect figure of the cellist Pamela Kent and two colleagues. Her haughty bearing was assisted by a striking blond appearance. Brenton's eyes returned to Sherry, whose own remained locked on Pamela Kent. "My God," he managed to breathe admiringly through his open mouth. He continued more confidentially, "She was one of the more outspoken members ... about Komorski, I mean."

Brenton's eyes narrowed. "In what sense?"

Sherry leaned forward and lowered his voice. "When I was on stage this morning, even I was able to pick up on the aggro between the musicians and Komorski. Whatever it is, they are full of it, and as near as I can make out, it has to do with the soloist – Maria what's-her-name."

Brenton rose from the table. "Back in a moment," he said briskly and headed towards Pamela Kent's table.

"Was it something I said," Sherry wondered, rubbing his chin. He watched expectantly as Brenton paused at the women's table, and was surprised when he received an invitation to sit down. In actual fact, it had not been an invitation because Brenton had asked them directly whether he might join them. The open curiosity on the three women's faces reflected Jim Sherry's interpretation. Without beating around the bush, Brenton told them he had heard vague disturbing rumours about Maria Wohlicka, and did they possess anything more concrete. Pamela Kent said that the orchestra only had rumours too, but they were strong, and they had originated from within the Polish group in the orchestra. Maria Wohlicka, it was being said, had had to enter hospital because of all the hassle she had received. The cellist went on to say that it was not difficult to know where to lay the blame. They had all seen, and heard, what had gone on between the soloist and that unspeakable creature Komorski.

"Do they know which hospital?"

"They said no one knew which hospital – not even the Polish members. And it wasn't because they hadn't tried to find out. Institutions can be very secretive nowadays," Pamela continued, "perhaps with just cause. But in this instance, all we wished to do was show our solidarity ... if that isn't too political an expression under the circumstances." Brenton thanked them for their time and returned to Sarah and Jim Sherry.

"You trying to upset me then?" Sherry asked with open curiosity, but before he could continue, a frown descended on Brenton's face. Komorski had just entered the canteen, accompanied by Lutowicz.

Blackmore was sharper than Brenton had expected. He entered shortly after. He engaged Komorski in conversation and, without sitting down, drew Lutowicz into the exchange. Blackmore then moved to the counter and purchased two coffees from Mrs Wheeler. His sudden movements disconcerted. They seemed to spell a negative response, but as he went to leave, carrying a coffee in each hand, Lutowicz rose from his table and joined him at the door. Blackmore handed a cup to Lutowicz and they disappeared down the corridor.

Komorski was now on his own. Which did not disturb him to any visible extent. Oblivious to the looks of scorn that assaulted his back from Pamela Kent's table, he extracted a long thin cheroot, which he lit with careful little puffs. He surveyed the urban rooftops through the large canteen window, cosseted within an aura of smug contentment.

Brenton broke off his attempt to decipher Komorski's change of mood and said to Sarah, "Let's ship out. We have a few pressing jobs in hand – not the least of which is to make contact with our BBC opposite number."

They bade Jim Sherry farewell.

At the side door they waited six minutes before Det Sgt Broadbent arrived to pick them up in an unmarked Branch car.

Brenton told Broadbent of his concern about Maria Wohlicka. The Polish group were staying at a hotel on the Cromwell Road, convenient to the West London Air Terminal and the Royal Albert Hall. If she had had to go to hospital it would have been from this address.

They eventually tracked her down in St Mary Abbot's Hospital on Marloe's Road, off the Cromwell Road.

Because of the absence of the administrator, they were received by his deputy, Mr Ribbleswaite. Introductions were made in his small office. He was sufficiently impressed by the authoritative nomenclature of detective sergeant and wing commander plus assistant to suggest a move to a plusher reception room. Within its more spacious surroundings, Brenton asked Ribbleswaite for discretion in the matter about which he was to be interviewed. With the acceptance that he would have to allow his administrator in on the problem, the interview commenced.

"Did you recently admit to your hospital", asked Brenton, "a middle-aged Polish national, Maria Wohlicka?"

Ribbleswaite reached for a telephone and, while picking out an internal extension, requested, "Would you spell that please?" Brenton obliged and the information was passed on.

"When do you think she was admitted?" Ribbleswaite asked, placing a hand across the mouthpiece of the telephone.

"Sometime between last Wednesday and today."

Silence fell as this information was acted on at the other end. Eventually Ribbleswaite replaced the receiver and said, "Maria Wohlicka was admitted to this hospital yesterday evening."

Even their suspicions had not prepared them for the confirmation. "May we visit her?" Brenton asked.

"That would be impossible," Mr Ribbleswaite said with surprise. "You are obviously unaware that Madame Wohlicka discharged herself at noon today."

Shock turned to confusion. Det Sgt Broadbent asked, "May we speak to the doctor who treated Madame Wohlicka?"

Ribbleswaite consulted his watch and said, "Doctor Swami may not be in attendance just now, but let's give it a try." He reached for the telephone and asked the switch to contact the doctor. Presently he joined them.

Madame Wohlicka, in Dr Swami's opinion, had been assaulted. The damage to the side of her face, her cheek bone and eye, could be explained by a heavy fall; but taken in conjunction with the bruising on her arm, which was likely produced by the crushing grasp of a pair of hands, he had no hesitation in saying the injuries bore all the hallmarks of common assault.

Madame Wohlicka, while appearing to be frail, was physically, and indeed mentally, very resilient. He had expected some damage other than bruising but this had not been the case. So the lady had been perfectly within her rights in requesting, and the hospital perfectly correct in granting, permission to discharge.

"Please don't misunderstand," Brenton reassured the young doctor. "I'm not for a moment suggesting there was any negligence on the hospital's part. What we are concerned about is the possible abuse of the lady by persons whom we may not as yet name. What you've told us substantiates our fears."

Dr Swami relaxed. "She's quite an extraordinary person," he said with subdued admiration. "She told me she is to play a concert at the Royal Albert Hall tomorrow?"

"Well, that was the original idea," said Brenton. "Now I'm beginning to wonder."

"If she does," Dr Swami warned them, "she will have to perform with a deal of pain."

"You've been very helpful," Brenton told the administrator and the doctor. "We've taken up enough of your valuable time." He rose and extended his hand. "May I ask who collected Madame Wohlicka?"

"A Mr Lutowicz," replied the doctor.

Outside, Broadbent had to ask twice where Brenton wished to go.

"King Charles Street," he said distractedly, still endeavouring to correlate the spectre of Maria Wohlicka's battered person with the complacent arrogance of Jan Komorski that morning. "He's a dangerous bastard," he concluded eventually as Broadbent moved the car out into the traffic.

CHAPTER 22

Friday March 27th 1981
Whitehall
3.45 pm

When they reached King Charles Street in Whitehall, Brenton had already agreed that Broadbent should accompany Sarah to her apartment to pick up some odds and ends. That left Brenton free to accompany Hempson to face the rigours of a ministerial inquisition. As he waved them off, and the car was absorbed by the Whitehall traffic, an unaccountable emptiness took hold of him. His feet felt leaden as he passed through the entrance, and he cast uncertain eyes in search of Hempson.

The major was nowhere in sight.

Brenton was about to make his way to reception when a crisp "Beg pardon, sir," interrupted him. He turned to find one of the porters.

"Mr Brenton?" It was more affable confirmation than a question.

"Yes," replied Brenton. The man's face was not new to him.

"You may not remember me," the man said. Brenton's face registered curiosity but he said nothing. "While you think about it," the man said, grinning, "I have a message from Major Hempson."

Brenton examined his face for some hint or clue to his identity, which he abandoned when the porter explained that Major Hempson had been summoned by the Home Secretary earlier than expected; he was already in session and required Brenton's assistance as quickly as possible.

The porter intimated that it was part of his function to escort his visitor to the location of the meeting. They had begun to move in that direction when Brenton clicked his fingers and said, "Golders Green. The BBC. Were you with the BBC before coming here?"

A smile of acknowledgement increased the porter's wrinkle ratio. "You're quite right, sir, that's where we met." Rubbing his chin, he said, "It must be ... oh ... about ten years ago."

They reached the end of a long high-ceilinged corridor.

"A lot of crotchets and quavers have hit the air waves since then," the porter added with philosophical regret, and directed Brenton towards a beautifully finished hardwood door. The music reference attracted Brenton's attention and he asked, "Were you in the music end of things in Golders Green?"

The porter nodded. "I used to play the trumpet before I got this nerve problem in my lips."

"I'm sure the BBC saw you right,"

"No, no," the porter shook his head, "You don't understand. I was an army bandsman, and any time you saw me out there, I was deputising."

"Ah ... I see." Brenton observed the man with new-found interest, subjecting him to a stare that prompted the porter to ask, "Everything ok, Mr Brenton?"

"Ok," Brenton repeated, lost in thought. "Why in God's name did I not think of that before now. Look – " he said, "I need to get to a telephone immediately."

The porter pointed in bewilderment to the door behind which the Home Secretary and Hempson were in session. "But I thought –"

"As quickly as possible," Brenton urged. He was ushered into an adjoining room where the porter explained Brenton's requirement to the girl behind the desk. Brenton thanked the man, who took his leave still in some bewilderment.

Brenton asked the girl for a phone call to be put through to Symphony Hall, Croydon. When the Hall answered he asked for Cranshaw.

"What's the story on the three extras for the percussion section?" Brenton asked brusquely. Cranshaw tried to determine the direction of Brenton's anxiety. "Not much movement on that front," he said. "Appleby has only managed to get one definite response."

"Tell Appleby you can get as many percussionists as he wants. Do it now, Tim. Now!"

Cranshaw's perplexity transpired in a silent pause.

"We can load as many army bandsmen into the percussion section as they can take," Brenton explained. "Bandsmen who can also handle firearms," he added, lowering his voice.

"I'm with you. Of course!" Cranshaw's voice hummed with excitement.

"Get going, Tim. I can't spend any further time here. I've Hempson breathing down my neck outside."

———

Brenton entered the Home Secretary's environs with a lighter heart. Hempson rose with obvious relief to introduce him to the Home Secretary; the minister's private secretary, Peter Jarvis; and the head of the department, Sir John Wescott.

The Home Secretary was flanked at both ends of his desk by the two civil servants. He resumed by saying, "Now that the man on the spot has arrived, perhaps he will enable us to blow away the cobwebs of intrigue which threaten to envelop this otherwise splendid evening of Polish music. Nothing I've heard through the week, even up to the present moment, has convinced me of anything other than electronic pranks and two sets of mutually antagonistic Poles."

As Brenton sat down on his chair, it was like having a basin of official cold water thrown over him. The Home Secretary's relentless affability only added to the difficulty of counteracting the sleight of hand underlying this position. There were two possibilities at work here: either the Home Secretary had had a political compromise imposed on him, or he had reached this conclusion off his own bat. If the latter, then they were still in with a chance. Either way, however, the Home Secretary was leaving the security service out on a limb. His whole focus was on playing diplomat and mediator between the factions. Brenton steadied himself and said, "Home Secretary, we've already lost one good man on the way to this evening of Polish music."

"Yes. Very regrettable," the Home Secretary said moodily, glancing quickly at his minions to left and right. "I take it", he went on, "you've established a firm connection between the man's death and what you suggest is about to happen?"

"That investigation", Hempson broke in, "is in the hands of the Metropolitan police."

Sir John Wescott joined the fray. "Are you suggesting, Major, that the Metropolitan police handling this matter represents an impediment?"

Hempson harumphed at the aspersion. "That sir, is not what I said. I do not indulge in double talk. What I did say –" He inclined towards the Home Secretary, "– if I may be forgiven for repeating myself – is that the matter is in the hands of the Metropolitan police by my choice." The last three words were again directed in Sir John Wescott's direction. Hempson turned back to the Home Secretary and informed him: "Normally, sir, that sort of business is the preserve of Special Branch."

The Home Secretary removed his hand from his forehead. "Let's not become side-tracked. Wg Cdr Brenton has, presumably, the latest on that score." He looked interrogatively at Brenton.

"Det Insp Blackmore is in charge of the case, Home Secretary, and he has managed to place Mr Lutowicz in the location of the crime, at the time the crime took place."

"That's an interesting if rather vague connection," the Home Secretary opined. "Surely Mr Lutowicz – whom I have met – has every right to be in or near Symphony Hall, in his capacity as liaison officer for the concert?"

"Every right," Hempson conceded. "He also has an ulterior motive in his capacity as the Polish embassy's resident intelligence chief."

"I see," the Home Secretary said evenly, while visually consulting with Sir John Wescott. He then asked Brenton, "Apart from that snippet, have you anything further, Wing Commander?"

Brenton told them Det Insp Blackmore would have finished an interview with Lutowicz by then, which should add to the growing dossier. The Home Secretary indicated a telephone and invited Brenton to find out what had been added to the dossier – if anything.

Because of the possibility of a breach in security by phone tap in

Croydon, Brenton explained across the table that the enquiry would have to be made via Blackmore's chief superintendent.

Brenton called the chief superintendent and explained the circumstances to him; then he replaced the receiver and waited for a reply.

"Let's try and put some shape on your happenings, shall we?" the Home Secretary suggested. "I've already heard from Major Hempson, so may we hear the story from you now, Wing Commander?"

Brenton outlined the background to the operation in Croydon and the circumstances surrounding the recording of the two eavesdrop tapes. He emphasised his conviction of their intent, the terror to which his assistant, Sarah Carlyle, had been subjected in St George's, and her further distress when told her flat had been broken into. This had been in pursuit of those same tapes, because of Miss Carlyle's inadvertent disclosure of their existence in Croydon. Then, most harrowing of all, there was Thompson's murder. Gunned down while phoning in a report. He had undoubtedly discovered the stolen two-way radios which were used during the eavesdrop transmissions.

"And who does all that point to?" Wescott asked.

Brenton and Hempson exchanged looks; Hempson answered. "It points to a disaffected group of Poles."

"Elaborate on that," the Home Secretary directed, leaning forward on the desk. "I must make a decision on this, and what you're presenting seems very vague." He flopped back into his armchair, his effort to bridge this information gap seemingly defeated. "I perceive some odd things have happened, Thompson and Miss Carlyle ..." His voice petered out; then he took up more impatiently, "I can't help feeling you're holding something back from me. Something that might make sense of what has happened." He sat up again and looked directly at Hempson. "Either that or you've little else to add."

"This business started to evolve only three days ago, on Tuesday," Hempson pointed out. "In the normal course of events, we would have had a longer gestation period. I assure you, sir, we are not holding back material. We been constrained by a very short space of time. The concert takes place tomorrow evening. And while we would normally present you with direct evidence, we feel sufficiently alarmed by this one as to present incomplete signposts. In all events, that is our obligation to you," Hempson emphasised.

"I could, I suppose, take the problem higher," the Home Secretary murmured, peering beyond the group through the mullioned windows to the prospect of his next meeting at which the prime minister would preside. The meeting had been postponed from that morning to late afternoon on account of a vote on a private member's bill in the House of Commons.

"One way or another she'll require a decision," the Home Secretary reasoned aloud. "Better now than later. She doesn't like procrastination," he told them. "You see gentlemen, we are all of us subject to varying and various pressures. Some of which even you may not be aware of, Major."

Hempson blinked rapidly. "I am open to correction," he said, with tempered modesty, "but that's part of my brief: to know what's happening and who is under pressure – and why."

The telephone rang; Peter Jarvis reached out to answer.

It was the chief superintendent's return call. The room remained silent while Brenton received the result of Blackmore's interview with Lutowicz. He thanked the chief superintendent, replaced the receiver, and returned to his seat.

"Blackmore has finished his interview with Lutowicz," Brenton began. He diplomatically tried to divide his delivery between Hempson and the Home Secretary. "The most important development is that Lutowicz has admitted to being in the immediate locality around the time the crime was committed. We know he had a companion, and although he initially said he had been alone, when faced with hard evidence, he rescinded, courtesy of a 'me-no-understand' smokescreen. His companion turned out to be Quentin Appleby, the orchestra manager –"

"There you are!" the Home Secretary exclaimed. "A perfectly innocuous association. I'm sure Mr Appleby will supply you with some reasonable explanation."

"That's precisely what I would be wary of, Home Secretary," warned Hempson, "a supplied explanation."

The Home Secretary smiled and glanced at his two civil servants before asking Hempson and Brenton, "Aren't you reading too much into this unprepossessing encounter?"

Hempson chose to ignore the question and instead asked Brenton if there had been anything else from Blackmore.

Brenton shrugged his shoulders in exasperation. He had begun to wonder what useful purpose he was serving with the Home Office. What remained from Blackmore would not have set Hempson's pipe alight, never mind the Home Office ablaze. He told them Lutowicz had picked up Appleby outside Symphony Hall at 8 pm and they had gone into Croydon for a meal. "That much is probably the truth," Brenton surmised, because Blackmore assured Lutowicz that it was easily verifiable with the restaurant. Lutowicz said that was ok by him. They returned to Symphony Hall about 9 pm. Lutowicz went inside with Appleby. Neither of them saw Thompson either inside or outside when they returned to their car.

Brenton gloomily regarded Hempson and added, "That's about it apart from the fact that Blackmore now has Appleby in, to see how Lutowicz's story stands up."

The Home Secretary again looked to his left at Peter Jarvis. When Jarvis removed pen from paper, the Home Secretary gathered himself for a pronouncement. "Gentlemen," he began, "I have heard nothing so far which would prompt me, in any way, to interfere in tomorrow's Anglo-Polish concert. Cognisance must be taken of the extraordinary effort the two main participants have expended on the project. Dr Michael Pecton and his excellent company in Croydon, in a forward-thinking collaboration with the government of Poland, have put together a unique occasion. The new man – General Jaruzelski – needs a helping hand if he isn't to die of fright, what with Brezhnev peering over his shoulder. Her Majesty's government wishes to play a significant role in the process, primarily because of the strong friendship that exists between the peoples..."

Time for a commercial break, thought Brenton, and took comfort in the glazed expression adorning Hempson's face.

"...and in my anxiety to encourage this process," the Home Secretary continued, "I may have overestimated the capacity of the Poles in Exile to foresee the possibilities. We've had to back down on the transfer of General Sikorski's remains to his native Poland. We are not, however, backing off on this concert, and on a number of other mutually beneficial projects. The Polish government minister, Mr Uginski, is arriving tomorrow, and shall attend the concert tomorrow evening. If there is the smallest possibility of a hiccup or deviation from the direction in which the government has decided to go..." There was a minatory glance from the Home Secretary at Hempson and Brenton. "I know I can count on you two gentlemen to smooth the way."

This then was the end of the road for any hope of a cancellation. Hempson had been less convinced of that probability, and so was more immediately responsive.

"We are not so much interested in a cancellation of the event, as we are in a cancellation of Mr Uginski's attendance at the event," he pointed out, but the Home Secretary was adamant. What, he demanded, was the point in saying the concert had the approval and support of both governments, if this support was seen to be one-sided.

"You may be placing Mr Uginski's life at risk." Brenton said flatly. "Doesn't that prospect enter into it at all?"

"There is no hard evidence to support your suspicions." The Home Secretary's tone sharpened. "And I place your hunch in the same category as a request to cancel the concert because Professor Komorski may walk out under a bus. It's a possibility, true – but highly unlikely."

Brenton folded his arms and Hempson sniffed loudly.

"Now look here," said the Home Secretary, returning to his more congenial manner of delivery, "This thing can't be as bad as you're painting it. After all, the Polish liaison for the occasion, Mr Lutowicz, the man you now say is a Polish intelligence officer, told me he had absolute faith in Britain's ability to protect Mr Uginski. Surely he would know what's best for his own minister?"

Hempson stirred uneasily within the arms of his chair. "I'm not sure that what I'm about to say will make the slightest difference, but I'll mention it in any event, if only for the record," he said, nodding towards Peter Jarvis' industry. "I've had a very recent communication from MI6 about our minister friend, Mr Anton Uginski. I found the information rather curious in the context of this concert."

Brenton turned to look at Hempson; he must have collected this info just before the meeting.

"In the context of Poland," Hempson said, "it's not surprising. We're all aware of the quagmire of paralysis and corruption afflicting communism. Courtesy of MI6 we now have in our possession a list of five top Polish government people who've been described as having fallen into disgrace. Mr Uginski's name used to be on the list. And yet, recently there's been a complete turnabout on that score: his name's been scotched and he appears to be flavour of the month."

The Home Secretary stared unblinkingly at Hempson. "What the deuce is that supposed to signify?" he demanded.

Hempson squeezed the tip of his chin and said, "You see, their new chap – Jaruzelski – is being referred to as Mr Clean. And a clean sweep he is making, by all accounts. We have every reason to believe this report. Already, two of Uginski's government colleagues have become non-persons, and the head of their television service is to go on trial next year on a number of corruption charges, not the least of which was the maintenance of two African mistresses. An intriguing achievement," he conceded, "in an ethnically-conservative society such as Poland. Now, I'm not suggesting Uginski was in that bracket; nevertheless, as a minister with responsibility, he must, at the very least, have heard what was going on and acquiesced. We *do* know his name was on the list, and then removed."

Sir John Wescott leaned forward. "Then they must have been rectifying a mistake," he challenged.

"Or damn well setting us up!" Brenton said.

"Conjecture...conjecture," the Home Secretary said dismissively. "You are again floundering in supposition. Give me facts gentlemen. I must have facts!"

The Home Secretary gave the desk an impatient little tap-tap with the palm of his hand, as if the piece of furniture had suddenly transformed into the collective knuckles of the security service. "Besides," he went on, "this thing is a much more elaborate device than the mere holding of a concert." He paused to purse his lips. When he took up again, it was clear that he was trying to maintain an even keel; but an underlying impatience seeped through. "We wish to take advantage", he said softly, just the slightest quiver in his voice, "of a divergence of purpose in the other camp." He flopped back in his chair with controlled exasperation. "Even if the precarious see-saw between Solidarity and the new government should tip over and the Soviets invade Poland, our friends in MI6 tell us we will derive great beneficial publicity as a result: the Soviets once again demonstrating what utter hypocrites they are."

"You said, sir, you were refusing the Polish application to transfer General Sikorski's remains to Poland?" asked Brenton.

"Yes, that decision has been agreed. The option was considered counter-productive, and the conclusion not to proceed was taken at the highest level."

"If that's the case," Brenton wondered, "when do you intend releasing the information? If the information were to be released now, it might have a steadying effect – supposing the threat centred on those who feel aggrieved at the transfer of General Sikorski's body to Poland."

"Do you honestly expect the Home Secretary to swallow a further supposition?" Westcott demanded.

"Besides," the Home Secretary intervened. "Suppose the opposite were true? That would present a fine pickle. I believe neither event is a possibility. Now if I may return to the facts of the matter. It was the unanimous decision of cabinet not to make any response to the Polish application. That way nobody can take offence, for the immediate future at least."

The Home Secretary glanced at his watch. "I think everybody has derived as much as can be derived from the meeting. I must now proceed to a postponed cabinet meeting, so if there is nothing further, gentlemen?" He shuffled his papers and put them away in his briefcase.

Hempson, who had not contributed for some time, quietly said that there was indeed a further item. Since the Home Secretary had said earlier that he had met Lutowicz, he was now obliged to reveal what had been said at this meeting, and under what circumstance the meeting had taken place.

The Home Secretary smiled in surprise. "That's a quaint role reversal," and consulting his two officials added, "Don't you think?"

The two chuckled obediently.

"Of course, I'm only too happy to oblige," the Home Secretary told Hempson. "Anything that might assist in dispelling this disagreeable hiatus is to be recommended. Peter –" he directed his private secretary, "make sure you get an accurate account of what follows. Now Major, what is it you particularly want to know?"

"Everything," Hempson replied coolly.

Sir John Wescott made to leave, since as he put it, "The matter doesn't concern me."

"I fully perceive how this business does not in any way make you feel concern," Hempson responded. "However, in the event of your having come into contact with Lutowicz, I would consider your presence of some interest."

Wescott sought the reassurance of solidarity from the Home Secretary, but the minister's eyes had never left Hempson. Sir John rose, and gathering his papers together said, "In order to assuage your worries, Major, I can say I have never met the gentleman."

As Sir John walked past him, Hempson said, "You have my permission to leave. I may also reassure you, Sir John, that you haven't missed anything – Lutowicz is no gentleman."

The door closed with a disgruntled clunk. The Home Secretary said, "That was unnecessary."

Hempson suggested they proceed with the interview. If the Home Secretary was short of time, then it must be said the security service was equally short of the same commodity – mainly because of the adverse political decisions that had been taken.

The Home Secretary, it transpired, had met Lutowicz twice. The first meeting had taken place three weeks ago and had included the Polish ambassador. They had made a formal request for the re-interment of General Sikorski's remains, which had taken the cabinet by surprise. And while they had had some unofficial soundings on the subject, a formal and official request from Poland could only mean the rehabilitation of General Sikorski in communist Poland.

Whether this process extended to Brezhnev's Russia was extremely doubtful, so, ipso facto they were being presented with a crack in the Eastern Bloc accord. Lutowicz, as the Home Secretary remembered it, did not have a lot to contribute at that meeting. Peter Jarvis supported this and said his notes of the meeting confirmed the observation – nothing of an incriminating nature at that meeting. Lutowicz had attended as resident Służba Bezpieczeństwa (SB) or state secruity man, which indicated the seriousness of the Polish request and Lutowicz's professional interest in its fulfilment.

The second meeting had convened two days ago on Wednesday afternoon, six hours before Thompson's murder. The purpose of this meeting was to finalise arrangements, already in train, for the Anton Uginski visit. In contrast with the previous encounter, Lutowicz made a considerable input to this meeting, and, the Home Secretary conceded, a major part of that contribution centred on security arrangements. Startled, Hempson at once asked who had represented British security, and was told – the head of Special Branch.

"I could continue this interview with Special Branch," Hempson told the Home Secretary. "However, if you could spare the time, I should prefer to hear the remainder from you."

The sudden information gap had dented Hempson's self-esteem. He pursued the unsavoury Mr Lutowicz through the person of the Home Secretary, asking him to produce a list of the Polish security requirements.

Tucked in at the tail end of the list, almost as an innocuous throwaway, was the seemingly unctuous request that Mr Uginski not be bothered with the intricacies or implications of any of the security arrangements. Lutowicz had then reiterated his supreme confidence in

Britain's security – not that he thought it would in any way be put to the test.

As the meeting broke up, Hempson and Brenton watched in silence the putting away of papers, agenda forms, and departmental bumph. They then endured the good-humoured leave-taking by the Home Secretary and his assistant. When the door closed behind them the silence continued, until Brenton broke the impasse. "This is like a bad bloody dream," he meditated aloud. Hempson rose abruptly to his feet. "Let's get out of here," he snapped irritably.

On the way to the entrance, Brenton reminded the major that he would be picking Sarah up in the lobby.

"Very good," Hempson absently responded; and then more energetically, "We have a few further things to clear up before we go our separate ways." They slowly traversed a busy intersection and made their way down a less populated corridor.

"My first priority is to contact and meet the head of Special Branch," Hempson said with discernible rancour. We must sort out this lapse in communications. While I'm there I'll ask the Branch to put a tail on Lutowicz. We can't afford to wait until tomorrow morning for one of our watchers."

Hempson stopped and looked directly at Brenton. "In either event – " he sombrely pointed out, "– bearing in mind the ludicrously short time available to us, I doubt the exercise worth the trouble. Nevertheless, we must keep trying and continue to plug every breach."

They recommenced their preoccupied walk.

"I should have elicited the more active assistance of the director general in the first instance. We lack clout on this, and the damnable thing is, the caravan has now gone too far down the road for any sort of political manoeuvre. We're stuck with it, and to a great extent, isolated."

Brenton read anxiety on Hempson's face. He had been about to present a more positive assessment when the thought that the more elevated had farther to fall took hold of him. It also altered their working relationship in some imperceptible yet defining way. In an endeavour to rid his mind of the disagreeable tangle, Brenton returned to the Home Secretary's inadvertent revelations.

"Lutowicz obviously wields considerable influence."

"Yes," Hempson agreed. "If he's not the controller, I'll eat my hat. So we must bear in mind he's not the gentleman designated to pull the trigger."

They moved further along in silence before Brenton said, "It seems incongruous that we've been placed in a position of having to defend the life of a corrupt communist government minister."

"What we're defending, David, is the integrity of the institutional ground on which we stand. Anton Uginski is just one other corrupt piece of political flotsam, which should have been dumped a long time ago. I hazard the man is an unwitting vehicle in a sordid piece of undercover one-upmanship."

"What d'you think Lutowicz and company hope to gain?" Brenton asked.

"First of all, let me say that if they succeed, then the immediate consequence will be our abject humiliation and embarrassment; but that in itself is hardly the object of their exercise. There has got to be something else, another dimension, something which might not otherwise succeed without the assistance of this precipitating lever."

"To force the return of Sikorski's remains?" Brenton suggested.

Hempson nodded. "A strong possibility."

"I imagine", Brenton continued, "that our lack of knowledge about their new party secretary, Jaruzelski, doesn't help,"

"We know very little about Jaruzelski," Hempson confirmed. "What we acquire shall build up slowly and methodically. At this point we're not even sure how the man came to power, or to whom he is beholden. We can only speculate. Certainly he owes a great deal to the Polish army. Brezhnev could have assisted, but that doesn't tally with Jaruzelski's present demand for the return of Sikorksi's body. After all, Sikorski was the one who earned Stalin's enmity with his constant accusations of the Soviet's part in the Katyn massacre."

Brenton shook his head sadly. "I find it incomprehensible that an otherwise pillar of the military establishment could take a chance with this incredible bit of barbarism."

"Of course," Hempson considered, "that's the away game. Here at home, things are a little more manifest. For one thing, our political masters tend to take cognisance of strong public pressure."

"Which might demand the return of Sikorski's body as some form of expiation," Brenton guessed.

Hempson grunted an acknowledgement. "I detect a tendency in you", he said pointedly, "to try and disentangle the moral and ethical basis for this adventure." He shot him a searching look. "Don't. First and foremost it's a waste of precious time, and goodness knows we have little enough of that. Secondly, it's a luxury, which is best indulged after the event. If I were to point up the futility of the exercise as succinctly as possible, I don't think I could do better than quote the head of the Soviets' international department, Boris Possomarev. That gentleman said – 'Violence in itself is not evil. It is a progressive force in the hands of socialists'."

Brenton said, "I hadn't realised I was poking around in that direction."

"A tendency," Hempson said. "A tendency. Any decent individual would ask the same question, and you've been out of the ordinary run of things in the rarefied atmosphere of Symphony Hall." Hempson paused to draw breath and then continued with a hint of impatience. "Just bear in mind that this sort of business is stated Soviet policy and is commonly referred to nowadays as stirring the shit. They haven't the guts to carry out the dirty work themselves, so they farm it out to their dependencies. The cesspit will collapse in on them someday. No ordinary human being would put up with the abuses meted out by these autocrats. They've given the word progressive a whole new meaning."

Brenton remembered his phone call to Cranshaw, and revealed the arrangement he had put in train to insert army bandsmen in the orchestra. Hempson's relief was instantaneous. He suggested they temporarily induct the bandsmen into Special Branch if, as seemed likely, a necessity arose to carry arms. It was one other point he would raise with the Branch. Hempson moved over to a window overlooking Parliament Street. He surveyed the Whitehall panorama outside the window. The Cenotaph in the middle of the street drew his attention. There was hardly a family in Britain untouched by the necessity to pay tribute to the fallen dead. "We'll make out, Brenton old man, we'll make out."

CHAPTER 23

Friday March 27th 1981
Whitehall
6.00 pm

Brenton was glad to find Sarah waiting for him in the entrance hall. Once again she was accompanied by Det Sgt Broadbent. They already knew the schedule, so without further ado they located the Branch car and Broadbent drove them north along Whitehall, through Picadilly Circus, to Broadcasting House in Portland Place.

A receptionist located Adam Fuller, their BBC opposite number. After introductions, Fuller launched into a summary of the attributes and pitfalls of recording in the Royal Albert Hall. Knowing Fuller's professional reputation, which centred on the Promenade Concerts in the Albert Hall, Brenton had no hesitation in proposing that he take the hot seat in the Hall. "I've already got the programme on tape," he explained, "which leaves the live transmission to Poland to contend with. We also have a secondary request for a recording of the concert. Sarah here, or Jim Sherry, will run a tape on your output, so that aspect shouldn't present a problem."

Fuller accepted the offer with the unruffled confidence Brenton associated with the BBC, and as they took their leave, he said he was looking forward to meeting them all tomorrow morning.

"Right," cried Brenton, "Nosebag time. There's a convenient place not far from Biggin Hill."

Broadbent was pressed to join them; he declined on the grounds of his workload, but dropped them off at the pub. It turned out to be of the nook and cranny variety. Brenton attentively steered Sarah in the direction of one of the nooks, which he hoped would meet his tête à tête requirements.

"You seem unusually content," observed Sarah. Brenton nodded. "I'm with you, aren't I?" He smiled. "How well you read me."

"If I felt I couldn't," Sarah said, a cloud passing across her face, "or if I felt there was no real communication between us, that would be the end of our development as a couple, I should imagine."

Brenton's self-esteem got a boost when he heard Sarah's reference to the collective – welcome confirmation of the direction in which they were headed. At that moment, within the flush of recognition of their togetherness, he would have done anything for her, but instead of fulfilling his first intention to do something for the object of his love, he bent across the table and did something *to* the object of his love.

His kiss caught Sarah completely unprepared. He held her face in his hands and after the initial forcefulness sustained the kiss in a lingering tenderness – until the sudden appearance of a waitress.

"Yes," Sarah said, adjusting her hair and eyeing the woman. "Just as well to have dispensed with the aperitif."

But Brenton's joy was unalloyed: he had completed an emotional quantum leap. Sarah's large incandescent eyes engaged him from the other side of the slim table. He hoped their darkness was less a sign of annoyance, and more a reflection of the excitement enveloping his own frame. The waitress, with middle-aged forbearance, arranged the cutlery on either side of the table. Before retreating she murmured indulgently that she would return shortly with their meal. Brenton took heed and restrained any further impulse. "We'd better cease operations for the moment," he said, smiling again.

"You're full of surprises," Sarah said, with the reverence of someone who has received revealed truth.

The waitress brought in their order of steaming beef garnished with vegetables, wished them an enjoyable meal and departed. A barman delivered a glass of ale and a mineral water, and after his departure, Sarah said, "I've often wondered why you bought a house so far from Symphony Hall."

The unexpectedness of the observation caught Brenton by surprise. He choked off a surge of defensive irritation. He knew his new direction depended on the goodwill of the figure sitting on the other side of the table; but redemption could only come from within himself. Sarah sat expectantly across from him.

It was an ingrained habit with him at this stage – clam up when asked for personal information. "I'm finding this … difficult," he said eventually.

"This business tomorrow night isn't helping," Sarah said soothingly, and smiled at him.

This business tomorrow night, Brenton knew, clung to him like a gorging leech. Its throbbing pulse was building up to Saturday night and he wondered at his ability to dissipate his time and energy on something that had no direct bearing on events. Maybe it was a wish to reach over and beyond the event to the future.

"Look, Sarah," he said, "There are things I need to tell you."

"Don't feel obliged to do what is obviously difficult for you just now," Sarah quietly suggested. "After all, intimacies usually come out in dribs and drabs, over a period of time; and while I do, dearly, wish to know everything about you –" she arched her eyebrows earnestly, "I have no plans to be anywhere, other than by your side. So let them come, when they come."

Brenton nodded. But something inside him wanted Sarah to know him – really know him – as no one had known him since he was a child. "There are a few details I need to fill you in on." He saw her worried expression and smiled. "Nothing heavy – it's just that the story I told you wasn't quite as linear as I made it out to be." He looked away, and then said, "Can you see anything unusual about my right eye?"

Sarah looked at it in concern. She extracted a tissue from her shoulder bag.

"Not dirt –" Brenton said, "– the eye itself."

Peering more closely, she detected the slight indentation on the circumference of his pupil.

"You see," he continued, "Three years after I got married, during a pre-flight check in the cockpit, the spring holding an adjustable air-conditioning nozzle fractured and a small segment entered my right eye. Surgery was unable to correct the damage. Although, maybe I should qualify that. The sight in the damaged eye is adequate for what I do today. In that regard the operations were a success, but not quite good enough for a flying career. So there I was – twenty-seven years of age, and grounded. Everything I believed in, and stood for, and held precious, had been taken from me." He took a deep breath and shook his head. "And two years before that my parents had been killed in a car crash on the M4." Sarah reached for his hands and clasped them. "I muddled through it as best I could, and my flying duties kept me on an even keel. But with the order to stand down, I didn't even have that – just a wife who was relieved that I wasn't involved in that 'silly business' any more."

He observed Sarah's anxious countenance; she now bore title to his sorrows and his joys. "I hope all this fuss doesn't appal you," he said self-consciously.

Sarah bent forward. "David, darling, let me be the judge of my ability to understand."

He leaned forward as well. "You're not just a pretty face, are you?"

Sarah's spontaneous laugh crinkled her eyes and in the dim lighting her teeth sparkled.

"Sarah," he said, reaching for her hand. "I love you – totally and completely."

Sarah placed her free hand over the clasped hands and said, "To hear you say that makes me wonderfully happy."

They stayed like that for some time, intently drinking one another in and amazed at the irrefutable emotion that had enveloped them.

It was dark outside when they got round to ordering coffee. They went over the subsequent turns in his career. Moscow, London and Croydon. His move to the security service, and then his divorce. He wondered why it had previously been such an impossible subject to broach. Talking it over with Sarah it seemed much less forbidding, if not actually mundane. The mistake had been his inability to detect the incompatibilities in the first instance. So what had been the impediment to rehabilitation?

"David," Sarah entreated, "You're inclined to be hard on those around you. It may be because you are so very hard on yourself. Driving yourself so relentlessly also begs the question – why?"

This time Sarah reached for Brenton's hand, which she held across the table. "Nobody's perfect, David. We're all human. Some mistakes are greater than others, and we feel a corresponding increase in remorse, but remember: sometimes the ability to say sorry, or to forgive, is overshadowed by an inability to forgive oneself." She squeezed his hand comfortingly. "Let the past take its own position in the sequence of things," she continued. "Don't try and distort its significance by insisting on its presence in the here and now; and most of all – try and forgive yourself."

Brenton braced himself for the mandatory prickle that would normally have taken hold of him. In the event nothing happened. And then, he felt the relief within and about himself. He was free. No further need for the guarded stance. His ghosts were retreating into their past. He raised Sarah's hands to his lips and gently kissed each hand. She was the conduit through which he would be enabled to redeem himself.

When his father and mother died, two thirds of his family had been removed from life. He had cursed his position as an only child. The sorrow and loss had been quite unbearable. Had he had brothers and sisters the burden might have been in some way diluted. As it was, the event condensed into something that seemed eager to consume him from the inside out. Maybe it had consumed some part of him. With his new shift in emotional perspective, he could see that now.

To this day, he could still recall precisely what he had been doing when news of the motorway accident was brought to him.

Brenton's calm earnestness reassured Sarah and she brightened. He sensed her response and continued, "I've been stagnating for years, without realising it. Yet, within me I've carried this niggling awareness that something was wrong. I won't pretend that the change completely hinged on you. What I am saying is – the change would be incomplete without you. It's like the curtain going up on a first night: excitement, anticipation, and a new experience. Thanks to you, I've been enabled to see my previous drudgery in a more perceptive light."

But Brenton also knew he was being torn in two: his feelings for Sarah on the one hand, and his apprehension about the Royal Albert Hall on the other. "After the event we shall have ample time to sort these things out at our leisure."

So earnest had the exchanges been that neither of them noticed the uniformed presence moving inquisitively from table to table until the constable stood directly over them.

"Excuse me, sir," he addressed Brenton. "I'm looking for a Mr David Brenton."

"That's me," Brenton acknowledged. The young policeman asked for identification. Satisfied, he then said he had information he wished to pass on – in confidence. Brenton introduced Sarah as his assistant. The constable responded with a request to give the information in the presence of another constable in the police car outside. The encounter, not unnaturally, attracted attention, much to Sarah's embarrassment. As the trio moved through the pub towards the main door, she noted a smug expression on the middle-aged waitress' face and knew they'd probably be watching with glee as she sat into the police car.

"I'm Peter Braithwaith, and this is PC Ken Wrotham," the constable indicated his driver. "Do you know, or know of, a Madame Maria Wohlicka?"

"What's happened?" Brenton responded sharply. Then more calmly, he affirmed, "Yes, of course I know Maria Wohlicka. What's the problem?"

"No problem that we know of," the PC said blandly, and then explained that the order to deliver the message had come from 'pretty high up', and notwithstanding its seemingly innocuous content, was to be treated and delivered with the utmost haste and care. He took conspiratorial satisfaction in disclosing that Special Branch had supplied their whereabouts.

"And Madame Wohlicka went to extraordinary lengths, sir, to ensure that this message should reach you."

The message was indeed simple. She had said that she would not attend the morning run-through at the Royal Albert Hall, but would definitely play the concert.

"Does that make sense, sir?" the PC asked.

Brenton was lost in the imponderables and did not answer.

"At least we know she'll be there," Sarah said.

"You're right," Brenton admitted, "we now know she's all right."

CHAPTER 24

Saturday March 28th 1981
RAF Biggin Hill
6.00 am

Saturday morning, grey and overcast, began with sullen reluctance, and Brenton had to reach for his watch to determine that a new day had indeed dawned. While he had slept well, it had taken him a good while to get off to sleep. Downstairs he had breakfast with Sarah. They both had a preoccupied air, focused as they were on the important events taking place later in the day. Brenton reminded Sarah in as jocular a fashion as he could muster, "You're my number one priority."

At the Albert Hall they were met by Adam Fuller of the BBC. Brenton and Sarah had both been to the Albert Hall on previous occasions, but as members of an audience. Now their appraisals were professional and, not surprisingly, Symphony Hall suffered by comparison.

Brenton, Sarah and Fuller surveyed the empty auditorium from the stage. The stillness was somehow imbued with its own sense of occasion and triggered quite different thoughts in each of the beholders. Adam Fuller elaborated on the efforts in recent times to provide more precise acoustics in the building. Brenton's eyes had been drawn to the two boxes to the right in which the VIPs would be seated that evening. He had a strong urge to stand within the sections of the orchestra to see their potential, but knew he would have to wait until the seating was laid out. The centre floor of the Hall, the promenade, was also without seats. This area extended right up to within eight feet of the stage. This was Pecton's express wish. It would effect a direct comparison with the Promenade Concerts held there annually, Pecton had reasoned, and hopefully open the way to Croydon's future participation in that prestigious event. Their preoccupations were cut short by a growing level of activity off stage, which suddenly erupted on stage when orchestral attendants bustled forward carrying chairs and music stands. Brenton asked Fuller to bring Sarah and Sherry upstairs and show them the facility and their functions in the evening's concert. He needed to inspect the stage area at close quarters; while doing this Cranshaw appeared. The librarian hurried across stage with as serious a countenance as Brenton had ever remembered. "David," he said briskly, "I'd like you to meet our two bandsmen." A new, more serious Cranshaw was apparent; or maybe he was just filled with the same apprehensions currently gripping Brenton.

On the way to the changing rooms Cranshaw told Brenton that the Ministry of Defence had given the ok for the bandsmen's temporary transfer. They had been chosen more for their martial capabilities than their musical gifts. "And quite right too," Brenton accepted, the criminal intent long having overtaken the musical occasion.

Inside the otherwise empty room stood two obvious military types. Apart from their erect bearing, the shine on their shoes almost blinded.

"Sergeant Williams, Corporal Pringle ... Wing Commander Brenton," Cranshaw introduced. They shook hands. Brenton thanked them for volunteering and warned that the necessity to carry arms indicated the gravity of the event. Sgt Williams explained that Capt Cranshaw had already filled them in on the general background, and both he and Cpl Pringle were delighted to be allowed the opportunity to assist. Not because of the seriousness of the intended crime, but more particularly because it was to take place within their field of operation, so to speak. They were anxious to prove themselves.

Cranshaw had already formally sworn them in. Now Brenton briefly set out their duties. Because of their possible proximity to the source of attack, Brenton asked Williams and Pringle to attend a final meeting for arrangements during the afternoon. In the meantime they were to attend rehearsals in their capacity as musicians – with a watching brief only. "And by the way, it's Mr Brenton for the duration of the concert."

The door swung open and two early arrivals entered. They were both Poles. Stanislaw Reptarski, bassoon, and Jerzy Kazimierz, percussion. Brenton allowed Cranshaw to make introductions. Kazimierz showed immediate interest, which was not surprising: he would have Williams and Pringle working alongside him during the final work of the evening. Reptarski was less cordial, but as a member of the woodwind section he did not have the same professional interest in the two transitory percussionists. Further musicians trickled on stage.

Brenton excused himself and left the integration of the bandsmen to Cranshaw.

———

Backstage a room had been set aside for Appleby, Cranshaw and Miss Maybury. Despite the intrusion of Cranshaw's large wicker baskets containing all the orchestral music scores, the room comfortably accommodated the trio at three separate desks.

The arrangement did not provide for any degree of privacy, nor was any expected, because thirteen hours was to be the maximum any of them would avail of the facility. Miss Maybury would not take possession of her desk until late afternoon. Before that, she would accompany Pecton to Heathrow, where the guest of honour, Anton Uginski, was expected at noon. They would not be alone. Apart from well wishers from the fields of music, politics and the Foreign Office, there would also be representation from the security service and Special Branch – both overt and covert; and maybe even an MI6 stringer.

———

Brenton located the office, with Quentin Appleby already in situ. He was sitting behind a desk facing the open door at the other end of the room.

"David!" Appleby said, endeavouring to conceal surprise. Brenton stood in the open doorway holding the door handle. The orchestra manager seemed to have difficulty in focusing on Brenton, which was explained when he suddenly said, "Have you met Witold Lutowicz?" and pointed to the other side of the open door. Lutowicz stepped from behind the door and extended his hand.

"David Brenton," Appleby introduced. "Our recording engineer."

Brenton shook hands and knew the man had never experienced a hard day's work in his life. Everything had been nice and easy for Mr Lutowicz, a combination of characteristics at odds with the rest of his physical appearance.

"Mr Lutowicz," Appleby went on, "is the intermediary between Croydon and the Polish embassy. Indeed, without Mr Lutowicz's assistance, tonight's concert might not have happened."

"Indeed," said Brenton, and then asked, "You in the music business?"

Appleby once again explained that if Mr Lutowicz was not in the music business before, he certainly was now.

Brenton asked, "Does he speak English?"

Appleby swallowed a further explanation. Lutowicz closed the door behind Brenton and with a heavy accent said, "A little."

Brenton thought the closing of the door very proprietorial. It confirmed information he had received that morning in Biggin Hill from Frank Hempson. Leaving Lutowicz with his back to the door Brenton walked to Appelby's desk.

"But surely that presents an incredible impediment in communications?" he artlessly suggested.

"It might," Appleby said affably, "were it not for the fact that I possess a smattering of Polish."

Brenton hoped the acquisition of this nugget did not show on his face. "Excellent," he said blandly. "Always considered you a man of many talents."

He knew he was looking at the author of the Polish instructions on tape. It was a gut feeling, aided and abetted by the knowledge that while it had been impossible to decipher the voice on tape, there was no denying its affability.

"There is one slight hiccup you'll have to contend with this morning," Appleby continued. "Maria Wohlicka is temporarily indisposed and shall not be available for the run-through."

Brenton expressed concern, to which Appleby made soothing reassurance. "Everything will be fine," he said, smoothing out the papers on the desk in front of him. "Possibly some slight woman's malady," he mumbled apologetically.

Brenton went on to explain that he would need a stand-in pianist to play part of the Chopin, for a balance. "It's going live to Poland, you see."

Appleby readily agreed and, glancing past Brenton, suggested they might get the Polish embassy to pay for it. Lutowicz shifted his body position uneasily. His shoes made dissenting squeaks on the linoleum floor. Which beat an uninhibited tattoo in Brenton's mind. 'Crepe soles!' He held Appleby's attention until the position on Maria Wohlicka's stand-in had been settled. Then, nonchalantly, he took his departure. On the way out he observed Lutowicz's crepe-soled brothel creepers, and reckoned, with their owner, their combined contribution to music in Britain had been an eerie nocturne in St George's followed by *Sturm und Drang* in Sarah's flat. Things were coming together.

Outside, he endeavoured to find Cranshaw as speedily as possible. He made contact on stage where Kazimierz had taken the two bandsmen to see the Kilar music score and receive their percussion instruments. He hustled Cranshaw off stage and upstairs where he revealed his convictions about Appleby and Lutowicz. Frank Hempson's early morning call to Biggin Hill had set the train rolling. Lutowicz's watcher had communicated that wherever Lutowicz went, so too went Appleby, including overnights in the same hotel on the Cromwell Road in which the entire Polish group stayed. Brenton knew this to be out of the ordinary for Appleby, who never strayed far from his family home in Croydon. There was nothing yet to link this duo to Thompson's murder, apart from proximity, which of itself was a promising indication. What disturbed were the possibilities. Brenton mentally gave himself a shake and asked Cranshaw where the nearest public telephone was.

It was not difficult to find 'Lesko' in the phone book. It was the only 'Lesko' listed, and in case there remained a residue of doubt, it gave both names – Jack and Ada. It was interesting to see Jan Lesko had succumbed to pressure of usage and become Jack, at least for the telephone. Why risk deflecting a possible gig for the sake of a name.

Lesko answered after three rings.

"Jack? ... David Brenton here."

Brenton thought he heard an intake of breath. "Yes?"

"I wish to enlist your assistance, Jack." Brenton paused, but there was no response. In this instance however, he was not seeking information, he was trying to sell it. "It concerns Komorski and company," he took up smoothly. "If I can persuade you to help, it'll enable you to take a swipe at our visitors."

"What's up David? I smell trouble from here."

"You're right, there is trouble. I should have listened more attentively to you when I went out to Bromley. Everything seems to be happening as you said it would. I want your help on a particular job, which I promise you will warm the cockles of your Polish heart.

"Has this anything to do with Appleby or Pecton?"

"I would consider Appleby and Pecton on the opposing side, Jack."

The Pole mumbled a reflective "good," and Brenton knew he was home, if not actually dry. The remaining obstacle was to persuade Lesko of the absolute necessity for secrecy until later that night. Then Ada would have to be told. To participate, Lesko must have the use of his car.

"I must ask one question," Lesko persisted.

Brenton did not relish a withdrawal from a point of near acceptance. "Ok, shoot," he said, endeavouring to control his exasperation. Lesko cleared his throat and asked, "Is this some anti-communist thing?" Brenton's palpable relief needed readjustment time, and then he said, "Yes. Yes, it is."

"Count me in," Lesko said unhesitatingly.

"Jack," Brenton said with revived spirit. "If you go to your front door you'll see a Mini parked across the road from your house. If you peer a little closer you'll quite possibly see the cretin behind the driving wheel is smoking. His name is Chisholme. Tell him David Brenton wishes to speak to him on your telephone."

"David, this is like some …" Lesko's voice petered out.

"Yes, I know," Brenton muttered. "When you speak to Chisholme you'll realise that Britain could only have become Great with God's help, so we're on a winning wicket." Brenton heard the handset placed gently on the hall table, and the hall door opened.

After what seemed a lengthy interval, he heard voices approach the hallway. Lesko was saying: "I assure you, it's David Brenton, and he does wish to speak to you." Chisholme lifted the phone and after a neutral "Hello," asked incredulously from the corner of his mouth, "What the fuck's going on?"

"Ok Chisholme, calm down. There's been a change of order for you."

"Says who?"

"Says I, sweetheart. And just in case I detect your usual indolence, I warn you – I shall say everything just once. I don't have time for explanations."

"This is highly irregular," Chisholme grumbled, casting a jaundiced eye over his shoulder at Lesko's baffled face.

"Hempson will know all about it as soon as you hang up."

"Oh, so he doesn't …"

"Shut up Chisholme and listen. Go to Gower Street and fix yourself up with a press pass. Get over here to the Albert Hall; report to Cranshaw. You're covering the background to this concert as a press stringer. The man in your sights is Quentin Appleby, the orchestra manager –"

"Hold it," Chisholme cried, flustered and irritated. "Give me that moniker again."

Brenton spelled out the name. "Chisholme," he warned, "We have until TONIGHT to get this right. I want to see you over here in one hour. Put Lesko back on and move!" He placed a hand over the telephone and turned to Cranshaw. "He'll link up with whoever is looking after Lutowicz. One inside – the other outside with wheels. Go and prepare the way for Chisholme backstage, in case somebody thinks it a sudden imposition."

As Brenton began to speak to Lesko, the finishing touches of an orchestral tune-up faded to a satisfied expectancy, which was fulfilled when Komorski came on stage accompanied by Appleby.

Appleby's appearance before the run-through lent weight to rumours that had held the orchestra's attention since Friday. They concerned Maria Wohlicka's state of health. The stories ranged from the bizarre to the quaint, depending on the disposition of the individual member; in the absence of any hard evidence, the possibility of an official explanation was keenly awaited.

Appleby stood on the podium and welcomed them all to the Royal Albert Hall.

"Madame Wohlicka is temporarily indisposed. That means –" he raised his hand to stifle a growing level of querulous sound, "– that means we shall not run Chopin this morning. Instead, a stand-in will provide a few bars from each movement for a microphone balance. If this is undertaken at the end of this morning's rehearsal, it will mean the piano is in position for tonight – when Madame Wohlicka will join us for the first part of the concert. Thank you for your patience," he diplomatically added and left the stage to Komorski.

The offhandedness of Appleby's explanation was convincing and almost placatory. After all, if the lady was definitely joining them for the concert, her affliction could only be minor and transient.

Ronald Shipsey took his place at the console of the Willis organ and, looking very small in comparison, gazed down nervously at Komorski to await events. The maestro raised his arms and launched into the programme run-through.

Elgar's *Polonia* did the honours and rang out across the empty floor of the promenade, up the elliptical ranks of the amphitheatre seats; into the first level boxes; above them the ten-seat boxes; and above that again the five-seaters; over which tiered the 1,783 seats of the balcony; and finally into the picture gallery which at this highest seating point in the building, also accommodated the BBC Broadcasting Suite.

Inside the control room Adam Fuller was startled to hear a sudden burst of electronic static on the control room speakers. He had only set about pulling a sound together when the short crackling intrusion sent a shiver of apprehension through him. He put his assemblage on hold and awaited a further burst of static. Nothing happened. This was the worst possible scenario for a studio manager. The rehearsal run-through had begun and he had received the first instalment on an intermittent fault account. Depending on what he heard in the following minutes, he would have to decide whether to restart the balance or initiate a methodical pursuit of the fault. Fuller looked anxiously at Sarah and Sherry for confirmation that he had heard correctly. They nodded their heads in agreement. But Sarah realised that this was the same noise she had picked up in Croydon, this time without the voice. "May I put on a tape?" she asked Fuller. "Yes, do," he said almost absentmindedly, still preoccupied with the possibility of a further burst. She slapped on a tape and told Fuller that Brenton had had similar problems during the week in Croydon.

"I'll find him and maybe he can explain," she said reassuringly, and left the control room.

She found Appleby and Cranshaw backstage standing side by side at the entrance door to the stage. The door was opened fractionally to give a visual, and Appleby was directing Cranshaw to return to the office in case of phone calls. Sarah asked Cranshaw to check for the Kilar music score because it had not arrived upstairs. On the way to the office she intimated that the Kilar reference was just a ploy. In fact she was desperately trying to locate Brenton because the two-way radio interference had re-started.

He took her to where he had last spoken to Brenton – but he was not there. They entered the auditorium from one of the side aisles and surveyed the lower seats without success; but Brenton saw them from a higher position opposite in one of the five-seater third level boxes. He also caught on to their anxiety and correctly guessed he was the reason for their foray. Slipping noiselessly out from the box, he made a spurt along the circular corridor to intercept them.

Sarah unburdened the control room episode, which took Brenton by surprise. On the other hand, why should they not transmit? It proved they were still oblivious to their detection and further supported Brenton's views that the trigger man was nervous and in need of support. More ominously, it signalled the job was still on.

"It's curious nothing was said during the transmission," Sarah said, giving vent to an aspect of the happening which had lain further down her priority list.

"Could have been a mistake," Brenton considered, "Could have been placing the radio in a pocket, and accidentally touched the 'speak' button. Could have been any one of such a large number of things that to try and follow it up now would take a disproportionate amount of time. I'm very glad you had the presence of mind to put on a tape," he said directly to Sarah.

"What I've got to do now", he addressed them both, "is reassure our friend Fuller that it is not a fault on his system. I'll say the police are checking out the Hall."

"In Polish?" Cranshaw wondered.

"Ok," Brenton acknowledged. "Working with Polish security."

Brenton asked was there any way Cranshaw could shadow Appleby. Cranshaw pointed out that his boss had asked him to stay in the office in case of phone calls.

"He would," Brenton said, annoyed. "Chisholme won't surface here until noon. Look, do the best you can, Tim. In the meantime I've got to get upstairs to reassure Fuller and make sure we get everything on tape."

He stopped in his move upstairs and turned back to Cranshaw. "I think we'd better have an officer up to Fuller to impress upon him the necessity for a tight mouth on what he may hear. "Can you arrange that from your office?"

———

As Brenton and Sarah returned to the gallery the nearest police officers were impatiently standing outside the Albert Hall and alongside Quentin Appleby's car. They were Det Insp Blackmore and PC James.

"Don't break the bloody window!" Blackmore growled, and grabbed the young constable's resourceful elbow.

"I thought you said –" PC James raised questioning eyebrows in the direction of Appleby's car, and then desisted.

Blackmore released James' elbow and considered him for a moment. He was torn between gratification at the constable's eagerness to please, and affront at his willingness to compromise. Righteousness won – easily.

"What I say and what I do – are two quite separate issues, lad." He adjusted his chin and added, "If I ever come across a move like that again – you're a goner!"

PC James shifted uneasily. To cover his embarrassment he fell back on tradition and clasped his hands behind his back. "Sorry sir," he proffered. "I thought we were into beating them at their own game."

"Their game is crime, lad," Blackmore rasped an emphasis on 'game' as if it bore some other more distasteful connotation. "If we go down that road, we throw out every civilised rule we have from the beginning. And worse still – we descend to their level." He rose fractionally on the balls of his toes to further remove that possibility. "If we descend to their level, we're no better than they are – criminal."

"So what do we do now, if we can't get into the car?" PC James asked.

Blackmore's chin shot a defiant protrusion into the Kensington air. "We wait," he said.

'We wait' seemed anti-climatic after the great pronouncement – almost ineffectual. But what he had on his side was time, unlike the shower in the Hall. If they didn't get it right tonight, they were damned. And in his case – and it was his case – patience was a virtue.

They had walked some distance from the car and were on the point of returning, when Blackmore's hand shot out and brought PC James to a halt beside him. He manoeuvred James and himself between two parked cars and then peered back towards Appleby's car.

"What's the problem, sir?" the constable asked, looking alternately from Blackmore to the parked car. He then saw a man approach and fiddle with the door key. "Our Mr Appleby?" he suggested, both pairs of eyes now firmly latched on the figure. With unrestrained satisfaction, Blackmore replied, "Our Mr Lutowicz."

Lutowicz's persistence paid off. He succeeded in opening the car door and slid in behind the wheel.

"Do we nab him?" James asked, preparing to do the twenty or so metres in record time.

"No!" Blackmore shot back, resting his hands on the bonnet of the car in front of him and squinting forward through the car windows.

Lutowicz started the engine and began to edge the car out from the parking space.

"Now!" Blackmore said, and started to saunter up the road. He was in time to present an imperturbable obstacle to the car's further progress.

"Ah, Mr Lutowicz," He waved in greeting through the windscreen at the surprised Pole behind the wheel. At the driver's window he shoved in his craggy face and, tutt-tutting amiably, pointed out, "And without your driving belt in place, sir."

"Yes," the SB man said, returning the smile and clicking the seat belt into position. "I go to Heathrow. I greet Comrade Minister Uginski."

Blackmore dropped the civility, straightened up and said, "May I see your insurance, sir?"

Lutowicz weakly repeated the question. Blackmore emitted an irritable rumble. "No, Mr Lutowicz, you may not see my insurance, but I demand to see yours."

The Pole looked behind Blackmore to PC James in the forlorn hope of a more sympathetic reaction from the uniformed presence, only to receive a blank non-committal stare. "I will see Mr Appleby," Lutowicz offered.

"Not interested in Mr Appleby," Blackmore shook his head.

"But this is Mr Appleby's car," Lutowicz protested.

Blackmore stepped back from the car door and with a mechanical delivery born of a durable repetitiveness said, "I see," and almost with the same breath, "Please step from the car Mr Lutowicz." Lutowicz became angry at the indignity. With the intention of returning to the sanctuary of the Albert Hall, he stepped from the car, but PC James cut off his route there. Blackmore waved towards the back seat of the car and suggested they both sit there and allow the constable to drive. Lutowicz misinterpreted this as an offer to be driven to Heathrow, and obliged.

The trio set out for a location Blackmore referred to as "The Yard."

CHAPTER 25

Saturday March 28th 1981
Croydon
11.00 am

Betty Fenwick had a natural talent on the keyboard – of the word processor variety. Her facility insured a steady demand for her expertise with a corresponding and gratifying increase in her overtime. Today was the second consecutive Saturday Betty had worked overtime at her branch office in the British and Continental Properties Insurance Company. It had been the same the previous year, due to the end of the financial year or some such.

Betty's dexterity had a compensatory dimension. While her fingers performed enviable cadenzas on the keyboard, her mind was able to dwell on the infinitely more pressing trifles that preoccupied her young life. She didn't mind the extra hours in the least. The money went a long way towards making her annual holiday in Benidorm the exhausting success it usually was. There was still a long way to go before August set her free to lie on the beach with the merry abandon she had become accustomed to. God, they were a fun crowd. She smiled in remembrance, and anticipation, perhaps for the first time in a few days. That murder outside the office during the week had disgusted her. And that prat Jeremy Trusworth didn't help either with his graphic details. Silly ass. Perverted, that's what! She'd seen the evil glint in his eyes as he pranced around the office with his gory details. She had insisted on turning her desk. She now sat with her back to the offending thing, as she afterwards referred to the telephone kiosk. It wasn't as if she enjoyed sitting with her back to the passing parade. She had enjoyed watching people through the window. The other typists had bitched about the change because everyone had had to move a little. You'd think she actually enjoyed her new position. She didn't. But honestly, some people had no feelings. She had thought about changing her job, and she just might too – after August. The only thing to come out of this whole episode and give some pleasure was her talisman. She still couldn't fathom why she had become so attached to it. It wasn't attachment like she felt for her succession of boyfriends. It was more a feeling of reverence. Like a feeling you had for a relic.

It had smacked down on her desk out of the brass lampshade. Apart from the 'ping' heralding its arrival, the proof that it had come from the shade was the heat the little brass object had held for a time after its arrival. She thought its shape attractive, like a tiny beehive. It hadn't warded off the disgusting murder, but then it may have guarded her in some other more secret way. She owed it something. What exactly, she wasn't sure. Possibly allegiance. She kept it in her purse, beside a photograph of Simon Le Bon.

That evening, the evening the murder had happened in the 'thing', they had been asked to remain inside in the office until the body had been removed by ambulance. It had seemed to her at the time that they had taken their time about it, but why should she worry about that, she was being paid for the extra time. The heating in the building had been stifling. After tea she had opened her window, so when the excitement started outside, they were able to hear as well as see everything. In fact they had been in on it from before the start, because it was Jeremy who'd discovered it. He'd actually gone over to the 'thing' and looked in! He'd glided back through the office door like the master of ceremonies in a funeral home and made his gulping phone call to the police. And then he'd started to throw his weight about with the gory details. How could he be so bloody childish? Take her talisman, for instance. Anyone else would have thrown it in the bin. She had seen it and cherished it. What she really would like to do was attach it on a gold chain and hang it around her neck.

When Jeremy next paraded through the office, she called him over and, placing the talisman on top of her screen, said, "Do you see that Jeremy?" Jeremy's eyes opened wide and he nodded his head in astonishment. Maybe Jeremy was a kindred spirit after all. "Where did you get that?" he asked disbelievingly, his mouth never quite closing.

"Never you mind where I got it," Betty replied, quite pleased with the reaction her talisman had provoked. "All that need concern you is that it's mine."

Jeremy's eyes darted between the object and Betty's self-satisfied expression. Before he was given an opportunity to pursue the point, Betty retold how her mascot had 'pinged' in the lampshade over her head and dropped onto her desk. Jeremy, whose aptitude in space relations equalled Betty's keyboard facility, noticed the dint on the street side of the lamp-shade, the open window in line, and the phone booth beyond.

"Jesus Christ!" he exploded. "That's the bullet that went through the man's head!"

The shriek that rent the air brought the British and Continental Properties Insurance Company to a halt for the second time in a week. Jeremy explained to their supervisor the direct cause of the flap. Betty was beyond explaining anything. So distraught was she that she immediately dispensed with her purse – Simon Le Bon notwithstanding – and went on a hand-washing binge to eradicate the 'debris' she had chipped from her talisman.

The police arrived and collected the bullet, which Jeremy had considerately thought to place in an envelope with a cellophane window.

———

The first phone call on Cranshaw's return to the office came from Lutowicz, who asked to speak to Appleby urgently. When Appleby took the call, for the first time Cranshaw saw uncomfortable anxiety on the manager's face. Appleby waved him out of the office with uncharacteristic impatience, and as he stood outside with his ear close to the door, all he could hear from inside were mumbled monosyllables. He withdrew his ear in the nick of time. The door whipped open and Appleby stood intimidatingly in the doorway. He may have mistaken Cranshaw's embarrassed countenance for hurt pride because he shuffled self-consciously and apologised.

"Look, er –" he began, regaining a modicum of his normal composure. "I've been landed with a rather tricky situation."

Two members of the Hall staff walked past engrossed in animated debate on the weekend's football fixtures.

"Come in, come in," Appleby stepped aside and invited Cranshaw back into his own office. Cranshaw walked straight to his desk and sat down. Appleby proceeded to pace the room, deep in thought. Eventually he stopped in front of Cranshaw's desk. "I've got caught up in something incredibly silly, Tim."

Cranshaw's stomach gave a lurch. This sounded like the tip of a comprehensive confession. "Mmm." Wishing to encourage the process, he added, "Is there anything I can do to help?"

Appleby said, "Perhaps there is." He unfolded the saga of Lutowicz and the car he had lent him to go to Heathrow. With the aid of his diplomatic status, Lutowicz had managed to get himself released and was on his way to the Polish embassy instead of Heathrow to meet Uginski – without Appleby's car. As a result, the problem that presented itself to Appleby was the continued and unofficial incarceration of his car.

"Could you", Appleby entreated, "go and retrieve the car for me?"

This was not the kind of help Cranshaw had envisaged, and maybe the quandary appeared on his face.

"I can't move from here," Appleby morosely went on, "and you do have open insurance. I've heard you say so," he insisted, cutting off a possible point of retreat.

"I'd love to," Cranshaw arranged his features into polite regret, "but I also have a lot to contend with – including that chap from the press," he suddenly remembered. "He'll be along shortly."

"I'll look after that," Appleby replied. "I'll look after everything," he added expansively. Cranshaw's phone rang in deliverance. He snapped it up and entered into serious discussion with Boosey and Hawks on the woodwind requirements for a work that Croydon were to perform in four weeks' time. Appleby heaved a disconsolate sigh, which was interrupted by a knock on the door. Kazimierz, the Polish percussionist, stuck his head in and seeing Appleby with nothing better to do than nurse a sullen expression, brought the rest of his body with him and parked the lot in front of his manager's desk.

"This cowbell is cracked," he said, tossing the bell onto the desk. Appleby's resentment was transparent. He looked at the instrument with obvious disdain and then at its guardian with equal candour. "Remove that from my desk!" he snapped. "What do you expect me to do, whip up super glue?"

Kazimierz realised he had failed to pick up on Appleby's mood, and hastened to explain that it was needed for the final work – the Kilar. One of the two extras would use it. Kazimierz stared stolidly at Appleby. To say another word would make it more difficult. He picked up the cowbell and waited. Appleby calmed down and heaved another sigh. He looked across to where Cranshaw was still engrossed on the phone and returned to Kazimierz with soulful resignation.

"What's called for?" he asked.

Kazimierz rattled off: "'Songali, sheep bells, triangoli, crotali, cencerros, *campanelli da messa*."

"What's that last item?" Appleby asked.

Kazimierz explained that they were small bells used at Mass.

"Why don't you go down to Brompton Oratory," suggested Appleby, "at the end of the road, and borrow theirs?"

Kazimierz made a grunting laugh. "Are you serious?"

"You're a Catholic, aren't you?"

Kazimierz was not sure what way to take this. In the end he said, "I am nothing."

"Nobody's nothing," Appleby chided. "Everybody's something."

Kazimierz decided that a rephrasing of his answer was allowable. "I have no religion."

"Ah, that's quite different," Appleby said pedantically.

"Why don't *you* go," Kazimierz suggested.

Appleby sighed once again. The human spirit's ability to sustain old gods, and when these were swept away, institute new ones like Marx, Lenin and the monster Stalin, was indefatigable. He looked across his desk at Kazimierz and wondered if indeed he was immune to this.

Apart from all philosophical considerations, it did look as if chance had just provided him with an opportunity to get away from this place. He should grab it. "I will take a turn around Brompton Oratory and get you your *campanelli da messa*," he announced to Kazimierz with the revived spirit of someone given a reprieve.

Kazimierz sloped towards the door with an indifferent shrug of his shoulders. Cranshaw grabbed his phone and hastily dialled a number.

"Tim," said Appleby, "I'm going down to Brompton Oratory to get a mass bell for that dullard Kazimierz."

"Capital!" said Cranshaw, with what Appleby considered uncalled-for enthusiasm, "I'll hold the fort."

Appleby was glad to leave the Albert Hall behind him. He would try and forget the bind he was in, and instead absorb the uncomplicated energy of early spring.

All around him Londoners went unknowingly about their business. The further he progressed and drank it in, the more the contrast hurt. Did he really have the right to walk amongst the population he was betraying? He had no stomach for the poppycock Lutowicz spouted in his rare moments of reflection. Lutowicz was not someone to be trifled with. He could not bear to think of the horror and upset he would cause if Lutowicz were to do what he had threatened to do. He felt extraordinary shame because he had joined in and taken part in those photographs, and the other stuff, with Lutowicz and his girlfriends.

He descended onto Prince Consort Road, and crossed over into Exhibition Road. It was a fifteen-minute walk, but at Appleby's slow pace – twenty to twenty-five. He took in the diversity of pedestrians: fathers, mothers, brothers, sisters and lovers.

He stopped outside Brompton Oratory, reluctant to enter. It was a much larger building than he had anticipated. He had never stood outside it before, never mind contemplated going in. He continued standing until he saw that there was a constant trickle of people going in and coming out. He mounted the steps and went inside.

The interior was covered in marble, and like the outside façade, the style was Italianate Baroque. At first he hardly dared look around but a sudden burst of choral polyphony dissipated his inhibitions. A mixed choir was gathered around an organ console on a recessed balcony halfway down the church on the right-hand side. He entered a pew and sat down. The seats were facing down the nave of the church, so he had to move to his left in order to see more fully the choir and their location. They stopped almost as soon as they had started, the organist cutting them short with a brisk, precise gesture. This happened several times in quick succession. Obviously, there was no service in progress, and the choir was in rehearsal. There was a fair amount of movement in the body of the church. He leaned out into the aisle and asked an elderly lady for directions to the priest's office. The lady pointed towards a door at the top of the church.

———

He made his way up the church and turned into a side aisle, at the end of which he knocked on the door. He had begun to feel nervous again and wondered had he been misdirected, when the door opened slowly and a tired elderly man said, "Yes?"

"My name is Quentin Appleby," he introduced himself, and then stated his reason for being there. The sacristan shook his head slowly and looked doubtful. "But you'd better come in." He stood aside and indicated the other man in the room. "Have a word with Father Welton."

Fr Welton sat at a long desk to one side of the room. He was going through marriage lists. Appleby once again introduced himself and explained his purpose.

"My word," said Fr Welton, "A rather unusual requirement, what?" The priest laughed and added, "But far be it from us to stand in the way of culture. Let's see what can be done."

Even the sacristan, taking his cue from the priest's reaction, managed a creaking smile. Fr Welton placed a marker between the pages of the large entry book and closed it. He then asked his sacristan what they had in the way of mass bells. "Three or four," he was told. The press door beside the sacristy door was then opened.

"Three collections of bells and a gong," the sacristan corrected, peering in.

Appleby ruled out the gong straight away. Its sombre tone would not have carried within the fortissimo of the finale.

"This is the bell we use," the sacristan said, "so that rules it out."

Appleby looked in across his shoulder and chose the one that had five small bells, arranged in a circle. He rang it vigorously and nodded his head.

The transaction had been uncomplicated and generous. In response he offered tickets to the concert, which the sacristan declined because of the lateness of the event, and Fr Welton because of a prior engagement. "Some of the choir should be delighted," he said, and propped the envelope against a small crucifix on the robing table.

———

Appleby retraced his steps through the church. He was glad the sacristan had thought to cover the bell in a plastic bag. As he neared the balcony, the choir began to sing a *Sanctus*. It was so immediately appealing, that he stopped and placed his hand on the end of a pew. The sound not just filled the church, it seemed to gather in allusive eddying waves and flutter about his person. He lifted his head to breath it in. In order to catch sight of the singers he moved to the other side and sat down. Their rapt young faces converged on the energetic form of the conductor. The last time he had felt like this about music was ... No, he couldn't remember.

He looked around. There was something here that hinted at an older England than the pragmatic one he was familiar with. The old persuasion at prayer. His head fell back to catch the ethereal close of the section. It had had a drowsy, beckoning effect. Its transcendence gave him momentary freedom from the hunted feeling that accompanied him always now, and he breathed a deep contented sigh of relief. It didn't last.

The sudden sharp clap of the conductor's hands brought the music to a halt. Appleby was instantly reminded of a similar sound. He had been standing beside his car, down from Symphony Hall Croydon, awaiting Lutowicz's return. He had heard this same sound and then Lutowicz had rushed up, jumped in the car, and ordered him to drive.

A short distance from the Hall, the SB man had pulled a small handgun from his overcoat pocket and stuffed into the back of the glove compartment. The smell of cordite had made his eyes blink and his mind blank. He asked no questions. Subsequent events surrounding the telephone booth meant he did not have to.

The gun! The car! The connection hit him with devastating suddenness. Lutowicz's gun was still in his car. The car that was at present in police custody. "Oh no," he groaned. He had spent so much time in Lutowicz's company recently. But he had not had the presence of mind to ask the Pole to remove the gun. Lutowicz might not have liked that request – but anything was better than the predicament he found himself in now. Maybe Lutowicz had removed the gun? He found the uncertainties unbearable. The bag bearing the bells dropped to the ground with a muffled tingle, and he buried his head in his hands. Why did he get involved in this? Why? That sex-mad bastard Lutowicz!

Appleby strode back towards the Albert Hall. This time it would take fifteen minutes. He collided with a number of pedestrians on the way who were not as accommodating as the residents of the Oratory. Appleby did not notice or care. When the manager entered the office, Cranshaw saw there was something awry. He made an attempt to introduce Chisholme as the newspaper reporter. Appleby ignored his librarian, dumped the mass bells on his desk, picked up his phone and rang the Polish embassy. He asked for Lutowicz. "Did you remove that bloody thing from my car?" he demanded.

There came a moment when Cranshaw knew there was no longer anyone at the other end of the telephone. But Appleby continued to hold the handset to his ear. His back was still turned to the others, and

Cranshaw was about to move forward when Appleby emitted a long low moan and replaced the receiver. He continued to face the back wall.

"I'd like you to meet the reporter from –" Cranshaw started.

Appleby wheeled around and pushed past them out the door.

———

This time Appleby headed in the opposite direction. He reached Kensington Gore and walked blindly across the road. The number of irate motorists who blew their car horns only succeeded in adding to the confusion in his mind.

He gained the relative safety of Hyde Park and struck out towards the shimmering waters of the Serpentine. When he reached the lake, he walked along its perimeter path until he reached the point where rowing boats were hired out. Twice he suppressed the urge to enter the water. He knew he would find satisfaction in its liquid embrace. He could either reject or accept that embrace. A boat would enable him to determine the moment. He gave the attendant a twenty-pound note and brushed aside the efforts to give change. It was accepted with alacrity, the man advising Appleby that he could stay out as long as he liked.

"I intend to," replied Appleby brusquely, and shoved off into the lake.

———

It felt sublime. Lapping water against the forward thrust of the boat. Floating upon a flexible benign medium; the unassailable bliss of it all. Marvellous! He stopped rowing when he reached the centre of the lake and pulled in the oars. It was so tranquil. He trailed his hand in the water, cool and welcoming. He heard sounds that mattered. Lapping water. Birds. Waterfowl. Children shouting and laughing. Bathers splashing about in the bathing section. And far away, the distant rumble of London traffic. Distant and far away.

He sank down onto the floor of the boat and rested his head on the seat. The sky was filled with slow–moving pillows of enormous white cloud. Here and there the blue sky peeped through, allowing occasional brisk blinding moments of joy as the clouds ponderously progressed eastwards. Somewhere above it all a jet echoed a carefree solitary journey in perpetual sunshine.

He began to weep. People should not be allowed to grow up. Life was too long. It was all so unnecessary. That was why he could not believe in a God. All that innocence for nothing. Just so they could lose it and grow up into grubby adults. There was the conundrum of reproduction. If there was a God, surely he could have organised it better than the dung heap that faced all children. Why were people so bloody awful? Sleaze. Filth. Corruption.

He closed his eyes defensively as the sun suddenly found the lake. When it passed, he reopened them to the sky. He saw a small sparrow hawk hovering perfectly against a white background of cloud. The survival of the shitiest, he brooded and closed his eyes again.

Agnieszka, Agnieszka... His first love. His only love. She'd left him all those years ago to return to her Polish homeland. Left him, and her disconsolate parents, to be a part of the new communist Poland. Had such a wrench been worth it?

He'd never heard from her again.

She'd left a gaping hole in his life. First love, last love.

'Some things are worth fighting for,' she had said.

'I want to be a part of a new and better Poland, a new and better world.'

'This is my dream. Come, mój drogi, and dream with me.'

At the time he hadn't been able to. But now he could. Appleby slipped into the water. As it went over his head, he heard Agnieszka again: 'Dream, always dream,' she whispered, 'dream...'

Sweet dreams... sweet... dreams... dream

CHAPTER 26

Saturday March 28th 1981
Gower Street
Conference Room 1
2.00 pm

In attendance

1. Maj F. Hempson (chair)

2. Chief Supt M. Laymott (Special Branch)

3. Wg Cdr D. Brenton (security)

4. Capt M.T. Cranshaw (security)

5. Det Insp P. Blackmore (Metropolitan police)

6. Mr B. Chisholme (security)

7. Sgt A. Williams

8. Cpl R. Pringle

9. Mrs S. Barrett (secretary)

Frank Hempson entered the Gower Street conference room and accepted an attendance sheet from Sheena Barrett. "All present," she was able to tell him sotto voce. Hempson nodded brusquely. In normal circumstances she might have added some innocuous social or in-house comment, which Hempson invariably responded to in kind; but the Polish week had purged their sociability. She was herself imbued with the same sombre anxiety gripping those already seated at the table.

Hempson saw the two new names on the sheet, Williams and Pringle, and lifted his eyes from the paper to see where they sat. He was in time to catch both men averting their eyes from his presence near the door. Instead, they applied themselves to their own sheets and realised, since there had been only one vacant and numbered position remaining, that this last person – Frank Hempson – equated in significance with the number opposite his position at the head of the table: numero uno. They had also figured correctly that the list was made out in a descending order of rank.

———

Hempson sat down at the head of the table. Sheena Barrett sat at her escritoire to his right. On Hempson's left-hand side sat Brenton, Cranshaw, Williams and Pringle, in that order. On his right sat Laymott, Blackmore, and Chisholme. Hempson 'harumped' and declared the purpose of the gathering was to prepare, correlate, and finalise their arrangements for the evening's concert.

"Have Sgt Williams and Cpl Pringle been briefed?" he asked Brenton. He had not wanted the two bandsmen to attend. Their very specific duties could be more adequately taken care of by Brenton and Laymott. Ultimately he was afraid that the meeting might become unwieldy. Brenton had said that the bandsmen would have in-depth briefings from Laymott, Cranshaw and himself, and argued that because they were to be the frontline troops, they might benefit from some snippet or morsel of information overheard at this final meeting.

Hempson could not but accede to Brenton's request. He had been too long in the game ever to leave himself willingly exposed on any flank. "Welcome aboard gentlemen," he nodded in their direction. "I wish to put on record", turning towards Sheena Barrett, "my appreciation of these two men's qualities, in presenting themselves for this undertaking. It does go beyond the normal line of duty. I also wish to put on record that the suggestion for this unusual approach came from Brenton. The two members in question are," he turned to Sheena Barrett again, "Sgt Williams and Cpl Pringle."

The bandsmen glowed in the warmth of welcome. Nothing would come between them and the success of their operation.

"Now gentlemen," Hempson continued less affably, "we apply ourselves to the meeting proper. I'm taking things mainly in chronological order, as opposed to order of importance. I think it's better that way. It will impart a modicum of perspective to the business, which can't be a bad thing. Brenton –" he waved his left hand, "take us from the beginning of the day at the Albert Hall."

Brenton shifted forward in his chair and placed his hands on each side of the attendance sheet in front of him. He went through his arrival at the Hall, his meeting with Williams and Pringle, and afterwards, his meeting with Appleby and Lutowicz. It was his firm conviction that Appleby was the voice on tape, and Lutowicz had been the intruder in St George's and Sarah Carlyle's flat. "As we now know, wherever one went, so did the other. I imagine Appleby became Lutowicz's chauffeur in effect."

Then there was the glitch of static recorded during the morning. "I've listened to the recording of the interruption, and without a shadow of a doubt, it was a two-way transmission. There's no voice on tape, but that's not to say there was no voice on the transmission. The electronic circuitry in the Albert Hall is different to that in Symphony Hall, Croydon. It's my opinion there *was* a verbal transmission. It couldn't have been a mistaken application of the transmission button. The period was too long, apparently 45 seconds."

"A pity," remarked Hempson. "Is there any way that could be enhanced? The speech, I mean."

Brenton did not think the time expended jigging up the content of the transmission would be worthwhile. He was, as it happened, on foreign soil, electronically speaking.

"Bloody marvellous, what?" Hempson laughed, "This shindig is going to be transmitted live on air in Poland – so the listeners to Polish radio will receive the inadvertent broadcast of the conversation as well."

Brenton then asked Cranshaw if he had noticed Appleby transmitting.

"Nothing much to go on there," Cranshaw said. He had crept up on Appleby who was standing with his foot in the door leading on stage, but he had been seen before he got near. It was a likely point for transmitting, and the times coincided. He had been back and forward a number of times after that, but there had not been a second transmission.

Hempson thanked Brenton and Cranshaw. Looking around the table he asked, "Any questions?" No one replied, so he consulted a second sheet of paper, the contents of which had been put together prior to the meeting.

"Right," Hempson said, looking in Blackmore's direction. "I think Det Insp Blackmore has something to tell us."

"Yes. I'd been anxious to take a look inside Mr Appleby's car," he began. Blackmore then recounted the episode outside the Albert Hall, and his retention of Appleby's car in New Scotland Yard. "Thankfully," he said, "Lutowicz was not possessed of the necessary insurance cover for Appleby's car." However they had had no option but to release the SB man after he claimed diplomatic immunity. In itself this had not presented a drawback because their intention was to gain access to the car, which they did.

Everybody's eyes honed in on Blackmore.

"We found a small calibre handgun in the glove compartment," he said with gruff satisfaction. A murmur of approval built up around the table.

"The weapon is presently with forensics," Blackmore took up again. "Before I shipped it in we were able to ascertain that the clip of ammo had had one round released. This is significant," Blackmore underlined the obvious, "but it is as nothing compared to the lucky break we had in Croydon this morning."

Blackmore's chin stabbed the air, bringing to heel the appreciative murmur around the table.

"Due to an unwitting set of circumstances, we had been unable to trace the round which killed Thompson. Until this morning, that is." He unfolded the saga of Betty Fenwick's inadvertent acquisition of a talisman, and her subsequent hasty and horrified abandonment of the same. "The talisman is of the same calibre as the weapon found in Appleby's car," Blackmore bluntly spelled out. "It too is with forensics." A smattering of applause grew to a crescendo with accompanying bravos, and a single "Three cheers for Betty!"

This was what they had needed to hear – something substantive. It had seemed to take such a long time to materialise. It hadn't of course; just six days, to be precise. Last Monday they had received the first inkling of possible trouble. And now they'd had their first breakthrough.

"I don't wish to put a damper," Hempson cautioned. "but do bear in mind that these things need to be correlated." Surveying the table, he added, "It is however a gratifying start." He turned back to Blackmore. "How soon do you expect a result?"

"Because of the concert," the inspector said, "I've pressed for an early response. Possibly early this evening."

"Good," replied Hempson. "Might I suggest you cobble together a warrant for Lutowicz's arrest?"

"What's the point?" Blackmore said. "He'll just slither out like he did this morning."

"He'll undoubtedly try that caper again. However, a situation may arise whereby Mr Lutowicz's diplomatic status is withdrawn. Not by Her Majesty's government, but by the Polish authorities."

"Seems like a long shot to me," Blackmore pessimistically opined.

"You may very well be proved correct," Hempson said. "On the other hand, why take a chance? If, for instance, the Polish government disowns Lutowicz's efforts, that will leave you open to prosecute a case."

Chief Supt Laymott asked sceptically, "Do you think that's likely?"

"Just one moment," Hempson said and scribbled a quick note. He flicked it across the table to Blackmore. It read: MI6 indicate this evening's effort may be an independent operation.

"All right?" Hempson asked after both Blackmore and Laymott had read the note.

Blackmore nodded agreement. "Two warrants presumably," he enquired.

For one instant Hempson seemed perplexed.

"Lutowicz and Appleby," Blackmore explained.

Hempson lowered his eyes in apology. "I'm afraid that won't be necessary." He delayed a moment to stitch together a more circumspect revelation, and then said bluntly. "That's one of the drawbacks to taking things in chronological order. However, I still think it important to reveal events in their correct order. In so far as that's possible." He turned to Cranshaw. "Fill us in on the lead up to what happened."

Cranshaw opened with his success in remaining in the Hall in spite of Appleby's entreaties about his car. "Appleby then became embroiled in a fuss with the percussionist Kazimierz about a broken percussion instrument." Cranshaw wasn't quite sure how it transpired – he had had a lot to contend with. Then out of the blue, Appleby had announced that he was popping down to Brompton Oratory for a replacement item on the percussion list – a mass bell – to replace the broken instrument. This seemed rather outlandish at the time, given Appleby's previous insistence that he was obliged stay in the Albert Hall. He didn't know what had happened in Brompton Oratory. That could be checked out. What was indisputable was his agitated state when he returned with the *campanelli da messa.*

Appleby had rung a telephone number from his desk in the Albert Hall, apparently to the Polish embassy. He had requested Lutowicz and then asked, 'Did you remove that bloody thing from my car?'

"He was acting very strangely; as if there was no one else in the room. I tried to introduce Chisholme as the expected reporter. Appleby wheeled around and without any reference to either Chisholme or myself, walked out the door. I instructed Chisholme to follow him."

"Something obviously happened to alter his state of mind," Hempson suggested, "Between leaving and returning from the Oratory."

Cranshaw nodded his head in agreement. "He was almost a different person – completely ignoring what was going on around him."

"Did you think of getting in touch with someone in the Oratory to find out what transpired?" Hempson enquired.

This drew a blank from Cranshaw. "I had my hands full in the Hall, and there was nothing I could do other than send Chisholme in pursuit."

"Chisholme in pursuit was correct. But I'm concerned about what happened to Appleby in the intervening period." Hempson looked for a response from Cranshaw; he got none.

"Very well," he said. "Use the phone outside. Ring Brompton Oratory and find out."

Cranshaw excused himself.

"Well, Chisholme," Hempson raised his eyes to the other side of the table,"Your moment has come." He sat back and took out his smoking equipment.

Chisholme said, "It didn't take long to deduce there was something amiss," and waited while Hempson put a match to his tobacco.

"Continue," Hempson prompted in between puffs.

"He left the Hall and made his way to Kensington Gore." Chisholme shook his head. "I'd never met Appleby before so I know nothing about his personality."

"Self-assured," intervened Brenton, "quiet, not pushy."

"Well," Chisholme said, giving himself a moment to digest Brenton's assessment. "I'd have to say Appleby was the opposite of that."

"You were in Kensington Gore," Hempson pressed.

"Yes … well … the first thing I know, Appleby strides out into the busy road without glancing to left or right. Like there was nothing there. Like he couldn't see or hear. The road was full of traffic, as it always is, and there were blokes blowing their hooters and shaking their fists. He nearly caused two pile-ups but he neither sees nor cares. I dodged my way over, to see him make a dash for the ring road in the park. We find ourselves on the path beside the Serpentine. Appleby stops and contemplates – several times. He picks up again and we find ourselves at the boat hire place. He steps up, pays his money, and pushes out onto the lake in a boat. I contemplate taking a boat out, but where could he go? I could see him wherever he went."

"You might have saved his life had you done so," Brenton said.

"I'm a watcher," Chisholme protested, "not a bloody lifeguard."

Hempson directed Chisholme to continue.

"Appleby slides onto the floor of the boat. I thought he'd passed out at first, but when I stood on one of the park benches beside the lake, I saw – when I stretched up a bit – I saw he was taking a nap."

The door opened. Cranshaw returned and took his place at the table. He made an attempt to speak to Hempson. The major held up a hand, and then directed Chisholme to continue.

"I sat on the bench most of the time. It wasn't necessary to do anything other than wait and see."

"Go on," Hempson urged.

"Well, I waited until I knew something was wrong. The boat appeared lighter in the water. It moved more buoyantly. Then I saw the boat was empty."

"I don't understand," Hempson turned his baffled features in Chisholme's direction. "Are you suggesting he somehow escaped through the bottom of the boat?"

"No, Major, I'm not. He … well … must have slipped over the side while I blinked. It must have been as quick as that … I never took my eyes off the boat."

The silence was intimidating. No one came to Chisholme's assistance. Hempson extracted his full pound of stony silence.

Chisholme continued. He had run to the boat hire, got a boat, and as best he could, made his way out to where Appleby's boat floated unattended. He drew in his oars and caught the side of the drifting boat. There was nobody there; and nothing in the boat to suggest there had ever been anybody there. He got the odd feeling he was being watched and with the sudden flush of sensation, looked briskly around the perimeter of the lake expecting to see a transported Appleby following his clumsy oarsmanship from the shore.

But Appleby was nowhere in sight.

He would never know what drew his eyes down between the boats. He started, and released his grip on the other boat, which began to drift away. By one of those dramatic quirks of nature, the sun split the heavens at that very moment. He saw Appleby's upturned face greeting him from the bottom of the murky waters. At that instant it had seemed as if Appleby was still alive. He nearly overturned the boat and quickly sat down. He shouted back to the boat hire crew who recognised that something was amiss. One of them rowed out and when he saw the body on the bottom of the lake, immediately went in. He resurfaced after half a minute and asked for assistance. A further member of the boat hire had to make the journey before Appleby was brought to the surface, very definitely dead.

They rowed the body back to shore. Chisholme helped bring it in and suggested they ring for an ambulance. Alone with the body, Chisholme removed Appleby's wallet and, while going through his other pockets, one of the boat crew surprised him. "Hey! What are you doing?" he had asked suspiciously. "We've got to find out who the bloke is," Chisholme had said, busily frisking the sodden body. "I'd leave that to the police," he was told, and he dutifully agreed. An ambulance arrived, and shortly after, the police.

Hempson laid his pipe aside. "Appleby's demise inserts an element of uncertainty into the business; and as with most things which become unstable, one can expect proceedings to take an unpredictable turn. Whether this is to our advantage or disadvantage remains to be seen. Whatever way we play it, it needs to be controlled. Chisholme here", Hempson indicated his watcher with a quick flick of his index finger, "has given us the option of an immediate or delayed announcement of Quentin Appleby's death. The body has no identification until we choose to reveal it."

"What's the point of all this?" Laymott asked.

"The point is," Hempson said, "Nothing is decided until we see where our advantage lies. We can release now, or after the concert. Anything after this evening is out of the question. I intend opening the matter for discussion, but before we start, there remains one unresolved side matter." He pointed a finger at Cranshaw. "What have you to tell us about Brompton Oratory?"

Cranshaw said he had rung the Oratory presbytery. He had contacted both priest and verger who had dealt with Appleby. When he arrived, he had been both agreeable and civilised. He had transacted the acquisition of the mass bells in a sane, and they stressed, jocular manner. They parted amicably, Appleby leaving them a number of tickets for tonight's concert.

Some ten minutes after Appleby had left them, they received a complaint of a disturbance in the church, and the verger went to investigate. Appleby was seen sitting in a pew in the body of the church, the mass bells at his feet, in obvious emotional distress. He'd been heard shouting about 'an effing bastard, like a witch' and had then stormed out of the church.

"There was no evidence that Appleby had met anyone in the body of the church where the alarming transformation took place," Cranshaw concluded.

"Thank you," Hempson said. "Let's open the discussion."

Brenton got the first nod. "Appleby's transformation, as Tim puts it, is directly attributable to Det Insp Blackmore's sequestering Appleby's car. I know Tim would possibly tell us again that Appleby was perfectly normal, if a little overwrought before he departed for the Oratory. But clearly the impounding of Appleby's car gave rise to a situation from which Appleby found it impossible to continue."

"Could we direct our thoughts to what might have plunged Appleby along the road to oblivion?" Chief Supt Morgan Laymott asked. "It may throw some light on tonight's job."

"Indeed," Hempson agreed. "Who'd like to kick off?"

Brenton rattled his pen against the foolscap sheet in front of him. "It's the verger's version of what Appleby shouted in the church – 'That effing bastard's like a witch'." He paused to allow the utterance time to sink in. "I lay a pound to a penny what he actually shouted was – 'That effing bastard Lutowicz.' There was a general murmur of assent. "Which suggests that the pressure on Appleby came from Lutowicz. And his transformation," Brenton added.

Cranshaw reminded them of Appleby's telephone question to Lutowicz on his return from the Oratory – 'Did you remove that bloody thing from my car?'

"So Appleby knew the weapon was in the car," Blackmore said.

"On the evidence so far," Laymott said, "I should think so."

"Which undoubtedly contributed to his premature departure," Brenton said.

"It does not, however, help us determine why he was doing what he was doing," Hempson pointed out. "We know Lutowicz is a member of Polish intelligence and would be conversant with all the tricks of harassment and coercion," he elaborated for those around the table less aware of that aspect. "Bearing this in mind, and remembering Appleby's last known sentiments to have been tinged with a combination of fear, remorse and frustrated anger, pressure of one sort or another from Lutowicz would appear to have been applied."

"In the context of available time," Brenton considered, "I don't think it matters what form the pressure took. Its effects are all too obvious. So I propose that we up Lutowicz's surveillance status from watcher to armed Branchman."

Hempson agreed. "That's a prudent move. What are the chances?" he asked Laymott.

"I don't have one extra member available," Laymott stated flatly. "Under the circumstances, I can see it's of the utmost importance that we do what Wg Cdr Brenton suggests. So –" he drew breath and reflectively adjusted his lips, "I'll detach one member from a seat in the Hall, put a revolver in his tight little holster, and stick him on Lutowicz's tail."

"Good," Hempson nodded. "So," he addressed the meeting generally, "do we release Appleby's details now or later?" There were two criteria to bear in mind, he reminded them: was it advantageous to security? Would it disadvantage Lutowicz and company?

In the end a decision to withhold until after the concert was accepted.

"Where are the remains being held?" Laymott wanted to know.

"Originally in St George's on Hyde Park corner," Hempson said. "I had them transferred across the river to St Thomas'. I felt St George's was a little too close to the scene for comfort."

Hempson flicked over a sheet of paper and, acknowledging its contents said, "Can you tell us what the seating arrangements for the VIPs are?

Brenton distributed floor plans and photographs. "They'll be accommodated in the first two ten-seater boxes … and the middle-row boxes on the left-hand side looking towards the stage. Instead of the normal box seating, four armchairs will be placed in both boxes with three or four ordinary chairs behind. The seating order in the first box will be Uginski; the Polish ambassador; the chairman of the board of Symphony Hall; and Michael Pecton. Two Polish embassy interpreters will sit behind this group."

"And a single armed Branch officer," Laymott added.

"In the next box the order will be: Lyle Butler, representing the government; the Polish ambassador's wife; Mrs Butler; and Mrs Pecton. Behind them will be positioned one Polish embassy interpreter."

"And again, a single armed officer," Laymott said. "– Mr Butler's personal security guard."

"As you see," Brenton said, referring to the layout plan, "Anton Uginski will sit in a very exposed position. We now know these positions were determined by Symphony Hall, Croydon in collaboration with the Polish embassy protocol section, assisted by Witold Lutowicz."

"They were also assisted by Special Branch," Hempson said testily, "who attended those meetings without telling anybody else. Luckily they passed on what had transpired after their omission was pointed out."

"I thought we'd moved on from that," Laymott grumbled.

"We have, we have," Hempson smiled thinly. "There's no harm in sticking it on record. Now tell us about Mr Uginski's arrival," he urged the chief superintendent.

Laymott lost himself in the diplomatic niceties and personalities surrounding Uginski's entry into the UK. There had been nothing unusual or untoward at the Heathrow reception, apart from the disproportionate expenditure of time and energy involved in greeting such a self-absorbed and impossibly dull politician. The question on most observers' lips was how Poland managed to trade with anyone under his stultifying hand.

At the Polish embassy Pecton had found it difficult to hide his disappointment when, pressed for a comment on the upcoming musical treat, Uginski had revealed without compunction that he was musically illiterate.

"He's not all bad," Laymott countered. "He's already enquired about the possibility of 'a nice girl' for tonight."

"Perhaps", suggested Brenton, "we should introduce him to Lina Zukowska?"

"Lina Zukowska!" said Hempson, "I was under the impression we were responsible for the man's safety."

Zukowska's forbidding presence hovered behind the flippancies and prompted Hempson to ask Brenton, "What about your pianist friend Maria Wohlicka?"

"Maria", Brenton said, "spent an overnight in hospital … from Thursday evening until noon yesterday. The doctor in charge gave it as his opinion that she had been assaulted. Significantly, she was collected from the hospital by Lutowicz and, with one exception, hasn't been seen outside the room of her Cromwell Road hotel. Whether this is due to recuperation or incarceration, no one knows. Shortly before six o'clock yesterday she appeared at the newsagent's kiosk in the hotel foyer and bought some cigarettes. The girl behind the counter found a scribbled note wrapped up in the five-pound note she was handed. She said afterwards that the message had read, 'Bring to police please.' Madame Wohlicka had disappeared by the time she looked back up.

"As it happened," Brenton told Hempson, "Special Branch also had a body in attendance."

Laymott smiled sheepishly in Hempson's direction.

"Luckily," Brenton continued, "IDs were quickly sorted out, when our man and the Branch bod converged on the kiosk."

"I can understand", Hempson sighed, "a certain amount of overlapping. It's inevitable. And of course it accords with Mrs Thatcher's free market ethos." Brenton and Cranshaw looked sharply to where Sheena Barrett was capturing every word on her note pad.

"This transcript goes to the DG," Hempson reassured them. "Where was I? Yes, the free market. It's difficult enough, Morgan," he said to the chief superintendent, "trying to cope with MI6's duplication, without the added burden of wondering what our friends are up to. As I've already said, while that free market element may coincide with Margaret Hilda's view of things, it hardly conforms to her *obiter dictum* – value for money."

Hempson slipped the pipe between his teeth and applied a match. Between unhurried puffs he told Laymott that they must meet *post bellum*, and come to some arrangement about double staffing. He heaved around on his chair, wreathing his person with tobacco smoke, and asked Brenton to continue.

"Our bod was able to identify that it was me the letter referred to," Brenton told Hempson, "and the Branch bod had the message delivered to Biggin Hill in record time. The message was simply that Maria Wohlicka would not be present for the run-through this morning, but would definitely play tonight's concert."

"Which means in effect," Hempson speculated, "that she'll be thumbing a lift afterwards."

"Quite," Brenton confirmed.

"I've said it before," Hempson warned, "and I'll say it again. Do not allow Madame Wohlicka to take up so much of your time as to jeopardise our one and *only* job this evening."

Brenton could only agree. He pointed out that it came so far down his priority list that he had yet to finalise an embryo plan with Laymott. The plan was a simple one with an underlying audacity. It would need the assistance of the Albert Hall management and staff. "Their passive assistance," Brenton clarified when he saw storm clouds massing on Hempson's face. The major listened attentively to Brenton's further elucidation and eventually erupted in a gruff phlegmy laugh of acceptance. "Sounds like fun – only wish the rest of it was in the same vein."

"How much do we give away?" Cranshaw asked.

"The quick answer is, as little as possible," Hempson said. "It is also the more sensible approach."

Brenton added, "I think I mentioned that the lady wished to demonstrate her affinity with a British audience and in the process, give her minders a hard time?"

"Yes," Hempson agreed, "That sounds convincing. I can leave the details of that little plan to you and Chief Superintendent Laymott."

Laymott expressed willingness to row in with this.

Hempson next asked for and got from Laymott the disposal of Branch people in the Hall. Not all would be armed, but where there were two members together, one would be armed. Which brought them to the subject of Williams and Pringle.

The two bandsmen shuffled self-consciously at the end of the table. Brenton proposed that one of them be armed. Laymott questioned the necessity for this saying that he thought there were sufficient armed officers in the vicinity.

"That's correct," Brenton said, consulting the layout plan, "but not actually on stage, and this is the area from which the attempt will be made."

Laymott capitulated. "Ok," he said, "but I want to know exactly how we communicate with Williams and Pringle."

"I can tell you how I'm communicating with them," Brenton said. "Neither Williams nor Pringle is needed on stage until the last piece of music – the Kilar. We know the attempt will be made during the final *ad lib* section of the work, which by lucky coincidence also requires the extra musicians. The bandsmen will have to hang around from the start of the concert but won't be needed until the last piece at the end. So there will be no problem communicating with them up to when they go on stage for the Kilar."

"And when they are on stage, how do you propose to communicate?" pressed Laymott.

"By two-way radio," Brenton replied. "Actually it will be one-way – from me to them. The restrictions that the other side have encountered will also apply to us."

Hempson intervened, saying that the systems used – whatever they were – had to be interlinked. "Everybody on our side of the fence must be made aware of the state of play – not least to prevent accidents.

An outline began to emerge from the discussion as to how communications between the two systems would function and link up all the parties. The details were to be finalised by Special Branch's electronics section. Hempson asked Laymott to contact management in the Albert Hall and, under the umbrella of security for the Polish minister, procure a backstage room within which all communication systems would pass. "That's where I'd like to be," Hempson said, "Instead of in here at one remove. How about you, Morgan?"

"Good idea," Laymott agreed. "What about closed-circuit surveillance television?"

"Excellent," Hempson nodded vigorously. "A camera on the VIP box and another on the orchestra?"

An air of satisfaction permeated the meeting as it drew to a conclusion. "Are there any further points?" Hempson enquired, "Before we go into our separate sub-committees?"

There was no response.

He was about to wrap up when his eye came to rest on Blackmore. "In case there should be any misunderstanding, Inspector, you're welcome to our proposed operations room. You shall be doubly welcome if the revolver found in Appleby's car proves your forensic prognosis correct. With those cheering results, the operations room will be your first port of call. We'll know the location of your adversary, and besides, the punters might not appreciate your interrupting their little climax. Now, because we have so much to complete, individually, I suggest we end this meeting and get stuck into our specialist groups."

CHAPTER 27

Saturday March 28th 1981
MI5 Gower Street
4.00 pm

After the meeting, Brenton rushed down to where he had left Sarah browsing through the day's newspapers. A late lunch had been laid on in the canteen for the people attending the meeting, so they made their way there and sat by themselves. Brenton particularly wished to be alone with Sarah. In four hours' time – at eight o'clock – this thing would begin. It gave him a tight nervy feeling, which he did not appreciate. His responsibilities had been accentuated by Frank Hempson giving his backing to Brenton's approach in preference to his own.

So it was good to be with Sarah. She eased the tension within him; all it took was the occasional meeting of eyes across the table. But time, which a few days ago had moved ponderously and darkly, now moved with galloping swiftness.

After lunch, it was time to bring Williams and Pringle downstairs and have them kitted out for the concert. Brenton invited Sarah to see how the bandsmen were to be prepared.

Mr Kent was in charge of fittings. He demonstrated the bullet-proof vests to Williams and Pringle, which they were obliged to wear under their dress shirts. Pringle, in a fluster of bravura, wondered whether they were absolutely necessary. Mr Kent's thin moustache twitched with distaste. "Anyone who has seen the effect a bullet has on the human body would not ask that question," he said in a tight unemotional monotone, snuffing further comment. Undivided attention was what he demanded in his domain. "Now then," he said with thin–lipped parsimoniousness, and held up a small portable radio transmitter. "This", he underlined to Brenton, "is the transmission end of your communications network. Transmission is locked onto a specific frequency, which is non–negotiable. Its power comes from these batteries, which need to be switched off when not in use. The transmitter takes an unusual amount of juice. I'll issue you", he informed Brenton, "with a second set of batteries. The output from this transmitter is split between your communications room backstage, and these." Kent held aloft Williams' and Pringle's receivers, which were about three-quarters the size of Brenton's transmitter. "These are unusual," he continued. "There is no connecting wire between the receiver and the earpiece – which fits snugly into one ear." He held out the palm of his hand, in which lay a tiny flesh coloured object, for inspection.

"Inside each receiver there is a further transmitter which transmits into the earpieces. Understand?" he enquired briskly and, without waiting for an answer, told them there would be a technician on duty in the Albert Hall. "Remove your shirts please," he instructed the two bandsmen. He fitted a leather belt through the backs of the receivers and strapped one around each soldier's midriff. Each receiver rested snugly in the small of their backs. "Now, pay particular attention," Kent requested glumly. "I've connected together, in series, the defensive metal of each vest with a wire bridge. While wearing the vest, each man will in effect have wrapped around him one long flexible yet continuous metal rod."

Kent permitted himself a self-congratulatory smile. "Or put another way … one long metal aerial. Look here –" He held up one of the bullet-proof vests and extracted a length of flex with a small plug attached. "This is the aerial and –" he placed the vest on Williams' frame, "– this is where it plugs into Sgt Williams' receiver." He did the same with Pringle.

"Switch your batteries on before going on stage," he warned. "That will ensure enough juice to carry you through the performance. Make sure you test reception between transmitter and receiver," he cautioned the three of them.

Brenton made arrangements to have Williams and Pringle kit out and dress before entering the Albert Hall. "There will be time to test equipment after that in the backstage communications room during the first half of the concert."

Chief Supt Laymott entered the room. "This goes over your dress shirt," he said, handing a leather holster to Williams. "You collect the revolver which goes with it in the communications room before you go on stage. There will be someone there to brief you on aspects of the weapon and deal with any questions you might have."

———

A short time later, Maria Wohlicka became equally preoccupied with the clothes she was to wear to the concert. She sat on the end of her bed and gazed in through the open door of her wardrobe. Ignoring the recently lit cigarette in the ashtray on the bedside table, she snatched another from a pack on the bed behind her and lit it. She resumed peering into the wardrobe.

Again and again her eyes returned to the piece of chiffon on the wardrobe floor. Still confused and disbelieving, she reached out and picked up the right-hand sleeve of the dress she was to have worn to the evening's performance. She held it aloft against the dull light from the window. Though no expert in needlework, Maria Wohlicka possessed an innate capacity to assess the finer points of sartorial workmanship. To reassure herself that she was not dreaming, she whisked out the hanger on which the dress floated and yes, there was one full-length chiffon sleeve missing. And yes, there inside the shoulder hole where the chiffon sleeve should have met the full-length taffeta dress was the frayed evidence of its forcible detachment.

The distraught pianist sank back down onto the bed, the sundered dress across her lap and a consoling cigarette in her mouth. She sat silently trying to put together a rescue plan. It had always been her ambition to learn the rudiments of sewing and carry the elements of a sewing kit. Now she bitterly regretted not having done so. The hotel did not possess a seamstress, and a search for one at this late hour was out of the question – quite simply there was not enough time.

The door opened. Lina Zukowska spanned the entrance. Madame

Wohlicka's anxiety changed to anger. She knew – here stood the perpetrator of this mean, despicable act. It did not take a great deal of intuition to work it out. The woman's brutalising performance to date, coupled with the sneering apparition which now blocked the doorway, left her in no doubt. Zukowska barked, "I have already told you, you are not leaving here before I've had a meal. If we are late, that will be your fault. Get into that silly dress quickly, or I'll darken your other eye." The pianist kept her temperament under rigid control; she didn't even deign the other woman with a glance. Instead, she stood up and went into the bathroom with the dress across her arm.

There was a click as Maria Wohlicka locked the bathroom door behind her. She consoled herself with the knowledge that the nightmare would finish that very night. With the assistance of Mr Brenton she would be free. At least, she hoped with his assistance. He had not contacted her yet, which was upsetting, but then how could he? She had been to hospital and from there on she had been in the custody of some one of the three reptiles – Zukowska, Komorski or Lutowicz. She clipped the clothes hanger onto a small shelf and stepped back to take in the depredation wrought on the dress. She fumed inwardly at the indignity, and nearly came to tears in the process.

If they thought they were going to make Maria Wohlicka bow her head, they were mistaken. Wearing only a slip, she wrapped her arms around herself in an attempt prevent her emotions getting the upper hand. Her fingers brushed the bruised and discoloured upper part of her arm. She released her hold with a jolt. Her arms must be covered. The humiliation! The ignominy!

Wait a moment. A humiliation for whom? She looked at her arm again and felt the side of her face. The nagging ache in her jaw would slowly disappear over a few days, she had been told. This was a humiliation without question; but not for her. She had been the victim of an assault – the object of ridicule – why? For what reason? It was unacceptable for whatever reason. Her resolve deepened as she opened the bathroom door.

Lina Zukowska stood up in anticipation and frowned when she saw Maria Wohlicka, still in her slip, open the wardrobe and extract her overcoat. "What are you doing, you stupid bitch!"

The pianist snatched up her tights and shoes and made a dash for the bathroom. She slipped the lock before Zukowska began to bang on the door. "What are you doing, you idiot? Do I have to show you how to dress?"

Maria Wohlicka worked quickly while the pounding on the door continued. She held the taffeta shoulder pad in one hand and grasped the remaining chiffon sleeve with the other. Even she was surprised at the ease with which she managed to detach the second sleeve. She wondered about her apportionment of blame, but only for a moment, and then threw the dress over her head and wriggled into its new shape, and finally into her tights and overcoat.

When she opened the door, everything seemed to be in place. Zukowska was not pleased with this transformation and angrily demanded to see what she had on under her overcoat. She was briefly shown the dress. "Move, bitch!" she ordered, satisfied. "I need to eat."

Maria Wohlicka was made to walk in front of the SB woman. She was spurred on with occasional and malicious bursts of "Move!", which disconcerted hotel guests in the vicinity, and bolstered the pianist's resolve to end – one way or the other – this pointless and painful existence that very night.

"I should be filling myself with thoughts about the music," she appealed to no one in particular. Instead of which she was full of fear, hate and contempt. Worst of all, she was battling with self-loathing because of what she considered her own complicity. She had accepted and acquiesced to everything those vile creatures had proposed. It was self-preservation, she tried to tell herself. That did not make her acceptance any easier to bear. But none of this should have any space in her mind at that particular point in time. She *must* exclude everything except the music. She would do that when she sat down in the dining room and had a coffee in her hand.

Seated in the dining room, Maria Wohlicka again found her need for silence denied her. Zukowska sat opposite, hunched over a plate filled to overflowing. Lutowicz approached, but instead of joining them, he swiftly took refuge in the men's room. He at least seemed to be imbued with some awareness of the importance of the concert, if not the music. When they reached the Hall, she would demand that she be given time and privacy to gather her diminished strength and soothe her tattered nerves.

An embassy car awaited them outside. Maria Wohlicka complained about the painful crush on her arm when the three of them got into the back seat, so Lutowicz ordered Zukowska into the front seat. This perceived slight was put to rights when the car pulled up close to their venue. As the trio made their way towards the Albert Hall, Zukowska resumed her role of custodian and took hold of the pianist's arm in precisely the position in which she had inflicted the initial injury two days previously. Maria Wohlicka gasped open-mouthed with instant pain, which doubled as the battered side of her face tried to cope with the sudden reaction.

Lutowicz had stridden forward several paces before it dawned on him that he was alone. Looking back sharply, he saw his soloist drop slowly to the ground, mouth open, eyes closed. He rushed back to where the pianist half lay on the concourse ground. Zukowska still held onto her charge's arm imparting a rag-doll effect to the tableau.

"What happened? What's the matter?" Lutowicz demanded, fearful that this one further mishap would finally deprive him of his goal.

"She fell down – fainted," Zukowska said contemptuously.

"Why are you holding her arm like that?" Lutowicz asked, awakening to the possibility of custodial rather than medical reasons.

"In case she runs away," Zukowska barked with belligerent scorn. A number of people had begun to gather around them. One man suggested ringing for an ambulance. Another requested that Zukowska release the lady's arm and allow her to lie horizontally. Lutowicz told Zukowska to release the pianist's arm and as the crowd increased, told those nearest him that they were going into the Albert Hall where there was a doctor on duty. "Lift her in your arms," Lutowicz ordered Zukowska.

Comrade Zukowska hesitated and Lutowicz seethed, "Before we're bloody lynched. Lift her up and get inside!" He smiled at those around him. "A little faintness," he apologised. "A little weakness."

"Why don't *you* carry the wretch?" Zukowska put to Lutowicz.

"Because," Lutowicz tried his best to appear charming, "You are the one who made her faint. I bet you caught her by her injured arm? Did you not, Comrade?"

Zukowska bent down and lifted the pianist in her arms. She held the same rank as Lutowicz, but there was one very important and salutary difference. Lutowicz ran this show. She'd heard his name mentioned when she arrived in Britain. Everything revolved around, and emanated from, Lutowicz. So she clamped her mouth shut and moved forward towards the entrance to the Hall, Lutowicz by her side.

———

Maria Wohlicka's eyes began to flutter. She looked around her. Apart from the two horrors Zukowska and Lutowicz, she did not recognise her surroundings. She tried to raise her head, but it flopped back onto the chaise longue on which she was lying.

"This is your room in the Albert Hall," Lutowicz explained. The nagging pain in her arm impinged and she asked for coffee and a cigarette. Lutowicz nodded at Zukowska and motioned towards the door.

"I don't speak English," Zukowska protested.

Lutowicz moved to go and irritably said, "If you as much as touch Comrade Wohlicka while I'm outside, I'll have your hide for lard!"

None of which in any way reassured or even convinced the pianist. It was all so squalid. Their meanness – even to one another. Their cruelty, so readily available, and their gratuitous malice. She could not bear to meet Zukowska's eyes. She turned her head in the opposite direction. How in God's name could she manage to extricate herself from this misery of fear and loathing? She would die rather than go back; and that was possibly the way it might end. No, she reassured herself, it would only end like that if she were forced to lie here and not perform. She must perform – and meet Mr Brenton. She would miss her homeland, the pianist suddenly thought. It was of the utmost importance that from this point on, she nurture an unwavering resolve about her escape. Escape from her homeland. Her Poland. She closed her eyes to elude the shame of her emotion. She would miss the cities, the landscape, and the towns. She would miss the people. But most of all – she would miss her young family of piano pupils. She hoped for their sakes they had not imbibed her impatience with the decrepit and rotten system with which Poland was burdened. A bright notion opened a view to the future – she might be able to help them from outside the system. The door opened and Lutowicz returned with coffee and cigarettes.

"I must speak with you alone," Maria Wohlicka murmured as she received the coffee from Lutowicz. He hesitated only a moment. "Out!" he dismissed Zukowska.

Neither of them troubled to see how Zukowska took this. Lutowicz assisted Comrade Wohlicka to a sitting position, and when the door closed said, "Don't pay any attention to that fat cow."

"Comrade Lutowicz," the pianist said, after a sip from her coffee. "It is not the attention I pay Comrade Zukowska that should concern you, but rather the attention your colleague pays me." She pointed to her face and arm.

"I feel very sorry for you Comrade Wohlicka," Lutowicz tried to reassure. "I do the best I can. But I can't be everywhere. May I see your arm?" he asked appeasingly.

"No, you may not." she said abruptly, pulling her overcoat more tightly. The pianist lit a cigarette and returned her spare hand to the coffee. "I'll explain the position," she said quietly, and lay back on the raised end of the chaise. "I normally spend time alone before a performance. Tonight I need that time more than ever before." She looked Lutowicz directly in the eyes. "If you can't provide this – I shall not go on."

"But of course," Lutowicz was all hurt sympathy. "Anything you want you may have. You are the star of the show," he soothed. He cocked a knowing head in the direction of the door. "She is more fitted for the Polish wrestling team. I am going to write a very severe report about her when we return to Poland."

"If she doesn't kill me before then," Maria Wohlicka said through a cloud of exhaled smoke. "I need my rest now, so if you don't mind..."

Lutowicz exited with what the pianist considered unsettling obsequiousness. They made an unlikely duo: one so brutally direct; the other, sly and two-faced.

Her head sank back onto the headrest. She raised her legs with difficulty onto the sofa and sighed. Alone for the first time that day, her recuperative powers set to work. "It is good," she told herself. "It will be better. All will be good and better," she repeated, and dropped the cigarette into the remains of the coffee. The quick sizzle as it extinguished was the last thing she remembered.

———

When the telephone rang it was as if she had dozed off only a moment since. She looked at her watch. Half past seven! Her body did not react as instantly as her mind. She clutched the end of the sofa and stood still for a moment, not fully erect. The telephone continued to ring. "Oh my God," she groaned, and slowly straightened up. "Hello," she said into the phone. There was a surprised pause at the other end. "Hello," Maria Wohlicka repeated with some irritation.

"I didn't think you were going to answer," a male voice said in English.

"Ah, Mr Brenton," she whispered into the phone with surprised gratification. "I have been snoozing, as you say."

"Is there anyone with you?"

"No."

"Good. Now listen to what I say. Don't speak unless you do not understand."

"Yes." Maria Wohlicka said, her eyes widening appreciatively. Salvation was at hand.

Brenton said, "I presume, and hope, you're well enough to perform?"

"Yes," in a colourless monotone.

"I see," Brenton said with slow deliberation. "You're not to worry. I've organised a simple exit for you." He allowed a pause for the pianist to get the drift.

"I understand," she murmured.

"When the concerto has finished and you go forward to take the applause, look directly below you, into the audience. I'll be there at the dividing rail. I'll give you an obvious direction as to what to do. Just follow that."

The door to Maria Wohlicka's room opened and Professor Komorski stood in the doorway, in white tie and tails. Behind him in the corridor lurked Lina Zukowska – with intent it seemed.

Maria Wohlicka said matter-of-factly into the phone, "Yes, thank you, I shall be ready," and replaced the receiver.

"Who was that?" Komorski wished to know.

"A person from the Hall. They wish to know if I am ready."

"And are you?" Komorski querulously asked. The soloist still wore her overcoat, which increased his doubts. He wondered why this was necessary. The room seemed adequately heated. Then he noticed she was wearing her evening dress underneath. She was ready to go on. "Very well," he said dismissively. "I shall expect to see you at the stage-entrance door after the Elgar."

The soloist endeavoured to understand why such emphasis was being laid on something so run-of-the-mill. She nodded her head. Lina Zukowska's imposing bulk hovered behind Komorski. Maria Wolicka could not help round off the encounter with a salvo of her own. "I shall be there, Professor," she said, "I shall be there. It may even be that I arrive on a stretcher! Either way, I shall be there." And she closed the door in his face.

She did not see the sneer that enveloped the professor's face. He turned to Zukowska. "She will live to regret her pro-West toadyism. Look after her well." He returned to his own room to collect his baton and then head to the stage-entrance door.

The Hall was packed. This was an out-of-season tribute to Michael Pecton's extensive advertisement campaign, which pointed up the international aspect of the occasion, particularly in light of the continuing political controversy in Poland. The concert's co-sponsor was the Polish communist government, yet Pecton, through a deft use of latent sympathy for the Solidarity Movement and its mentor Lech Walesa, was able to set the Royal Albert Hall as a focal point for support of the workers and students of Poland. Not surprisingly, the promenade section of the Hall was crowded with young people in favour of Solidarity and the hope that Poland's new prime minister, Jaruzelski, might see his way to giving official recognition to the movement. On all sides of the Polish spectrum anxieties were heightened by the prolonged Warsaw Pact manoeuvres taking place across the borders in East Germany and Czeckoslovakia – a potent warning to the same prime minister not to overstep the mark. All of which had assisted Pecton's pursuit of a focal point. While he greatly sympathised with his guests' domestic dilemma, he was equally thankful for the publicity the same dilemma imparted in terms of bottoms-on-seats. What he was not chuffed about was the inexplicable disappearance of his orchestra manager. He was torn between consternation and concern, between his immediate needs, and Appleby's uncharacteristic absence. One necessary decision was Cranshaw's elevation to fill the gap. He was competent, if less pliant; perhaps in the same mould as Brenton. But competence and steadiness were what was required right now, and Cranshaw had these qualities in abundance.

However, from his position in the box, everything looked and felt marvellous. He had greeted and welcomed Uginski and the Polish ambassador and his wife at the front entrance. The Polish party had arrived together in the ambassador's car. Cranshaw had been designated to greet their own government minister, Lyle Butler, Mrs Butler, and the Croydon chairman. There had been pre-concert drinks where everyone had met. What he had previously considered a strange imposition – the outlandish separation of spouses in the two concert boxes – was now an irrelevance.

In the first box, and closest to the stage, sat Uginski. He seemed gratifyingly impressed. Next sat the Polish ambassador. Then the chairman of the board, and last but by no means least – himself, Dr Michael Pecton. In the next box sat Lyle Butler. Had they wished, they could have stretched their hands out and touched! It was all very congenial and comfortable. Mrs Pecton sat three down from Butler, with Mrs Butler and Mrs ambassador in between.

The excited pre-concert chatter stilled a little when the oboe initiated the tuning, and moments later the leader of the orchestra, Arthur Liddel, came on stage to polite applause. Michael Pecton could hardly contain the euphoria surging through his body. To think the people of Poland were joining them on radio for this groundbreaking event. It was, without a shadow of doubt, the crowning achievement of his career. There would be others, he flattered himself, but for the moment, he would sit back and bask.

Pecton's eyes roamed further afield. Directly below the boxes in two of the parterre seats that rose from the oval of the promenade, sat the Reverend Rupert Pryce and his sister Mildred. When their eyes met Dr Pecton smiled. There was the custodian of his other project, the organ-recording contract in St George's. With a curt nod of his head, he acknowledged the clergyman's wave. "Nice man," murmured Mildred, an avid music fan who had greatly appreciated the gift of tickets to the concert.

There was a sudden hush and then the auditorium resounded with applause. Komorski walked briskly between the violin stands and halted at the podium. Rupert Pryce beckoned Mildred's attention and guardedly drew her eyes to Ronald Shipsey's form at the console of the Willis organ high above the orchestra. Mildred had already noted the organist's arrival, so she quickly returned to Komorski, who was waiting for absolute silence. When it came, he gave the signal for the opening clarion of Elgar's *Polonia*. It rang out with dramatic suddenness to start the concert, releasing the pre-concert tensions.

Up in the control room Brenton's tensions had other more uncertain triggers; the same was true for Hempson and Laymott in the communications centre behind the orchestra, as well as the collection of Branch men and women seated and tucked away in various positions around the auditorium. They endeared themselves to Michael Pecton in so far as they were accountable bottoms-on-seats. His tolerance might have been short-lived had he known their inability to take any enjoyment in his concert. In that respect they had more in common with Minister Uginski.

After the opening *forte*, Brenton checked with Adam Fuller on the desk and, receiving an ok, took a pair of binoculars outside to the deserted top level. He focused on the first box. Uginski sat in prime position. His admiring attention settled on everything and everybody except the music–making below him. His ambassador knew precisely where his eyes should rest and seldom deviated from that. Croydon's chairman was essentially an opera buff, but nevertheless enjoyed a good orchestral bash. Elgar would always have been included in that category. Honest English stuff. A trifle odd to hear this Polish side to him…

Pecton sat head back, eyes closed. He breathed in his choice of overture, and then to make sure it was not a figment of his imagination, re-opened his eyes and concentrated on Komorski's swaying form. Yes, it was really happening there in front of him. Brenton followed Pecton's line of vision and picked up Komorski in the binoculars. The conductor's autocratic bearing and concise gestures looked convincing. From that angle Brenton could not wholly see Komorski's face, except when he turned directly towards the first strings to his left or the cellos to his right. It only took a short time moving through the strings to realise that the orchestra was on auto. If the members were looking anywhere apart from their music scores it was at Arthur Liddel. Komorski, if anything, was following them. Brenton swept the glasses through the percussion, the woodwind, and the brass. Which of them would be capable of executing a wet job? Everything seemed so bloody normal, but then why wouldn't it.

Polonia had about three minutes to run so he replaced the binoculars and moved downstairs. He had to place himself in position for the concerto. At the exit from the promenade furthest from the stage, Brenton spoke to two Branchmen and the chief usher. It was more a communication of nods, indicating prior arrangements.

When the Elgar finished and the applause enveloped them, Brenton walked down the parterre stairs and into the standing mass of mainly young people in the promenade. He pressed on towards the front rail and eventually found himself directly under the piano keyboard. There was guard space between the audience rail and the stage. Brenton rested his elbows on the rail, which brought his head below the bulk of the boy and girl to his left. The audience awaited the appearance of the renowned concert pianist with the usual Albert Hall good-humoured impatience, which included a rash of variety hall and political catch cries, and when someone stuck a pin in a large balloon, the bang was greeted with a roar of approval.

No one noticed the diminutive pianist's arrival at the piano. The sudden sustained hush concentrated minds and the audience stared in disbelief at the waif-like figure before them. For one uncharacteristic instant, Maria Wohlicka became unnerved by the stunned reception. She had, moments before, eluded Komorski's offensive clutches and now she stood alone. Komorski had been flabbergasted when he saw her exposed arms before going on. On its own, the yellow and mauve surrounding her eye might have been seen as an unfortunate accident. But together with the large area of bruising on her naked arm, there was no doubting the implications, which sparked his acute embarrassment. Komorski had been under the impression Wohlicka had sleeves to her dress. That very point had been discussed with Lutowicz: Lutowicz had asked Zukowska, and the bulbous idiot had said, "Yes".

Yesterday Komorski had experienced a hungry satisfaction when he saw the injuries on the viper. He did not give a curse if that affected her playing. If she did not play well, it was as much as she deserved. And there she was – out on stage!

Standing beside the piano…

Every part of the bruising on view...

And these imbeciles around him shouting that he must go on...

Lutowicz's nails bit into Komorski's arm. He pressed his mouth close to the conductor's ear. "Uginski," he rasped, with the bereft anguish of someone watching a lover walk out on them. "Uginski," he whispered hoarsely, tugging on the arm.

Komorski shook himself free of the grasp and returned to the necessities of the occasion. "Yes," he nodded in agreement. "Yes – of course."

He gathered himself together, imperiously dismissed those surrounding him, and walked on stage.

The applause had been long and sustained. It had been initiated when the orchestra stood, and it ceased when the conductor reached front stage and the orchestra abruptly re-seated. Maria Wohlicka also sat, and rather more quickly than was appropriate, Komorski precipitated the orchestra into Chopin's *Concerto No 2 for Pianoforte and Orchestra in F minor*. Maria Wohlicka shrugged her shoulders. Why should she care? But she did care! It was insulting to open the apotheosis of all that was romantic in such a brusque, unfeeling way.

She had seventy bars of orchestral introduction to regain her composure and play. And how would she play? As one who would never again play in or for Poland. Never again was an impossibly long time. She felt overwhelmed, and struggled for mastery. Her double forte entry at bar 71 was almost upon her. She readjusted her position on the piano stool, and as the fingers of both hands impacted on the ivory, the jarring reminder in her left arm was no match for her state of mind.

Maria Wohlicka, the darling of Poland's music world, was saying good-bye. Good-bye to her friends, her relations, her pupils. Good-bye to her possessions, what little there were, but most of all good-bye to her Poland, the amalgam of all she loved – and loathed.

After the piano entry, the audience nearest the stage became caught up in an emotional response. Young people, as the great majority of them were, might have responded more to the inherent romanticism of the music. But an incongruity in the performance, which captured their imaginations, was the austerity of the interpretation. It gave to the music a nobility and poignancy never before heard in the work. In their minds it equated with the spectre the soloist had presented when she first appeared before them. Their eyes never left the soloist's controlled performance. To do so would have amounted to an act of betrayal. So it continued through the 1st Movement and into the poetic 2nd Movement. Finally, the allegro of the 3rd Movement produced an almost audible relief of tension. It sparkled along vivaciously, the opposite of what had gone before. 'Light at the end of the tunnel,' Brenton thought, and when they emerged into the tumultuousness of the subsequent applause, Maria Wohlicka rose from the piano, a very tired but gratified soloist. She looked out and into her enthusiastic audience. She was afraid to bow, not being absolutely sure she was capable of returning to the vertical, so with tired nods of her head she accepted the jubilation surrounding her. When she raised her bruised arm in a wide sweep of the orchestra, the cheers, if possible, increased. She pointed towards the joint sponsors in the first box and here Komorski, standing motionless behind her, felt he could join the applause.

Brenton was a little disconcerted because as yet, Maria Wohlicka had chosen not to seek him out. Had she changed her mind, or was the adrenalin still flowing to the detriment of the plan?

The pianist made to move off stage. The audience reacted vociferously, which immediately denied her the opportunity. She returned to the piano and sat down. Komorski continued off stage correctly assuming an encore in the offing. The clamour died instantly.

Maria Wohlicka returned to Chopin. With tiredness clearly visible on her face, she threw off the exuberant 5th of the twenty-four *Preludes*. The crowd found the snippet greatly to their liking. It seemed to beg a further contribution, but that was not to be. Standing beside the piano, she sought and found Brenton directly below her. He acknowledged contact, and with the applause still ringing in his ears, directed the soloist's attention to a small movable stairs, which he had arranged not to be removed during the concert. Maria Wohlicka looked down apprehensively at the maintenance facility, which enabled Albert Hall staff easy access to the stage from the ground floor. Brenton slipped over the rail and from the bottom of the steps, extended his arm towards the soloist. She grasped his hand but before she could descend, she received a tap on her shoulder. Behind her stood Cranshaw with a bouquet of flowers. Maria Wohlicka released Brenton's hand and accepted the bouquet to further applause. The applause reached new heights when Cranshaw planted a kiss on both the soloist's cheeks. She returned to the edge of the stage with the bouquet in one arm and Brenton assisting the other, and then moved cautiously down the steps and into the dividing area between stage and audience. Brenton guided her towards the rail behind which a youthful clamour for autographs had started. Madame Wohlicka transferred the bouquet to Brenton and proceeded to oblige. The delay made Brenton anxious, he wished to get the manoeuvre over as quickly as possible. Maria Wohlicka's obvious joy on contact with young people helped to prolong the signings, until a glance over his shoulder confirmed his worst fears – Lina Zukowska was edging out through the orchestra to find out where her charge had disappeared to. Brenton grabbed the soloist, lifted her across the rail, threw the bouquet after her and jumped over himself. He turned to see Zokowska taking determined strides towards the front of the stage.

"She's defecting," he told the heaving crowd surrounding Wohlicka. "She's defecting! Spread the word!" The enthusiasm with which this was greeted was infectious and the word spread quickly.

"Block Bessie Bunter there," Brenton pointed back towards the stage as he pushed and guided the pianist towards the far end of the Hall. The response was instantaneous. Zukowska found it almost impossible to breach the guardrail. They waved their programmes in her face, demanding her autograph. Inevitably those closest to her received more than her autograph, and soon Zukowska had opened a wedge in the crowd, eventually shoving and battering her way into the audience. It was not any easier for her in the audience, as she was then surrounded on all sides; but she seemed impervious to physical curtailment. The promenaders had taken up the taunting chant, "Defecting! Defecting!" and this was what rang in Maria Wohlicka's ears as she walked out into Kensington Gore.

Brenton escorted her, and her bouquet, to the first of two cars parked at the kerbside. Two constables emerged from the second car to supervise proceedings and Jack Lesko jumped out from behind the driving wheel of the first.

"Dobry Wieczór Pani!" he shouted joyfully to the pianist and then, extending both hands, he added more formally, "Good evening and welcome, Madame."

Maria Wohlicka held both his hands and said, "Thank you, thank you. I hope I am not a burden." They embraced and reverted to Polish, not even noticing that it had started to rain softly. Brenton hurried them into Lesko's car and, as it moved out into traffic, signalled the police car to follow. He had no sooner done so than a panting Zukowska rushed up and joined him at the kerbside. He ostentatiously waved as the cars disappeared in the direction of Bromley. With her back to Brenton, Zukowska peered after what was now physically beyond her. Within the rush of disappointment she endeavoured to see beyond the cavalcade and into the meaning of a system – the soul of a country – that could somehow attract wayward bitches such as Wohlicka away from their motherland. Where everything was done for them. From cradle to grave. Everything. Every damn thing!

What she perceived and smelt was a people become self-indulgent. Wrapped up in their own particularities, their own fulfilments, and nothing of the collective. It was hell. Brenton could hear her short gasping breath, which, as he turned to go back inside, contrived to sound disturbed. When he reached the entrance to the Albert Hall and looked back, Lina Zukowska had begun to walk dejectedly in the same direction as the traffic. There was little point in returning. She knew what awaited her if she did.

CHAPTER 28

Saturday March 28th 1981
The Royal Albert Hall
9.15 pm

Brenton bumped into Cranshaw backstage on his way to the communications room. He was still smiling. Cranshaw knew immediately how the 'exit' had gone and smiled broadly. "A job well done," he said, "although Pecton rang down to find out what in hell's name David Brenton was up to escorting Maria Wohlicka out through the promenade!" They both laughed.

"You denied any involvement?" said Brenton.

Before Cranshaw could reply, Pecton stalked in. "What the deuce are you up to?" He glared at them with predictable hostility. Cranshaw immediately availed himself of the opportunity to impress Brenton with his degree of uninvolvement. "I was asking the same question," he said, turning to meet Pecton. A flickering glance showed that Pecton had taken in Cranshaw's fealty; the litmus test had been passed and his future secured. The eyes swivelled back to Brenton. "Well?" Pecton demanded. "Yes-yes-and-" he began to splutter, but Brenton interjected, "There's a perfectly reasonable explanation for an absolutely shameful episode."

"Try me – try me," Pecton badgered. "I demand to know."

"Half an hour before the concert started, we had an enquiry upstairs from Poland via the BBC to know was Maria Wohlicka going to play."

"What has that to do with Madame Wohlicka jumping into the audience?"

"Briefly," Brenton said, with a growing awareness of time passing, "the BBC received the query from Poland, who some way or another had became aware of the second reason. Namely, that Lina Zukowska had physically abused Maria Wohlicka. I rang down to her room here to find out if everything was all right. The soloist requested not to have to face Zukowska again."

The fluster disappeared from Pecton's face. He looked to Cranshaw for confirmation. Cranshaw said, "So that's what it was all about."

Pecton asked Brenton, "Why didn't you call the police?"

"I did," Brenton told him. "I arranged to have them meet her outside."

"Ye-es," Pecton said, more reflectively than he had ever been known to pronounce the affirmative. "I must confess – yes, I had an inkling – that something unsavoury was going on. Where may I contact her?"

"I presume", Brenton said, starting to move in the opposite direction, "that you'll be told in good time."

Pecton looked at his watch and made to return to his guests. "I take it we may look forward to a relatively uneventful second half."

"I wouldn't bank on it," Brenton muttered, and pressed on to the communications room. Cranshaw had attached himself to Pecton, so Brenton entered alone.

He met the anxious looks from Hempson, Laymott and two operators and said, "Everything went ok." Williams and Pringle sat by themselves to one side. The two operators faced four vision-monitors, the first of which could be directed to all sections of the hall. It had a zoom lens. The other three were fixed on the VIP box, the woodwind and percussion sections, and the third on a general view of the orchestra.

"We were watching your caper on the televisions," Hempson nodded towards the bank of flickering monitors. "How did you make out outside?"

"She's on her way to a safe-house in Bromley," Brenton stated with satisfaction.

"I'd like to keep an eye on her," the chief superintendent suggested, "until things cool down."

Brenton scribbled Jack Lesko's Bromley address on a piece of paper and handed it to Laymott. "There are two constables in attendance tonight. Presumably you'll make your own arrangements for a transfer?"

Laymott said it could be left with him.

"Right," Hempson redirected their attention. "Part two of the concert." He turned towards Williams and Pringle and extended an arm. "And here are our front-line yeomanry. Let's make sure they're adequately furnished."

The two bandsmen stood up. Brenton asked if their vests presented any problem. The vests had been covered in a white cotton material to diminish detection under the dress shirts. Pringle said he felt like an American footballer. Hempson thought the extra 'beef' might present a visual deterrent to a potential adversary. Williams felt safe. "And that's a good way to feel going in," he said.

"Orchestra coming back on stage," one of the operators advised.

"Now," Brenton addressed the bandsmen. "A preliminary test of the radios while the symphony gets under way. You'll be standing by for the Kilar in about half an hour.

They connected in and switched on. "I shan't speak loudly," Brenton said, and pressed the transmission button. Even before he spoke, both bandsmen signalled reception of the room ambience.

"Leader of the orchestra coming on stage," the first operator spoke into the desk microphone. Everything, vision and sound, was being recorded. Hempson and Laymott turned their attention to what was happening in the Hall. The orchestra leader, Arthur Liddel, took a bow and sat down. An expectant hush was only relieved when Komorski came on to renewed applause.

"Conductor on stage," the operator said for the record. After a moment or two, Szymanowski's Second Symphony got underway. Hempson and Laymott remained glued to the monitors, occasionally exchanging a sparse comment.

"Before you go into the musicians' dressing room," Brenton told Williams and Pringle, "there's a colleague of yours in the entrance hall from armaments waiting to deliver a pistol to you and explain its statistics. When you've finished, I'll slip around to the front of the Hall and give the communication mic a test from there."

At the Kensington Gore entrance Brenton placed the transmitter close to his mouth and whispered, "Testing from the Hyde Park side of the Hall. Testing with very low volume ... mouth close to mic ... testing testing ... over and out."

Back in the communications room, the operator confirmed that all had gone well. But an intuitive spark had been niggling away at Brenton during his transmission to Williams and Pringle. It had taken root with the hope that his transmission would not be picked up by Lutowicz or his accomplice. Out of this hope emerged the corollary – access to the opposition's transmission system – but to what effect? He grabbed the internal hall phone.

"Start of 2nd and final Movement of Szymanowski," the operator said into his desk mic. Brenton dialled the BBC control room in the gallery. Sarah answered. "Is Jim Sherry there?" Brenton asked. "He is," Sarah said with discernible diffidence, "and so is Mr Lutowicz."

"Lutowicz!" Brenton's incredulity jumped down the phone. "What the hell is he doing there?"

"He is acting as the phone liaison to Poland to let them know when the music finishes and restarts."

Brenton's momentary silence conveyed his astonishment. Lutowicz was proving to be an exceptional adversary. "What's he doing now?"

"Still speaking to Poland," Sarah said quietly.

"Put Sherry on," Brenton said, his edginess apparent.

Sherry's eager bonhomie came across as something of an affront until Brenton remembered he was an innocent participant. He impressed on Sherry the necessity for caution where Lutowicz was concerned. "He may be the new owner of our two-way radios," he warned. "Do not repeat any part of what I discuss with you. Understood, Jim?" He got immediate agreement from Sherry. Brenton continued, "We originally had four corresponding radios?"

"Yes," Sherry confirmed monosyllabically.

"Do we still have the fourth?"

"It wouldn't work with the new set," Sherry tried to explain. "It's on a different frequency – the same frequency as the original –"

"Shut up!" Brenton cut in.

"Oh yeah, right," Sherry belatedly remembered. Brenton asked again, "Do we still have the fourth one?"

"I last saw it in the back of my van – but that was some time ago."

"And it must still be there."

"Unless I threw it out."

"Christ," Brenton fumed, "You'd remember doing that, Jim. Supposing it's there in the van. Would it transmit a high volume blast of tone at 1000 Hertz? Don't give me details –" Brenton warned, "– just a yes or no."

Sherry turned this over and then said, "Yes."

"Fetch the radio and whatever else is needed in the control room. Ring me at –" Brenton searched for and gave his extension number. "Don't let that bastard see the equipment if he's there when you get back."

Brenton turned to Hempson. "Lutowicz is upstairs in the control room." Hempson raised his eyebrows questioningly. "I thought something was afoot," he said. "An enterprising chap, is our Mr Lutowicz."

Brenton muttered, "Let's hope Chisholme still has him in his sights."

"Who's that we have looking after him?" Hempson became a little fidgety.

"I transferred Chisholme from Bromley to keep a close eye on him in the Hall," Brenton said. "You have an armed Branch man on his car outside."

"Would you check that that arrangement is still in place – Chisholme, I mean."

———

There was nobody at the entrance to the stage. Brenton rushed back to the room where the Croydon office was located. Miss Maybury was the only one there.

"Where's Cranshaw?" Brenton asked without preliminaries, which did not go down well with Miss Maybury. "I need to know urgently," he added by way of explanation. He hovered impatiently in the doorway, which may have lent credence, because Miss Maybury suddenly assured him that Mr Cranshaw had left the office after receiving a telephone call from Dr Pecton during the interval.

Brenton entered the office and rang the BBC control room. Sarah again answered.

"Is Lutowicz still there?"

"He's now outside in the gallery looking down into the Hall," replied Sarah. "Adam Fuller asked him to stop chattering on the phone during the performance."

"Good for Fuller," Brenton brightened. "If he arrives there before me, tell Jim I'm on my way up."

Brenton turned to Miss Maybury. "That chap Lutowicz is upstairs in the BBC room making a nuisance of himself. I have to go upstairs and make sure he observes the niceties. Tell Cranshaw where I am. Mention why I'm upstairs and say I'm particularly disturbed because the newspaperman Chisholme seems to have disappeared and needs to be located."

Brenton made his way directly to the BBC room. There was no sign of Chisholme on the way. He had passed Lutowicz half way round the gallery. The Pole had feigned an adequate nonchalance and continued to look down into the Hall.

"Will he be returning?" Brenton asked Sarah and Fuller.

"I'm afraid so," Fuller said. "For the interlude between the Szymanowski and the final piece, the Kilar. He won't be back for the finale, you'll be glad to hear," he added.

The phone rang. Sarah answered and held the handset in Brenton's direction. "Do you mind?" Brenton asked Fuller.

"Provided it doesn't go on for ever."

"Cranshaw," Sarah murmured as she handed over.

"We've lost contact with Chisholme," Brenton said. "I think we have a problem."

Cranshaw digested this. "What do you want me to do?"

Brenton asked Fuller how much longer the Szymanowski had to run.

"Five minutes," Fuller said, after a hasty glance at the studio clock.

"You've got five minutes for a quick sweep backstage. Tell Hempson and Laymott what you're about, and ask them to get the armed officer on Lutowicz's car up here in the gallery area.

"How could Chisholme have gone astray at this critical moment?"

"I wouldn't say too much, Tim. This could be Thompson mark two."

Jim Sherry entered the control room. He carried a plastic holdall and wore an engaging smile. Brenton directed him to the equipment room off the control room. "What did you manage?"

"Everything," Sherry said, holding aloft the bag. "I found the fourth two-way. I have a good length of lead to patch us from the BBC tone source into this." He rummaged deeper into the bag. "Look at this neat little amplifier."

"Excellent," said Brenton. "Lutowicz is expected back for the interlude between the symphony and the Kilar, so work in here. You'll see him through the window. Don't let him see the two-way."

Sherry produced an electric soldering iron.

"What have you got to do?" Brenton quizzed.

"This end of the lead goes to the tone source –"

"Will it reach the balcony wall in the gallery?" Brenton cut in.

"Ample," Sherry assured. "At the wall you'll have the amplifier and the two-way. Whoever your customer is, the release of tone should blow his bloody head off!" Sherry smirked, and then became deadpan. "The bastard returns," he whispered between clenched teeth. Brenton looked through the dividing window and saw Lutowicz enter the control room. "Ok Jim, a low profile. I'll see what the story is inside."

When Brenton entered the control room the applause had already started for the finish of the Szymanowski symphony. Lutowicz sat at the end of the control desk speaking quietly into the control line to Poland. Fuller nodded to Brenton indicating a satisfactory transmission, and Sarah threaded in a further tape at the tape console. Brenton's attention returned to Lutowicz. The Pole spoke almost continuously to Poland with an unconcerned intentness. Then again, he was unaware that he was under surveillance. The internal phone rang. Brenton answered: Cranshaw stated that Chisholme was definitely missing. Before Brenton could respond, Cranshaw whispered that he had to go. Komorski was about to return to the podium for the Kilar. When Brenton turned back to the audio desk to replace the phone, he caught a glimpse of Lutowicz's crepe-soled shoes and straight away felt concern that Sarah should not see them.

"Do you have tape-machine remotes on your desk?" Brenton asked Fuller. The BBC man said he had. "Then you won't mind if I take Sarah from you for the moment."

In the adjacent room Brenton asked Sarah if she possessed a large handbag. Sarah wondered whether her shoulder bag qualified. With Brenton's nod she said, "It's next door, behind Adam Fuller. Shall I get it?" and made to move into the control room. "Not yet," Brenton arrested her eagerness. "I want to carry the two-way radio outside to the gallery. I don't want our friend inside", he indicated towards the dividing window, "to see what we're about."

"What about the holdall?" Sherry interjected, without lifting his head.

"Excellent," Brenton agreed and asked Sarah, "Is there an internal phone?"

Sarah pointed into the far corner and said it was an extension of the internal phone on the audio desk. Brenton rang the communications room backstage. One of the operators answered. Brenton asked for Hempson. "Any sign of that warrant?" he asked quickly.

"No," Hempson replied tersely.

Brenton explained that the 'intruder' was still in the vicinity.

"The buffer should have left by now!" Hempson grumbled. "The final music has already started. Look, old man," he said abruptly, "I've sent out for the armed Branchman for you. Cranshaw has been in to say there's no sign of Chisholme. I'm not taking any further chances with Lutowicz. He's an irritating nuisance roaming around the place. I'm suggesting to Laymott that we take him in; diplomatic status notwithstanding. If it turns out we were mistaken – it can be explained as all in a good cause."

Sarah tugged Brenton's sleeve. "He's gone," she nodded towards the dividing window. Brenton relayed the information to Hempson.

"Right, we'll try and intercept him. You get on with your business. We have everything else covered down here."

———

Fuller shouted from the control room, "I need Sarah to read the score for me. The dynamic markings are giving me trouble."

Brenton indicated to Sarah to oblige.

"David," Sherry beckoned from the litter of electronics on the table. "If I attach the amplifier to the two-way, I'm certain some of the wiring will break when you go to use it. Would it make any difference if I inserted the amplifier beside the tone source in the control room?"

Brenton saw no reason why not. Sherry quickly soldered the wires into the two-way and brought the amplifier into the control room jack-field to complete the circuit. Brenton stuck his head outside into the gallery causeway. It was dimly lit and deserted. He lifted the holdall and, trailing the connecting wire, made his way around to a point where he had a good view of the stage and VIP box. Kilar's music surged up from below. Brenton placed the holdall against the waist-high wall separating the gallery from the balcony underneath. He extracted his own two-way and prepared to speak to Williams and Pringle on stage. When a quiet section arrived he pressed the speak button and said, "If you're receiving me – one of you stand."

Brenton raised the binoculars and saw Williams give Pringle the nod: Cpl Pringle stood. Time was in short supply, but at least this was one less thing to worry about.

He lifted out Jim Sherry's two-way radio from the holdall. The extra wires bulged from its side. The instrument was now held together by tape. The connecting wire stretched back along the gallery and into the control room to what he hoped was a piercing volume of tone. By inserting himself on the same wavelength as Lutowicz, he could hope to get through to the trigger-man and identify him. And – he hoped against hope – also neutralise him. Sherry's amplifier would deliver a deafening blast to the trigger-man's earpiece and incapacitate him. He found that his hands were shaking, so he knelt down and placed the binoculars on the gallery wall to steady his view. He concentrated on the woodwind and percussion sections of the orchestra and, his heart pounding, pressed the transmission button. The response from within the woodwind was immediate and frantic. Reptarski dropped his bassoon and grabbed his head in agony. In the binoculars his convulsed features dramatically underlined the volume he had taken.

"Bingo," Brenton exhaled. He wiped the sweat from his forehead and then lowered the binoculars. He must inform the bandsmen on his own two-way. There was a movement behind him. He had expected Jim Sherry, but was shaken to find Lutowicz standing there. The Pole had installed himself further along the gallery behind a pillar and had been speaking to Reptarski when his compatriot's agonised reaction alerted him to possible extraneous interference. He looked over to see Brenton using a two-way.

Lutowicz's suspicions showed clearly on his face. "What are you doing?" he demanded in halting English. Brenton faced Lutowicz and said, "I could well ask the same of you, and perhaps with more reason."

"I am Polish security," Lutowicz stated flatly. Brenton felt Lutowicz was playing for time. If nothing else intervened, then what the SB man had planned would take place.

But before Brenton could achieve extrication from the verbal dance, Lutowicz withdrew a small pistol from his inside pocket and placed it to Brenton's temple. "Tell me," he said, with the assured menace of one who held the upper hand, "Why you do this?" He indicated towards the binoculars and two-way. Brenton tried to calculate how much of the Kilar remained, but with the cold tip of the gun barrel against his head, every note in the score dissolved in a jumble. Note by note that fateful last bar was inching closer and closer, pulling them towards an abyss.

"Why don't we call the Hall security?" Brenton suggested.

Lutowicz grunted dismissively. "I am security," he said, tapping the pistol against Brenton's head. "Tell me what you are doing, before I hurt you."

The control room door opened. Lutowicz glanced behind, but Brenton's hand shot out and cracked into the SB man's larynx, karate style. The pistol shot a round and Lutowicz fell back gasping and coughing towards the open door. Jim Sherry stood in the doorway not sure whether to come forward or take cover.

"Call security!" Brenton shouted, and moved in the opposite direction towards a door in the gallery wall. He staggered out through it, and then a second door onto an encircling roof. A soft drizzle of rain enveloped him. He searched for a hiding place, without success, and wondered how the rain had managed to soak his person so rapidly. He held up his dripping hand close to his face in the dim light. It was covered in blood! He could not believe what he was seeing. He felt no pain. There had been no feeling of impact. No indication of any sort. He tried to source the blood, but heard the first door to the Hall opening behind him. He would be seen immediately at the back of any one of the skylights. He slipped behind the door that opened out onto the roof. He had hardly done so when he felt Lutowicz's presence on the other side. He tried to control his breathing. The strain imbued the distant music with menace and his heart beat a syncopated accompaniment to its insistent rhythm.

Before his staring eyes, Lutowicz's pistol edged out between the door and the doorframe; Brenton's breathing stopped. Then, with a sudden exhalation, he slammed the door on the pistol barrel and held the pressure on the door. Nothing happened for a number of seconds. Then centimetre-by-centimetre, the nose of the barrel began to jerk back inside. Brenton exerted further pressure but the gun continued to jerk and jolt its way back inside the door. In desperation he grabbed the barrel. A round shot between his fingers into the Kensington night – the pistol vanished, and the door snapped shut. Brenton put his back to the door and braced his feet against the ground. The door handle rattled at his back, then the door itself began to bump threateningly. Brenton wrested the two-way from his jacket. "It's Reptarski!" he yelled into the transmitter. "Reptarski!" he repeated, "On bassoon!"

Lutowicz blasted a hole in the door between Brenton's shoulder and his head. Brenton pitched sideways. As he picked himself from the ground, Lutowicz emerged onto the roof. They eyed one another silently. Lutowicz smiled appreciatively.

"I could kill you now," he said. He waved the pistol towards the parapet wall. "But I have a better plan." He positioned himself between the exit door and Brenton's position at the parapet wall. "Move!" he shouted. "I give you chance," Contempt etched itself on the SB man's face. "I shoot – or you jump?"

Brenton did not bother to assess the odds. "Shoot, you bastard. You'll pay for it." Lutowicz raised the pistol in Brenton's direction. Brenton felt a need to close his eyes. Behind his lids he confronted his anguish, and within it, the lost opportunity to find fulfilment.

The blast shattered the air. He stood there frozen to the spot, until the strangeness of it impinged: he was indeed still standing. His eyes shot open to see Lutowicz collapsed on the ground. This was a reversal of such proportions that it took time to connect what had happened – and the Branchman who had stepped from the shadow of the doorway, revolver in hand.

"Glad you could make it," Brenton said stiffly as the Branchman reholstered.

"Sorry sir," the policeman said, bending over Lutowicz's body. "I came as quickly as I could, are you all right?"

Brenton nodded and moved across to where the Branchman was pocketing Lutowicz's pistol. His foot came in contact with his two-way transmitter where it had fallen after he had jumped aside from the door. "Jesus!" Brenton gasped and snatched up the transmitter. The Kilar was drawing to a close.

The two-way was still switched on, so Brenton pressed the speak button and shouted, "It's Reptarski, on the bassoon – in front of you." But the battery had faded to a point where both transmissions from outside the Hall were a mere crackle on the bandsmen's earpieces.

Brenton turned to the Branchman. "I've business downstairs," and stumbled towards the door. His limbs would not obey him, and he suddenly felt so weak as he bumped and staggered his way back onto the gallery.

There, Det Sgt Broadbent could not hold Sarah or Jim Sherry back, and all three surged around Brenton to find out what had happened. Brenton's anxiety was immediately obvious. All his focus was on reaching the point in the gallery where he had last communicated with Williams and Pringle with his own two-way radio. The whole evening – the whole operation – depended on it.

On stage the Kilar was drawing to a vigorous climax – *molto rustico* – and first the brass and then the woodwind rose to their feet at Professor Komorski's direction. They began to wave their instruments around – *ad lib*. Ronald Shipsey at the organ console steadied himself in order to deliver the massive C major chord in the final bar, and Reptarski pointed his second bassoon – directly at the VIP box.

In the cacophonous tumult, nothing seemed out of place – except Reptarski's bassoon, the only steady instrument in the orchestra. Its mouthpiece was straight and larger than normal and culminated in a round eyeglass, which Reptarski placed to his right eye. A colleague, who did notice, thought the displacement wonderfully amusing, all part of the hilarity of the occasion.

"Reptarski!" Brenton shouted into the two-way. "It's Reptarski! The outside bassoon! Reptarski – nail him!" He snatched up his binoculars: Williams and Pringle had snapped into action. They lunged at Reptarski and grabbed an arm each; his feet didn't even touch the ground as the two bandsmen lifted him bodily and disappeared at the double through the on-stage door – just as Shipsey forcefully struck the C major chord.

CHAPTER 29

Saturday March 28th 1981
The Royal Albert Hall
9.55 pm

Brenton's command about the bassoonist had also been received in the backstage communications room and as he slid exhaustedly onto a chair in the control room, hastily provided by Sherry, Hempson and Laymott raced to meet Reptarski as he was escorted off stage. Laymott produced his identification and informed Reptarski that he was being detained.

Hempson congratulated the army bandsmen and asked them to go back on stage and collect both of Reptarski's instruments. The applause for the Kilar had commenced and before Williams and Pringle had a chance to go back on stage, Cranshaw opened the door for Komorski's first exit.

The professor glowered at the bandsmen and then more apprehensively took in Reptarski's state of detention. He mopped his brow and hurriedly made his way back to the podium and the consolation of continuous applause. Williams' and Pringle's music etiquette made them reluctant to follow a conductor back on stage to further loud applause. "The buffer's part of their set-up," Hempson snapped, and pushed them back on stage. Their reservations dissolved, they sidled through the on-stage door, picked up a bassoon each, and awaited the general exodus of the orchestra. Hempson peered through the partly opened door to make sure his material evidence was in safe hands. He had nothing yet on Reptarski, so Brenton was going to need some pertinent reason for his order to apprehend him. All appeared to be in safe hands on stage.

"Take Reptarski inside to the communications room and search him," he ordered the custodial detective. In his capacity as detaining officer, Morgan Laymott went to oversee the search. Hempson and two Branch men awaited the orchestra, but before the orchestra had completely come off, Laymott rushed back to Hempson and muttered in his ear,

"Two down in the gallery, one of them Brenton."

"Good God!" Hempson wheeled around to Laymott, and then to Cranshaw. "Get on stage and make sure no one disturbs the site around Reptarski's seat." Cranshaw moved before Hempson had even finished. Hempson then turned to the Branchmen. "When the orchestra comes off, escort the bandsmen to the communications room here."

Laymott said Det Sgt Broadbent had radioed in the message. "The gallery should be sealed off by now," Laymott looked at the wall clock, "and the medics are on their way. They'll be met at the Kensington Gore entrance and brought up."

"Good," Hempson responded, and then hesitantly, "What's Brenton's condition?"

"He's been hit high up on his arm – lost a lot of blood."

"He'll survive," Hempson said with some relief.

"Orchestra off stage," the operator spoke into the desk mic.

The door opened and Williams and Pringle entered, still escorting Reptarski and with an accompanying escort of Branchmen. They laid the two bassoons on a table at the back of the room.

"Find anything on Reptarski?" Hempson wanted to know.

"Nothing substantial," Laymott had to admit. "But he was wearing a two-way radio strapped to his trouser belt, with a listening lead sewn inside his jacket."

"That's what we're looking for," Hempson said, approaching the table. "Could we attach Mr Reptarski", Hempson wondered, "to something solid? Such as his arresting officer or –" He swung his arm in the direction of the corner, "– perhaps one of those water pipes?" He glanced at Laymott. "He seems a trifle malevolent standing there."

Laymott caught Hempson's unease and moved to allay it. He ordered the detective sergeant to handcuff Reptarski to one of the down pipes. Reptarski did not take this lightly, and his blustering protestations increased when Hempson picked up one of the bassoons from the table. "Lighter than I thought," Hempson mused and passed the instrument to Laymott. He picked up the second instrument and immediately felt the extra weight. "Oh?" he said interrogatively, and moved round to more direct light.

Reptarski ceased protestations. Instead he tried desperately, within the confines of his handcuffs, to avoid the position in which an intent Hempson was pointing the instrument. Eventually the distraught musician could not contain himself and screamed – "Stop! Stop! Don't press the B flat. Turn it away! Don't press the keys!"

Hempson withdrew his hands and turned his attention to Reptarski. The Pole heaved a shuddering sigh and closed his eyes.

"Is there some reason I shouldn't touch the keys?" Hempson asked and moved closer. Reptarski's eyes opened to find the top of the bassoon beside his head. "Don't – no!" he shouted, and frantically moved his head away from the swaying top of the instrument. "No, no, please," he wailed. Hempson replaced the bassoon on the table and glanced over at the two bandsmen; they immediately averted their eyes.

"I think", said Hempson, "you're needed back in the dressing room." He nodded slowly. "And er, pick up all stray conversation while you're at it." He pointed to the radios. "Strip the two-way from your persons and leave them here," he indicated the Branch technician. "If anyone enquires about Reptarski – say he was taken ill." He rapidly ushered them out the door.

"Thanks Morgan," Hempson turned back to the handcuffed Pole. He jammed the top of the bassoon under Reptarski's chin and said, "Now sir, tell me why I should not place my hand down here on what you call the B flat?"

"No, no, don't. Don't do that," cried Reptarski hoarsely, his eyes shooting down to where Hempson's fingers had begun to poke at the keys of the instrument.

"Don't!" Reptarski roared, and then weakly whispered, "Ok – I tell you."

"Yes," Hempson agreed, "you certainly will." He encouraged this with a jab of the bassoon. "I'm waiting."

Reptarski swallowed and said, "I don't know what they will do to me."

"They?" Hempson responded with grim amusement. "Do you think it will be any worse than what I'll do if you don't open your mouth?" He rammed the instrument in tighter on Reptarski's throat.

"If I were you, Reptarski," Laymott intervened, "I should make my own arrangements. Lutowicz has already made his upstairs."

"I don't give a tuppenny damn", Hempson goaded Reptarski, "whether you live or die. It would give me a great deal of pleasure to press this B flat and dispatch you into the bargain. It would save a great deal of paper work, so get on with it."

"Ok, ok," said Reptarski. "There's a gun inside that." The words came out grudgingly as he jerked his head towards the instrument under his chin.

"We bloody well know that," Hempson barked scornfully. "Tell us something we don't know." This took Reptarski aback; it also prompted him to undertake a comprehensive reassessment of his part in the undertaking. Hempson motioned that the operator keep a tape rolling.

Reptarski's second bassoon, as it transpired, had spent time in the expert hands of an established Afghan gunsmith whose ingenuity had enabled him to insert a precision rifle, accommodating two rounds, inside the long cylindrical barrel of the instrument. A very precise periscopic lens within its straightened mouthpiece was Russian. The trigger was activated by the lowest note on the bassoon, B flat, as he had already told them.

Hempson removed the bassoon from under Reptarski's chin and replaced it on the table. "Take him down to your place and charge him," Hempson said. "Though, come to think of it, it may be wiser to keep him here until the dust has settled."

The door opened and Det Insp Blackmore came in. "Let's take this outside," Laymott suggested straightaway. "I don't want Reptarski picking up any floating info." Blackmore glowered. "Well?" Hempson prompted impatiently. The detective inspector looked at Hempson. "Sorry about the late arrival."

"Bugger the late arrival," Hempson snorted, "Have you got Lutowicz's warrant?"

"I don't," Blackmore bluntly responded. "Bullet and weapon didn't match."

Hempson and Laymott were dumbstruck. Laymott managed, "But how can that be?"

"That's what delayed me," Blackmore shook his head. Hempson and Laymott both saw that Blackmore's bluff awkwardness was directed against himself. He could not hold either of their disbelieving looks and shifted from one leg to the other. "When the first negative test came in," he said, eyeing the tips of his size twelves, "I could not believe it. I asked them to do it again." He removed one hand from his overcoat pocket in a gesture of uselessness, and quickly stuffed it back in. "I forced them to do it again," he said, raising his head to the lights. He expected their admonition, and in some deep dark repository of his being, he needed their admonition. He would accept it in a spirit of atonement. "The second test confirmed the first," he ploughed on. "The round which killed Thompson was not fired from the weapon found in Appleby's car."

The trio mulled over the implications. Hempson and Laymott dwelt on what they had thought were the pre-concert certainties, Blackmore on the post-concert prognosis.

"Look here, Blackmore," Hempson said, "You appear to be taking to yourself responsibility for a train of events which did not, as it were, bear fruit. I think you should hold onto the fact that this was not a mistake on your part."

"Major Hempson is right," Laymott joined in.

"But I started the train of events," Blackmore countered. He turned on his heel and walked away.

Det Sgt Broadbent then rushed in. "I didn't want to say over the radio, but Lutowicz is dead."

"Well," Hempson said to Laymott, "It turns out Blackmore's warrant might have been a life saver."

Broadbent said, "I wouldn't give it a thought, sir. Lutowicz was shot when about to shoot David Brenton. Brenton had already taken a round in the Hall. He escaped onto the roof. Lutowicz followed and was blocked just in time."

"Who pressed the trigger?" Laymott asked.

"Det Sgt Griggins, sir. He'd been ordered in from Lutowicz's car."

"Yes, we know about that," Laymott said. "How is he?"

"The medics gave him a sedative. He's sitting with Brenton in the gallery until the audience goes. Then they'll be taken to hospital."

Det Sgt Broadbent reached into his pocket and took out a transparent plastic bag. It held a small calibre pistol, of the same type as had been found in Appleby's car.

"This is Lutowicz's pistol," the detective sergeant told them.

"I'm sure Blackmore will be interested in this," Laymott smiled.

"A word of caution," Hempson interjected. "May we speak?"

Laymott immediately relieved Broadbent of Lutowicz's pistol. "Get back upstairs and let them know that Major Hempson will be up shortly to see David Brenton."

Broadbent turned and retreated.

Laymott wearily acceded to Hempson's request. "What's on your mind?"

"I would consider it prudent not to pass that weapon to Blackmore just yet." He nodded towards the pocket in which Laymott had pocketed the plastic bag.

"Why so?" Laymott emitted a nervous laugh. "Earlier you were the essence of sympathy and compassion where Blackmore was concerned. Are we back to the wars?"

"Oh no, not at all," Hempson hastened to reassure. "I was sympathetic. Still am," he emphasised. "What I'm suggesting has nothing to do with Blackmore."

"I'm sorry," Laymott's expression hardened. "I was under the impression it had everything to do with Blackmore. You said so yourself. I heard you with my own ears at one of those meetings during the week. Due process," he added, with growing exasperation, "and a lot more besides."

Hempson nodded and listened as the chief superintendent pointed out, "I know Blackmore can be awkward, but he's also as straight as a die."

"A characteristic that should be nurtured rather than sidetracked," Hempson said. "We are as one on that, but, and I am loath to remind you, there is another strand to the business we're both engaged in, and –" his voice rose slightly in case Laymott felt tempted to jump in "– if there's one tenet I've learned to value more than another it is – never close a door. The most searching appraisal of any given moment in time will never match its subsequent qualified review. It may be draughty under the circumstances; better that, than closing off a solution for the sake of being tidy."

"What are you saying?" Laymott demanded.

"I said my suggestion has nothing to do with Blackmore. What it concerns is the further evolution of this international business we have on our hands. I'm not suggesting that we withdraw that article permanently." Hempson's eyes again sought Laymott's pocket. "What I am suggesting, and I emphasise it's only a suggestion, is leaving it in abeyance for a time to be mutually agreed."

"I can't see the point in all of this," said Laymott, still nettled. "What the hell difference will it make if Blackmore wraps up his due process?"

"I can only answer that it may make not the slightest difference. On the other hand …" Hempson left it hanging ominously.

"Very well," Laymott yielded irritably. "What time scale are we talking about?"

"Monday evening suit?"

"I haven't a bloody idea whether it does or doesn't," Laymott muttered. "I do know it shall quite possibly suit you." The communications room door banged after him.

"Much obliged, Morgan," Hempson murmured.

CHAPTER 30

Saturday March 28th 1981
The Royal Albert Hall
10.30 pm

Hempson bent down to where Brenton was sitting in the gallery; the extent of his torpor was startling. His injured arm had been withdrawn from his jacket sleeve and strapped to his body. "Why hasn't he been taken to hospital?" he demanded. The doctor looked up from his kneeling position in front of Brenton and said, "We've been prevented from moving because there's a clampdown on this area for security reasons."

Hempson returned to Brenton, "How are you feeling, old man?"

Brenton found it difficult to focus on the major, but managed to mumble, "Fine ... Major ... fine."

"He should be in hospital," Sarah said anxiously. "The doctor says he needs a transfusion."

"Damn it all," Hempson fumed to Det Sgt Broadbent, "Who's in charge up here?" Broadbent pointed to the exit and said there was an inspector there in contact with the communications room.

"Right," A muscle twitched in Hemspon's jaw. "Beat along in there. Get the damned lights turned up around here, and let's get Brenton on the way. The audience has gone. There should be no impediment." He leaned forward to Brenton again and said, "We'll have you in a good clean bed presently."

Brenton responded with a sleepy smile.

"What's been happening?" Adam Fuller asked Hempson. This was the third time he had asked the same question without receiving a rational explanation.

"Who are you?" Hempson asked.

"I'm the one who normally asks the questions round here," Fuller said, a slight touch of pique in his voice. "My name is Adam Fuller, and that is my area of operation," He pointed towards the control room. "I work for the BBC." But before Hempson could respond, the lights came on and the inspector was at his side.

"I want Brenton out of here and into hospital," Hempson ordered. He turned to the doctor. "Get your orderlies in and let's get moving." The doctor rose from his kneeling position and asked the inspector to radio down for the ambulance orderlies and a stretcher.

When he'd finished, Hempson asked the inspector to let Chief Supt Laymott know what was happening. "I passed on the info before coming over," the inspector said. Hempson turned to Sarah, hoping that she had suffered no ill effects. He wondered whether or not she might accompany Brenton to hospital. "Try and stop me," Sarah laughed, perhaps for the first time that evening.

"Good, good," Hempson approved. She found it difficult to remove her eyes from Brenton's for any length of time, and when they returned she saw that they had closed. She drew the doctor's attention and went to kneel beside Brenton's chair.

The ambulance men arrived and Brenton was transferred to a stretcher. "Off you go," said Hempson, bending over the stretcher. "Good luck, David, thanks for everything. I'll drop by later."

Sarah's concern had also made a good impression on him. "Good girl," he said, and squeezed her arm. "Look after him," as the group set off for the exit.

"Now who have we here?" Hempson addressed the remainder. Fuller stepped forward. "I've already introduced myself," he said, his curiosity tempered by Hempson's augustness. "I've yet to find out who you are."

Hempson took sardonic account of the faces around him and reached into his pockets for smoking utensils. "I'm Frank Hempson," he said, opening his tobacco pouch. "I represent the security service."

"I don't think you are allowed smoke here," Fuller pointed out.

"Who's going to stop me?" Hempson struck a match. "I haven't had a smoke since the whole thing started this evening. Now then,"

Hempson harumphed and directed Det Sgt Broadbent to take a list of names. "First of all, David Brenton," Hempson said with a visible degree of satisfaction. "And his assistant, Sarah Carlyle. They've left the Hall for hospital," he stated, reiterating the obvious. He relit his pipe and addressed the quiet member of the group. "And you are?" he questioned.

"I'm Jim Sherry," Sherry said with unusual solemnity. "I look after the technical end of things for Symphony Hall, Croydon."

"Very good," Hempson said, and turning to Det Sgt Broadbent added, "And of course, Adam Fuller of the BBC."

"Is this some kind of –" Fuller started, and then changed his mind. "Are we under arrest, or suspicion or something?"

"Nothing of the kind," Hempson assured. "I apologise if that's the impression you got." He pulled indulgently on his pipe, which beguiled Fuller and Sherry, who then wondered how they could ever have thought anything except the very best of Hempson. "I wish to ask you a few questions," Hempson told them and leaned against the balcony wall. It was all so laid back and easy. A while ago Hempson had instilled anxiety – even fear. Now he was their favourite uncle. Hempson tucked a hand under his arm, which steadied his pipe.

"Questions about what?" Fuller's puzzlement surfaced again.

"What you were doing and saw during the concert," Hempson said. For the first time during the interview, Sherry's eyes lit up. "I saw Lutowicz with a gun in his hand," he said enthusiastically. "Falling around the place like he was drunk, when I came out onto the gallery from the control room."

"Now that's the sort of thing I'm looking for," Hempson congratulated Sherry who, thus encouraged, added for good measure, "He fired a shot."

"I saw or heard nothing of this," Fuller opened up. "I was busy inside flying the desk – with Sarah Carlyle's assistance. If I knew what you were looking for I might be able to assist more positively."

Hempson said, "Thanks just the same. Even that morsel is of assistance because it places you and Miss Carlyle in a certain place at a particular time." Hempson moved away from the balcony wall to relight his pipe. "Obviously neither of you is aware of the big story of the evening, and I'm sorry I didn't fill you in at the beginning. Frankly, I wished to find out what your in-concert impressions were, unadulterated so to speak, by the underlying drama."

While re-lighting his pipe, he told Fuller and Sherry, between puffs, that the story of the evening had been Maria Wohlicka's defection. During Fuller's and Sherry's surprised reaction, Hempson again managed a comprehensive ignition. "Yes," he said in a more relaxed mien. "All went relatively smoothly, but if I may issue a word of caution: do not be tempted to open your mouths to the media on the subject. The lady in question is not yet out of danger, and won't be for some time."

Hempson looked sternly at the two in front of him. "You saw for yourselves the lengths these people were prepared to go to, to try and prevent this talented lady from gaining freedom."

The major turned to Sherry. "Your description of Lutowicz captures that individual's disposition precisely."

"And now he is no more," mused Sherry.

Hempson's teeth ground on the stem of his pipe. "What do you mean?"

"I heard someone say Lutowicz was dead when Brenton came in from the roof."

"Ah." Hempson turned aside to dislodge the moisture from the bowl of his pipe. After a thorough shaking, he jammed the pipe between his teeth and whipped out a handkerchief to wipe his hands. "What you possibly heard was – Lutowicz is DID." Hempson spelt out the letters. He looked to Broadbent for support and then back to Sherry.

"What's DID?" Fuller wanted to know.

"I really shouldn't be getting into this," Hempson said more tightly. "But if it eases your minds," he said, putting caution aside, "it means Diplomatic Immunity Delete." He studied their two faces for receptiveness and when satisfied, elaborated, "The bugger's on his way back to Poland."

Jim Sherry became furious at this avoidance of just deserts. "I hope they bury him," he hissed.

"That may be just what they'll do," Hempson remarked. "Now chaps," he addressed them more briskly, "we have some cleaning up to do so we want you out of here. Broadbent will take you downstairs and organise a lift home for you – on us. I may be in touch with you again for further details. The bones of the story will possibly make the Sunday papers tomorrow, but for Maria Wohlicka's sake, keep it quiet."

He shook hands and they departed with Det Sgt Broadbent. Sherry to his van with the recordings; Fuller to accept the offer of a lift.

The inspector turned to Hempson and said, "DID, sir? I hadn't heard of that one before."

"Neither had I," Hempson murmured.

———

Morgan Laymott got back to the gallery and reported that the orchestra instruments were being packed into the transporters downstairs. Hempson grasped his arm. "Is there any chance", he wondered, "that we might borrow one of Cranshaw's double bass zipped coverings, for half an hour at the most? To remove Lutowicz unobtrusively," he explained.

Cranshaw dutifully obliged, and a double bass case materialised. Lutowicz was quickly zipped inside a body bag and squeezed into the instrument container, and the case was rapidly taken outside, its contents unceremoniously dumped inside a dark anonymous van. There was a certain satisfaction in the crudeness of transport with which Lutowicz departed. The first stage of the SB man's last journey had begun, and the way was now clear for a search of the Hall from top to bottom. They knew the truth of Chisholme's whereabouts lay behind Lutowicz's cold tightening jaws.

They tried the roof area first, without result. The equipment left behind in the gallery by both Lutowicz and Brenton was collected and stored. Hempson and Laymott ushered the troop of detectives out the exit and down to the next level. They re-assembled at the bottom of the stairs and the surrounding foyer. Laymott ordered their search locations and then rejoined Hempson. They were on the point of entering the balcony to oversee the operation inside the auditorium, when both were drawn by an intermittent yet persistent rattle from somewhere alongside the stairs. They traced it to a small utility cupboard, which opened easily and quietly. Inside Chisholme lay prostrate on the floor, bound and gagged, back to the wall, feet outstretched, and out to the world. Like a tired ratchet, his snores bubbled up to them. Hempson looked at Laymott's surprised face. "The alternative concert," he suggested, and tapped the soles of Chisholme's shoes with his foot. Chisholme awakened with a jolt, and then they saw the trickle of congealed blood from his temple.

Inside the auditorium the search was ordered to stand down. Within minutes the only activity was the remaining instrumental cleanout at the side door. In the office, Cranshaw was putting away the last of his papers when Hempson entered. The wicker baskets full of music scores had already departed. Cranshaw jangled the mass bells at Hempson and said, "I have to bring these back to Brompton Oratory tomorrow."

Hempson had come from the communications room where he had overseen the departure of the two operators with their final trolley-load of equipment. Reptarski had been escorted to detention. "The place seems oddly forlorn in the end," Hempson said to Cranshaw. "Or is that the after-effect of this particular concert?"

"No," Cranshaw said, "that's the usual wind-down after a programme. The fun and games have moved to another venue."

Hempson raised interrogative eyebrows.

"The reception at the Polish embassy," Cranshaw said briskly.

"Are you going?"

"Yes, of course I'm going, I'm expected to attend."

Hempson looked at Cranshaw more closely. A number of possibilities jumped to mind. "Is Komorski attending?" he asked.

"Naturally," Cranshaw replied. "Look," He snatched a sheet of paper from a desk. "Here's the list."

"Are you under some sort of pressure?" Hempson enquired. Cranshaw hesitated knowing that his curtain had been raised. "I mean," the major continued, "apart from the pressure we've all been under this evening?"

"Pecton was in here before he left for the reception, and I'm not sure he doesn't smell a rat."

"Good God Cranshaw, we've spent a lot of time and money putting you in position; what's happened?"

"He wants a written report on the Maria Wohlicka episode."

"So – you write a report saying you know bugger all about what happened. You pressed a bouquet into her arms and she jumped into the audience. You didn't push her – she jumped," Hempson emphasised, jabbing his index finger at him. "*He* saw what happened. Ask him for a bloody report."

Cranshaw sighed. "He wants another one on Reptarksi."

"What did you say to him about Reptarski?"

"I said what I was instructed to say," Cranshaw said reasonably. "I said Reptarski was taken ill."

"And what's the problem with that?" Hempson demanded.

"No problem," Cranshaw said with growing alarm at the rise in temperature, "But –"

"But nothing. Don't make me nostalgic for the return of David Brenton. There's nothing amiss here that a little arrogance won't circumvent. Get off your knees and remember your master resides in Gower Street." Hempson picked up the invitation list. "What's the ambassador like?"

"A career diplomat. Cultured. Kindly."

"Is he mixed up in this business?"

"Doubt it," Cranshaw considered. "I shouldn't think so."

"Any chance of an invitation?"

"To the reception?"

"Cranshaw!" Hempson exploded, "No – to the Mad Hatter's tea party. For God's sake keep your mind on the job."

"Sorry sir – sorry."

Hempson sighed in exasperation. "Ambassadors, by and large, are penny-boys to the real representatives; usually some thug such as Lutowicz. I'd like to take a look at Mr ambassador and, come to think of it, Professor Komorski. I'd like to see them on their home ground."

"You might also look over this evening's guest – Uginski?"

"Yes. How do I get in?"

"You could use Brenton's invitation. I have it here." He rummaged in his papers and extracted a white envelope. "It should be perfectly feasible to scratch out Brenton's name and insert yours. Major Frank Hempson would look quite well. Albert Hall security wouldn't be too far away from the truth. I can initial the change." Cranshaw laid his pile of material back on his desk and opened the envelope. He changed the names with a flourish.

"What's the best way to travel, and more importantly, to arrive?" Hempson deferred to Cranshaw.

"I'll go first," Cranshaw said. "I should be there now, actually." He hastily gathered up his things. "I'll explain at the door that you'll be arriving sometime later."

He departed leaving the door wide open. Hempson looked around at three empty desks. This once busy office had witnessed unusual and strange comings and goings during a short intense period of time. Brenton had first caught sight of Lutowicz's crepe-soled shoes in here. He had tumbled to the voice on tape being Appleby's in here, and Cranshaw had seen Appleby's exit to eternity from this room.

'Yes,' Hempson conceded, 'all under such pressure of time.' But that had been the problem all week. And why start to slow things down now? To enter the winners' enclosure and find the prize had been forfeited would not do. He turned and walked through the open door.

CHAPTER 31

Saturday March 28th 1981
The Polish Embassy, London
11 pm

The after-concert reception at the embassy was a jolly affair. The principals were able to come down off their interpretive high in congenial surroundings; the more prestigious recipients of their interpretation were happy to have an opportunity to mix with the interpreters; and smiling benignly over all were the organisers, delighted with the active social mix their enterprise had engendered.

Hempson looked around the soirée, obligatory glass of wine in hand. The only satisfied faces in the crowd were British, he found. Michael Pecton had also noticed Hempson and wondered who he was. At one point, Pecton found himself close by the seemingly unattached Hempson. "May I ask who you are?" he enquired, as Hempson tried to squeeze through. "No offence," he added, "I thought I knew everyone since I sent out the invitations."

"Major Frank Hempson,"

"Michael Pecton, Dr Michael Pecton."

They shook hands unenthusiastically. Pecton stared unblinkingly through his glasses at Hempson for some explanation. Hempson said, "Security."

"Ah." Pecton pursed his lips. "Every retired army officer in the country seems to be in security of one sort or another. Either that or doormen in large hotels. So, security in the Albert Hall?"

"Yes," Hempson confirmed.

"How could you have allowed that debacle to occur in front of the ambassador?" Pecton admonished, indicating the distinguished man beside him while ostentatiously refraining from introducing Hempson.

"Whatever are you referring to?"

"I refer to Maria Wohlicka galloping out through the audience," Pecton's voice rose irritatedly. "Security sadly lacking there!"

Hempson felt affronted. "Are you suggesting I should have hauled her back?"

Croydon's general manager shifted a little. "I would like to know who left those steps in position, for instance. In fact, yes, I demand to know why they were left there. I have never seen utility steps there during a concert." Pecton eased sideways to allow Lyle Butler access to the group. The junior minister had represented the government at the concert and was happy that to all outward appearances at any rate, the occasion was a success.

Pecton turned his back on Hempson to prevent his inclusion in the company of a government minister.

"Frank," Butler said with obvious surprise. "Just the man I've been thinking about. How did you get mixed up with this rum lot?" The minister promptly moved over beside Hempson and administered a discreet clap on the back. "Glad to see you, old chap. Need to have a word." He turned to Pecton and the ambassador. "Would you mind excusing us?"

It was difficult to find a conveniently quiet spot, so Butler suggested the entrance hall. Hempson pointed out that if the conversation was important, then they were better off in the clamour of their immediate surroundings. Butler readily agreed and asked, "So what happened?"

Hempson unobtrusively took cognisance of who was where, and said quietly, "We have an assassin and his weapon in custody. Witold Lutowicz has been shot and killed –"

Butler blanched and reached for Hempson's elbow. Hempson continued, "David Brenton has been shot and injured." Hempson nodded in the Polish ambassador's direction. "Their *chef de equipage*, Lina Zukowska, stumbled at the last fence, so to speak, and has bolted. The good news is the pianist Maria Wohlicka has defected and is safe and sound until this blows over. Apart from that…" Hempson allowed the unsaid corollary to hang between them.

Lyle Butler had had some intimation from his personal detective that something of an unusual nature had taken place, but it had been no preparation for the facts. After what seemed like an unduly long period of time, which Hempson had no intention of disturbing, the minister eventually whispered, "Good God!"

Hempson stonily took account of the minister's pious inclinations. "You may put your trust in God," he said. "Unfortunately, it falls to us to interpret his intentions. We are not infallible you know," he quietly but pointedly put to Butler. "On this occasion the government were lucky – our scramble paid off."

"May I nab you for a moment, Lyle?" Michael Pecton's sharp voice cut through the party hub-hub. "I'd like to introduce you to some ardent admirers of your political acumen."

Hempson preferred not to have to witness this jollification. Butler leaned towards Pecton and still in the serious and confidential tone with which he had received Hempson's news, said, "Michael, can it wait? I have some important aspects to take on board here with Frank."

Pecton was surprised. Yet he was sufficiently in awe of, and innately predisposed towards, the aura of political power as to be able to quickly overcome what he realised had been his bad judgement. "Of course, of course," he chirped gamely. "Sorry to intrude, Frank," he whispered to Hempson's back and melted into the crowd.

Butler returned with renewed attention to Hempson. "Maybe I shouldn't be here," he looked about him furtively.

"Maybe you should not," Hempson decided to be unhelpful. "Politicians usually have their own way in these matters and because our advice with regard to this event has to a great extent already been put aside, I forbear to cast my pearls once again."

Butler ignored the allusion and continued to await Hempson's imparted wisdom. "I will say this," Hempson took up, gratifying the minister's patience. "My function here tonight is to observe and correlate the attitudes and reactions of those within and without the relevant entourage."

"Good grief, I'm off." Butler made to depart.

"May I ask a favour?" Hempson intercepted. "Presumably you're about to contact the Home Secretary?" Butler nodded his head vigorously at the mention of their mutual overlord.

"You might convey the need of some small get-together tomorrow?"

The prospect of proposing a meeting that the Home Secretary would be obliged to attend fazed Butler momentarily.

Hempson said, "I have at least two cadavers to dispose of, and I'm not moving on that until I get a political green light."

"Very well," Butler replied. "I'll put that to the Home Secretary."

"Could I also warn you that Pecton knows nothing of this, and that is the way it should remain."

"I understand."

"Have you children?"

Butler nodded.

"One of them has suddenly taken ill," Hempson suggested.

———

Hempson noticed that there had been no contact between the two Poles, Minister Uginski and the orchestra conductor, Professor Komorski. They were opposites: the minister gross and porcine; the conductor aesthetically emaciated; the fat cat and the thin catapult. The ambassador had engaged both in social chitchat with equal amounts of attentive charm of the diplomatic variety. Either he was not taking sides, or more likely, he had been kept in the dark. Hempson moved closer to try and have a word. "Frank Hempson – Home Office," he managed to say eventually. The ambassador smiled thinly. Hempson said, "I've been asked to apologise."

The ambassador became concerned. "One of his children, I believe," he said sympathetically. "Are they very young?"

"I'm afraid I don't know," Hempson said and then asked, "Were you satisfied with the response to your concert?"

The ambassador's geniality returned. "I thought it a wonderful concert of fine music," he said delightedly, but then became concerned again. "This is a dreadful affair about Maria Wohlicka." He patently did not wish to indulge in speculation and seemed genuinely bewildered. "All these nice people have missed her presence most terribly." He unclasped his hands and the long fingers of one hand fluttered unostentatiously towards his guests.

"You must also be aware why she fled," Hempson remarked with unctuous civility.

"That is the distressing part. Embarrassing even. And it is twice as distressing because all those who might have thrown some light on the happening are not here, with the exception of Professor Komorski, and he says he knows nothing." The long fingers fluttered again, this time in exasperation. Hempson saw Komorski detach himself from a group of admirers and make his way towards the door. It was time to say goodnight. He assured His Excellency that this distressing episode would fade. The good memory of the concert would prevail. The diplomat thanked him for his kind words.

They did not sooth however, because while he could contend with Maria Wohlicka's defection – even understand it – (he involuntarily glanced around the room seeking the one person who had entrée to one's unthinkable thoughts) what he could not contend with was Lutowicz's absence. And because of that absence, he did not know what to do. He paused, unable to make up his mind. Should he contact the ministry for foreign affairs in Warsaw? Or ring the Party offices? Suppose he did, and then Lutowicz reappeared... That would be totally and completely terrifying. He certainly could not contend with that. The possibilities appeared to gather momentum 'That dog, Lutowicz!' he thought with malice, and then agonisingly squeezed the well-manicured nails of one hand into the palm of the other. He was losing the run of himself. These were thoughts that could not be permitted.

———

"Good evening, Professor," Hempson saluted Komorski in the embassy entrance hall. "Congratulations on an extremely interesting, indeed stimulating, concert."

Komorski eyed Hempson with hostility, and speculated on his intention. He was in no mood for small talk. He could not abide it at the best of times and the evening had turned into the worst of times. That bitch Wohlicka had destroyed him. In his moment of triumph she had grabbed the spotlight and his triumph was forgotten, while her defection would be remembered. If he had her in his control now he would smash every finger on her wretched hands; or better again, have Zukowska smash them. But that was another aspect that rankled. Where was Comrade Zukowska? And for that matter, Lutowicz? He had had to endure everything on his own, and now this fawning imbecile in front of him.

"Yes," he said to Hempson and took up his overcoat to leave. He had to get away from the atmosphere of apology and commiseration and back to his hotel, if only to find out if Zukowska or Lutowicz were there.

"May I offer you a lift?" Hempson enquired benevolently.

Komorski's immediate impulse was to reject this impertinence out of hand, but on considered reflection, he did not know where he was, relative to his hotel. And here was instant relief from the cloying condolences.

"Yes." He reiterated the monosyllable to Hempson.

"I'll ring for my car," Hempson indicated in the direction of the reception area, which was manned by a porter who sat and a more gloomy type who stood. Hempson assumed the man standing to be one of their SB people. The onerousness of his office appeared on his face. It combined a dullness of intellect, resulting from four decades of repression, with the contemptuous arrogance of those who had abandoned the rank-and-file of the oppressed, and joined the oppressors.

"I wish to make a telephone call," Hempson put to the seated one.

"Down the hall," he waved vaguely, "a call box."

"See here, old chap," Hempson's voice rose assertively. "I am driving Professor Komorski to his hotel. I do not carry small change. Do I have to ask the ambassador's permission?"

The seated one looked fractionally to his left. The gloomy one nodded imperceptibly. "What is the number?" the seated one asked with weary irritation. Hempson trotted out his car-phone number.

"What telephone is this?" the seated one asked, seemingly confused by the unusual combination of numbers. "My car phone," Hempson said. The SB type looked across his compatriot's shoulder to where the phone number had been inserted in a logbook.

"Pfeff!" the seated one exclaimed. "Another Western plaything," he said dismissively in Polish.

Komorski strode up impatiently. "What is the delay?" he asked Hempson.

"You'd better ask this gentleman," Hempson pointed towards the seated one. Komorski's foul humour erupted instantaneously. He knew he was on home ground and his ability to withhold his pent-up frustrations evaporated. The exhibition gave Hempson a measure of Komorski's standing in the embassy.

The car arrived quickly. Hempson escorted Komorski outside and the two sat into the back seat. The Rover sped off through the darkened streets. Hempson said, "Marvellous crowd at the concert." Komorski could not but agree. A further silence ensued which Hempson knew he must break.

"Maria Wohlicka has a large following in Britain," he said provocatively. "And you were of such wonderful assistance to her."

Komorski glowered. "I do not wish to speak of that."

Hempson felt the moment slipping from him. "Why ever not? You two make such wonderful music. You're an exceptional combination."

The car sped on through the fitful nocturnal traffic. Komorski's head of steam was beginning to build again. He fumed sullenly beside Hempson as the major unloaded one seemingly innocuous platitude after another. Komorski tried, and to an extent succeeded, in blocking out Hempson's intermittent inanities. They must be near his hotel, so he should not have to endure the claptrap for much longer.

Then two things happened almost simultaneously. Hempson, he recalled, had not asked him for the address of his hotel; and the intercom on the Branch car squawked.

"Stop!" Komorski shouted, cutting short yet another of Hempson's trite observations. "Where are you taking me?" he demanded, with an awakening surge of anxiety. Hempson looked out the car window and, without changing demeanour, said, "We'll see." It was almost a chummy reassurance that they were all in this together. The car tyres rumbled over the cobblestones of a dark tight archway, and then they were parking in a square formed by high-rise modern buildings, half of which had their lights on.

"Where am I?" Komorski asked.

Hempson turned to his guest. "Where we are doesn't really matter. It's who we are that matters – wouldn't you agree?"

The conductor mulled this over. "I claim diplomatic immunity," he said undiplomatically. Hempson suggested they move inside to put the veracity of the claim to the test. Komorski said he wished to contact the ambassador, which Hempson said could also be achieved from inside.

———

The detective sergeant brought two coffees into the interview room for Hempson and Komorski. The major thought Komorski might be more forthcoming on a one-to-one basis, and so kept the interview as cosy as possible. The first item to be disposed of was diplomatic immunity.

"You're not on the list," Hempson pointed out.

"But that is why I wish to speak to the ambassador," Komorski irritably repeated. "It is a mistake, and he will fix it."

The suggestion was so monumentally naive that Hempson perceived Komorski's position in the run of things. Or did he? "You don't understand," said Hempson. "It's not possible to jump on and off the list whenever you please. The number of people on the list is an agreed number, and the people chosen are agreed bilaterally."

Komorski kept up the pretext a while longer but eventually accepted the inevitable. Hempson said, "Which means in effect, that you can be held and charged on an official warrant."

The conductor's arrogance had gradually subsided during the verbal chess game until silence signalled his assent. He clasped the half mug of coffee before him on the table. Hempson allowed Komorski's uncommunicative preoccupation to continue until he suggested, "You do know what I'm getting at, don't you?"

The man peered into the cooling coffee for half a minute or more. A feeling of betrayal erupted within him and he banged the mug on the table. Ignoring the spilt liquid on his hands, he cried, "She is still a bitch, and whatever has been done to her, she deserved. She deserved it!" He was still smarting. Hempson encouraged this outpouring of unsought material with a soft manipulative "Indeed." It was true, Komorski confirmed, that Wohlicka has been chosen because of her professional standing in Britain. But that did not give her the right to impose her musical tastes on those of the conductor. That was an intolerable imposition, which he found grossly offensive. "How dare she!"

Hempson let the vituperative flow of hatred continue until he perceived that Komorski was repeating himself.

"Madame Wohlicka was assaulted. She had to be admitted to hospital," the Major reminded. For Komorski this was the logical inevitability of her outlandish and very personal music interpretation. The first was the cause of the second; as logical as night follows day. It could be described as musical justice. She got what she deserved. It was not like the mindless violence one reads about in the West. Justice was done. Wohlicka was an anti-social musical mischief-maker.

Hempson found the tirade a mite tedious and tried to push the interview along. "Obviously you have a quite different system of justice in Poland," he said sardonically. "In Britain, the individual has recourse to an array of protective legislation, Professor, and as you may have noticed, you are now in Britain, and are subject therefore to the laws of this country."

Komorski appeared both uncomprehending and once again sullenly intractable.

"Look," Hempson tried to be more precise. "If you assaulted the pianist, you're in trouble. You are still in trouble if you know who assaulted the pianist and withhold the information; it could mean prison."

"I did not assault her," Komorski said at once.

"Good," Hempson remarked. "You can put that obstacle behind you. Now, do you know who assaulted her?"

"I did not see her being assaulted," Komorski responded in protest.

"No," Hempson said, wagging his finger negatively. "You misunderstand. That is the answer to the next question. I asked you – do you know who assaulted her?" Komorski felt trapped. He could not bear to think of betraying names. He also felt the plan had come to grief. Apart from the non-event in the Hall, the disappearance of Lutowicz and Zukowska after the concert did not auger well. He could not think what to do – or say. What a wretched misalliance. When he had seen the bassoonist Reptarski behind the on-stage door looking helpless in detention, the sudden slump in the pit of his stomach had taken his breath away.

"Perhaps I should help you," Hempson put to the beleaguered Pole.

"Would you?" For the first time a hint of ingratiation seeped into Komorski's voice. Hempson wondered had the professor mistaken his offer of assistance for a lifeline.

"I don't think", said Hempson, "I shall be breaking any secrets if I tell you Lutowicz and Reptarski are in custody."

Komorski tried to look beyond Hempson to the implications of this information. Was Hempson attempting to deceive? The expression on Reptarski's face he would long remember; and then the absence of the others from the embassy party, which substantiated what Hempson had said.

"Where is Lina Zukowska?" Komorski hoped for some good news.

Hempson sighed. "Lina has decided to leg it," he said, but before the puzzled look on Komorski's face found audible expression, Hempson apologised and explained that Zukowska had fled. "It won't be long before we pick her up. So…" Hempson spread the outstretched palms of his hands along the table towards Komorski. "How did a person of your standing become involved in such a sordid piece of chicanery?"

"I tell you, I did not assault Maria Wohlicka."

Hempson bent forward across the table. "Who did?" he quietly demanded. Komorski knew it was self-preservation time.

"Lina Zukowska," he said.

Hempson drew back. "Good," he said, and asked Komorski if he would like another mug of coffee. Komorski agreed and Hempson found his pipe, tobacco, and matches. He rang the bell on the wall behind him, put in the order, and with his pipe well alight said, "I'm glad we're through that. Now we must deal with the more serious problem of assassination."

Alarm showed in Komorski's face. He looked at Hempson through a veil of tobacco smoke. What did this English prig mean? More serious? More serious than what? This was the end of the world as far as he, Jan Komorski, was concerned, and to be confronted by this self-satisfied know-all, sucking on his pipe like a soother, was the last straw.

"Before we proceed further," Hempson said, "I think it incumbent upon me to put to you certain possibilities in the matter of evidence that you might be disposed to provide. For instance –" Hempson harrumphed, "– if you provide us with an explanation of this unfortunate business… it might be possible…" Hempson moved accommodatingly on his chair. "A tincture of a possibility," he held up the small finger on his hand, "that arrangements other than prison might be offered in settlement. I am not without influence," he stressed, while contriving to look self-deprecating. "I can say without fear, if your version of events proves truthful and satisfactory – something in the shape of deportation to Poland could be arranged."

Hempson leaned back on his chair and grimaced, his pipe had gone out.

The two coffees arrived. Hempson told the detective sergeant that he would need paper and pen.

———

The day had passed into Sunday. The new day was young and darkly fresh – unlike the two who faced one another across the table. It was as nothing compared to the tiredness they would feel when finally they separated for breakfast later that morning.

CHAPTER 32

Sunday March 29th 1981
7.30 am

Sarah started to clear the breakfast things off her hospital bed. As she moved around, she bumped against David's case history board, which rattled at the bottom of his bed. She picked it up again, savouring the flush of pride that once more engulfed her. Earlier that morning on her way to the bathroom she had taken a quick look as Brenton slept and, after taking in the name at the top of the sheet, she had clasped the clipboard to her and gazed down at Wing Commander David Brenton. It had filled her with such pride she almost forgot to put it back. How had it happened? And in such a short space of time. The previous Sunday the possibility had seemed so remote. She had been hoping so earnestly, it had almost begged disappointment; yet here she was, not just involved with David, but a spectator of the extraordinary events that had ultimately nearly deprived her of her love. She observed the still figure in the bed. Up to this, Sarah had perceived Brenton as approachable yet distant; forthcoming and at the same time reticent. This was the Brenton she had fallen in love with: this shadowy, and she had to admit, austere figure; she had been assured from every side, including herself, that to try and change him would be self-defeating.

She looked at him intently, hoping to decipher some hint of what might lie in the future – there must be hundreds of things she didn't know about him – and whether through force of intent or accident, Brenton's eyes opened to see Sarah clasping the clipboard. He murmured, "My guardian angel."

"What a very beautiful thing to say," She glowed with the compliment. "I love you, David," she then said, simply and straightforwardly. His drowsy helplessness suddenly impelled her to kiss him. A slow smile of beatification spread over his face.

Major Hempson knocked softly on the door and came into the private room. He held his trilby deferentially in both hands, smiled tiredly at Sarah and Brenton, and asked how the patient was. There were two beds in the room and Sarah said she had been allowed to stay and keep an eye on him through the night. Oblivious to the tubes attached to him and aided by medication, he had slept through the night.

Brenton noted the major's weary appearance. "I've been talking to Komorski all night," said Hempson, "Only finished a short time ago."

Sarah escorted the major to an armchair beside Brenton's bed. "I have a few telephone calls to make, so if you'll excuse me," she said, and left them to whatever it was they so obviously had to discuss.

"Damned nice gel," Hempson said reflectively. "How are you feeling?" He surveyed the remains of a plastic bag of blood hanging over his head. Brenton felt amused. He had never seen this careworn side of Hempson before. By all appearances, Hempson was the one in need of rest. "I feel fine," Brenton said. "I've never felt so relaxed and unconcerned. You're the one should be in bed."

"I intend," Hempson returned the smile. "Thought I'd drop by before putting my head down. I've a meeting with the Home Secretary later this afternoon, so I must have my wits about me."

"I know I should be concerned," Brenton sighed comfortably. "But I find it difficult to focus on any subject for any length of time."

"Any discomfort?" Hempson peered over at Brenton's injured shoulder. The bullet hole had been very close to more vulnerable parts of his body.

"A dull stiffness," Brenton said. "But that may be because it's been trussed up."

Hempson leaned forward. "You've been lucky." He nodded his head towards the injured arm. "That was a close–run thing. Anybody who's taken a round has good reason to feel euphoric if they survive the experience." He sat back in the armchair as if he were about to produce his pipe – but didn't. "What I really want to say is thank you," he said, with a stab at intimacy.

Brenton's mind went blank and he found he couldn't respond. He lay rigidly in the bed.

"Damn fine show," Hempson mumbled, struggling to his feet to break the rush of emotion which threatened to undermine his dignity. "Must be off." He rapped his knuckles on the bedside table to bring himself to order. "I'll be in touch," he promised, and walked briskly from the room without looking back.

Brenton knew a particular cadence point had been sounded and passed. Time would not make the recollection of this moment any less uncomfortable; but, despite all the torpor and coldness, he knew he would never forget it.

The door opened and Sarah returned. He smiled back at her bright face.

Hempson made a dash for the Home Office at 4.30 in the afternoon, having managed six hours sleep. His driver had forewarned him of the necessity to take a longer route to avoid the remnants of the London Marathon. "The London what?" Hempson had irritably demanded.

"The first London Marathon," his driver had said with some surprise. The papers had been full of it during the week, but Hempson had had other things on his mind. Explanations had accompanied maps of the route, with prognostications about those taking part, and the role the weather might play in the comfort or discomfort of the 6,700 competitors. The weather scored a draw on this last Sunday in March. London was enveloped in a fairly persistent drizzle of rain to the relief of the runners and the disappointment of the very large attendance.

Hempson's satisfaction with the outcome of the previous night's caper, as he was then more confidently disposed to think of it, might encourage him to expect apologies all round. But that was not how things worked. He wondered how they would work and what temper the Home Secretary would be in when he arrived. He already knew Morgan Laymott was to attend the meeting, as well as the director general of the security service. So it seemed the big guns were being wheeled out. Which meant in effect that he and Laymott would take a back seat. Whether this was a strategy to protect the Home Secretary remained to be seen. All of which occupied his mind in the back seat of the official car. He consoled himself with the reassurance that he was not being brought to account. If there was any accounting to be done it would come from the Home Secretary and John Wescott.

When Hempson was shown into the Home Office meeting room, he found Chief Supt Laymott already there. He was reading Saturday's *Times*. The attendant pointed to another copy of the newspaper lying on the table, which the Home Secretary had suggested Hempson might like to peruse before the meeting started.

"Is there a hidden message in Saturday's *Times*?" Hempson wondered.

"If there is," Laymott assertively shook his newspaper, "I'll leave it to you to determine precisely what it is."

Hempson detected the tattered edges of Laymott's due process still fluttering between them. He sat down on the chair beside Laymott with his name on the table in front of him. He pushed the nametag to one side and spread the *Times* out. When he saw the photograph of the Queen, Prince Charles, and Lady Diana Spencer across the top right hand of the front page, he abruptly remembered that he had not seen a newspaper for some days. Had he misjudged the Home Secretary's intentions? Why Saturday's paper rather than Sunday's? He eagerly set about catching up. Under the photo it said: 'The Queen photographed yesterday with the Prince of Wales and Lady Diana at Buckingham Palace after giving formal consent to their marriage at a meeting of the Privy Council'. Hempson felt sympathy for his DG, and looked across the table at the vacant chair on which he would sit. He caught the heading on the left–hand side of the page: 'Polish tension rising as strike brings country to standstill'. Underneath he was told, 'Lech Walesa appeals for moderation'. He began to read: 'Tension in Poland appeared yesterday to have reached its highest point since the Solidarity Trade Union Organisation first confronted the government and the Communist Party nine months ago, according to reports from Warsaw reaching the West. Against a background of indefinitely extended

Warsaw Pact manoeuvres in the border regions between Poland and the Soviet Union, dwindling national food supplies are reduced to barely enough for 12 days. Attention is now focused on Sunday's crisis plenary session of the central committee of the Polish Communist Party. The immediate cause of the present crisis is the violent intervention by police at a meeting between Solidarity representatives and the state regional council of Bydgoszcz where three union men were badly beaten. The incident led national Solidarity officials to call off the 90-day truce concluded with the new government of General Jaruzelski on February 12th. Mr Walesa opposed strike action but conceded yesterday's four-hour stoppage, believed by observers to be the greatest organised labour protest in the post-war history of Eastern Europe. Solidarity claims the support of 10 million workers. According to these reports, the whole of Poland came to a virtual standstill'.

Hempson turned to Laymott. "Pretty heavy stuff in Poland at the moment."

At the bottom of page one it said, 'Russians say political instigators now controlling Solidarity'. He turned the page. The *Times* had laid out a map of the route taken in the Marathon. "Bloody lunatics," Hempson muttered. He turned the page again. 'Washington sounds alarm on Poland', page 4 warned, and to point up the gravity of the situation, a photograph in the middle of the page showed Soviet tanks trundling across a pontoon bridge on manoeuvres. 'NATO remains calm in face of Pact exercises' another article began. Hempson cut to page 13 to see how the leading article presented the situation. 'Poland in peril again', it said. It would be a tragic absurdity if Poland were brought to ruin by the lunacy of a few security police in Bydgoszcz – or by the irresponsibility of those who gave them their orders.

Hempson heard approaching voices outside in the corridor. He tried to skim the remainder of the article. Prime Minister Jaruzelski has already made a sensible move by rejecting the first report by the minister for justice... The system could learn to accommodate new union structures... In the long run it is more likely to be swept away if it does not do so... Part of the trouble is that Moscow does not believe this...

The door opened and the Home Secretary breezed in followed by the director general of security and the director general of intelligence. No civil servants, not even the Home Secretary's private secretary Peter Jarvis.

'Curious,' Hempson thought, and awaited events.

The Home Secretary sat down at the head of the table and beamed benevolently at Hempson and Laymott. He then addressed the two DGs who sat across the table from Hempson and Laymott. "Thank you for making the effort to come to the meeting at such short notice gentlemen, and –" he turned to DG intelligence, "at great personal inconvenience. We've all been taken aback by the, er, happenings during and following Saturday's concert."

Here he again ingratiated himself to Hempson and Laymott.

"I travelled down from the North this morning – as soon as I was informed of what had happened." The Home Secretary extended a hand in the direction of those sitting on either side of the table. "This is a… how shall I put it? … a select, and of necessity, confined gathering. I'm following the suggestion of the director general of security here," he acknowledged the other side of the table, "so it's not a meeting in the normal sense. Rather a gathering of friends to toss around the implications of what has happened. Before we start, I'd like to thank Major Hempson and Chief Supt Laymott most heartily for their quite extraordinary perceptiveness in the first instance and their astute handling of the matter."

Laymott thanked the Home Secretary but pointed out that the alarm bells had originated in the security service. Hempson added that the break had come from Wg Cdr Brenton.

"How is Wg Cdr Brenton?" the Home Secretary enquired solicitously. Hempson enlightened the meeting and then for whatever record there was, mentioned Thompson and Chisholme in the list of casualties – in Thompson's case a fatal encounter.

Hempson was asked how the attempt had unfolded, and how it had been dealt with. Without elaboration, he trotted out the salient features and then the countermeasures that had been taken. "I presume it shall now become the responsibility of the director of public prosecutions," he rounded off.

"Yes," the Home Secretary said with a certain preoccupation. "However, I'd prefer to address that problem later on, as there are equally pressing elements demanding our attention."

At the use of the word 'problem', Hempson turned to look at the Home Secretary who, realising that he'd given something of an unpalatable preview, turned to Hempson and added, "In so far as it is within my powers, Major, your efforts shall not go unheralded." This produced the desired effect. Hempson was momentarily distracted wondering what, if anything, might drop his way. During the diversion the Home Secretary asked DG intelligence for his assessment of Poland's internal social and political problems.

DG intelligence said these were of such diversity and magnitude that it would take a day to cover everything adequately. He would therefore give a much-curtailed version, with which the Home Secretary quickly agreed. Hempson's instinct told him that the evaluation was for his benefit, or maybe Laymott. Or maybe both of them.

He sought his own DG's eyes and was rewarded with a casual blink. Security was going along with whatever it might be.

"The first thing one should bear in mind about Poland today is that its economy is basically ruined," DG intelligence opened his assessment. Hempson noticed the delivery appeared to be directed at Laymott. "To the extent that they are about to introduce ration cards. In one decade their indebtedness has jumped tenfold – to everybody. Russia, their neighbours, the West. They have dumped First Secretary Gierek and most of his cabinet. They were responsible for the mess. The new man is Jaruzelski. He has begun to try and root out the endemic corruption. Mr Uginski, our recent guest, was one of those whom he sacked." DG intelligence lifted his eyes from his notes and looked around the table. "Notwithstanding this attempt at reform, it is my opinion that communism is incapable of reform from within. There is a new feeling running through Poland that is challenging communism's inability to reform. The Foreign Secretary, Lord Carrington, has recently returned from a trip to Eastern Europe. A truculent change was discernible in Poland, he has said. The intelligence service has also taken note of a further movement in very recent times, and that is the persistent stream of Poles who visit the Vatican to confer with Karol Wojtyła, the Polish Pope. He has, in their eyes, redeemed Polish self-respect in the world and wields an inordinate influence in Poland. Russia has very deep reservations about this development, and it is my opinion they will do something to try and stop it. Ironically, we think John Paul II is in fact dishing out placatory advice because when Lech Walesa, the secretary of the new independent trade union Solidarity, returned to Poland after a visit to the Vatican, he straightaway appealed to his national co-ordinating committee not to confront the authorities. The advice has been largely ignored. This left Walesa exposed, but as a possible quid pro quo, the authorities have made a breathtaking number of concessions. For instance, the Mass has been broadcast on Polish radio again. Mr Jerzy Ozdowski, a member of parliament from the Roman Catholic group ZNAC, has been appointed deputy prime minister. This came a week after Ozdowski arrived home following a visit to the Vatican."

DG intelligence raised his head to look around the table. There was a pause, then he added bemusedly, "It's almost as if the Pope were making the Polish communist government appointments…"

This provided a patter of chuckles from around the table, with the exception of Hempson and Laymott. "As recently as February 13th", DG intelligence continued, "former First Secretary Gierek was denounced and removed from the council of state." He looked pointedly across the table at Hempson and Laymott. "The surprising thing is that he was replaced by a Mr Ryszard Reiff, who is chairman of the Roman Catholic group, Pax."

The Home Secretary clasped his hands together. "Strange and unusual things are happening in Poland. And without letting any cats out of the bag, I can say that there is a Polish delegation at present in the City of London negotiating a British loan. The PM is robustly enthusiastic about the possibilities emerging from this new scenario. She and President Reagan, whom she met in Washington on February 25th, have agreed to the formation of a Rapid Deployment Force. This is in response to the Russian invasion of Afghanistan. Hopefully the Russians may have second thoughts about walking into Poland." The Home Secretary turned to Hempson. With slow deliberation he added, "Therefore, we still wish to encourage – and help." The Home Secretary paused to elicit a response from Hempson or Laymott; in the ensuing silence he was moved to clarify, " - as I've already expounded on during the week."

The silence continued. Eventually Hempson enquired, "Am I missing something here?" His head swivelled up and down the table interrogatively. "If this is a for-your-information session – good enough. But I get the impression Laymott and I are here for a lecture. It should also be unnecessary to point out that I implement expounded government policy. I have no problem with that. I do have problems, as you may have noticed, when governments ignore my warnings."

The Home Secretary raised both hands to put a brake on Hempson.

"You have my apologies for that," he said, nodding. "Particularly because of Thompson's death. If he died for anything, it was in defence of his country. It's up to us to ensure that his death shall not be in vain. That's why we five are here. To implement and carry through that change."

"You've already expounded on that Home Secretary. We already know about the new direction." Hempson felt the unease across the table from him. "Unless you have a further element to elucidate?"

"My dear Major," the Home Secretary acknowledged with a rueful smile, "you are ahead of me. I confess to feeling somewhat chastened. I admit to having had this preamble inserted. In the first place to mollify your battle-weariness, and secondly your susceptibilities." The Home Secretary now leaned across the table in Hempson's and Laymott's direction. "In fact," he continued. "this follow up or follow through – whatever you like to call it – has more to do with Chief Supt Laymott than it has with you, Major." The Home Secretary turned to DG intelligence. "I think we've had enough background. Perhaps you might air your proposition?"

"I beg your pardon, Home Secretary," DG security intervened,

"Frank is correct when he says the momentum should now be moving into the area of the director of public prosecutions. However, a unique and ultimately clean solution to the problem presented itself to MI6. DG intelligence and I mulled it over early this morning, and put it to the Home Secretary, who then got authority to implement. Before I pass back to intelligence, I'd like to say that I know Frank and Morgan will assist in whatever way they can."

"I heartily agree," The Home Secretary enthusiastically nodded his head.

Hempson and Laymott glanced at each other.

"Could we have sight of what we are so heartily assisting?" Hempson enquired. The Home Secretary extended a hand in invitation to DG intelligence.

"You weren't the only one working late last night," the DG said to Hempson. "Before the concert, intelligence gave it as an opinion that the group involved in the wet job seemed to be an independent group, or a group acting independently from within Polish intelligence. The time seemed right: a new leadership struggling to come to terms with economic and social breakdown. Last night we received tentative confirmation that our guest, Minister Uginski, had indeed been sacked in the cleanout, and so far as the new government is concerned, he has remained sacked. From that premise, and with further probing, it transpired that the attempt was unauthorised."

Laymott commented, "They would say that, wouldn't they?"

"They would, and they did," the Home Secretary interjected. "We were obliged to take note, because they reckoned there would be a trial and immediately offered to supply all evidence of intent."

"Are they by chance dumping these people", asked Hempson, "for the more heady attractions of mammon?"

"If they are," DG security stressed, "that would place them in a position of adding to their own trauma."

"Besides which," DG intelligence chipped in, "they've offered quite an extraordinary opportunity to British interests, which we are about to put to you.

The Home Secretary indicated that DG intelligence continue.

"Straight off, I have to say I'm not free to divulge everything that transpired. It's a little too hot at the moment, but –" he started to smile in the Home Secretary's direction, "I think I can say that the Conservative government has dropped its ideological barriers sufficiently to allow itself an opportunity to give fulsome support to the future prosperity and empirical success of the new Polish trade union Solidarity."

The Home Secretary tut-tutted to a ripple of amusement.

"Essentially," the DG said, becoming serious again, "We've agreed to send back the remaining group of Poles plus the trigger man – the musician Reptarski. They shall be dealt with by the new Polish government and, I stress, they are not to be informed of the reception that awaits them."

"You must have received a very substantial enticement," Hempson surmised.

"In time you shall make your own judgment," DG intelligence said. "In the interim, I can only say – very interesting. The reason we're not releasing information down the line is because only a handful in Poland know about this meeting of minds. If any part of the détente gets out, it would have calamitous consequences. There is great alarm among communist hardliners in Poland. They are clamouring for Moscow to unleash the Soviet army. So you see a very tight rein must be applied."

"Thank you, gentlemen," the Home Secretary addressed the two DGs and, turning to Hempson and Laymott, asked, "Do you know of any reason or impediment as to why this undertaking should not be set in motion? How many know about last night's real objective for instance?"

Hempson's head was not as clear as he would have liked. And like a footballer in the dressing room after a hard match, only the highlights jumped to mind. It would take a day's rest before the incidentals could be recalled. He did remember his interview with the personnel in the gallery before leaving the hall and his launch of a new acronym, DID – Diplomatic Immunity Delete…

"Luckily, not many," Hempson considered. "Where civilians made peripheral contact, I turned Maria Wohlicka's defection into the main event. So I think we're clear on that front."

"Excellent," the Home Secretary congratulated. "What about you, Chief Superintendent?"

Laymott said, "The most obvious impediment to exporting the judicial outcome is the due process which is already in train. Det Insp Blackmore is in charge." Laymott cast sidelong, disgruntled looks at Hempson beside him, whom he considered had had prior knowledge of this turn of events. Something of Laymott's feelings crossed an awareness frontier within Hempson, who said, "I hope you're not holding foresight against me?"

Laymott turned on his chair to face Hempson directly. "You knew about this! You must have had inside information to have made the suggestion you did."

Hempson turned to those across the table. "Do you mind if I smoke?" Before they could respond, he was already extracting a match to relight the embers in his pipe bowl.

"What's the matter?" the Home Secretary asked, his head turning in puzzlement between the two DGs and their subordinates.

"I think that should be plain to everyone," Laymott challenged. "Hempson here knew what you were about yesterday." Laymott addressed the others. "And I now understand why: you're trying to sidetrack the due process."

The Home Secretary addressed the DGs. "Would someone please explain sharpish, how Major Hempson came to be in possession of information on a government directive before a decision on that directive had been taken?"

"Perhaps we should ask the major," DG security said. "*I* didn't know about the result of the meeting until later this morning. Major?"

Now safely alight, Hempson eased back into his chair and considered those around him.

"Do please explain," the Home Secretary insisted. "You had access to the secret agenda of a government meeting, and more bizarrely, knew the outcome of a decision taken at that meeting before that decision had been taken. How come, Major?" he demanded. "It does indeed look as if you had prior knowledge."

Hempson retold the episode where Det Insp Blackmore had, on the same day, retrieved the pistol from Appelby's car, and the expended round from the British and Continental Insurance Company in Croydon. How their hopes had been raised for the first time and then dashed, when bullet and pistol had not matched. "After last night's concert a similar pistol was retrieved from Lutowicz's body. It was handed to Morgan for evidence, and I suggested it not be passed to Det Insp Blackmore until a more complete perspective arrived." Hempson shrugged his shoulders and relit his pipe.

Nodding slowly, DG security said, "Fortunately, as it transpired."

"Isn't all of this rather academic?" DG intelligence wondered. "After all, the recipient of the proposed warrant is dead."

"Good point," the Home Secretary quickly responded. "What about that aspect, Chief Superintendent? Surely the greater good being offered the West rates above the dotting of i's and crossing of t's? Lutowicz has already paid the ultimate price. Justice has in effect been done." Laymott's resolve crumbled. He diverted the thrust of the meeting with a demand for the rationale behind the assassination attempt.

Two possibilities had been suggested during the night. A maverick group of opportunists from within Polish intelligence bent on making a name for themselves during a lull in political direction, or similar hardliners in the pay of Russia with the intention of souring Anglo-Polish détente. "Had they succeeded," DG intelligence ventured, "quite a lot of things would have been put on hold, including the loan for instance, and the re-interment of General Sikorski's remains."

"I have to say at this point," Hempson intervened, "our operatives in security are of the idea that this group would have made the demand for a massive loan and the return of Sikorski had they succeeded. Our embarrassment would have been so great, we would have agreed to anything."

There was a sudden freeze in proceedings at this unexpected reversal of perception. Eventually the Home Secretary said, "Yes, that's another convincing scenario which shall be put to the test over the next few days. It has the advantage of allowing me the opportunity of stating categorically that we are not allowing the transfer of General Sikorski's remains to Poland. Cognisance is being taken of Polish sentiment in Britain in this regard. To have acceded to the Polish government's request would have raised more problems than it would have resolved. For the moment we shall say nothing, but next June I shall make a statement refusing permission. This is to distance their request from last night's concert. In the interim, and through the Foreign Office, we shall intimate to our new friends that their wishes are unlikely to be granted. This is a cabinet decision."

The Home Secretary looked Hempson full in the face. "Not taking sides for obvious reasons, I can say, however, that this decision might have been quite different had we been presented with the assassination of a Polish government minister this morning. Luckily that is not the case."

DG security suggested that Hempson deliver himself of any relevant debriefing information gathered from his overnight sojourn with Komorski.

"I am convinced that Komorski had no direct input into the attempt," Hempson began. "That's not to say that he didn't know anything about it. His egocentricity is of such monumental proportions, that he saw the concert only as a vehicle for the advancement of his ambitions in the music world. He very quickly came to terms with the dispatch of a minister in his own government. It was easily explained, he told me. Uginski was corrupt and his elimination would have contributed to the advancement of music and the welfare of his country. He also told me at some other point in the interview that if he could lay his hands on Maria Wohlicka he would have every finger on *her* hands broken. Which substantiates his warped point of view. She took the spotlight away from him by defecting."

Hempson raised both hands fractionally above the table in an extenuating gesture. "So far as Komorski is concerned, he is the assassinated martyr; nothing else matters. It must have been child's play to recruit someone that perverse. All they had to do was to dangle before him a Polish concert, held before an international audience, in one of the international music centres of the world. What musician with the tunnel-vision of meglomania could have refused?"

"Any reason why the government proposal should not go ahead?" the Home Secretary asked. This was the problem he would have to address again at cabinet level on Monday morning.

Hempson considered for a moment and then said, "No – but two things jump to mind. I gave Komorski some intimation at the start of the interview that it might be possible to substitute deportation in lieu of a prison sentence, provided his de-briefing proved to be substantial and of real value. This proved to be the case. He was prepared to dump his new-found associates provided he could return to Poland and his music. This offer can be rescinded at any time. It does, however, tie-in neatly with the government proposal to send the lot of them back." Hempson leaned forward on his chair, hands clasped, eyes closed. He opened his eyes again and sat back on his chair. "The other item is of greater importance and concerns those who may be making contact with people in Poland," he said directly to DG intelligence. "Komorski told me Lutowicz had a paymaster in Polish intelligence."

"Does this mean trouble?" the Home Secretary asked anxiously.

"Not so far," DG intelligence reassured the Home Secretary.

"Do you have a name?" DG security asked his director.

"No," Hempson disappointed the table. "However, I do have a description of his right hand. Two fingers are missing."

"How accurate is this?" DG security demanded.

"No, wait. This is good," DG intelligence said. "What did Komorski tell you?"

"I take it to be an accurate description," Hempson said. "The only time Komorski expressed curiosity about their intelligence mentor to Lutowicz, he was told he could not have his name. And let's face it, they could not have mounted an operation of that magnitude without the active assistance of someone with monetary clout – someone who controlled a large budget. In jest, Lutowicz said that their master could never have been a musician because he had had two of his right-hand fingers detached in an accident."

"Sounds convincing," the Home Secretary remarked and looked to the DGs for confirmation.

"That description rings a faint bell in my memory box," DG intelligence pondered. "It can be checked out. We shall require guarantees from our contacts that those who are to be sent back shall not be dealt with by the wrong people and for the wrong reasons."

Laymott said, "We hold all the aces and should not let go until we have those guarantees."

DG intelligence said, "That should be easily achieved, from a position of strength."

The Home Secretary shuffled the papers on the table in front of him. "Look gentlemen, I don't wish to enter too deeply into the intricacies and technicalities. This is your department. I have a cabinet meeting tomorrow to attend, and this proposal is on the agenda. Do I say it's on or off?" He looked to the two DGs on his left for an answer.

DG security eventually observed, "With all due respect, sir, that's not a question I would ever be prepared to give an answer on. You will, after all, be in the company of the PM, the person authorised in law to make that kind of a decision. We carry out your decision. I can understand that you may feel you got your fingers burned during this week. The thing to hold onto, sir, is that your making the decision is what makes the difference between us as a nation, and the collection of mavericks we were pitted against during the week."

"Yes," DG intelligence joined his colleague. "We can't guarantee success. Nobody knows what the outcome of the Polish thing will be. It could be, in the end, just more of the same. On the other hand..." The DG left the prospect up in the air with a slight shrug of his shoulders. "What we possess is a priceless jump on the more alarming elements in Poland as a result of Saturday's concert. We don't guarantee success, but I think what we are saying is – the prospect looks too good to miss."

"That's what I want to hear," the Home Secretary replied, gathering his papers together. "I'll leave you now, gentlemen. There are one or two other matters I wish to attend to before tomorrow. Thank you for a very interesting meeting."

———

DG security took the chair. Most of the matters to be dealt with were in the security area. First on the improvised agenda was Hempson's task of disposing of Lutowicz's and Appleby's cadavers.

They agreed to release Appleby's remains forthwith. Laymott was asked to make the arrangements and immediately left the meeting to make the way smooth for a clean transfer to the Metropolitan police and other relevant agencies. This enabled the remaining trio to put their heads together on the transfer to Poland of what was left of the group responsible for the wet job.

As they dotted i's and crossed t's a phone call came through to the effect that a Lina Zukowska had been picked up during the afternoon while endeavouring to board an East German merchant ship. The call neatly placed a full stop at the end of the meeting. The three men rose, shook hands and left the building to go their separate ways. Hempson dispensed with his official car and hailed a taxi.

———

The taxi man lowered his meter as Hempson clambered aboard. With professional good humour, he asked, "You been to the marathon, then?"

"No," Hempson said wearily. "I just look like I have."

"Marvellous finish to the race," the driver said, wondering whether Hempson had heard. When he got no reply, he raised his voice. The first two home – the American, Dick Beardaley and a Norweigan girl, Inge Simonsen – ran across the finishing line hand in hand. Bloody lovely gesture! 2 hours 11 minutes."

Hempson judiciously nodded to the driver in his mirror. But his attention was drawn to the littered streets outside. A small army of cleaners was busily making inroads into the mass of litter. There was still a discernible carnival air about the streets notwithstanding the damp conditions. In many ways the afternoon's meeting had concluded satisfactorily. The taxi gathered pace as it left behind the debris of the marathon.

EPILOGUE

January 1982
Symphony Hall
Croydon

Michael Pecton rang Miss Maybury for his coffee. He normally did not indulge until 11 o'clock or thereabouts, but today was different. The preview box of the newspaper on his desk heralded the New Year's Honours List and he wished to peruse the list before Cranshaw came in with the schedules. It was not that he expected to see his name there – just a wish to know and acknowledge those whom he would be joining at some stage, which he hoped would be sooner rather than later. He would not begin to go through the lists until his coffee arrived.

His eyes skimmed the front page, not really settling on any one item. Something on Poland caught his attention, which instantly triggered a remembrance of his astute follow-up to the Polish Week. He smiled at the memory, sank back into his armchair, and congratulated himself on the successful chance he had taken. Within the enfolding wings of his armchair, Pecton's reverie assumed a complacent smugness; but the Polish allusion in the newspaper broke back in on this. He leaned over the paper spread out on his desk and picked out the reference. It said the martial law that had been imposed in Poland late last year was not likely to be lifted in the immediate future. Lech Walesa and thousands of other trade unionists and intellectuals had been imprisoned. Pecton swore softly to himself. He had been told by his government contact, Lyle Butler, that any reciprocal arrangement he might come to with Poland was "not on" while martial law remained in operation. "It would be wholly inappropriate," Butler had intimated.

"It can't go on for ever," Pecton thought, seeking further information in the article.

The door opened and Miss Maybury entered. After Pecton had removed the newspaper from the desk, she deftly placed the coffee and biscuit in front of him.

"Thank you," he said perfunctorily, more important things on his mind. The real pleasure could commence. "Hold everything until I've finished, Miss Maybury."

"Very well, Dr Pecton," Miss Maybury replied, wondering what had precipitated the taste for extended elevenses in the otherwise predictably zealous general manager.

Pecton moved the coffee to one side and again smoothed out the paper in front of him. He unfolded the wrapper on the biscuit and busily bit into the chocolate-covered shortbread. Munching happily, he found the page with the lists of elevated recipients proudly laid out. His eyes searched the photos for familiar faces. A gasp of surprise induced his chocolate-covered shortbread to go down the wrong way, and the resultant coughing fit then sprayed it all over his paper and desk. Ignoring the eruption, Pecton sat transfixed by the centre photograph in a group of three pictures in the middle of the page. He forced his eyes from the photo to read the caption beneath. 'Wg Cdr David and Mrs Brenton', it said of the smiling and happy couple in the photo. To his growing amazement it continued, "Wg Cdr Brenton was one of those who received an MBE yesterday. He farms 700 acres in Somerset'.

Pecton brushed away some of the crumbs and returned to the photo. "Wing Commander," he muttered, resenting the superior smiles from the picture of the two individuals who had until last April been minions in his organisation. "700 acres," he repeated, with chastened mystification. He did a hasty calculation at contemporary prices and blanched. "Damned riffraff, pushing up the stakes!" he spluttered. "Very well. It's a knighthood or nothing."

Satisfied with his decision, he lay back in his armchair and removed his glasses. With a silk handkerchief he removed pieces of shortbread that had attached themselves. Yes, he agreed with this strategy. Replacing his glasses, he shook the residue of crumbs from the newspaper to the floor. He spread the newspaper out before him to see who had received the real honours. Before his eye found the list of new Knights, it alighted on one further photo. 'Sir Frank Hempson, Home Office', it said succinctly. "Bloody civil servant!" Pecton exploded. From within the photograph, Hempson jovially held out his insignia of investiture for inspection. Pecton tossed the newspaper to the floor and stormed into the outer office, which took Miss Maybury and Cranshaw by surprise. "Look after it yourselves," he barked at nobody in particular. "I'm off for the day."

This was so startlingly uncharacteristic that Cranshaw and Miss Maybury could only look open-mouthed at one another after he had gone. Miss Maybury rose and entered Pecton's office to see if it contained some clue to his intemperate performance. Cranshaw followed, to find her taking in the disarray around the desk. "Most extraordinary," she muttered, looking from one item of confusion to another. "Did the biscuit blow up or some such?" she asked sceptically, as Cranshaw came to stand beside her.

"Look," Cranshaw pointed to the newspaper on the ground. "There's a photo of David Brenton and Sarah Carlyle."

He retrieved the newspaper from the floor and spread out page 2 over the remaining crumbs on the desk. "You know Brenton picked up an MBE yesterday?"

They both looked at the photo. Miss Maybury clasped her hands. "How absolutely splendid, Sarah Carlyle looks wonderfully happy," Miss Maybury gushed. She drew up a chair beside Cranshaw.

"What a day that was," Cranshaw said. "Their wedding day," he elaborated. "They were both very sorry you weren't there." He explained that St George's had been chosen because Sarah and David felt it was special for them, and they had also formed a special regard for the rector, Rupert Pryce.

"I remember that name on the recording contracts," Miss Maybury said.

"As you know, they held the reception in the rectory, at the rector's insistence. Jim Sherry's after-dinner speech caught the festive occasion beautifully."

"How did David pick up an MBE?"

"You may not know, but he's on the board of the RAF Museum in Hendon."

"Is he indeed," Miss Maybury's eyes widened. "Presumably he gave of his expertise and was suitably rewarded."

"Presumably," Cranshaw cheerfully agreed.

"I must say, he's quite the dark horse, isn't he?"

"I'll say,"

"And young Miss Carlyle – or should I say, Mrs Brenton – well! I'm lost in admiration at her resourcefulness."

Cranshaw pursed his lips and flicked a few crumbs from the photographs.

Miss Maybury delicately cleared her throat. "If David's presence on the board of the RAF Museum was so beneficial to all concerned, perhaps we might induce him to become a patron of Symphony Hall, Croydon. I must suggest it to Dr Pecton. The poor man works so tirelessly for the common good – he could do with all the assistance he can get. What do you think?"

"Undoubtedly, an interesting prospect."

Miss Maybury cast a frosty eye over the office. "I'll have to get the cleaners up here to put this shambles to rights. Well then," she sniffed and moved briskly over to the door. "– no call to shilly-shally about. There's work to be done."

Cranshaw stood back to let Miss Maybury by and, with a final glance around Pecton's office, closed the door behind them.